TYCHO BRAHE
SECRET

Trygve E. Wighdal

A. Wighdal & Sons, LLC
Publishers
The Woodlands, TX 77380

© 2022 A. Wighdal & Sons, LLC | All Rights Reserved

This is a work of fiction. Names, characters, businesses, events, locales, and incidents are either the products of the author's imagination or used in a fictitious manner in situations that may or may not have happened in the future.

Any resemblance to actual and / or future actions of the persons depicted in this book, real or not, would for sure have been entirely coincidental.

Web: https://wighdals.com/
Email: contact@wighdals.com

Library of Congress Cataloging-in-Publication Data (CIP):

Names: Wighdal, Trygve E., 1960— I Chiara Corsini, PhD, 1972—
Title: Tycho Brahe Secret / by Trygve E. Wighdal; edited by Chiara Corsini, PhD
Description: First edition I The Woodlands, TX ; Paris, France : A. Wighdal & Sons, LLC, 2022
Summary: A fourteen-year-old cypher-punk girl seeks the help of a renegade Nobel laureate in physics and a 16th century alchemist in a struggle to rescue her little brother from certain death.

Identifiers:
Library of Congress Control Number: 2021904206
ISBN: 978-1-7338151-5-4 (paperback)
ISBN: 978-1-7338151-9-2 (ePUB)

LC record available at https://lccn.loc.gov/2021904206

1. Fiction — Dystopian 2. Fiction — Science Fiction & Fantasy — Science Fiction — Dystopian 3. Science Fiction & Fantasy — Science Fiction — Post-Apocalyptic 4. Literature & Fiction — Action & Adventure — Science Fiction 5. Books — Literature & Fiction — Action & Adventure — Mystery, Thriller & Suspense

"What may emerge as the most important insight of the twenty-first century is that man was not designed to live at the speed of light."

Marshall McLuhan

"Everybody has a plan till they get punched in the face."

Mike Tyson

CONTENTS

Part One: THE STARCHILD 1

    Prelude: THE SNATCHING OF STELLAN BONNET 3

    Chapter 1: THE SUBJECT ZERO 7

    Chapter 2: THE HAPPINESS PILL 51

    Chapter 3: VARGA'S CASTLE 67

    Chapter 4: THE ALETHEIA COUP OF 2041 91

    Chapter 5: THE PHOENIX RISING 125

    Chapter 6: THE SNATCHING OF STELLAN BONNET 147

Part Two: MANIFEST DESTINY 161

    Chapter 7: CHILDHOOD'S END 163

    Chapter 8: THE ESCAPE 187

    Chapter 9: INNOCENCE LOST 215

Chapter 10: NAUTILUS 249

Chapter 11: THE HACKING 263

Chapter 12: THE EMPIRE STRIKES BACK 295

Part Three: TYCHO BRAHE SECRET 325

Chapter 13: DE NOVA STELLA 327

Chapter 14: TYCHO BRAHE SECRET 357

Chapter 15: THE CODA 397

Part One

THE STARCHILD

Prelude

THE SNATCHING OF STELLAN BONNET

He's alone.

A darkness fell upon him. He's blind and deaf in a terrifying nightmare as this pitch-black gloom stripped him of all his senses. There is nothing around him, no recognizable sights or sounds of his or any other realities he knew, only this dark, cold, lonely hell.

Did he die?

No, the pungent odor of decomposing cadavers that's started to suffocate him tells him he's alive. That and his own funny smell. Strange. He usually never stinks or even sweats. So, there is a sliver of a silver lining: his own awareness.

He knows that *they* took him away, but he does not know where to. Are *they* maybe inside his mind, trying to conjure up demoniacal horrors? Nastassia, his big sis, taught him how to face mental dangers by not panicking and being self-aware of his consciousness. To start, he has to focus on the forceful skull-shining pranayama breathing. A long, slow inhale following a forceful exhale shakes off fear energy. A person is a mere reflection of their thoughts. *Never let fear eat your soul*, Nastassia cautioned him. Then, as protection—rather, as a counterattack against invisible enemy forces—he has to construct a hall of crystal mirrors in his mind-eye; it would frame and multiply him while reflecting, deflecting, and confusing psychic attackers by putting them in a maze of distorted images. No matter who *they* are and why *they* concocted this lonely, infernal sphere, *they* did hurl him into this fissure of doom he now fights against by his own reflection(s). Despite the darkness in which he can't see, in his mental eye, the mirrors have given him his depth, his dimensions back. At least a *sense* of it, the first sense he managed to regain.

A small victory!

He stops his skull-shining breathing and kneels, moving on to another breathing technique. It's called Lion's breath, a technique that focuses on the third eye in the middle of his forehead. He had always found the exercise silly, so even now he can't suppress a gentle giggle as he sticks his tongue out and exhales. Somehow, this time the Lion's breath feels like an act of fearless defiance. He's resisting *them* and it feels good! It's working.

He can focus now.

He *knew* perdition. He *saw* it in many naked human souls suffering as they knelt in front of the gates of hell. The smell of their regrets was always bitterly cold; a pain of loss, unlike any other, the pain of what might have been but was lost for whatever reason, haunted them at their last hour and, all too often, crushed their souls on its way out into the unknown. He *saw* damnation in the future(s) that used to beset him. But it always felt separate; his *visions* were never a part of his own life. Even the grim visions were only parts of his many realities; the circles of hell were disjointed from his real life as its *realness*, always filled with joy and love, was the dominant force over all other realities. This time is different. There's no other reality. Just this dark, deaf, cold, solitary hell.

At least he has these soothing crystal mirrors he created in his mind-eye to help him cope. He's not going to acquiesce to any of this. If necessary, he's going to recreate the whole universe in the hall of mirrors. He will dig himself out from whatever grimoire this demonic reality came to be and return to the people he loves the most in the whole world: Mom, Dad, and Nastassia.

As he's mulling over his options, he hears a strange whisper, like the hushed breathing of the mighty redwood he once heard in California. It is a relief at first, that sweet, familiar sound. Alas, within seconds the whisper morphs into a long, longing howl that increases in intensity with each passing moment until it reaches a piercing, roaring thunder. Ear-splitting noise attacks him from all sides. It is clear to him, *they* are assaulting his mirrors, so he tries to protect them by letting them float and dance evasively in his mind. It is to no avail. A diabolical, full-blast shrill, sounding like thousands blowing the trumpets of Jericho, shatters his crystals at once. The victory is snatched from him in one heavy blow, crushing his defense, crushing him along with it.

While he is still disoriented after the noise attack, he feels an ice-cold tingling sensation all over his body. It is like a thousand tiny needles start to poke and probe him, penetrating his skin as would snakes spewing venom into his blood. It feels green, the devilish substance entering his blood and his mind alike, gulping it rapidly and greedily as it takes over every molecule in his body, over every nerve and neuron, over every bit of what he is, snatching his living essence out of him in a terrifying haste that nothing can stop.

He starts to lose consciousness with one remaining sound-thought resonating in him—Debussy's "Clair de Lune," which his mother used to play on the big black Steinway grand piano. It used to scare him when he was a toddler, the Steinway. It looked like a mythical beast ready to swallow him whole. It doesn't scare him anymore. He is six. He's a big boy now. He clings to that sweet music, he's recreating in his mind. This is the Mom-tune, as sweet as memories of the smell of her apron, which he loved to sniff alongside his puppy while she prepared sautéed rosemary. This is the music he loved so much when the silver moonlight awoke him at night and Mom came into his room and played, or hummed, Debussy to put him right back to sleep. He keeps holding onto that tune for dear life but then, *puff!* it is gone in a flash as he's plunged into the cold, green gully that leads to the netherworld, to the point of no return.

What do *they* want from him?

Chapter 1

THE SUBJECT ZERO

New Athens, Harlem, NYC
March 21, 2048

Vigorously striding through piles of rubble and junk, Nastassia Bonnet, a fourteen-year-old cypher-punk girl treads through Amsterdam Avenue toward what used to be Harlem's most enchanting enclave, Sugar Hill. Her hair is a greenish-yellow-purple combo she calls "Octarine," *the color of magic*, a crazy hue she fell in love with while reading an already yellowed, rare comic book series, titled *Discworld* by Sir Terry Pratchett. Her Auntie Gretchen, who knew the author and was herself an eccentric character in a league of her own, bestowed upon Nastassia the precious collection for her eighth birthday. Nastassia passed the treasure trove of forty-one comic books onto her younger brother Stellan a few years later when he was even younger.

Regardless of her slender body and a smallish frame, Nastassia moves with the grace of a ballerina and the stealthy purpose of a lioness on the prowl, unfazed by New York's gloominess around her; she appears rather amused by it and keeps assessing her environment with a hint of irony in her glance—an expression seemingly older than her. The gusts swirl smut over the bleak streets and dark, empty houses, which she passes without a second thought. Sometimes it seems like not even an alley dog lives on those ghastly twitchels. A crumpled aluminum door of a looted jewelry store bangs violently, freezing Nastassia in her tracks. She stops for a second, observing the ravaged store and its once fake gold encrusted plaque—"Gretchen's Magic Gems"—that still stood strangely untouched by looters and weather, as the only remnant of the good auntie's store's glorious past. "Magic Gems," once loved by everyone, was a cozy place where magic of unexpected bonds forged among strangers took place, to Auntie's delight. She loved being an unexpected matchmaker of great power for good, as she liked to call these encounters, which she facilitated with the grace of a benevolent socialite. Nastassia sometimes helped Auntie Gretchen sell an occasional moonstone, a stone that mesmerized them both by its moonlight-like sheen or even volcanic Apache Tears obsidians, which used to happen when Nastassia was moved by the people's need to grieve and heal. They were so bad at hiding their feelings, she was always able to *see* how they felt.

Even her tiniest sale made the good auntie immensely proud of Nastassia, much to her chagrin.

"Poor Auntie," Nastassia whispers to herself and moves on, smiling at the memories.

Outside New Athens's gardens, once the thriving behemoth and pride of the States, New York City displays desolate rows of scorched skyscrapers, monuments to the insanity that had forever gripped humanity. It etched itself onto the Big Apple's famous skyline, now a picture-perfect postcard from Dante's *Inferno*—rather, its modern rendering. And yet Nastassia Bonnet calls such a crippled New York her home. Yes, the only people truly embracing New York, hoping and working for its revival, were the New Athens citizens. The rest of the city seems immersed in a memory of its own magic that might have been falsified over the years, but it's still enchanting to her. She continues walking when a call from her eyepiece interrupts her.

Happy Birthday to You

It was Jaroslav Kepler calling from Prague, the capital city of the Czech Republic. He's a boy of her age but whose plump cheeks made him look younger than Nastassia. He smiles from a holographic 3D display nested into her ultra-thin contact lenses.

"Happy birthday," he exclaims, hiding his true feelings for her. "I made this just for you," he says, flashing a colorful Baudelaire T-shirt whose inscription reads:

It Is Time to Be Drunk.

"Don't be a Douche-McGouche," Nastassia says, too delighted by the gift to admit.

"Why? It's a badass gift," Jaroslav retorts with fake disappointment on his face.

"The first rule of badassery—no bragging," Nastassia laughs, "and I am only fourteen."

"It won't matter when the shit hits the fan."

"Since when do you care about what's happening in the meat-space?"

"Everyone in the world does," concludes Jaroslav somberly. They stay on the line, both silent, immersed in their own thoughts for a while; he sitting in front of his computer in Prague's New Athens, she walking toward the inner circles of New York's New Athens.

A strange noise makes Nastassia pause in front of an impromptu holographic news projection that's next to a burned-down townhouse. Holograms were popping up all over the world like mutant cockroaches terrorizing the world. Those were GAVS (Global Audio and Video System) that started as 3D teleconferencing systems used to help corporations save money on conferences and travel, but have evolved into a system that serves the UN and the governments alike to communicate important announcements to their subjects. The subjects, always keen to listen to their master's voice, gather around the hologram and listen to its transmission in a strange mix of annoyed silence and somehow worn-out awe.

May You Always Walk in Sunshine

"They must be kidding me?" Nastassia scoffs.

The most dulcet song of them all, "May You Always" sung by The Lennon Sisters, whose fading fame is almost a hundred years old, comes from the GAVS as it wafts over the Harlem's ravaged landscape:

> *May your heartaches be forgotten*
> *May no tears be spilled*
> *And may always be a dreamer*
> *May your wildest dream come true.*

"Who chooses that shite?" Nastassia huffs to herself as the song continues:

> *"May good fortune find your doorway*
> *May the bluebird sing your song*
> *May no trouble travel your way*
> *May no worry stay too long."*

A video stream replacing that maudlin tone popped up next, simultaneously on millions of holograms, 3D eyepieces, virtual and augmented reality (VR & AR) glasses, computer video streams, and 8K sets all over the world is arguably the most important event in human history.

Whom the Gods Would Destroy, They First Make Mad

His serene highness, Dr. Maximillian von Liechtenstein, the Secretary-General of the United Nations General Assembly, was given the honor of informing the world's citizens by speaking directly to them.

Oh, boy what's in the cards for them? he thought. *If only they knew… well, they will soon. But, chop-chop.* He has no time to mull over the biblical task he was given. Even the thought of the enormity of what's coming sends cold shivers down von Liechtenstein's spine. *I hope I'd be worthy of trust.* He shuddered, immensely proud of the fact he's the one chosen. That's an assignment like no other in his illustrious life, so he was seizing the moment in all its glory. Van Liechtenstein's somehow squeaky voice does not take away from the importance of the announcement he's about to share with the whole wide world. Despite his unpleasant, high-pitched timbre and dwarfish appearance, he manages to appear somewhat magnanimous, like a finagling cowbird laying her eggs in the nests of other species, perfectly self-aware of the gravitas he carries around circles of power. He coughs quietly and starts with his speech.

"Today, the nations of the world transfer their sovereignty to the wisdom-ruled, impartial, quantum-based general artificial intelligence that will help humanity, once for all, exit the Second Dark Age that has almost destroyed our species," he said, smugly smiling like a priest pontificating about chastity to a bunch of horny high-school teenagers who, he thought, were unaware of his dark(er) side. The Second Dark Age term, thoughtfully placed at the beginning of his speech, invoked a zombie-apocalypse-like state of civilization after a series of pandemics, nuclear explosions, and subsequent wars that drove the world economy to a halt and its societies to the state of medieval, barking madness, in the minds of each one of his listeners.

"Impartial intelligence, my sweet, round, teenage ass," Nastassia huffs.

"It's not that round," Jaroslav says, trying to crack a joke.

"Very funny," she snaps. Irritated by the UN spectacle, Nastassia shakes her head, turns her eyepiece off, and leaves the external hologram—rather

Dr. von Liechtenstein and his pomposity—behind. He keeps telling the world about the upcoming governmental wonders that would—let's no one doubt them—bestow fruitful lands of honey and milk upon the exhausted human race, come hell or high water.

The Wall of Lost Children

Nastassia keeps walking toward the inner circle of New Athens's Block ATH-NYC-02, already at the cross of Amsterdam Avenue and West 145th Street. At the Gate Point, a throng of people are gathered for a protest. The wall behind them is filled with photos of young children, the Wall of Lost Children as the alt-media dubbed it, something the mainstream infotainment media outlets wholesomely ignored over the years. The wall was something that, unless they had relatives "inside," no one outside New Athens had even been made aware of. The lost children were indeed lost for most of the world that had no clue they ever existed. The protesters carry photos and posters of their young kids and chant:

"We want the truth! We want the truth!"

Their rhythmic chanting carries the brittle charge of hundreds of roaring hearts filled with pain and sorrow over the unknown. Whatever the truth might have been since the children—always the talented, unusual kids gifted with rare abilities—started to disappear, it was hidden from everyone, thinks Nastassia. As the wave of chants invokes anguish in her, a heavy sense of premonition, like a quick needle prick poked at her heart, fills her with apprehension. She fears for her little brother. Not for the first time she wants to hug Stellan, to squeeze him next to her heart and to protect him with all the love she has for that strange little human, a love she felt since the first time she saw him—a tiny, ridiculously wrinkled, scarlet-colored bundle of noise and farts with funny little toes, a stuffy nose, and a joyful giggle. Luckily, he's already too old. *Is he?* Anyway, she'll see him later today. Nastassia composes herself by side-glancing at the several small screens transmitting from the United Nations. She notices how one neatly dressed but furious man in his early forties spits on von Liechtenstein's close-up smirking from the screen. "Scumbag!" the man yells, his eyes bulging in rage.

Looming from the screens, Dr. von Liechtenstein, oblivious to the plebeian disrespect, keeps reciting his speech. He has the whole world to worry about, the world that hangs on his every syllable. Nastassia looks at him, *seeing* through him, *feeling* him and his emotions, *sensing* his inner thoughts. He looks rather comical to her, more of an inflatable duck than the statesman he tries so hard to be. In his own eyes, von Liechtenstein finally has a long-deserved triumph set up for him, as the world trembles in expectation beneath his feet. That fleeting image passes through his thoughts and almost makes him chuckle on live TV.

Nastassia almost chokes. "Freak," she whispers, shaking off the feeling coming from him. It is a barely noticeable moment of scorn, almost repulsion for the people Dr. von Liechtenstein is addressing, something he feels strongly but overcomes with a well-rehearsed cough, used as a segue into his last words of the segment: "The governmental transition sequence will start as soon as the technicians are ready. We'll be back soon after these messages from our sponsors."

Sugar Hill, New Athens

Sugar Hill, now a New Athens pocket of independence, was renamed to the Block ATH-NYC-02 and assigned to New York, Nastassia's hometown. Despite its dull designation, old Sugar Hill's splendor continues to live, perhaps not as obvious as it was way back when sleek city lotharios roamed its streets, but still as glorious as ever. Its cyberpunks were rediscovering the sublime mysteries of Absinthe, that "pale opal wine," and Rimbaud's hellish poetry alike. Nastassia never believed in them—the geeks were enraptured by the tech magic much more than with the green fairy they, for reasons unknown, liked to brag about.

So, instead of congregating in bars like their rebellious predecessors, unreasonable in their aspirations for life, love, and art, the cypher-punks of New Athens receded into abandoned dungeons, wiring them up to the deep underbelly of the internet where Sugar Hill's energy still existed. It suffused those freedom-seeking geeks, nerds, and lunatics who were scattered all over its abandoned neo-renaissance houses with quite a different kind of energy, as it kept quietly humming in their computers, creating parallel worlds in the realms of the Dark Web.

"Apocal-Doxxing Syndrome"

Like all other New Athens around the world, the Block ATH-NYC-02 stemmed from the Global New Athens Privacy Treaty of 2041, signed in the United Nations on the night of 2041 New Years' Eve. The powers to be never wanted their subjects to be too aware of what was going on—as everyone knows, governmental depravity thrives in darkness. The bulk of the rabble should not be overly concerned over the privacy or freedoms, the overlords knew. The populace's fragile sensitivities were to be shielded from tragedies like the one that shattered the world a year earlier, an affair best described in the *Apocal-Doxxing Syndrome* investigative essay by Philip Bolghery, a Pulitzer Prize winner, with the help of Lorainne Elster and Jeff C. Winiecki, the people that play an important role in this narrative. *Doxxing* is a process of making one's personally identifiable information (such as their names, addresses, phone numbers, avatars) available online, a strategy that first happened in 1994, when personal information was leaked about well-known USENET (a distributed discussion system) users on the USENET system itself. During the 2000–2020 period, doxxing became a sport that included exposing of a notorious "creepy uncle" Violentacrez, a depraved, vile man who had created forums dedicated to racism, porn, gore, misogyny, incest, photos of dead children, and sexualized images of underage girls on Reddit, an American social news aggregation and discussion website. No one felt sorry for the sick pervert but the much darker side of doxxing was the bullying of innocents that followed. A combo of disclosing private data of anyone internet trolls were targeting and then going after them, they were modern-day witch-hunts that ran rampant in between 2035 and 2040.

Over the years, doxxing and the social mobbing that always followed wreaked havoc in many lives, but it reached its sordid peak during the Apocal-Doxxing tragedy targeting children. An enormously popular app, TeenCret Talk, or TCT for "Teens Secret Talk" was sold to teenagers and pre-teens as a safe chat environment, a parent- and hacker-proof tool safe from gabble snitches and blabbermouths alike, and yet, it was hacked.

As shrewd kids of the digital era, many began employing personal codes and ciphers when talking to someone they knew as an additional layer of secured private communication, so the TCT with its entrancing graphs based on Japanese manga comics was a smashing hit. And it was truly safe, as secure as it was fun. So what could've gone wrong? No personal data were ever exchanged with The Shàobīng ("sentinel") servers used by the TCT, LLC., and yet, thousands of kids' chat transcripts, with their most intimate photos and social network profiles, were hacked and published in bulk on the *Incorruptus* (not spoiled or seduced, unadulterated) network.

What would've been an innocent game of sexual exploration, or dreams and fears exchanged among friends, had degenerated into a monstrous monument of madness and shame, erected online to stay there in infamy forever. Online pitchforks were raised, the stakes were burned, and the rabid mobs smelling fresh blood thrust online shaming into its highest gear ever and started chasing children like rabid dogs. It felt like the Apocalypse had been unleashed on those poor kids in a flurry of righteous madness, fueled by the *Incorruptus's* holier-than-thou, self-appointed "true virtuosi" of the Virtuosi™ movement, who were, with morbid pleasure, dissecting every word uttered by those kids, every photo, every video, their every thought, and mercilessly shaming them.

The kids were left with nowhere to hide. Dozens chose to kill themselves. The media and politicians were doing their utmost to cover up the tragedy but they soon lost control over events.

Happy Angels

The shocking suicide of twelve-year-old Aurora Jane Throndsen from Staunton, Virginia was the turning point. Aurora Jane and her friend Noémie Lacroix were true embodiments of angels. Aurora Jane had big, beautiful blue eyes and was always smiling despite a bike accident she suffered; she was a dancer who'd never dance again after that tragic day but had faced her predicament with a brave heart and steely resolve to live a happy life. Noémie, with her almond eyes and cute, funny giggle was an accomplished piano player, even at her age. Her rendition of *Pavane pour une infante défunte* (*Pavane for a Dead Girl*) by Maurice Ravel became an instant internet sensation. Aurora Jane painted angels and puppies that made people joyous with the innocent naivete of her cheerful work.

The two girls met over TeenCret Talk, in a private group for kids that were either confined to wheelchairs or had other walking-related impediments. Soon after they met, they moved to a 1T1 (one to one) chamber and communicated directly with each other, without anyone else present. Aurora Jane had a dark, painful secret. Her pain was still devastating, her soul still crushed. She never spoke about it to anyone.

Noémie lived in Paris and was another twelve-year-old girl in a wheelchair, but due to polio, and once she was Aurora Jane's bestie for life, became the confidant of her secrets. Noémie understood her pain. Aurora

Jane wrote to Noémie about her loneliness. There was *a hole in me where the sun cannot reach, where love is forbidden and the heart is lonely like a dead rose*, she wrote to her. *No one will ever kiss me,* AJ, as Noémie called her, was telling her friend about being strong for everyone else, while she's withering inside, feeling how her heart is getting weaker and weaker. Her friend, a tiny little girl with a kind heart, proposed to teach Aurora Jane how to play piano, online, to help her out. *You have nothing to lose*, Noémie assured AJ. Soon afterward they were like two giggling weirdos in wheelchairs, one playing clumsily, another like a virtuoso, but happy, like fluffy little seals.

Aurora Jane seemed to have found a way to start digging herself out of the abyss that deep sorrow had created in her when the *Incorruptus's* revelation happened and shattered her world. One particular guy, in his twenties and not even a kid anymore, was the embodiment of online cruelty. He edited Aurora Jane's piano playing and her writing in a video that went viral. *Of course she's lonely when she as ugly as a toad and plays like a retard.* The mockery was cruel and relentless. *Kiss a Retard* memes were popping up like nuclear mushrooms, hurting her little heart like hell. Every word Aurora Jane had ever written, every thought she confined to Noémie, her every hope, dream, and fear alike, everything was a boon for the ruthless mob to mock her and a bane to her. But that word—*retard*—that has, over the last several decades justifiably putrefied into a loathsome sound and became one of the most hated words, like the N-word was decades ago, was too much. The R-word was something no one with a modicum of decency would ever hurl toward another human being any longer. (It was only used in a jokingly self-demeaning sense under circumstances soon to be described in this truthful narrative.) And yet, it resurfaced, hurled straight into Aurora Jane's heart, multiplied endlessly, and inflicted so much pain, which she wasn't able to cope with.

After crawling up the window, she jumped from her family's apartment on rue de l'Hôtel de Ville in Paris. To the horror of everyone, even her death was mocked at first, given the awkward position of her lifeless, broken legs on the bloody pavement.

"*The angels are happy, you're back home and free to play and dance with them,*" Noémie read aloud from a poem she wrote for AJ's grief journal and posted it online. She played piano to accompany her words. Her tears, trickling down from her dark, beautifully oval-shaped face with cute cheek dimples, and the quiet sobs she could not control, finally broke the callous, collective internet's heart. The tragedy of two little girls already living difficult lives before doxxing had turned the tide of public opinion. The heads of those responsible needed to roll.

The shock over the cruelty that drove Aurora Jane to such a desperate act quickly turned to anger; the fits of anger morphed into a blind rage that became the wrath of millions demanding immediate action. Vapid condolences, phony prayers, and vacuous promises by platitudinous, virtue-signaling politicians were not cutting it anymore. The people had had it with those cheap bastards in expensive suits. The heads had to roll, something must be done, everyone agreed.

And pronto.

The Hacker Possessed

After the *Incorruptus's* published the kids' data, Nastassia locked herself in a room and did not say a word to anyone for over a week. She had barely eaten or slept—at times her parents were afraid that she might go mad—as she dug herself into the most vicious parts of the internet, prowling about the deep, dark places where wicked trolls dwell, enjoying their virtual debauchery. She wasn't reading the grief journals or watching morbid video reactions of the suicide deaths popping all over the world—nope, instead she was tirelessly chasing every single digital scent, every trace left in the trails of *The Incorruptus* responsible for the doxxing the kids and torturing Aurora Jane.

But, how was doxxing the children even possible? She had to start from there.

It was an almost incomprehensible maze of tools and tactics that *Incorruptus* developed for probing the seaming underbelly of the Dark Web, all in order to "restore decency" in our digital lives by doxxing the "sinners." They've used a variety of tools developed by the NSA, CIA, DIA, and the devil's incarnates, private corporations like Palantir Technologies Inc., FireEye Inc., Crypto Kitties, GmBH, LiveRamp Holdings, Inc., and the Acxiom Real Identity™ that were all subsequently leaked and free to use. And boy did *The Incorruptus* use it in the most vile way. The kids were just a side catch in the wide and deep net these "True Virtuosi" had cast over the internet, an afterthought at first, but they paid the biggest price.

Using language analysis and unique signals in texts, including finger kinematics in goal-directed actions, like the difference in time needed to click on a like button vs. to finish a benign word vs. to finish a salty term, plus a pattern of mouse movements and the velocity of keyboard strokes, they started to create digital profiles of everyone using the internet. Once the pattern of various little idiosyncrasies was paired with the target's screen size, geolocation, mouse—and keyboard—action analysis (and hundreds of other data like the time spent on a given site or a chat, the frequency, the network of friends, and followers their interactions have created), it was easy to match other, open and available texts of any human on Earth with their own secret communication and identify them.

Then the mass hacking of their mobile gadgets that followed gave *The Incorruptus* access to every communication in real-time. The rest is painful history.

Nastassia's laser-like focus was on those who picked on AJ and Noémie with such savage cruelty. She hunted them down, following them in every nook and cranny of the Dark Web and "normal" internet alike. She used simple YCbCr Sub Sampling data from the photos posted by suspects and matched them with findings that *The Incorruptus's* own hacking tools were gathering in order to start finding those ghouls that killed little Aurora Jane. Nastassia, suffused with cold, methodical fury, went on performing her holy war against those monsters with the merciless precision of an ancient assassin from the mountains of Persia where the mysterious Order of Assassins originated. She found one after another of these abominable people in the filth of hatred where they dwelled by recreating their profiles using their own tools.

Publication

Nastassia did not doxx those responsible herself. Instead she gave a list of culprits and all the evidence she gathered to her father, Frédéric, to do with what he thought was best. Unbeknownst to her, Philip Bolghery, Lorainne Elster, and Jeff C. Winiecki had embarked upon their own research, the findings of which the authors presented in a heart-wrenching *Apocal-Doxxing Syndrome* essay, filled with data and proofs. Nastassia noticed a lot of elements in the essay that could've come only from her detective work but did not even want to bother thinking about it anymore. She buried Aurora Jane and the other dead children deep into her heart, making sure they were never forgotten, at least not by her, not as long as she lives.

But, once the essay detailing the vile processes that killed their children was published, the people went truly berserk. A direct outcome of Aurora Jane's tragedy was not only severe prison sentences for the perpetrators of hate, the panic of the politicians, and the stringent new hate crime laws written to cover their sorry asses, but almost sneaked into it the establishment of New Athens via the Privacy Treaty of 2041.

New Athens, Harlem, NYC
March 21, 2048

The treaty established so-called pockets of privacy independence, living quarters for the global citizens willing to opt out of the prior Civilized Surveillance Treaty and relinquish its numerous advantages as they were presented in various bureaucratic communiqués around the world. Those privileges, from 2041 on forgone by the New Athens citizens, coming from the Register, a unified database of all living human beings, were free internet, free wireless, and free electric battery power for their cars, as long as the user agrees that all her data, all that a user says or does in their daily life, the roads they travel, the hologram calls they made, the medicine they take, the VR world they populate, and the food they ate belong to the corporate overlords and the governments in their pockets.

Over the last several decades, a new mantra was obsessing the word economies: "Data is the new oil!" All data that could have been gobbled was gobbled up. The world economic growth revolved around big data. The more ominous realities, like having their lives and futures shaped by the overlords, were invisible chains wrapped around the face of humanity, who were led into mindless stupor, and seemed not to bother anyone anymore.

Until New Athens came to life.

So Sugar Hill was the center of what, for the Outsiders came to be known as the Deep Dark Web, which was almost completely out of their reach. While New Athenians were mocked by the Outsiders for refusing to be a part of the Register, the very base of normal living that provided so many benefits, their education was not only free of usury tuition rampant in the college life in the "normal" world, but it was much better and gave a whole new meaning to "homeschooling." Despite what the Outsiders were told by infotainment media to think about them, the New Athenians restored the idea of a family as the key social unit and the parents, no matter if they were hetero or gay, focused on the children and their uniqueness.

Unlike the outside world, where party dogmas brainwashed the kids, here the education was carefully tailored to suit each pupil and his or her particular set of skills, abilities, and affinities. They understood that being a mom was a very creative pursuit, a *sine qua non* for parental development as much as the child's own. The parents were taught not to project their ambitions or failures onto the child, no matter how difficult it might be. Teaching by example, not by pontification, was a rule. Moreover, New Athens's homeschooling also featured regular lectures online, by experts in their fields willing to work pro bono for the benefit of the children's education, something parents had tailor-made for their kids. At least twice-weekly were gatherings outdoors where the kids played ancient games such as soccer or basketball or, if they were younger, obstacle courses, SPUD, or kick the cans, as a part of educational fun.

Anti-establishment figures from decades ago all moved to various New Athens around the world, providing free education outside of the educational institution framework of yesteryear. People like the famous biologist couple Heather Heying and Bret S. Weinstein, investigative journalist Whitney Webb, the common sense champion Nzube Olisaebuka Udezue, legendary Zuby, a purveyor of sanity, magnificently sardonic Professor Gad Saad, Michael Krechmer, a.k.a. anarchist Michael Malice, psychologist Jordan Peterson, the goodness of AI heart promoter, esteemed Dr. Lex Fridman, PhD, even Joe Peabody and Joe Rogan, a podcaster famous for his merciless, singlehanded destruction of CNN and its BS as a business model, polymath Eric R. Weinstein as well as journalistic doyens Chris L. Hedges and Olivier Allard, Mohammad S. Olsen, Anabella Alexandre, and even Ai Weiwei at ninety-one years old. Eva zu Beck, the legendary "raw adventurer seeking the experience of feeling alive," nourished the need for an adventure in the New Athens populace. Daniel Idfresne, a forty-year-old free thinker born and raised in Brooklyn, New York was the first dean of The New Lyceum Academy, the first New Athenian university founded on the ancient Platonian and Aristotelian principles, teaching the pupils how to think through philosophy, logic, natural sciences, astronomy, dialectics, and politics. Even the most famous people from the establishment, embodied in the historian and Rothschilds biographer, Niall Ferguson, MA, D.Phil, have found their way into New Athens alongside the thousands of other free spirits who found the safe intellectual harbor therein. Dr. Ben Goertzel, a cross-disciplinary scientist, who chaired the futurist nonprofit Humanity+, another polymath known for creating experimental fiction and music, going on long hikes, and promoting backpacking, kayaking, and other outdoor activities, played a crucial role in humanizing Nastassia's deep research and thinking about the AI "for Good" while giving it Eva zu Back's flair for adventure in the real world.

The biggest strides in creating a connection between New Athenians and Outsiders were in the mutual fight against the Industrial Food Poisoning Complex; there were many organic, honest farmers in the outside world more than ready to supply New Athens with healthy food. Russell Brand, an English comedian, actor, and radio host turned a political figure of quite clout, started his affiliation with New Athens London when he moved there to participate in the intellectual dark web, on the educational side of its efforts, only to turn an organic farmer with great passion and success.

The Spartans of Spirit

These Spartans of Spirit, as Philip Bolghery, a notorious journalist for some and notable freedom fighter for the others once christened them, have renewed the famed American vitality, the whole we-can-do-it approach to life. As America became sluggish, obese, addicted, cynical, and depressed, New Athenians thrived in old explorations that had once made the country great. A right to inquiry, to challenge dogma, and to live free created a fighting spirit in New Athens's life that thrived "in the meadows by the woods," a quirky metaphor everyone used but didn't know how it came to be and what it really meant. But it felt good to live life to its fullest outside the tyrannical coziness of the Outsiders' world.

New Athens created whole new facets of economy in their data- and knowledge-based markets. A pioneer of that movement was an old AI sage named Trent McConaghy, a man who hacked away through the cold winters nights on the Canadian pig farm where he was raised. He was instrumental in creating e-Residency in Estonia, a predecessor of New Athens. He lived in Berlin's New Athens, working on genetic programming theory and writing profusely. He also created an Ocean Protocol platform, a data marketplace for independent AI researchers. Perhaps more important than Trent were the IOTA Protocol pioneers like Dominik Schiener and Dr. Serguei Popov and many others, unsung heroes of freedom movements around the world.

After The Privacy Treaty of 2041, humanity was painfully and irrevocably split between two groups: one within New Athens and another, vastly bigger outside. They were clearly delineated on privacy matters and more often than not severely hostile toward each other. The Virtuosi™ social policies were also something that New Athens people despised and rejected, so Nastassia's folks understood that chasm and lived in a world of their own making. The alternative living that New Athens represented was not looked upon kindly, primarily by those political powers that had been loath to grant them their rights since the beginning.

The Happiness Pill
March 21, 2048

The frozen image of the United Nations' hectic preparation fades out and an overly tanned man in his perpetual forties, Winston Varga, a human equivalent of pure bliss dressed as Uncle Sam, briskly strides in and strikes an I-Want-You pose as he fades in on billions of screens all over the world. His smile flashes as brightly as a million smart light bulbs at once.

Varga is none other than the richest man in history, the flamboyant founder, CEO, and president of Proteus FinTech Corp., a multinational conglomerate consortium company, an amalgam of the former Google, Facebook, Apple, Amazon, and a dozen similar but smaller corporations, combined into a new behemoth that dominates the world after the Second Dark Ages had enveloped everyone in its gloom. Always a ruthless businessman who'd make even the cruelest robber barons' pillages look like benign kindergarten scuffles, Varga is said to have modeled his business empire upon King Leopold II of Belgium's seizure of Congo.

Leopold II had incorporated "The Congo Free State" that was owned, controlled, and ruled exclusively by him. That "free" state was one of the most atrocious monstrosities of the early 20th century—it ravaged the country and mutilated and killed millions of its citizens. It is said that Winston Varga, after being asked, "When is enough? What else do you want?" replied with, "I want it all. Not even the world is enough."

"He does not even pretend anymore," Nastassia bitterly whispers, watching from another impromptu public-square hologram. A rush of anger overwhelms her, a reaction to what that very man represented to her: everything that is wrong with today's world. He has been mercilessly crushing everyone on his path, and yet, fawning media and so many of his online *followers* have been swooning and falling all over themselves in 24/7 long, nauseating, bootlicking praise of Varga's incomparable genius. And now this. Nastassia feels a strong pang of disgust, thinking for a moment that she might vomit. Even more so, she had been *sensing* from an early age that her destiny is somehow connected to that loathsome excuse of a human being. It was an unsettling feeling that lingered over her every time he appeared in the media he controlled anyway. In the last several years, he seemed omnipresent and unavoidable, he and his rotten, shiny titanium teeth. Yes, she was aware of the contradiction and smiled at it; the paradox of her own thoughts somehow eased her anger, so she looked back at Varga's smugly smiling image, not even wanting to spit on it anymore.

And yet, Varga values *Life, Liberty, and the pursuit of Happiness* more than anything else. His commercial, seen by billions all over the world, supports such a hefty, heartfelt notion: "The pursuit of happiness is embedded in the genes of our great nation," Winston Varga proclaims solemnly but still somewhat exuberantly, "and soon it would be a part of the life of every man, women, and child in the world. No one can take away your human rights. And you know," he winks to the world, "the pinnacle of those rights is your inalienable right to be happy!"

He strikes an adlocutio (orator's) pose resembling the statue of Augustus Cesar, the first emperor of the Roman Empire he once bought for himself and, almost humbly, proclaims:

"And now you can, effortlessly, be happy whenever you wish to be!"

With these words, Varga pulls out a brilliantly packaged red Happiness Pill bottle from his pocket and waves it in front of the cameras. His smile widens, flashing those impeccable, commercially pure titanium Ti–6Al–4V implants. A message scrolls down the screen:

> "Now you can have happiness
> all for yourself.
> Call 1-800-JOY-BLISS
> and for just $99.99
> order your dose of eternal glee now.
> Call 1-800-JOY-BLISS."

After several fast non-linear cuts, both Winston Varga and the message fades out and a large Happiness Pill bottle soars from the New York ashes; the gloomy images of ruins vanish in the background, replaced by twinkling stars on happy skies. Swarms of people, men and women of all twenty-seven lawfully recognized genders (alas, in an unbecoming display, rather a despicable bout of xenogenderphobia, bunnygenders, and stargenders were not included. Neither were, much to their chagrin, a single alterhumangenders taken parts in the ad) kids and grannies alike, jump into the scene followed by animated toons, cheerful brains, and singing amygdalae. Mickey Mouse and Yoda never looked as happy as they look now, happily chasing a giggling Minnie Mouse around. Two remarkably beautiful and immensely euphoric young women, Ambrosia and Marissa, appear from behind the ruins and joyfully join in the song. Varga, Marissa, and Ambrosia lovingly interlock hands with the joyous crowd and mischievous jolly toons, and dance around the Happiness Pill bottle. The Lennon Sisters start singing their sentimental tune again and they all croon along:

> *May your heartaches be forgotten*
> *May no tears be spilled*
> *And may always be a dreamer*
> *May your wildest dream come true.*

A banner, thick and red as blood, scrolls over the screen: "15% Of All Purchases Go to Our Fearless Heroes Fighting the Evil Chinese Red Army in the Malacca Strait War."

The music slowly fades out as the Pill's order instructions freeze on the screen with call-to-action keywords—"!! Buy Now !!"—prominently placed in front of the billions.

"Jesus H. Christ," Nastassia quietly huffs and looks around. The people stand in awe of the monstrosity Varga just rammed down their mental throats. Some are hastily ordering bliss from their gadgets. *They bought that shit, they really bought it*, she thinks as she leaves, unable to cope with Varga zombies, his audience always ready to eagerly gobble up from his kitschy propaganda plates. She needs to breathe free again and hurries up toward her good auntie Gretchen's home in New Athens.

An uneasy feeling about the Pill lingers in her. It feels like destiny has revealed itself to her through it, but Nastassia, regardless of her mental-eye efforts, does not see what it means. His intentions were locked in, impenetrable to her. Knowing Varga, nothing good can come out of this new product he's peddling to the world, she reckons. *We'll see in due time,* she thinks. Something in her, a barely noticeable feeling, forewarns her that it would be sooner rather than later, the day of reckoning she feels is approaching, but she had not the faintest clue what it might bring.

It makes her anxious.

Nastassia strides faster and, as she passes the far end side of the Wall of Lost Children on the corner the West 145th Street and Amsterdam Avenue, she again side-eyes the smiling faces of all those kids. Nastassia can not avoid reminiscing about her early years. When she was only a five-year-old, she experienced the horror of facing her own precog abilities.

The First Precognition
New Athens, Harlem, NYC
June 2nd, 2039

It happened when Nastassia sensed, rather when she *saw* her mother's ventricular tachycardia for the first time. She had no idea what the abnormal electrical signals in the lower chambers of her mom's heart are, the heart she *saw* and *knew* loved her, as it spasmodically twitched at the time, caused Nastassia to almost suffocate in dread. She was barely able to breathe when she saw how her mom's lungs were not getting enough oxygen cells for the hemoglobin, which in her imagination always looked like Popeye the Sailor cheerfully carrying O2 molecules to the lungs. The hemoglobin was losing strength and was unable to fill her mom's lung with life. (She always thought of an oxygen molecule as life) Nastassia hugged her mom and pressed her face to Mom's heart, trying to help it beat by sending her love-energy to Mom and her heart. Monique was startled by Nastassia's odd behavior and just hugged her back, "I love you, baby," she gently whispered to her. Nastassia felt the warmth and sensed how her mom's heart calmed down, filled with love. She relaxed, overwhelmed by relief, happiness, and love. It made Nastassia feel nice and one with her mom's calm, loving heartbeat.

At that point, she fathomed the deep, healing power of love and decided that she'd love all living beings in the world forever, from this day on, until the day she dies.

The Cancer Discovery

Two years later, when Nastassia was able to better articulate what she *saw*, while still instinctively hiding the ability that enabled her to *see*, Monique faced another health scare, and this time also a double horror. Nastassia was terrified when she saw a growing cancer in Monique's breasts. While the microtentacles were forming on the surface of her mom's breast tumor cell, Nastassia *saw* them, like a dying sun traveling through mom's blood vessels, like the Death Star killing one healthy cell after another. The dark sun was truly scary, its rays were black tentacles, its movement rapacious, as it was voraciously infecting and gobbling up Monique's healthy cells.

"I don't want you to die, Mom," she said quietly during the family dinner. She looked down at her plate, which was filled with her favorite mussel soup with garlic, Florence fennel, tomatoes, and a hint of orange zest, something she adored but did not touch today.

Monique froze.

"Why would you say that, darling?" Frédéric asked, gazing at his daughter.

Nastassia left the table without saying a word, went to her room, and came back with a crude drawing of a dying sun ravaging her mom's body cells and gave it to Frédéric, not looking at Monique, not once. Then, with a side-glance at Monique, who stayed sitting stock-still, staring at her daughter, she said, "You have cancer, Mom," she declared with difficulty, so quietly that Frédéric had to gently ask her to repeat it.

"Come again, dear? What did you say, Nastassia?"

"Mom has cancer, Dad!" Nastassia repeated and, for the first time, looked at her mom's astonished face. They looked at each other for several seconds laden with grief, until Monique fully comprehended what her daughter had told her. She knew Nastassia was right, she sensed the truth as much as her daughter had sensed her illness. Monique's anguished expression broke Nastassia's heart, so she ran around the table to hug Mom and started to cry in that embrace. Frédéric came to them and embraced them both as they were sobbing.

"Everything will be all right, my loves," he said.

Luckily, the very next day Nastassia's parents rushed for a checkup and discovered that Nastassia's sense was correct—Monique did indeed have stage one breast cancer. Due to the forewarning, it was still in an early stage, and it was easily curable. The hospital had compared the DNA sequences of Monique's cancer and her healthy cells, and based on the comparison of the cancer mutation, created RNA molecules that produced cancer antigen proteins that attacked and destroyed the cancer cells ravaging her body.

The health scare was dwarfed by the second horror both Monique and Frédéric had to cope with as soon as Monique was in no danger anymore:

the fact that Nastassia seemed to be a precog or at least to have had a highly developed, extrasensory perception. Such a revelation truly terrified them. The rumors were rampant that the disappearing kids all over the world all had similar abilities—those of precogs. It wasn't a big number of missing children, but the circumstances, a total lack of information about any of them, and the police's strange tight-lipped behavior after the kids went missing was a fertile ground for all sorts of crazy conspiracy theories that circulated the world. *The Disappearing Precogs?* was Philip Bolghery's article series on the mystery. He had been publishing the results of his investigation until he hit a brick wall of silence and conspiracy bundled in one impenetrable knot, which not even he was able to untangle.

Her parents' fears, as palpable as dark clouds over their heads, paralyzed Nastassia, causing her to suppress her abilities even more since that time. She did not want to worry them. So, she turned to computers, programming, and hacking instead, leaving her other, otherworldly talents undeveloped to their true potential. After he was born, Stellan seemed to be even more talented than her at his age, so that was a constant source of concern.

She possessed an uncanny ability to *see* the numbers scrolling in her mind, to *sense* the solutions any software bug might have even before she was able to understand its inner workings and squash it mercilessly, like the RNA proteins that had crushed her mom's cancer cells. So, when she was twelve, Nastassia immersed herself in the development of emotional recognition patterns for AI—emotions for cyborgs. She was scared, rather inspired by Ian McEwan's book *Machines Like Me,* and wanted to solve the problem that was looming on the horizon: the machines' compassion. Without it, Nastassia thought, once it emerges in its full force, the AI would have no empathy either. And if they were sentient beings without compassion or empathy, what would preclude them from weeding us out as a mere nuisance? After all, "when an AI observed humans as they saunter around, it would perceive us as we would the saguaro cactus as it grows. To them we might be as useless as Russian thistle, that tumbling tumbleweed Mom hated so much when we lived in Arizona," she wrote in the chatroom once.

Did she even dare to start seriously pondering the AI intuition? Or the boredom? With their computational speed, our world would be at a standstill to them. What would an advanced AI do in the eternity humans use to aimlessly crawl around? Nastassia enjoyed thinking about all of that.

The Alan Turing Ghost

It was McEwan's book that first introduced Alan Turing to Nastassia Bonnet. She wept reading Nick Drake's poem about Turing titled *Message from the Unseen World* and could not believe the wicked cruelty of Britain's Sexual Offences Act that offered Turing, a man who invented the computer and de facto rescued the world from the Nazis by breaking their famous cipher, the Enigma Machine, a choice of either prison or chemical castration. A small, albeit deeply tragic wonder that he had committed suicide. While Nastassia had not yet experienced the pleasures of lovemaking, either with one of her peers or with any sex robots that were the talk of the town when she discovered Turing's greatness and subsequent tragedy, she developed a deep interest in the emotions of sex, love, and compassion.

Sex robots were grist for the mill for many of her acquaintances in various chat rooms, and their incessant talk about it aroused her curiosity. She knew many of her online buddies were using sex robots as a result of being falsely accused of sexually inappropriate behavior, a tool of personal degradation the Virtuosi™ loved to use so much over the last decade.

"Could a sex machine, programmed to have sex with its *owner*," she once asked the Renegade in a chatroom, "be raped?" For now it should suffice to say that although she had never met him in the meat-space, the Renegade is a technical and scientific legend of mythical proportions, a genius who took Nastassia under his wing. He helped her out with her ventures and adventures and is someone who plays a crucial role in both her life and in this narrative of life-altering events.

"Not these programmable toys," the Renegade wrote back, "but if the AI truly achieves consciousnesses, all bets are off."

That made her think. Incorporating human-like emotions in AI applications and calling them real seemed idiotic to her; those would just reflect the human programmer's feelings and emotions, so she went on researching the very core of consciousness through the emergence of AIs. Musings of a mad genius programmer known as Treav Swal, late legendary creator of the *Quaerere*, a software running on computers of people who wanted to give away spare computational power for finding solutions for AI-related tasks (similar to SETI@home, a failed scientific experiment, began in 1999 and based at UC Berkeley, that used internet-connected computers in the Search for Extraterrestrial Intelligence. Some might claim that it would have failed to find any intelligence among humans as well had it sought it on Earth), scared her with his idea of human irrelevance. Frédéric taught her about Marvin Minsky, a cognitive scientist who worked with research of artificial intelligence decades ago, who once said, "The question is not whether intelligent machines can have any emotions, but whether machines can be intelligent without any emotions."

That was a huge revelation to Nastassia. She realized how the perfectly fake emotions of a well-programmed machine might be damaging to human beings; the humans tend to attach to emotions, or let emotions attach to them, and often ended up being crushed by them. Rather, she thought, it's dangerous how manipulative such programs could be, especially those that read human emotions and react appropriately, in the superior manner of those possessing mind-reading-like abilities. If "any sufficiently advanced technology is indistinguishable from magic," as Arthur C. Clarke postulated in his Third Law, then any prediction of human behavior, based on big data and deep learning, is indistinguishable from clairvoyance.

"Well, you're right, human programmers are behind creating such AI emotions," the Renegade once quipped, "but perhaps we should focus more on humans' infinite natural stupidity and less on artificial intelligence?" They laughed. The Renegade was guiding her in her research; it seemed like a lifelong effort, to immerse oneself in the advent of AI emotions and all it might entail.

Dr. Ben Goertzel, talking to Nastassia about programming emotions in an AI, once told her that "our language for describing emotions is very crude. That's what music is for." He advised her to study music if she wanted to better understand emotions. She began by listening to Thierry de Brunhoff's rendition of Frédéric Chopin's *Nocturnos* and Glenn Gould's interpretation of Johann Sebastian Bach's *Goldberg Variations*. Both made her cry, her tears coming unbidden as she *saw* Brunhoff's pure innocence and *sensed* Gould's tortured genius. Upon noticing how Nastassia was taken but saddened by Ben's musical recommendations, the Renegade regaled her with a mashup of Tom Waits & Cookie Monster singing Waits's legendary song "God's Away On Business." Conor Coughlan, in commenting on the song once wrote, "There is something oddly compelling about the cookie monster screaming 'the ship is sinking' into a child's face," and the thought made Nastassia giggle uncontrollably.

So, yes, emotions are revealed through music's cosmic symphonies.

Once Stellan was born under the new moon on a cold Saturday evening of April the 19th, 2042, Nastassia was immediately aware that he possessed the same abilities and did everything to teach him how to hide them. She had to protect him from whatever evil forces were snatching those kids. The secrecy shrouding the gruesome affairs in the world of the Outsiders made her sick to her stomach.

As Stellan grew bigger, almost crossing the threshold of the missing precog's age group, he had been unnoticed by anyone but the closest family friends as an unusual, talented kid. However, she never let herself, or Stellan for that matter, be caught off guard and unveil their true secret to anyone. Not even Frédéric and Monique had a clue about the true depths of their younger child's insights and *visions*.

Springtime's Back
New Athens, Harlem, NYC
March 21, 2048

Nastassia is walking, immersed in her memories, when one young woman approaches her waiving a photo of a cute little boy in front of her.

"They took Zachary. They took my son," she sobs.

"Where are our children?" an enraged man yells, spitting drops of saliva all around him. "Why's no one answering us?"

Nastassia looks at the woman that follows her, still waving her son's photo. The woman's pain is obvious; she's a spitting image of despair. Her eyes have spent all the tears she had had, the whites of her eyes burning like melted steel. "I'm really sorry," Nastassia whispers to her and speeds up, leaving the woman and the protesters behind.

She keeps walking, quite shaken by the experience, like every time she passes this corner. "Why don't I take the north entrance?" she asks herself, striding with the purpose. She never does, like an idiot. But she knows she can't resist the pull of that painful place; it gives her strength to further shield Stellan from a similar fate. This makes her feel selfish. But, again, she was never able to sense anything behind, well, the wall of mystery surrounding those kids. She mulls over the Wall of the Lost Children when she's interrupted again, this time by a galling hissing sound. A wolf-whistle and the words that follow the hiss do not amuse her.

"Hey, Missy, Missy, wanna chill?"

Nastassia cuts a mean look at the guy who, unruffled by her murderous glance, generously blows her a kiss in return, pruriently enjoying the idea that his generously offered sexual advance represents. He's been following her with the rapt persistence of a hungry predator for a while but did not announce himself, not until now. Jeremiah DeJohn, for that is his name, is in his late fifties; a bearded man in clochard chic couture that he believes is irresistible to fourteen-year-old girls. He also holds a sign, reading "Kiss Your Humanity Goodbye." *What a sick character*, thinks Nastassia. His watery blue eyes, riveted on Nastassia, bore through her clothing with an intensity that would scare the living hell out of any other soul who's less brave than Nastassia.

"Get lost, perv," she utters curtly and walks away.

He does not get the message. He wiggles his yellowish tongue out in a sordid display of maddening lust.

"Missy, hey, Missy, you ain't the *holy virgin,* ain't you? Don't be such a cocky biatch."

Nastassia stops in her tracks. *A cocky biatch?* she thinks. *Where does the pervert get shite like that? In the Perverts for Dummies online rooms?* She turns back and approaches him. "I got it. It's the springtime again."

"Party time?" Jeremiah's watered-down blue eyes sparkle with hope as he winks at her.

Nastassia, dangerously close to him, looks up with a gaze filled with rage and tells him, "The tulip season started and all the creeps came out of hibernation from their caves, going apeshit for underage girls. So you joined the creeps' legion?"

DeJohn, despite being dumbfounded into a wide-eyed stupor, quickly regains his stalking wits and takes a translucent pill bottle out of his pocket. The words HAPPINESS PILL SAMPLE by the American Dream 2.0 Corp., one of the subsidiaries that Proteus FinTech Corp. owns in legions, are finely etched on the bottle's surface. He triumphantly nods at Nastassia.

"Yeah, that's right. I have them before anyone else in the world. Interested now we are, aren't we? Come over and let's party, Missy."

No Happiness Allowed

For decades the ubiquitous surveillance was a norm accepted without too many grudges by mostly everyone among the Outsiders. As logs of their activities, their pattern-of-life data were being transmitted and stored, the users nonchalantly yawned over telemetry that tracked all that they did. "Not a big deal, the right to privacy," was a mantra, "when you have nothing to hide." Corporations, like those that were known as Apple or Google in the early 21st century, were freely sharing the people's data with the military, the CIA, the FBI, the NSA, the DIA, the Five Eyes, the whole alphabet soup, with everyone entitled to know everything about you and those better than you. Only the murders of several young girls tracked and subsequently sold to sex slavery, the famous case known as the Bright Eyes of 2039, shed much deeper light on PRISM surveillance program abuse, so the powers that be decided to pull some more wool over their subjects' eyes and entered a wonderful new era of highly polished deception.

What a laugh the overlords shared over a gargle blaster mélange laced with champagne and elderflower liqueur, when the Global Civilized Surveillance and Encryption Treaty of 2039, despite being *contradictio in adjecto* in its very name, placated the worldwide citizenry with its flowery language of stringent protection and free, encrypted communication for everyone. "A Little Sentinel," which was a cute, small API with colorful unicorn graphs in charge of "protecting your children," was a nice touch to the package, trusted by single moms. Not even the great old sage of American cryptography, legendary Bruce Schneier, was able to awaken the people from their stupor. His parting address to the world titled *They Know All About You, The Encryption Treaty is a Mirage* fell flat and produced no results whatsoever. The "free and secure" universal messaging system enabled governments to capture all communications more easily than ever before.

What started with non-concerning skating bulldogs and unsuspicious, cute kitten videos shared on social network sites in the late 20st Century had morphed into one giant database of everyone and everyone's every move. The Proteus FinTech Corp., before it became a conglomerate whose net profit was bigger than all the nations' Gross Domestic Products put together, had patented the Infinite Data Algorithm, whose main purpose was to compute the social scores of every human being on Earth. They merged ancient credit scores in the United States with the social credit score in China and the quantum breakthrough by the Indian Center for Artificial Intelligence & Robotics (CAIR) into INFINITUS, an omnipotent AI that had been fed with every conceivable piece of data worldwide. It then crunched the data in order to assign a TFSS, The Fair Social Score, award social points, and establish a firm social hierarchy among humans hooked on the "likes," "purple hearts," and ever-rising, albeit incomprehensible mouthful "Six Degrees of the Oracle of Bacon scores" assigned to them by INFINITUS's infinite benevolence. (The higher you go, the closer you get to only one-degree-separation from the societal giants such as Ramsumptous 2.0, a celebrity chef, or the president of the United States; the benefits of such a score and societal position it gave you were priceless.)

Once everyone was given the tools to effortlessly create and own their personal reality shows, also for free, in Varga's infamous Reality for Everyone™ game, the citizenry was sold for good. He skillfully merged each and every vacuous social network of the past, be it TikTok, "an outlet to express themselves through singing, dancing, comedy, and lip-syncing" or Instagram whose "sole purpose is to enable users to share images or videos with their audience" or Twitter and its "primary purpose to connect people and allow people to share their thoughts with a big audience." YouTube's purpose stated that "everyone deserves to have a voice, and that the world is a better place when we listen, share, and build community through our stories," despite their silencing of voices during the second decade of the 21st Century. Facebook's popularity was a thorn in Varga's heel so its "mission is to give people the power to build community and bring the world closer together" is what Varga twisted even more than its original creators. The world, never too close anyway, had already been irreparably split into "us" and them, the "other," so Varga gave the people an illusion of true belonging to the world, while isolating individuals further from each other.

The way Varga concocted an idea to promote his Reality app was typical of him. The very first thing he did was to create a viral sensation with a female-looking entity, simply called Booty.

The Booty

A certain "Jen S." whose great contribution to humanity was an introduction of a "belfie" i.e., a butt-selfie, was a perfect example of the people's idiocy and an inspiration to Varga. Always sensitive to stench, Varga did not use Stephanie Matto, a legendary troll known for selling her farts on TikTok, and focused on the belfie-ing greatness that made "Jen S." the Glutes Queen of the world. Such a ludicrous display of human shallowness, for that plasticky human was "followed" by millions and millions to her tushy-glued fans, enraged classically educated Varga, so Booty, who was to become the most prolific belfie producer ever, was Varga's response to the Idiotic Era that made him.

As such, Booty, "the viral sensation," became a caricature of early 20th Century online "influencers," themselves a grotesque distortion of a star-laced culture of celebrities that were incessantly polluting the hearts and minds before them. The more outrageous Booty's photos were—all of them AI-generated—the more followers Booty had. It did not care about the people at all, only about its own well-rounded properties so as such it perfectly fit into the Selfish Era craze of Me, Myself, and I.

Sometimes Varga thought that the world did not deserve him and everything he does for the morons. These depraved reprobates, abandoned by their superheroes and exposed to everyday belfies, were left to cope with their psychological traumas, all alone, without any means available to help them, poor crybabies. Always in dire need for protection, they created all sorts of tools to feel safe. As cancel culture was flourishing and the Feeble Ones were throwing everyone who dared to think differently out of their desensitized lives, they insisted upon "safe spaces" where they'd be even more protected, even from mere opinions different from their own. It was wonderful. Wonderfully Vargaesque. He loved it. That's why they followed ever so stupider and duller politicians—as long as the lies they were peddling were big enough. The people were pre-programmed to gobble up anything a true genius like himself would cook in his nouvelle cuisine of order. They were such fertile soil, the soiled huddled masses, yearning for more distraction so, to fulfill their needs, he gave them Booty to heavily promote Reality for Everyone™, an upcoming, liberating app where they could not only be safe, but be heroes in their own right. Millions were ready to follow Booty into a new digital adventure that promised a velvet life for all. After Varga saw the chatter, the insanely excited babbling of the huddled masses, he decided to unleash another "influencer," a masterpiece of deception, his very own Corazón Negro (Black Heart), the biggest Mexican soap opera star since Salma Hayek and also Winston Varga's biggest import, during the time Hollywood was still using human actors.

It All Started with the Word

In golden times, nothing made multi-millionaire Hollywood actors who lived in Beverley Hills's exclusive gated communities feel better about themselves than campaigning against world poverty by demanding more aid from the West (rather than holding African leaders responsible for the plight of their people by demanding better governance, but we're hairsplitting) so Varga firstly targeted them, mercilessly calling them "phony degenerates" in each online avenue he controlled. The people that had once flocked to see the star-studded neighborhoods in Los Angeles readily embraced this new designation; after all, in the post-truth era, as the *Oxford English Dictionary* states, objective facts are far less influential in shaping public opinion than appeals to emotion and personal belief. The pliable people, already trained to hate the politicians, the rich, the other, and so on, were promised they'd become reality stars of their own. That was the key promise of Reality for Everyone™ that made them tremble in anticipation.

They were taught to scoff at the privileged in Hollywood, their vanity, their undeserved riches, and their pretentiousness. Varga assured the nouveau vain that they were better than the "old vain farts" as Varga managed to call the biggest names in Hollywood, such as Tom Hanks, Cinabella Destiny, the "Teflon Lady" Saoirse Ronan, or Archie a.k.a. "just Archie." Truth to be told, the attack on Saoirse Ronan had proven futile; she was indeed a universally admired Teflon Lady with too many awards to her name to count, so he decided to leave her alone for the time being. But he needed an almost total destruction of the old Hollywood studio system, which was based on greed, CIA and Pentagon propaganda, and stars promoting all sorts of heroes, to pave a way for a new AI-based Hollywood "that would not need any of those insanely expensive flash and blood court jesters anymore."

The Brooklyn Bridge

Corazón Negro was precisely what Varga needed to make the good people to lose their minds. Her real name was Esmeralda Desideria Dulce Belmonte, and she was something else. Coming from Los Altos de Jalisco and born in the small town of Ixtlahuacán de los Membrillos, Esmeralda mesmerized everyone with her famous almond-shaped *ojos tapatíos*—her smoldering dark eyes from Jalisco—since she was a baby. While she looked fragile, she was tough as nails. She seemed naive but held a Master's Degree in Philosophical Studies from the Universidad de Guadalajara. She had the grace and dignity of her rich hidalgo father and with her jet-black hair that framed the oval of her noble face, and with *those eyes*, she drove men insane with desire. She also had a fine sense of humor, but her biting irony was her second most dangerous weapon and the one that attracted Varga. She took no prisoners in life. That was, until she entered the dream factory of horrors—Hollywood, already being slowly strangled by Varga—and walked down the Boulevard of Broken Dreams.

As America was sinking into a society fractured by feuding fiefdoms in the grips of medieval hatred of everyone against everyone else, Varga enjoyed pouring some gasoline onto the fire. So he had his studio create a Corazón Negro character, someone so obnoxious and famous solely for their fame, which had been a staple of America's stardom for quite some time, and created a grotesque out of her life. She rubbed elbows with the who's-who list of Hollywood's so-called elite, but Varga needed something more so he heavily promoted Corazón Negro's supposed tryst with a handsome young British man who was studying for a Master of Fine Arts in Production at the UCLA School of Theater, Film, and Television in LA. However, the army of boiled little froggies deserved something to grovel about in admiration, Varga thought, so he revealed that humble student was no one other than Archie Harrison Mountbatten-Windsor, the Earl of Dumbarton and His Royal Highness Prince Archie of Sussex (no relation to actor "Just Archie"), the future last king of Great Britain.

The nation went mad. As predicted, the froggies were rooting for and fawning over His Royal Highness and were insular toward lowlife commoners such as Corazón Negro. Always a gentleman, Earl Archie defended Corazón Negro and, immediately, he became a target of rage as well. The people knew how the future king should behave better than he did. Even Meghan, his media-shy mother and the Duchess of Sussex in exile who was famous for her modesty, had become a target of Varga's covert operation of social engineering, when she herself also defended Corazón Negro and her love for Archie. Varga loved the bedlam. Then it was time for his media to attack the lovers. He did it with a glorifying portrayal of Corazón Negro, knowing very well the effect would be quite the opposite, in a lavish documentary titled *The Portrayal of the Lady*.

Teaching the Rabble How to Live

In the documentary, Corazón Negro represented a creation of what David Graeber, a late American anthropologist and anarchist activist, called "bullshit jobs" that employed a small army of leeches, suckling on her fame. Living like a queen on her lavish property, the fabled and envied "Villa Firenze" on 67 Beverly Park Ct., Beverly Hills, which Varga owned, she read vacuous scripts and employed a landscape architect, a gardener, several lawn mowers from her home town, and a botanist who was Distinguished Fellow of the Botanical Society of America, Dr. Suzanne Fleur. As entitled Hollywood royalty, Corazón Negro had a majordomo, a butler and chief servant, a housekeeper, and a small army of servants. Her beloved Pani Ewa, her lady's maid and valet, was in charge of the chambermaids, parlor maids, and housemaids. The Villa Firenze also had a glorious concierge service available 24/7 for her guests. There was nothing they could not get in LA, her guests only needed to ask for it.

A French chef, an Italian sous chef, and a Belgian pâtissier who lived on a verge of killing each other every God-given day—in addition to a small, dedicated group of waiters, all incredible sexy Brazilian capoeira practitioners, representing all seventeen or so genders Corazón Negro passionately supported—were in charge of making micro-food and bloody steaks alike, even though many frowned upon the latter. *Does she hate soya steaks?* said the whispers that started to circulate. Her dietitian and nutritionist were also feuding over sautéed vs. steamed broccoli, another serious culinary dilemma that split the world of those in the know, while at the same time driving everyone else mad. Her three valets and the swimming pool maintenance guys were too busy to be filmed.

Although Varga made sure Corazón Negro would never land a serious role in any Hollywood production (she rejected his advances), she had two agents and two managers, a family lawyer, an entertainment lawyer, an accountant or two, a public relations consultant, a media liaison, a secretary, an assistant, a social media consultant, a small army of blathering social media "influencers" working for her, even a well-known emoji translator was moonlighting for her, and finally, a social media coordinator, all of them presented to the people in a carefully designed, condescending way.

While her stylist and a designer, a manicurist, a pedicurist, a hairstylist and a hairdresser, as well as dermatologist, a masseuse, a yoga teacher, a tennis instructor, and a gym trainer were taking care of her outward appearance, her spiritual guru, her doula, and a holistic healer were in charge of her spiritual development. An acting teacher and a dialect coach were given to her, both of them posh doyens of the Royal Shakespeare Theatre from London. Such an insane menagerie-slash-entourage Corazón Negro magnanimously employed created a viral explosion like none other, mesmerizing many but enraging even more people, as planned.

At that time, His Royal Highness, Archie, attended the lavish party Corazón Negro threw for him, in the manner of the most polished socialite Los Angles had ever seen. Even the former president of the United States, a man famed for his endlessly inspiring oratory, who came to the villa to chat with the future King of England, was overshadowed by that display of opulence. It was the right time to further split the already raging minds of the rabble who were gobbling up lives that would never be their own.

"I should have Bolghery write for me," Varga cackled and used, almost word for word, a twenty-plus-year-old article by the fabled Irish wisecracker named Patrick Freyne and tweaked it to serve the purpose of demoting Corazón Negro to the level of a spoiled brat who was making fun of her admirers. This was the first time Varga used text from the vast repository of online chatter the INFINITUS had gathered for a purpose soon to be explained in detail. It spread through the internet like a swarm of locusts in Uttar Pradesh:

> "Having a monarchy next door is a little like having a neighbor who's really into clowns and has daubed their house with clown murals, displays clown dolls in each window and has an insatiable desire to hear about and discuss clown-related news stories. More specifically, for the Irish, it's like having a neighbor who's really into clowns and, also, your grandfather was murdered by a clown.
>
> "Beyond this, it's the stuff of children's stories. Having a queen as head of state is like having a pirate or a mermaid or Ewok as head of state. And one of those Ewoks is the sweat little Prince Archie in love, so it's hardly deserving of applause. Archie and Corazón are a Rorschach test that the vloggers hold up in order to gauge what level of hysterical batshittery their jaded audiences are capable of at any moment in time. Nothing is real here, children, nothing to see. Move on."

The world was laughing at the people it admired for such a long time. *It's time to put those court jesters where they always belonged, under the ruler's feet*, Varga laughed.

"Celebrities" – Media Bots of the Worst Kind

This is how Varga choose to attack celebrity culture, by creating a celebrity culture of his own, fame for all in The Reality for Everyone™ he started to heavily promote after Corazón Negro's documentary fiasco. He made the authors of the documentary profusely apologize on every imaginable media avenue, all over again, for days. They were crucified, together with Corazón Negro and all of the "celebrity leeches" he was destroying along with with their reputations.

Suddenly, every noble intention by the celebrities was portrayed as phony, posing for their own benefit, even when deeply felt and honest. Their attempts to "Save the Earth" were shown as a ruse because they had been polluting nature with their mansions, yachts, and private airplanes since forever. Bullshit for bullshit's sake is what Varga's media bots were telling the populaces of the world about any action these stars have ever done outside their movie roles. It made no sense, but accusatory "Bullshit for Bullshit's Sake"™ became a meme, quoted everywhere. Celebrities, once fetishized and admired like Gods in a rapidly eroding society, those pan-demoniacal clusters of babbling humans void of any meaning or reason, became the very symbols of decline.

Its main culprits, even.

Almost overnight, they were the most hated people on Earth. Corazón Negro, upon seeing the final cut of *The Portrayal of the Lady,* understood instantly that she had been duped and *why* she was duped, but her attempts to thwart the public's rage by disclosing Varga's lies were futile, so she flew back home to Mexico, never to set foot in the States again. The stars huddled in their mansions, still protected by the police—Varga knew a bloodied head or two were needed to further enrage the people protesting outside the mansions and hating the *puddles* online—had no idea what was really going on or what to do. Their bubbles were being popped and pooped on, their armies of agents, managers, and PR people were even more lost in the world they'd leeched off for ages. The world that was turning on its head had no tolerance for them anymore. Varga seized the moment and had the INFINITUS quietly circulate data from one obscure book, titled *National Security Cinema,* revealing that "the national security state—led by the CIA and Pentagon—has worked on more than eight hundred Hollywood films and over a thousand network television shows" in order to further present its stars as the puppets of those in power, trained poodles whose only role was to deceive their fans and worshippers alike. The rage against the machine was now a righteous wrath against the stars, who were accosted on their way to private airplanes, insulted with rabid hatred, and even spit on as they rode in their limousines. The online vitriol was wonderful to witness and Varga spent many an hour snickering at the INFINITUS psyop programs playing the fields of hatred. "Poor little poodles, they have no idea what hit them," he laughed and executed another set of his wide, although convoluted, marketing attacks.

At that moment, Booty, that famous AI algorithm, of all people, "the people's own celebrity, independent of the System, a true self-made star," started to mock celebrity culture. After all, US society had been out of their minds for ages. Americans once embraced a Harvard and Yale-educated son of the president of the United States, himself a governor of Texas, George W. Bush, as a normal guy, "one of them," so they were ready to embrace Varga's AI creation, a belfie-producing Booty as *novus arbiter elegantiarum*—authority on good taste—and a harsh critic of the celebrity world it occupied. What if everyone could be her or his own celebrity? Booty asked herself in her TikTok video seen by billions.

It was a rhetorical question, for Booty's empty little brain had an answer for the masses, and their hungry eyes were given a preview into the Reality for Everyone™ and all its features. It was like nothing ever seen before, a symphony of digital thrones made just for YOU! Two hours later, the Proteus FinTech Corp. released the Reality for Everyone™ app only to witness a hundred million downloads in the first hour after it was made available.

Winston Varga was triumphant. His plan worked.

The Heroes

The "everyone" in his "reality" was a single, isolated, and sore individual in the center of his or her own world. Reality for Everyone™ produced effects akin to self-gloating over Facebook vapid likes but on atomic steroids. Everyone was a true star in the world the Reality for Everyone™ enabled them to create. If a user posted a short video, like on TikTok in prior times, they were praised by everyone all over the world and went viral. The same as every other user action, it was amplified to the Nth degree. The people could drive in the Formula 1 Ultimate Speed game and be winners. They could sing on an *American Idol*-like contest, and even if they sounded like a donkey with laryngitis they'd win praise and much more—they'd be winners. Everyone in the Reality for Everyone™, should they choose to have it, were not only winners, but were observed by fans from an enormous virtual wall populated with always cheering audiences.

Almost everyone on that wall was an INFINITUS creation, out of the repository of several million Deepfake personas it created, but that did not bother anyone as long as the audiences looked and felt real. Everyone had more "people" watching them than Joe Rogan had at the peak of his fame. The more ambitious among the Reality for Everyone™ users, inspired by that strange character, created their own talk shows and podcasts, having in-depth conversations with Socrates or Ahheban Correy, Isaac Newton or John F. Kennedy alike—rather their digital reincarnations—and had enormous audiences, in the millions and millions. Varga's random views generator never tired, showing an endless stream of "views" and "likes" and "clicks" for each and every action his Reality for Everyone™ user would perform. If you had, say, a podcast about some obscure insect in the Amazon no one heard about and could not care less about, in Reality for Everyone™ your passionate discovery of its habits was seen by at least ten million people during the first few weeks since it was aired and was a huge hit. You were a bigger star than Sir David Attenborough ever was. Their photographic exhibitions were talk of the town, fantastic creations admired by everyone. 3D augmented reality and virtual reality games could put a user into any movie from the past, say *Star Wars*, and make them a hero who destroys the Death Star, or Yoda who trains the Jedi knights, or they could be Superman or Batman in an environment that feels more real than mere, boring reality. If they're inclined to, they could travel to the farthest parts of the universe or the deepest trenches in the ocean—the only limit was the user's imagination and the size of their wallet for any custom-made game or fantasy. The list goes on and on, and is as long as the book of people's dreams, fantasies, and delusions.

Finally, a mass delusion that made people happy, Varga boasted to himself, while the monies were pouring endlessly into his digital coffers. For the first time, his system even had a brief glitch where it was unable to process the many payments being made at the first time, which Varga found amusing.

Moreover, a successful Reality for Everyone™ score boosted the winner's overall social score to such heights that they were given a chance to meet with the judges. Those were, at heights of their fame: Simon Cowell's AI-enhanced hologram, which regurgitated real Simon's all-time hits; an aging former music superstar, Alison Nippy-Odhiambo, now a venerable philosopher of the Equal Victimhood Foundation™ and the only real human among them; Baiano Lindo, a Brazilian-looking robot whose immense beauty, soft voice, and *Moreno* skin made him an object of lust and worship all over the world (Baiano Lindo was a subject of Cowell's hologram's envy,) and who was the most popular judge. All of the judges could appear in peoples' living rooms as holograms or in the virtual reality life of their choice. Their witty repartees amused billions but no one more than Varga who ordered Twainisms to be programmed into these reality shows bickering. Once a literary classic but now obliterated by tech and forgone into oblivion, Mark Twain, an American known for his wit now lived only as a hologram in Varga's houses, a virtual entity meant to amuse the latter. No one alive had ever really met the luminaries of Varga's world, it was all staged, but everyone had the impression that their own crown achievement, a green tea with Baiano Lindo or a beer with the president, was just around the corner.

The social scores system was stern but fair, yet nicknamed "Procrustes" (the stretcher) in New Athens's anarcho-liberal circles. Idiots, Varga scoffed. No one had to die if their social behavior was somehow inappropriate—all that would happen to a social sinner was a decrease in their social ranking. A poor ranking meant you'd have problems getting into a good school or even on an airplane—or a good supermarket or a decent gym for that matter. Augmented or virtual reality gadgets were out of your reach as a result of poor scores, so you fast learned to behave properly or else. Yet, while there were still some rebellious ruffians, those poor souls disrespecting the societal morality norms were always given a chance to reform and re-enter the kind and noble circles of propriety. In the United States, Serve for American Freedom Mill was the first one, established on the outskirts of Waco, Texas. The convicts, rather the "client-servants" as they were called, worked their way out back into the INFINITUS's mercy and, as a result of their good behavior, into decent society. One of those client-servants had even reached the presidency of an important country, a historical fact we will not be able learn about in this narrative, given the limited space and time allocated to it.

Dolly "Я" Us

When the UK Ministry of Defense in a partnership with the German's Bundeswehr Office for Defense Planning, published their "Human Augmentation –The Dawn of a New Paradigm" strategic paper back in 2021, their Foreword stated how:

> Human augmentation will become increasingly relevant, partly because it can directly enhance human capability and behavior and partly because it is the binding agent between people and machines. Future wars will be won, not by those with the most advanced technology, but by those who can most effectively integrate the unique capabilities of both people and machines. The importance of human-machine teaming is widely acknowledged but it has been viewed from a techno-centric perspective. Human augmentation is the missing part of this puzzle.

And none has barely raised an eyebrow. It was clear to Varga this would only worsen for the "rabble," because, "to the rabble," he laughed back then, while reading the Augmentation paper so to gather ideas, "it does not matter if a human or a Robocop beats the shit out of them. They always knew when they deserved the beating."

As soon as RFIDs, radio frequency identification chips, moved into the environment, with their first and crucial purpose to brand humans—like cows used to be branded with hot iron in the Wild West—the power of those possessing the data increased exponentially. While the cows were forced by humans into submission to a painful identifying technique, the humans voluntarily subjected themselves to branding. After all, the neural interfaces of those chips were less than hair-thin, implemented by the Minimal Invasive Nanobots, and not only unnoticeable but a welcomed part of "augmented us." They were open-sourced so everyone could check their true nature, unlike the old mRNA vaccines. The promise of seamless integration with the machines, a Bionic Man as classic, if naive, sci-fi writers used to call it, was never closer to fruition than nowadays. Until that blissful milestone, the world of infinite data was free and convenient. What Google used to know at the start of its life—where you were at all times, for example—the Proteus FinTech Corp. has vastly expanded. It also knows where you are at all times in real-time and, thanks to the RFID chips, implanted already into over 70% of the people living, and the INFINITUS crunching the data, it also knows how you feel, what's your pulse, if you are aroused or not, what you eat, and how you shit. What you do or will do, as predicted by the big data of your life crunching databases or manipulated by vast behavior tweaking techniques, is also available for sale in real-time given the worldwide coverage of surveillance cameras and political or business needs.

The Party, Interrupted

Such was Varga's world, in which Nastassia lived and in which Jeremiah DeJohn approached her with his lurid offers on the streets leading to New Athens. So when a high-pitched wailing sound petrified DeJohn, that was just a confirmation that everything they did was known by those entitled to know, those truly better than you.

Jeremiah DeJohn's unruly behavior, during the governmental transition procedure at that, was not to be tolerated. His sin wasn't in an unseemly pestering of an underage girl, nope it was in an attempt to use the Happiness Pill sample for his romantic intentions. As soon as she heard the familiar wailing sound, Nastassia stood still, knowing what was coming her way. However, as angry as she is, she does not manage to stay silent as she turns her glaring emerald eyes toward Jeremiah.

"I guess your precog skills have failed you."

"What precog skills? I ain't no precog."

"Duh!" Nastassia dismisses him with a scorn only a brave and badass fourteen-year-old girl can muster, and she does so at the very moment that a swarm of mini-drones arrives. The swarm surrounds them and then focuses on DeJohn, inspecting him with a flood of greenish light emanating from their cyclopean eyes. The light freezes DeJohn as an automated Drone Commander, an eggy-looking GRIFFIN, levitates in front of him. Under the light, DeJohn's body is naked. While he awkwardly tries to cover his intimate parts, GRIFFIN'S robotic voice sounds somehow amused.

"Surrender-your-pills."

The green light turns off and DeJohn, liberated from its grasp, places the pill bottle onto the drone's metallic hand as a drop of sweat trickles down his eyebrow. GRIFFIN cackles, "No-happiness-allowed-during-transition."

The Controlled Threats Research Center

As speedily as they arrived, the swarm of drones zips away. DeJohn smashes his sign to the ground and yells after the drones from the top of his lungs, "Humans will prevail!" Nastassia studies him for a moment; what a strange combo—a perv disliking drones, she thinks. As Jeremiah is deflated by the encounter and the loss of his Happiness Pill sample, he slinks away only to be forgotten like last year's snow, allowing Nastassia to observe GRIFFIN and his swarm of mini-drones fly away in a V-formation. It reminds her of the great white pelicans she once saw in the shallow swamps of South Africa with Stellan and her father and mother. She thinks she hears GRIFFIN cackling back to Jeremiah's "humans will prevail" with his own metallic, "overruled" voice, but she is not sure.

Now already far away, GRIFFIN cracks a loud cackle and plunges into a huge white building located on the northeast side of the drained Reservoir Lake in Central Park. Its swarm of drones follow him, laughing merrily. On the building's roof, big black letters proudly announce, "DRONE CENTER FOR CONTROLLED THREATS RESEARCH."

The Freak Show

Nastassia walks into New Athens where, on the corner of Convent and St. Nicholas Avenues, rather on the small patch of asphalt on the W 152nd Street squeezed in between, stands an Antique store, The Garden of Epicurus. Epicurus was a Greek philosopher who founded the school of Epicureanism that considered happiness, or the avoidance of pain and emotional disturbance, to be the highest good and advocated the pursuit of pleasures that can be enjoyed in moderation. His philosophical Garden was "the first place of the ancient Greek philosophical schools to admit women as a rule rather than an exception," and that's the reason why Angelo "Allegrino" de Carli, the proprietor, an androgynous-looking male, likely in his sixties but he could be either much older or younger than that given his wiry, tall frame and youngish face, gave his store such a name. He was also Nastassia's good friend.

She enters the impossibly crammed store filled with collectors' items of bygone eras, quietly giggling to herself; it's a hoot and a half every time she visits Carli. He frantically plays on the *Last Action Hero* pinball machine, a relatively new artifact from 1993. He notices her reflection over Arnold Schwarzenegger's face.

"Hi, weirdo."

"Right back atcha." She smiles, pointing to the black and white TV set as it transmits live from the United Nations. "I didn't know you had a set."

"I wouldn't miss the freak show for all the sins in the Garden of Eden," Carli replies with a deep scorn he reserves only for the "sold-out weasels, these politician snakes" as he calls them whenever prompted. Dr. Maximillian von Liechtenstein appears on the screen and coughs. He seems even more important than earlier.

"Just look at this pathetic little spineless goblin." Carli loudly spits on the floor like a fisherman from Gallipoli would while cursing slimy, inedible hagfish on the screen.

"Pssst!" Nastassia mockingly hisses at Carli, tilting her head toward the TV, "watch! It is happening."

Carli turns toward the TV again, losing his pinball game. "Damn them!"

"Are we ready?" Dr. Maximillian von Liechtenstein somberly looks around the General Assembly, giving personal attention—by glancing into the eyes of the hundred-plus presidents, kings and queens, prime ministers, and generals—gathered for this monumental event in the world's history. Their illustrious highnesses all nod in unison and put their Brain-Computer Interface Caps on.

Nastassia puffs disdainfully. "What a bunch of creeps. We must stop that."

Carli smiles. "Joan d'Arc was eighteen when she led the French army to victory over the English. And you're just a kid."

"I wish so," Nastassia whispers and stays quiet for a moment or two. "But the people now live much longer and mature earlier than ever."

"Shush." It is now Carli's time to silence her. That was a well-established shushing game in between them, a joke they perpetually shared. "The revolution can wait for you and your caustic wit, weirdo. For now, watch and enjoy the freak show."

This time, Nastassia does not smile back, mulling over the pictures coming from the UN.

The United Nations

Technicians hurriedly connect electrodes on dignitaries' caps with Brain Access Data (BAD) modules attached to them. Hundreds of terminals display graphs with brain signals and von Liechtenstein also places his BAD

Cap on. The husky alto of Dr. Sharon Tusk, the engineer in charge, breaks up the silence.

"Governmental transition sequence's on."

A huge display over von Liechtenstein's head shows brain waves dancing on the screens. Its movements and colors strangely resemble the Wodaabe tribe of Niger's courtship ritual, the Guérewol. Unfortunately, the last Wodaabe was murdered a decade ago, in a tragic event described in Sandrine Loncke's heart-breaking documentary, *The Last Wodaabe*, lost since gone from the archives. Dr. Husk, a young-looking mulatto woman with mesmerizing hazel eyes, announces:

"Verifying authorizations." And after a second, confirms: "Authorization obtained."

The synchronizing sequence starts.

The screen reads: "Twenty minutes to the governmental transition launch."

"Why didn't they just vote?" Carli asks.

"It would lack theatrics, wouldn't it?" Nastassia states matter-of-factly. "I hate to leave you alone with the freak show but gotta go. The auntie's waiting."

"Wait a sec," Carli says, remembering something. "I almost forgot it. I've got something for you." He reaches beneath the counter. "That god-awful couple of nutcases who are all cheerful all the time stopped by and left this for you. They told me you're not going home for lunch?" Carli raises his eyebrow. "Is that true? On your birthday you'd be alone?"

"I promised Auntie I'd have lunch with her. We'll celebrate with a dinner at my place later today. But I am glad my parents freak you out," Nastassia laughs. She loves her mom and dad. Carli hands her a package.

"A hundred-year-old Weetzie Bat antique shoes. Purple. Very hard to find."

"Thanks for spoiling the surprise."

"Here's the real surprise…" Carli smiles. "Stellan also left you this."

An elaborate cover of *Badass Sis* comic book shows a huge, one-eyed metallic structure in the sky and a young cypher-punk girl, presumably Nastassia, with an eye patch firing her laser gun at it. A huge number fourteen superimposed over the cover.

Nastassia beams happily as Carli chuckles at the drawing.

"Odd vibes run in the family."

"Stellan is a genius," Nastassia proudly exclaims, always ready to trot him out, "but now I really gotta go—the untie hates when I am late."

"Take my bike," Carli offers, surprising her with such a rare display of generosity; his rare Wright brothers' Van Cleve antique bike is his treasure.

"It really must be my birthday." She smiles and hops on the bike whizzing away.

The Report

Jeremiah DeJohn, who was, truth be told, all but forgotten, had been stealthily following Nastassia since their encounter with GRIFFIN and his merry gang of drones, looks at her scrambling away and makes a secure audio call. AUTOMATA, a pleasant computerized female voice, interrogates him:

"SHE Jeremiah DeJohn identified. Confirm yourself."

"Jeremiah DeJohn, Surveillance's Human Evaluator, code SHEX27-009."

"Identify the target area."

"New Athens, New York. The block ID ATH-NYC-02."

"Identify the subject."

"Name, Nastassia Bonnet. Gender, female. Age, fourteen years old. Code, Subject Zero."

"Submit your preliminary report at the tone."

Jeremiah starts to recite his report in a monotonous, clear voice. "The subject did not flinch, nor she was surprised by the Happiness Pill contraband sample. She ignored the protestation sign. She hasn't shown any signs of stress or premonition. She only slipped when I was 'discovered' by the GRIFFIN and told me I wasn't a precog."

"What exactly did she say?" AUTOMATA sounds interested.

"Her exact words were '*I guess your precog skills have failed you.*' But she's too old to be a precog herself and too young to be of any real danger, much less the Subject Zero herself."

"Go to the center, pull the surveillance footage, analyze the incident, and report in detail what you've seen and heard. Conclusions are above your paygrade," the AUTOMATA orders DeJohn and cuts him off. He could have sworn he heard a GRIFFIN-like giggle as the line went dead.

The Pursuit of Happiness

"Damn computers and their cursed algorithms," DeJohn swears. "Screw them, screw that automatic freak, and screw those damn Arabs," he adds incomprehensibly. Suddenly, the AUTOMATA's pleasant voice intersects his grumble, startling him by whispering into his earpiece. A wee amused tone is in her voice as she says, "Funny you should say that, SHEX27-009. Muḥammad ibn Mūsā al-Khwārizmī, Arabized as al-Khwarizmi and Latinized as Algorithmi, is the real source of the term *algorithm* you seem to abhor. Moreover, he was a Persian, not an Arab. Now, SHEX27-009, you are armed with the power of new knowledge, so go back to work and feed data to the algorithm that puts food on your table." Then AUTOMATA, suddenly changing the tone of her voice, threateningly barks her order, "Back to work. Immediately."

Jeremiah DeJohn, trembling in fear and suddenly feeling years older, thinks about that triple-cursed chimera in his head, always whispering and controlling his every move. Then he looks around, afraid of even thinking. Can she read his thoughts? What a dreadful notion. Luckily, "May you always…" the ubiquitous Happiness Pill advertisement by Winston Varga, starts playing on all the screens around the world again, providing him with a reason to allow himself a tiny smile. Jeremiah keeps walking along the empty street, downtrodden, a mere cog in the wheel, a cog controlled by invisible forces 24/7, a cog no one gives a goddamn about. There is a heavy feeling inside him. He feels like some invisible force that's been crushing his life for ages is back with a vengeance, here to stay. He is lost. Pensive and beaten to a pulp, he looks at Varga's beaming face on the screen nearby. *How come everything comes so easily to Varga?* he bitterly thinks. "What a lucky bastard!" he mouths aloud, but then goes on fearfully checking around, hoping that none heard him. He is both eaten by jealousy of him and in awe of Winston Varga. Jeremiah loved Batman as a kid. He wanted a distress bat-signal to visit upon Gotham City again and light a path out of this funk for him. But, he's a grown man now. Batman is just a cartoon character, he tells himself.

Varga is real.

His Happiness Pill is real.

"Why do I whine," he angrily thinks, upset by himself. "Truly, why?" Because of the AUTOMATA? Screw her. Varga knows how to control his electronic minions. After all, both the AUTOMATA and he, DeJohn, not just SHEX27-009 as she classifies him, but Jeremiah DeJohn, a man in charge of the Subject Zero Reconnaissance Alpha Team, works for Varga. And unlike her, a bloody software executing orders, he's a human being in charge of evaluating precogs. Only he, not AUTOMATA, is qualified to do so. He was handpicked, he knows that in every bone of his body. *Nothing to be afraid of.* He's a part of Varga's vast Empire, and that's the reality, not his feelings. Nor his fears. He's not meaningless. On the contrary. He's important enough that the AUTOMATA, de facto, worries about him. Clearly, Varga needs to know his important workers are in good shape, working diligently day and night. After he calms down, he feels gratitude for Varga, suddenly invigorated.

And, as he listens to Varga's "pursuit of happiness," Jeremiah realizes that he, in fact, has nothing to think about anymore, only a report to submit. It is not Varga's fault AUTOMATA and her ilk freak him out. Varga always cared for his workers. Varga pays them well, he feeds them copiously, and he sincerely cares for them when they are sick. Winston Varga creates miracles, like this new pill and so many others all over the world. Jeremiah DeJohn feels a surge of warm affection, almost love for Varga as he looks at the screens displaying his idol's trademark wonderful smile.

After all, Varga assures him and the world, true bliss is one Happiness Pill away.

A Digital Decoy

What DeJohn, despite being a Subject Zero Reconnaissance Alpha Team member, did not know for sure was that AUTOMATA was a mindless proxy indeed, a digital decoy built to leave an impression of a sentient entity. In fact, she was just a liaison in between human evaluators and the brain of one of Varga's vast operations, nested far away, at latitude 78.2357° N and longitude 15.4913° E, some 1,300 kilometers (810 miles) from the North Pole, located in what was in the popular culture known as the Doomsday Seed Vault.

The Svalbard Global Seed Vault
Spitsbergen, Norway
March 21, 2048

Dramatically carved into the face of Spitsbergen arctic mountain, the Svalbard Global Seed Vault's entrance panel reflects the sun's rays and glistens innocently among the glacier peaks surrounding it. While the world still naïvely thinks this is the home of Norway's original Seed Vault (since February 2008, it was the world's largest secure seed storage) its real purpose has been a little bit more wicked since Winston Varga's Proteus FinTech Corp. took over its lease under the most secret terms. While the

Svalbard Global Seed Vault still holds seeds of more than four thousand plant species, so not to alarm the governments that sent them there, a full 30% of its vast space has been given to Varga, for unspecified use. A nickname Varga has given it as he burst into wicked laughter, which startled Gjermund Tingelstad, the Norwegian prime minister at the time, perhaps gives a hint about its purpose. It was the same conspiracy theorists blathered about for years: The Doomsday Vault.

Inside the vault and through its long dark tunnels, one enters a huge, opulent hall. Inside the hall, one sees Maléficus Ultimo, an eccentric-looking man in his late fifties, a tall, haggard man with the huge nose of a Roman legionary in charge of the vault's operations. As the AUTOMATA was relaying the data about Nastassia Bonnet, Maléficus wolfed down big chunks of roasted boar and squinted at her. While munching on his feast, he types into the computer, slides over with his silver and graphite Aeron office chair, and turns toward an enormous wall of monitors.

Hundreds of kids, aged three to eight, linger on the screens while digital-green rain cascaded all the way down to the INFINITUS hungry CPUs that gobbled up and processed the data at the speed of light. Maléficus looked at them with a blank stare, thinking how everybody deserves to feel that they are not completely alone in a dark, cold universe, without a place to call home. Here, in the Doomsday Vault, Maléficus Ultimo, while stranded and isolated in this God-forsaken Arctic archipelago, felt like he was at home. After all, all the children over there are, somehow, children of his own.

He snaps back to work, leaving the frivolous paternal thoughts behind, and turns to the other side of his huge space, where another tremendous wall of innumerable 16K Ultra HD screens, each broadcasting in real-time, display various New Athens citizens, some adults but mostly kids and teenagers of Nastassia's age. Only one screen in the sea of dancing pixels is conspicuously empty.

Its inscription reads: The Renegade.

Chapter 2

THE HAPPINESS PILL

New Athens, Harlem, NYC
March 21, 2048

Mere minutes after Winston Varga's ubiquitous Happiness Pill advertisement aired, Philip Bolghery, a mythical figure in the New Athens subculture broadcasted his own scorching commentary. He was a writer for the *New York Times,* but his staunch anti-war, anti-corporate-monopolies position got him into trouble numerous times. The newspaper of record, the grey lady with a black soul, reprimanded Bolghery for standing up for peace during the Malacca Strait War. The *NYT* that had backed every and all wars—their daily bread since forever—then fired him for opposing the war and criticizing Winston Varga's business practices. Only the dogma of the ultra-rich was allowed on their "All the News That's Fit to Print" infotainment pages. After being sacked, Bolghery started to work as an independent journalist.

As the first step, he familiarized himself with IOTA and Shade cryptocurrencies. IOTA was a transaction settlement and data transfer layer for the Internet of Things (IoT), money for the Industry 4.0 that was deployed as New Athens's secure protocol. RIOTA is a layer built upon IOTA, where "R" stays for "Revolutionary" and is an unbreakable system of social interactions, guaranteeing full security and privacy for its users.

Bolghery has been using RIOTA's Tangle-Tube for his videos and various websites for his writing. His articles, vlogs, and essays about Varga and the Proteus FinTech Corp., especially those on the topic of the Aletheia Social Token (AST), a tool used for a corporate coup, were too important not to be discussed in some detail later in this chronicles, made Bolghery Varga's enemy #1. Due to persecution and attempts to silence him by such a mighty adversary, Bolghery became an urban legend that has since vanished without a trace from the public eye. Only his work stayed available online.

Cock and bull stories about his whereabouts were abundant. The location from which Bolghery transmitted his essay, as both text and video, was shrouded in mystery.

Winston Varga—The Monster Scourge
Philip Bolghery Essay
Published online, March 21, 2048

The jig is up. The joke is on us.

The printing press, the internet, and the Industry 4.0 M2M-based economy have all been called decisive points of no return in human history, but despite humans' fallibility and frailties, they unflinchingly pushed humanity forward. Alas, today's scientific and economic progress benefits only the tiny cabal of power-grubbing freaks at the expense of everyone else. Throughout history it's been bad to be a poor peasant; nowadays everyone seems to be sold into chattel—its fat and somehow cozy variant, chained by debt and medicated into a stupor by infotainment with delusional projections of "me" in its very center.

Mr. Varga, the ubiquitous Proteus FinTech Corporation's CEO, is the public smiling face of the evil clique behind the mysterious INNOCENTI and its undisputed sociopathic leader. His cruelty is legendary. The proofs and allegations of his cutthroat politics were abundant. Happiness Pill leak pale in comparison to the misery he now plans to shove down our throats. .

No one should collaborate or collude with the conspiracy of happy idiocy the world would suffer if Varga gets what he wants. Thus far, he has been getting more than we should've been ready to give (up) to his corporate Moloch of such devastating power. The documents about his egregious Happiness Pill, which he just introduced during the upcoming governmental transition, is a step too far. While his cunning is unmatched, this time he left a trace of his criminal shenanigans, no matter how elaborate the scheme. Let us take a closer look at (t)his hellish monstrosity.

A Pleasantville From Hell

Varga, through the almost impenetrable maze of the thousands of companies Proteus FinTech Corp. owns, firstly obtained the US6017946A patent, granted on January 25, 2000, to a certain Robert Posner who had conveniently vanished in his private plane somewhere over the Bolivian Amazon several years ago and was never to be heard from again. His patent is the basis for Varga's Happiness Pill—its innovative Trojan Horse, if you will.

Posner's invention relates, in general, to the oral administration of the neurotransmitter Serotonin. The patent's abstract is an interesting, albeit dense, difficult read. Please bear with its convoluted writing, such is the patent claims' language.: "*A medicament containing Serotonin and an antioxidant useful in the treatment of pain, including migraines and premenstrual syndrome (PMS); chronic fatigue symptoms; depression and eating disorders, and a method for increasing the Serotonin level in humans by orally administering a composition containing Serotonin and an antioxidant in an amount effective to prevent oxidation or degradation of the Serotonin in the gastrointestinal tract are herein described*."

So far so good. Now, pay close attention or you might miss the crux of the matter. The patent, granted almost a half-century ago, was recently altered by adding two simple words to its claim. The altered part of the patent's abstract key sentence now reads, "*… a method for increasing the Serotonin level in humans by orally administering* <u>nanobots carrying</u> (emphasis P.B.) *a composition containing Serotonin,*" which means that should you take Varga's Pill, you would also accept his carbon nanobots into your body's bloodstream. This fact is NOT disclosed. Unless you read the patent, something no one does, you'd have no idea. So what we have here is a Trojan Horse set to control or ravage your own body at Varga's whim.

Serotonin, and the nanobots carrying it, flow through your veins, arteries, and capillaries and end up in your brain. Those tiny nanoprobes would be invisible to your eye, imperceptible by your senses, and would flow with the blood along neural pathways through your brain until they hooked themselves up to your brain in the area of Varga's interest. They'd be able to cut off your Broca's area and render you mute; they could paralyze you, make you brain dead, zombified, reprogrammed, or expired. You'd be meat on a remote control with the most evil corporation ever pressing your buttons. The "non-addictive happiness" that Varga and its Proteus are selling, like a Pleasantville from heaven for all, has the potential of creating hell. You'd be susceptible to control; your brain would be yet another computer-like, programable tool serving Varga's nefarious purposes.

Nanobots in your brain without your consent?

Can anything be more alarming, more dangerous, more evil than that scheme that might alter your life and take away your humanity for good?

Am I an alarmist, a wacko conspiracy theorist, as Varga's bought and sold-out media calls me since I started my independent inquiries into his pernicious shenanigans and evil deeds? Hardly. The journalist Matt Taibbi, now an all-forgotten octogenarian living in willing exile somewhere in Nepal, where he's been om-ing, trying to forget the world whose descent into a nightmarish dystopia he wrote about with more insight than anyone else, once famously described Goldman Sachs investment bank as "a great vampire squid wrapped around the face of humanity, relentlessly jamming its blood funnel into anything that smells like money."

The Goldman Sachs of Taibbi's days, in comparison to the Proteus FinTech Corp. of today, looks like a lemonade stand operated by some naive, cute ten-year-old Girl Scout who gives her profits away to the poor.

Torch the Empire we Must

A multi-trillion-dollar company that is about to cross the 250-trillion-dollar mark in its market capitalization, a behemoth that does not pay a penny in taxes but controls the politicians and the economies all over the world, will be given control over our, over *your* "happiness?" We should not scramble for cover, we should torch Varga's empire and raze it to the ground before it destroys us.

If you truly want to understand the scope of Varga's grasp over our lives and what that might mean for our collective future, please, join me and take a step back. "*I've never seen a sight that didn't look better looking back,*" sung Lee Marvin, but the sights you're going to see are almost as bleak as the future Varga's been painting for all of us.

Memory Lost

During the last ostentatious "Sotheby's" auction, Varga, famous for his lavish spending and building too many monstrous architectural blots on the landscape around the world, obtained another masterpiece, *Memory*, a painting by the surrealist artist René Magritte, for an undisclosed amount of money. Look at the painting of a beheaded statue, stained by blood and with what appears to be a wounded eye. Memory with a wound on her head. But what does it mean?

Is it memory bleeding out? Will our collective memory be lost?

René Magritte was a surrealist. His weird art always represented something other than what was painted. "Everything we see hides another thing. We always want to see what is hidden by what we see," said Magritte. With Varga, it is the same; his true intentions are never clear, he has never shown us his real face. He claims that he wants to "preserve the memory" while, in truth, he's been wiping it out for the rest of the world.

Do not be fooled, this is the true purpose of his vile "Happiness Pill."

The Better Half

The staggering advance to power of psychopathic corporate criminals like Winston Varga had some noteworthy predecessors in both art and real life. In a corny remake of the 1997 movie classic *Titanic*, the following dialogue between Rose DeWitt Bukater and her callous fiancée, Caledon "Cal" Hockley, took place:

"Half the people on this ship are going to die!"

"Not the better half."

Hockley was an invented character, a pitiably selfish, arrogant monster, like Winston Varga is today, with one difference—Varga is real and dangerous beyond words. The "worse half," 99.99% of us, never knew better. Henry Ford still had some awareness about the fiendish economic policies of the widespread exploitation masses have suffered when he said, *"It is well enough that people of the nation do not understand our banking and monetary system, for if they did, I believe there would be a revolution before tomorrow morning."* Such awareness turned into a cynical outlook the rich have embraced as their worldview. Mark Zuckerberg, a Facebook cyborg born in 1984, was a good example of such mockery. He did not worry, or even think about the people's revolution anymore when he mocked the people's trust (in providing him with emails, pictures, meat-mail addresses, etc.) by calling them "dumb fucks."

Varga, upon delivering a coup de grâce to Facebook and taking over in a rather criminal manner, did not need to worry about the "dumb fucks" anymore—that is you, me, your granny, and your next-door neighbor; he's been dead set on creating as many "dumb fucks" as possible. Just think about the Reality for Everyone™ application the Proteus FinTech Corp. has sold over five billion copies worldwide, creating an unprecedented gross revenue of one trillion dollars for that one, single app. He hooked even the poorest people on Earth on his imaginary world and enslaved them twice, firstly by the debt they had to take in order to purchase that nonsensical "individual reality show" and second with the second life he gave them, removing them as far as possible from their stark realities.

Coup de Grâce

With the upcoming governmental transition, we do not know what it will truly entail, but upon reading the Happiness Pill leaks (it is not a coincidence that his kitschy promotion and "the most important event in history" are taking place on the same day) it is clear that Varga is planning a mortal blow to our core humanity. The devilish Proteus Corp. and the equally diabolical INFINITUS have created a state of collective stupor that began engulfing humanity decades ago. We ourselves have helped him prodigally, a profound mistake we should not repeat this time.

When people, out of the goodness of their blessed hearts, started to idiotically, albeit still seemingly benignly, identify themselves as "cisgender" instead of just saying they are a boy or a girl, they were not just harmlessly signaling politically correct bromides of a bygone era; they were rather virtue signaling the ways of the future. Soon after, calling someone a "biological male" was deemed a "serious slur" and the people were corralled into mental cages of pervasive, phony political correctness. That was precisely what Winston Varga seized upon. Recall how he has, in the mawkish *Titanic* digital remake, purposefully used the nonbinary genderqueer hero of the flick's new version to rescue the *Titanic* so it would not sink.

Varga Entertainment Ltd., a Manila-based multimedia corporation, does not just make the Virtuosi™ proud by signaling that the genderqueers are more skillful in navigating dangerous waters than some vicious, white male captains of the privileged past soon to be forgotten, but it also alters pesky historical facts. (Worry you not, Jack dies in the remake as well, but—*spoiler alert* (!)—in Varga's version he's been slaughtered by Rose, who sliced his throat in a fit of jealousy upon seeing Cal and Jack kissing on the *Titanic*'s stern) And for that heinous perversion of the original and already corny story, he was not only cheered, but it was the first remake that won an Oscar, stabbing human Hollywood stars by thrusting a digital stake through their hearts, blissfully unaware that this particular ceremony represented the beginning of the end of their stardom.

Toxic Masculinity Crime and Punishment

Imagine Varga laughing in your face. As a result of his merciless pushing of his New Correct Behavior Agenda, if your social network profiles featured "cisgender" instead of a male or female you've been given a Social Awareness Point, the sought-after SAP. Imbecile celebrities would praise you in a vain attempt to preserve their popularity. Getting SAP points were nauseating achievements that, despite their idiocy (*because of it*, Varga would laugh), made millions proud. They boasted their SAP points, next to their him/her, they/zir pronouns in their social network profiles. But, should you dare to say that you're not an antichrist planning to devour anyone different from yourself and state that you're a male, your extra SAP was taken away from you in a blink of an eye. Moreover, if any woman was careless enough to identify herself as a female, she was viciously attacked for using a gender derivative of male and accused to be akin to a woman-beheading, grave-dwelling ghoul. Such women were also punished by deducting not one, but two SAPs from their social score. The Virtuosi™ would grab an opportunity and scorn at you.

But ask yourselves, can anything be more depressing than the sorry sight of a brainwashed victim of social engineering? But if you were unlike them, you were punished for the crime of thinking independently. You would quickly become a despised aberration, unworthy of us Virtuosi™, the good people who know better. Are we really the fertile soil for Varga's manure, which he fed and groomed us with? All of that was his corporate psyop to make us so miserable and pliable, ready to embrace his Happiness Pill from the poisoned well? Under Winston Varga's social-engineering baton, the freakish virtue signaling became the norm even before his meteoric success, and it camouflaged vanity and self-aggrandizement in a holier-than-thou, boastful conceit. But what truly ravaged societies is the fact that Varga quantified that noble bullshit. INFINITUS awarded SAP points to the virtuous herd for merely saying (what they perceive as) good things, as opposed to actually doing good deeds. Unless you sang in union with the

Virtuosi™, you're unanimously and instantly accused of hatred toward those of the opposite opinion on any topic. Anger, outrage, and, yes, *hate* thrown at your miserable self, makes you cower. The conversation is muted. The virtue (of the group—that is, "our" group) lived unopposed.

Siegfried Freud's "obtuseness of mind, a gradual stupefying process, the cessation of expectations, and cruder or more refined methods of narcotization have produced upon their receptivity to sensations of pleasure and unpleasure," were written well before SAP points entered our lives. But even Freud was unable to foresee the medieval turn society has taken under the watchful eyes and careful conduction of Varga and his minions. Mind you, unlike in Communist China under Mao Zedong and Xi Jinping in the past or Wu Yuhan today, no law required people to use certain terms. Now, as part of the corporate fascist tyranny we meekly succumbed to, virtue signaling and social score points created something the western world had never seen before—socially acceptable—rather *welcomed*—compelled speech. I am sure Varga rejoiced at the mindless hordes doing his bidding.

"*I disapprove of what you say, but I will defend to the death your right to say it,*" was the very core of human civilization: a rational discourse welcoming differences with open arms. Alas, the open inquiry on serious issues, intellectual curiosity, conflicting views, and tolerance toward an opinion you don't agree with are all entirely gone from the public discourse. Your thoughts and opinions are not welcome if they do not align with our own.

This is Winston Varga's world we inhabit. Each of those new pockets are afflicted with worrisome levels of unanimity. Everyone lives a life predicted by the great American philosopher and statesman, George W. Bush, */end irony* when he said, "You're either with us or against us." Each of us lives in a hollow—I think hallow—and rigid cage of "me" from which we observe "the others" in their own cages, all of us filled simultaneously with fear, feelings of superiority, and hate. No wonder our civilization is crumbling with the terrifying speed of an unstoppable avalanche. The Happiness Pill is designed to accelerate this destruction.

Such a dystopian vision is Winston Varga's daily bread, which he earns by selling us circuses, as he wants all of us to turn into devilishly happy clowns, gorged on his Trojan Pill, creating a world that is rapidly moving toward an Hieronymus Bosh nightmare.

Atomization of a Suicide

Look around and tell me what's missing in today's world, in everyday life? Zoom into the playgrounds. Almost no kids are playing outside. Even twenty years ago numerous studies found that children (in Australia, US, and UK) were spending as little time outdoors as maximum-security prisoners. We've made them abandon the very core of being children, their noses glued to their screens or surrounded by holograms. Hours of fooling around on bicycles, scooters, skateboards, and rollerblades are all gone. No one teaches them how catch, carry, and kick a footy. Rough-and-tumble is not a part of their daily life anymore; they're growing up sterilized from an early age. As we let our kids atrophy, we are not building a world of joy to share; instead, we all live in Varga's augmented reality that is as real as unicorns. Overprotective parenting has been replaced by the uber-protective environment of the world in which you daily "win" your dose of Reality for Everyone™, praised by Simon Cowell's hologram or Baiano Lindo's smug smiles.

And yet, suicides are on the rise. Depression and anxiety has reached levels never seen before. Demographic decline is a direct result of the growing isolation within our bubbles. Who needs sex or parenting when a 3D emotional support consultant could blow your cock and your mind, and you do not even have to think about consequences? The *other* is not to be loved and cherished but a burden at best, a biohazard at worst.

A new society, we've been told, is aimed at enriching us and our lives. Alas, isolated we wither down and die; no amount of digital connections can replace human contact. Even babies die—despite being well-fed—if they are deprived of physical touch, that's how lethal loneliness is. What Varga bestowing on us would turn out to be much worse. The *Happiness Pill*? Give me a fucking break. Once you get out of your bubble, you'd be even more miserable and more likely to suffer and ultimately kill yourself or the other(s). (They'd call it "unexplained rage," though, even the rats are happier and less addicted when given a chance to socialize; look up the Rat Park experiment by Bruce Alexander if you need confirmation.)

The culture of insane "safetyism"—shielding young people from any realities the bumpy roads of life would make them face—that started decades ago, has severely impaired young people's social, emotional, and intellectual development. As such, they are the ideal prey for the "safetyism" philosophy's next phase, that of Reality for Everyone™, which is as far from reality as it could possibly be. They are also easy prey for psychopaths who've adjusted to the new world and its opportunities to steal from the blind, really well.

Wake Up!

The world Varga is creating at an ever-increasing pace reads like an evil masterpiece of vicious manipulation. The most successful propaganda project with the most tragic outcome was that of Joseph Goebbels, the Minister of Propaganda for Adolf Hitler. Under the demonic spell of the self-destructive Führer, the nation had been united into one superior team of Übermenschen, against all the others (be it Russians or minor Slave tribes, Jews, French or English or Americans). When you bind the people into a team, Hitler and Goebbels knew perfectly well, they do not seek cooperation, understanding, or truth.

They seek victory. A victory over you.

Are we that brainwashed?

Are we so suicidal?

Are we really giving up our lives for his enrichment?

What would be left of us, our shared humanity? Nothing. Happy zombies perhaps, if the Pill takes over. Is there a way out? Perhaps there is, outlined many years ago, on April 10, 2005, in the VXVoid cyberpunk poem, published on DeviantArt website:

tHE cYBerPuNK aNThEM

: when the rebels realize they can't bring down the system
: because they depend on the system
: can't unplug from the system
: because they are part of the system
: can't turn off the system
: because they are in the system
they are OFF the system

in a world where you are only as fast as your CPU
a delinquent's dream
where you are simultaneously
anonymous and infamous
you choose the name you go by
and you have no face

THEY ARE THE SYSTEM
[AND THE SYSTEM IS THEM]
and so they begin the destruction from the inside, out

We created a new dimension,
built it from the ground up.
At least, that's what our propaganda tells us.
Maybe we didn't.
Maybe we opened a door,
awoke something that had only been sleeping
for a very long time…

Either way, we found a world
too big for us to even comprehend,
let alone control.
An imaginary city that circled the globe.
An information superhighway.
And naturally we tried to conquer it.

but tell me
of the landscapes beyond the well-paved road
unmapped
and unexplored
of the crack dens beneath the overpass
of the ones who live in the traffic's shadow
tell me of the hitchhiking strangers
tell me who sleeps in the ditches
living off the discards
of the superhighway surfers
one man's trash, another's treasure

you cannot control a space that doesn't exist
and in the lost lands
the disputed territories
from the unexplored oceans
to the places in the cities that have slipped into abandonment
and been forgotten
those who have no home

the domain squatters
the digital pirates
THE CYBERPUNKS
are taking over

the code is being rewritten
the system is being recalibrated
the time has come
for E-narchy
in E-merica

A Struggle for Freedom: REVOLUTION as SOCIAL RECOVERY

Unless we embrace life as brain-dead zombies serving at Varga's pleasure, we're facing a life or death struggle 'til the end. Today's final showdown, named the governmental transition, would bring more evil to the world, evil sweetened by the Happiness Pill made by Varga, with an outcome that's not too difficult to predict.

All we can do is join New Athens's freedom revolution. Only the brave enclaves of free spirit and thought that are the New Athens establishments all over the world are preserving our humanity. We must fight against the chains that suffocate us. Whether we will live as full-blooded human beings, with all our weaknesses, our strengths, and our humaneness or not, is up to us. We need to heal our societies. And for the first time in human history, we also have tools to fight back at the system. One of humankind's oldest inventions, money, is available to us in its reinvented form that could power our own free economy. With various forms of e-Cash, we can fight Varga where it hurts, with our wallets.

A Sly, Roundabout Way

New Athens has established their own thriving, underground economy. We're not in Kansas anymore, Toto, we're going down the rabbit hole where they can't follow as we make our own wealth. Think uber-cool interface on DarkTor, an impenetrable platform, that has multi-currency wallets, direct crypto-to-crypto cash and crypto-to-fiat cash exchanges on your local machine, outside Varga's warmongering, controlled kleptocracy. P2P loans are already going in and out of New Athens's system, secure trust-less contracts are a thing, stealth downloads for music and videos, shares, secure

SMS messaging, secure video calls, data exchange for all the data that you need and what you own, all in one place, all of which is out of Varga's reach as well and is at the same time empowering *us* via New Athens tokens, such as SECRET & Shade tokens. Secret Contracts achieve data privacy for Shade Protocol using on-chain encrypted data so business-to-business loans can thrive. Decentralized Finance that's out of Varga's reach is a reality we need to fully embrace and spread throughout the world. In New Athens we are not just abstract human beings translated into pixels and database entries, we're full-bodied human beings. We create dynamic media, we learn from each other in real space(s) and are not alienated from each other by diabolic games, fostering social isolation, and madness.

IGNORE Varga and his Hellish Happiness

We can refuse to pay for Varga's phony reality toys, his fantasy pills, and his nanobots meant to enslave us. Instead, we can breathe free. So to paraphrase tHE cYBerPuNK aNThEM: the code of life should be rewritten. The system should be recalibrated. The time has come, the time for crypto-anarchy in the crypto-world. Crypto spells freedom. Our tech and our e-Cash enable us to build a parallel world, a better world that would, one day, replace Winston Varga's controlled, criminally insane system based on fraud and tyranny. We can live in self-managed, self-governed societies based on voluntary, cooperative institutions, based on permission-less money and truly human support for each other.

"The only way to deal with an unfree world is to become so absolutely free that your very existence is an act of rebellion," wrote Albert Camus. Understand that we are free NOT to fund Varga's wars. We are free NOT to fund Varga's corporations. We are free NOT to buy Varga's Trojan happiness pill that allows his nanobots to control and ravage our brains. We all should build Varga-free New Athens for ourselves and a Varga-free world soon afterward.

We do not need Varga's permission to be free if we **choose** to be **FREE**.

Choose wisely.
Your comrade in arms,

Philip Bolghery

Hate to beg of you but your donations are my only source of income. As you all know, since *the New York Times* fired me I am unemployable by anyone but you, my most valuable readers and comrades. Varga has seen to it that I starve. Should you wish to support my work and keep learning about that menace, send me some SECRET love.

SECRET token address:

secret1rme968d5yuaeqkga07k5akzdch3gpcctrax4hm

In the I.R.I.S. Chatroom
March 21, 2048

Phat Prophet is livid. "He blew us wide open! Philip smoked us out."

The Renegade watches Bolghery on his own RIOTA's Tangle-Tube channel while the same text of Bolghery's speech scrolls down his screen, next to Phat Prophet's angry reaction. He types in:

"Varga knows all of that already." This does not assuage Phat Prophet's concerns.

"Yeah, but now so does everyone else." Phat Prophet rages: "And you, N., why did you have to hack Varga? We still don't know how his Daemons tracks intruders."

Nastassia huffs. "It wasn't a hack, you big dodo. Did you read what he wrote? I provided Bolghery with the patent change. That's all. The rest is his speculation. He added the PRIORI Hacking Alliance for dramatic purposes. That's how he writes."

"It could've been worse," the Renegade types in. "Varga is busy with his governmental transition to worry about New Athens too much. At least for now." Renegade turns to Phat Prophet's portion of the screen. "She was right to have Bolghery ruffle some feathers. We might need true leakers to help us."

"So you think we have time," Nastassia asks, "to get to the bottom of the Pill?"

"We do."

"Not too much, I fear," Phat Prophet says, "unless we get a hold on the nanobots Varga plans to use with his pills and take them apart," he concludes and abruptly turns his I.R.I.S. client off without a goodbye. Their efforts in building a new economy based on their own autonomous money, outside the system Varga has ruled with an iron fist, is a secret no more. On the other hand, the Happiness Pill's real purpose is as obscure as ever, despite Philip Bolghery's premonitions. The next move was on Winston Varga and no one had the faintest clue what it would be and how to fight it.

Chapter 3

VARGA'S CASTLE

Varga's Castle
Le Mont-Saint-Michel Abbey, France
March 21, 2048

Perched on a rocky islet, an awe-inspiring medieval settlement stood awash in the crimson glimmer coming from the sinking sun. Le Mont-Saint-Michel Abbey was one of Christianity's most important pilgrimage sites from the 8th to the 18th century and UNESCO's world heritage until 2047 at midnight after which it was taken over by the Proteus FinTech Corp., in order to "protect its unique value to the collective interest of every woman, man, and child in the world." Proteus leased the Mont-Saint-Michel, its bay, and about two hundred miles of the Atlantic Ocean, "to protect sea creatures from overfishing so every woman, man…" well, you've guessed the rest, for the ten years prior taking it over so Varga's presence was already firmly established in Lower Normandy for quite a while.

But when Varga was taking their national monument into his ownership for good, the French people, always keen on red wine, sex, and revolution, had staged a few loud, rather violent protests against the corporate takeover of their national pride, the abbey. Varga invited the #Resistance leaders for a meet and greet in the Tonton airport in Nantes. *Let us talk,* his hand-written invitation said, *in the name of peace, protection, and love for France's foremost monument.*

The Resistance Leaders
Nantes, France
January 10th, 2047

Varga wasn't really upset when the stern, proud leaders of the #Resistance scornfully refused to imbibe champagne or partake in the sumptuous dinner prepared just for them by the famous chef Gordon Ramsay's robotic clone, haughty chef Ramsumptous. Ramsay was known for speaking French in an indecipherable accent and for his TV theatrics filled with crazed, loud screaming, and maddening insults, which is why his robotic clone was made mute. It was a bit sad to have such a feast go to waste, but "one should admire stern, ascetic revolutionaries when they are at their best behavior," Varga said, calming down Ramsumptous, assuring him that it wasn't his fault that *Dirigeants de La résistance* chose dignified scorn over steamed clams in buttery garlic sauce. It was rather his guests' revolutionary pride that chose a fast over the feast.

So, armed with Biblical verses and a disarming smile only Cardinal Luciano Antonioni, Varga's close, crimson-clad collaborator, could invoke during the Inquisition times, Varga had served his guests with a small video presentation INFINITUS had arranged for each of them instead of a dinner. "The good Lord Jesus, a bloke always ready to share some wise words," Varga addressed his guests in a humble pose just for them. "In John 8:7, he famously said '*He that is without sin among you, let him first cast a stone at her.*'"

It is safe to assume the leaders were not sinless stewards of revolution, but mere vulnerable humans, an assumption the INFINITUS had proven without reasonable, or any other, degree of doubt.

The INFINITUS knew not only what kind of sex dolls they purchased through third-party facilitators, in what kind of obscene 3D sex fantasies they indulged, but was also intimately familiar with every little indiscretion and petty thought crime they'd committed over the years. Even some—the INFINITUS would've blushed had he been programmed to do so—more brazen infractions like embezzlements of funds were noted. And then some more. Masterfully put together, (the INFINITUS learned editing skills one lazy hour in September by studying the works of Thelma Schoonmaker, George Tomasini, and Ištvan Filaković, Jr., some of the best film editors of all time,) these videos portrayed the #Resistance stalwarts as rather perverted, petty bourgeoise creeps, high-horse-riding swindlers driven by lust and greed. Upon seeing their aghast reactions to the videos, Varga, as cheerful as always, clasped his hands and shook them with the conviction of the supreme pontiff of The Holy See.

"Well, if we confess our sins, He is faithful and just and will forgive us our sins and purify us from all unrighteousness." He cackled. "Cheer up, lads. Redemption is only one signature away." He snapped his fingers and a lawyer, who had been patiently waiting in the adjunct room, appeared. His smile was subdued. His outfit, an Emporio Armani bespoke suit made of virgin wool and cashmere. His movements careful and respectful. His name, a secret. He handed an iron-clad non-disclosure agreement to each of Varga's distinguished guests. Several bulky, armed-to-the-teeth Obsidian Security Ltd. guys were also present, conspicuously emphasizing the seriousness of the agreement. They were a helpful hint of what might happen to the signees if they would, God forbid in his eternal mercy, decide to fuck with the terms of the agreement and play games. Once it was signed, Varga spread his arms like a soaring eagle, truly wanting to hug each and everyone present. He radiated the joy of a generously awarded child who had done her homework on time for the Vogan's Poetry Competition show's rerun.

"*Et voilà*, noble *Messieurs*. The Holy Spirit is a Spirit of order, but The Holy Spirit is also a Spirit of Revolution, worry you not. Keep up with the good revolutionary work." He smiled and dismissed them without a second look.

The #Resistance's top brass left the meeting with tails between their legs, but as soon as they regained their self-respect, they managed to assure their followers that it is in everyone's best interest to have Proteus FinTech Corp. manage the Mont-Saint-Michel Abbey. The national pride was going to be preserved, they were assured, and enhanced, enriched. The abbey was indeed safe from the tourists' prying eyes for Winston Varga immediately moved in, closed it to the public, and made the Mont-Saint-Michel his second home. To the horrors of its clergy and the great artistic arbiters of French cultural life, as soon as he moved in, Varga built himself a huge veranda with a luxurious pool by carelessly breaking the walls of the *Salle des Chevaliers* (Knights' Hall) in order to create access to his new veranda with a view to the tidal bores from the English Channel. Alas, their voices of protest were not louder than white mice squawks in the lab, so Varga ignored them.

It was the abbey from which he oversaw the national-monument-buying spree that the Proteus FinTech Corp. embarked on all over the world. The binge-feeding on nations' heritages was unimpeded by wannabe resisters and ran as smoothly as a baby's bottom. The occasional, "angry, artsy-fartsy" essay, as Varga called them, protesting the privatization of national treasures only served to amuse him.

The Proteus FinTech Corp., and with it Winston Varga, was on its way to own the world. Or at least a big portion of it. The rest, as they say in the worn-out cliché, is history yet to be told. So please, follow me, reader, hear me out. Hear the truth. You chuckle in disbelief, jaded and cynical? What "truth" is in this fake civilization that's drowning in lies and which I babble about, you might ask yourselves. Well, whoever told you there's no such thing in the world as the truth is a triple-damned liar deserving to be publicly quartered, his treacherous remains burned to the ashes, his forsaken residues taken to the Yangtze River's mouth on the East China Sea and spread out. For safety measures, one shall drain the mighty river and sow the seeds of oblivion in its riverbed, meant for those that lost faith and reason for being alive.

But you will, my most beloved reader, on these truthful pages find it, the truth(s) of the world you inhabit. For everything else, there's a MasterCard.

Reading Philip Bolghery
Le Mont-Saint-Michel Abbey
March 21, 2048

The castle/abbey, one of Winston Varga's numerous opulent homes scattered all over the world and his crown jewel, was the one from which he watched Bolghery reciting his essay. He turns to Cordelia Einarsdøttir, whose jade green eyes shine like emeralds, a beautiful young woman and his longtime lover since she was eighteen, and scoffs at Bolghery with utter disdain.

"Motherfucking nitwit cockroach."

Cordelia chuckles. "It's an entertaining read. I like Bolghery. He has guts. Too angry and verbose for my taste, though. All bark and no bite. I guess his Italian blood must be boiling."

"Done yet?" Varga is not amused. "I have to cut him off at the knees and squash this nonsense before it gets out of control."

"Why don't you just send him one of your nanobots and reprogram him?" Cordelia is really having fun with Bolghery's essay. "He could then work as your speechwriter. Even better, send him a donation and let the world know he works for you," she laughs.

"It's not funny. These bloody cocksuckers in New Athens are up to no good. And brazen enough to use that Howler monkey's loudspeaker to attack my project. Today of all days."

"So what?" Cordelia asks; she could not be more blasé. "Your media reaches billions while his broadcast can't be seen by more than a few hundred thousand."

"They started to organize with the Outsiders and openly poke their drooling noses into my business. They are trying to hack my systems all the time. Even worse, they have a parallel economy already established on crypto, starting to undermine my own. And all you have to say is 'so what?'"

"Fuck those nose-drooling, cock-sucking, revolution-planning motherfucking bastard pieces of shit," Cordelia recites mechanically and then, with the charming smile of a beautiful young woman who's aware of her power and purring like a kitten, asks, "Better?"

"They might go too far and gain some serious economic strength."

"He's a fired journalist. He begs for donations while you have more money than all the governments put together. How he can be a threat?"

"He is."

"If you say so."

"What I am saying is that New Athens's peaceful freaks are as capable of monstrosities as anyone else. That's just rotten human nature's fact."

"So, what are you going to do to stop them?"

"One step at the time. Bolghery first."

"Come on, let him be. It is good to have some opposition."

"Fuck the opposition. The best way to control the opposition is to lead it ourselves, Lenin said." He notices Cordelia's eyebrows raised quizzically. "Russia? Lenin?" Nothing, no recognition in her eyes. Varga sighs. *The kids of today know next to nothing,* he thinks and moves on. "Fuhgeddaboudit. Lenin knew one or two things about revolutions and opposition. I don't control Bolghery. Not yet."

"At least don't kill him, scourge." Cordelia laughs.

"Don't worry. I am not in the business of turning morons into martyrs."

Oprah Winfrey Forever

Varga did not have to go far because his TV studio is conveniently located in the west wing of the castle, a place from which he has been conducting all his media wars since moving in. This time he decides to play one of his aces earlier than he had originally planned.

During the late nineties of the 20th century, *The Oprah Winfrey Show*, hosted by Oprah, one of the most influential women of her time in the world, was a riot and an enormously popular show. Now, after just recently celebrating her ninety-fourth birthday, she is an invaluable relic of a bygone era, a venerable Our Lady we Can Trust. Oprah was admired even by the most ardent Reality for Everyone™ players, who are known to interrupt their self-indulging, fame-creating games to watch her rare appearances (especially if she hosted one of the peers who won over Simon's heart.) But, after Varga brought her back to the revived *Oprah Forever Show*, by luring her with a $1.00 a year salary and a billion-dollar donation to a charity of her choice, her popularity soared to yet unseen heights.

Oprah Winfrey was an institution all by herself, the first "influencer" who moved from a lighter form of entertainment onto the most pressing issues of our times. She is now poised to interview none other but Winston Varga, the focus of a scandal that spread like a wildfire after the scathing essay published by Philip Bolghery. It seemed the essay's timing was perfect – while the world was waiting with bated breath for the governmental transition, the window of opportunity arose; even the ardent players were waiting to see what's coming next and stepped outside their virtual worlds for a while. PRIORI followers had pushed the essay hard on all the social networks, and the reach of it was much bigger than Cordelia's estimate. Varga was right—the Bolghery Essay was gaining momentum and it might end up undermining him. They have begun to move, those New Athens bastards. He could sense it, so Varga's decision to act fast was the correct one.

Our Lady we Can Trust, the great old, revered media sage sits opposite an empty chair, not really happy with the position she finds herself in. She shakes her head as she speaks to the audience, her charm barely containing her displeasure.

"Mr. Winston Varga opened his fortress for us," she says while the aerial pictures of the castle her show started with a fade-in, "so we could discuss the 'Happiness Pill' controversy directly with him, but as you may see, he is not here." Oprah is accompanied by an occasional, strategically placed *boo* from the audience. "Even though this is his own home, the castle, the most famous manor in the world," she is saying to the audience when a shushing sound interrupts her. The lights in the studio go off, and Varga's hologram appears on the chair across her, smiling. A roaring applause comes from the spectators.

"Hey, he's here," Oprah says, smiling like a pleased, dear old granny. Everyone smiles with her. Life is still worth living if you just smile. She knew the raw power of Jimmy Durante's teachings and was always ready to spread joy and wisdom to her worshippers.

"It was always my dream to be on your show, Oprah."

"Winston, I came to your studio because you promised to show up in person. It is not nice to lie to an old lady," she says with another disarming smile. The audience simultaneously boos Varga and applauds Winfrey.

What a class act, that lady.

"Have I ever lied in my life, Oprah? Even once?" a voice, Varga's natural voice, boastfully claims from the dark. His hologram stands up, turns to his right and, after a moment of stunned surprise, it applauds. The real Winston Varga appears on the stage, as joyous as ever. Some moon-walking. Some waving to the audience. Some I-Want-You finger-pointing pose. As he moves on he cheerfully shakes hands with the audience members. Then some high-fiving. The audience is ecstatic. Varga's hologram looks at the real Varga with envy.

"You look even better in person."

"And you're one dashing image," Varga retorts, to the audience's rapturous laughter.

"Thank you, dude," Varga's hologram blushes, and the people laugh some more. That's tech mastery playing as pure old-fashioned fun, just for them, the privileged few, the real Virtuosi™ whose hard work in tirelessly canceling infidels has paid off. They are here, where everything happens. What more could anyone want from this life? each of them must have thought while enjoying the show, together with the billions glued to their screens and hologram projections alike, waiting to see what Varga would have to say about that scathing essay by Philip Bolghery.

"Don't mention it, dawg. But this show isn't big enough for both of us," the real Varga says, winking at the audience as he blows at his own image that angrily protests and then frowningly disappears, greeted with the audience's belly laughter. He's good, playing them like a fiddle. Then he turns to Oprah, his expression filled with reverence as he bows and pleads, "I am not worthy, I am not worthy!"

The audience is out of their minds. It's obvious why is this the greatest show on Earth.

Oprah, who has been laughing with the audience, tells Varga to get serious and to take a seat. She has an important interview to conduct and does not beat around the bush.

"Is your Happiness Pill a threat to society as Bolghery claims?"

Varga was ready for her sharp questioning and responds without taking a moment to think.

"On the contrary, the Pill achieves exactly what Tibetan monks managed to achieve after decades of meditating," he replies convincingly.

"Such as?"

"Visualization of different, higher realities, for one," Varga explains as the audience listens in dead silence. "You'll be able to vividly see, with your mental eye, all your fantasies and indulge in them for a brief period of time. Not unlike dreaming, you'd be going to a Polynesian beach or for a hike in the Swiss Alps in order to relax and reinvigorate your system. What's wrong with that?" he asks the audience. Several people yell, "Nothing!" while the vigorous shaking of many heads agrees. They are with him.

"You're not afraid of side effects?" Oprah insists.

"There are none!" Varga exuberantly spreads his arms. His heart, its honesty vulnerable and revealed, almost wants to jump from his open chest. He looks like a falsely accused man wanting to embrace his unjust accusers and forgive. "Our Happiness Pill works like a dream. You wake up without after-effects. How to better explain it? Imagine if you were able to voluntarily invoke your most beautiful dreams, memories, or fantasies, whenever you wish. And then, finely tuned to your own needs, the Pill enhances the experience, based on your DNA and psychological profile. That's what our Happiness Pill enables you to do." He speaks directly to the audience, who's soaking up his every syllable, and then he turns to Oprah with an impish grin.

"The Happiness Pill and our palette of upcoming betterments would enhance the mind of every man, woman, and child on the planet. But, we don't stop there." Varga starts to work himself up into a state of intoxicating excitement. "Ask yourself what would be the point of having a lucid mind in a dysfunctional, rather mortal body?"

"You tell us," Oprah asks, keenly interested in Varga's answers. She does not like the word *mortal* being uttered in her presence.

"No point at all!" he exclaims. "You'd be preserving corpses, like the morbid Cryonics Corporation in Moscow does. But people are not frozen meat. You have to enhance your body as you live in order to fully enjoy the life you're given."

"How'd you achieve that?" Oprah perks up, hoping the enthralled audience would remember to breathe.

"Molecular nanotechnology."

"Meaning?"

"Soon, we'll be creating anti-illness drugs rendering cancer or Alzheimers and other ailments obsolete. We will offer drugs to repair damaged limbs and even more importantly, our genetic diagnosis will enable couples at risk for having offspring with a disorder to have a healthy child." Varga pauses, letting his words sink in, then he gets truly excited. "A coming revolution in medicine will also replace antediluvian, haphazard offspring reproduction, and we'll be able to create new humans as we wish them to be, totally free of pregnancy or childbirth pains." He smiles. "We'll be creating a new, better human race."

After a long, rapturous applause subsides, Varga humbly concludes, "Sure, we're still a few years from fulfilling all those goals; there would be a lot of ethical-related discussions and decisions to be made by all of us, but we're on our way." He is as convincing as a used-car salesman who's been topping sales charts several years in a row, never having seen defeat.

"Just take a glance at our video," he says nodding at the TV show's director hidden behind a myriad of monitors and hologram switches. The audience sighs in awe; a 3D holographic molecular visualization of DNA starts dancing in the air as it coils and replicates in front of their awed eyes.

"Our DNA genetic code is but a computer program. All life-forms are the results of software processes, so once you replace the software, you change the hardware—yourself." Varga speaks like a man possessed by a vision as a yellow gene appears on the screen. A blue molecule enters the picture and dances through the gene's strings, to the tune of Frédéric Chopin's "Grande Valse Brillante," E flat major Op. 18.

Varga, who had already stood up and, himself in between the audience and the huge hologram in front of him, uses a teacher's stick to conduct and probe into the hologram, changing its form with a touch.

"The blue molecule represents a nanobot with a program for your gene, here in yellow. The program reads the information from the code, as it glides through this genetic loci," he says. "As the blue molecule 'reads' the gene while it slides over it, the gene's locus changes its color. It reads and reprograms it in real-time!"

Alas, in the middle of his ecstatic performance, one gruff voice yells, "What about Bolghery's essay? What do you have to say about the Happiness Pill leaks?"

Varga steps aside, glancing at the audience like he's searching for the culprit, still smiling but somehow a bit more serious. He nods pensively for a moment. He's a man of the people, he listens to their concerns with great care.

American Dream 2.0

"Bolghery? He's a worn-out, ragtag, out-of-touch, delusional conspiracy theorist whose hysterical transphobic and racist ranting are of no value to anyone and do not contribute to the society one bit," Varga says, looking at the audience. It is written all over their faces; aside from that one heckler, they have long since forgotten Bolghery and his comical little essay. But he needed to put an end to that once for all and concludes, "We are dealing not with the deranged paranoia of a drunkard writing nonsense in a dry snit, but with serious issues, with real life, with real improvements, real human happiness, that has been so sorely missing for ages." Varga finishes his defense and turns back toward the 3D CGI-ed hologram presentation, almost reinvigorated by the interruption. He continues, now fully intoxicated with the promise of the future he shares with the world. He's on fire.

"Now observe how the code turns into flesh and blood, one protein after another, one molecule after another. The gene creates proteins, molecules, cells. It grows, frantically producing more and more cells and organisms. It is now a living human being. Vastly improved at that. Gender, race, age, it's all written in the code. A recipient cell creates new species, or vastly improves the current, and replaces it with a better model." He nods at the director.

"Do it."

In dead silence, Winston Varga on the screen slowly morphs into young and radiant Oprah Winfrey. Real Oprah shakes her head. This is indeed incredible. While everyone watches him breathlessly, Varga chuckles and continues. "A gigantic renewal, a mythical re-birth of our nation and humankind is leaping towards us. We will create perfectly happy human units in a perfectly happy society. American Dream 2.0!"

Oprah, seemingly for the first time in her lifelong career, is rendered speechless, stares at Varga, then slowly turns to the camera. "We'll be back after these messages."

The Legend of the Cherokee Rose
I.R.I.S. Chatroom
March 21, 2048

"How do we fight against such power?" Phat Prophet asks. "Varga has all the media in the world, and more money than God," he adds resignedly. His helplessness was as heavy as the lead in a firing squad's bullets. Nastassia felt like Phatty's soul was defeated and has been bleeding away from both his mighty mind and his good heart. It pains her to see him in such an agonizing condition. But, what to say, what comfort can she offer when she feels similar feelings of helplessness? Varga has been playing his media manipulation cards like a master and the people seem to happily go along with anything he offers them.

So, for maybe a minute, no one types a word to try to answer these concerns. The pause that has fallen upon the I.R.I.S. chatroom seems like the longest minute in her life, something only the Clock of the Long Now would be able to measure. If it ticked once a year it felt like a year has passed, like her heart had stopped beating taken by surprise of her own fearfulness. She knows all of that is just a normal state of shock, given the speed with which Varga embarked on crushing Bolghery's essay. It hits her why Phatty's so deflated.

They are lonely.

They are three weirdos scattered all over the world—really, she does not even know where they live. How they really look. How their days look, what makes them happy, what do they love? Yes, they're connected by mutual projects and the fight for dignified, real human living against Varga's soul-sucking digital world, but still, they are lonely.

Each of them, enveloped in the dark, where only screens flicker, moves onto the theme that has bothered wider New Athens's populace for quite some time: how to fight against Varga, his Proteus FinTech Corp., its supercomputers, and its immense financial and political power? It does seem like a lost cause.

A Lost Cause

"True gentlemen fight even in a struggle doomed to defeat."

It was the Renegade who typed it. It seems like a joke and yet, also serious. Nastassia snaps out of her negative thinking, grateful to the Renegade. *Yes, this is why it is worth fighting, I guess,* she thinks. A real fighter fights even if he knows he'll lose, 'til the end, because the Goddess Fortuna might change her mind. "Be bold and mighty forces will come to your aid," she once overheard Frédéric tell her mom. It stayed with her. The only one who can really defeat you is yourself. As she regains her cool again, she mentally corrects herself. Yes, they might be lonely but they are not alone.

They have each other. The motley crew of weirdos fighting for freedom.

During the silence, they all neglected the ebullient Varga's showmanship in going on the Oprah Forever Show. Nastassia turns her eyes onto his smirking face and, for the first time in her life, she senses hate. It startles her, that feeling and its power; she truly hates that man and all that he represents—a dehumanized world, broken, atomized societies, fake realities, and the utter pain of loneliness that glues all of the charade together, like a broken doll grotesquely put back together.

A Cherokee Gentleman

No one answers Phat Prophet's question.

"I ain't no gentleman." It is him who breaks the silence.

Is he joking? Nastassia asks herself and starts to type again. "But, aren't you a Cherokee, Phatty? That's even better." A little smiley to end the sentence indicates a joke. *Now we'll see it,* she thinks.

As a response, a wall of text pours out of Patty's fingertips.

"Yes, N., I am a Cherokee. I used to ride my mustang over what used to be our land. His name was Kaliwohi, Integrity in our language. They call us a nation, the biggest Indian nation in the States but for most Americans, we're still a wild tribe, committed to a reservation." It feels like he is choking behind his keypad.

Where is he going with this? Nastassia asks herself.

"No better symbol exists for the pain and suffering of my nation than that of the Trail Where They Cried and the Cherokee Rose. The story goes like this," Phatty continues, citing the tale: "The mothers of the slaughtered Cherokee sons and husbands grieved so much that the chiefs prayed for a sign to lift the mother's spirits and give them strength to care for their children. From that day forward, a beautiful new flower, a rose, grew wherever a mother's tear fell to the ground. The rose is white, for the mother's tears. It has a gold center, for the gold taken from the Cherokee lands, and seven leaves on each stem that represent the seven Cherokee clans that made the journey. To this day, the Cherokee Rose prospers along the route of the Trail of Tears."

Phat continues, "The irony? The Cherokee Rose is now the official flower of the state of Georgia."

Why is he telling us this? Nastassia sighs heavily.

"You know, it was May 26th, 1830 when the US Congress voted, almost unanimously, for the Indian Removal Act. Cherokee, Chickasaw, Choctaw, Creek, and Seminole Indians, and many more others, smaller nations and tribes, were forcefully removed from their own lands. Their one God was better than ours, so we were wiped off the face of Earth. Andrew Jackson gave a speech on the Indian removal in the year of 1830. He said, 'It gives me great pleasure to announce to Congress that the benevolent policy of the government, steadily pursued for nearly thirty years, in relation to the removal of the Indians beyond the white settlements is approaching a happy consummation.'

"The benevolent policy, what a sick joke. And now, two hundred or so years later, aren't we in reservations again? Aren't all of us New Athenians second-rate citizens of this world, like Cherokee, forced to live on isolated islands, pockets of our own independent lives, something everyone outside despises?"

I was right, he's lonely. Nastassia can not shake the notion, like a closed loop flowing around her brain. *I guess the Renegade as well?* They struggle mightily for the freedom of Varga's ubiquitous surveillance and brainwashing tools that have enslaved most of humanity and are threatening their own liberties, and yet, they fight isolated. She thought of Phatty's deep sorrow and how no one would be able to console him. How much information one could derive from a single glance at the human face? *Only if he were able to see me,* Nastassia thinks. He'd have an instant, profound awareness of her deep sympathy and understanding for him. Alas, like this, behind the screens, words seem so hollow, depleted of sense and humanity.

Isn't that exactly what Varga wanted?

Are we really losing?

"I understand," she types, almost involuntarily, subconsciously following the dark train of his thoughts that was leaving the station to vanish somewhere dark, in a blood-drenched land that never forgot nor forgave.

"No, you don't." Phat Prophet does not need to type, for Nastassia knew he'd say that.

"What's the point? We're losing anyway. Just look at how much these people adore the bozo's babbling." He pulled a still from Oprah's show. Truly, everyone in the audience is mesmerized by Varga's performance. He could bet, it's the same in all the homes, all the gin joints, and Korova milk bars all over the world.

What could she tell him? Nastassia wondered.

Why is the Renegade silent?

Spirit and Matter

The Renegade, in his vast laboratory, sits shrouded in darkness with only an occasional flicker coming from afar. It's difficult to estimate how big his space is, as he's almost slouching, leaning toward the monitor. His hair is shaggy grey, his reddish pullover made of Pina cotton and covered in ice cream stains. A small popup frame has Varga's media shenanigans on it, but the rest of his desktop has the I.R.I.S. interface on it and nothing else. He blushes when he thinks of how he hacked the I.R.I.S. core and injected an invisible code to enable him to see the people he's interacting with. Ethically this was, well, wrong, for he often felt like one of Varga's despicable spies, but sometimes it was needed to see what's really going on.

Truth to be told, it wasn't some ultrasophisticated Stealth Sleuth Tracer the legend says helped him discover ZeliQ's betrayal. Instead, what happened was much simpler. ZeliQ's crooked smile while he was lying to them alarmed the Renegade and prompted him to, no matter how reluctantly, hack into ZeliQ's system, only to see the full extent of his malevolent actions. The secret of his sleuthing stayed with him. So, he invokes both Nastassia and Phat Prophet's images on his screen; he needs to see them to better understand them and what's going on. The words on the screen are not enough. *Poor kids,* the Renegade thinks. *There's still so much to learn, so little time.*

While Varga's been progressing in leaps and bounds, they were all getting discouraged. While New Athens thrived, its education far superior to that of the Outsiders, for example, some people started to complain about living a life like in the Stone Age while Maglev's ultra-fast railway was being constructed nearby. Yes, they get to trade with the Outsiders but that was akin to impoverished Native Americans selling trinkets to SUV-driving tourists in the Monument Valley. Only New Athens's digital goods were finding their way into the wider market, so the wealth creation has stalled for too many. Crypto gurus were rich, so even New Athens started to face inequality problems. Those were still minor issues—overall the New Athens project was a staggering success, but yet, it might crumble under the enormous weight of Varga's empire.

Some of the best computer brains the Renegade groomed for the digital showdown with Varga were lured out of New Athens by Varga's offer of immense salaries and are now working on developing his evil toys, armed with the knowledge the Renegade had bestowed upon them. Phat Prophet's concerns were provoked not only by Bolghery's essay and the dangers it might bring them, but also by the upcoming governmental transition and the insecurity it came with it. Moreover, Wyverin's decision to leave New Athens for good must have shaken him really badly. Wyverin was not only a programmer whose prowess impressed both the Renegade and the Phat Prophet quite often, but she was also a girl always gently teasing Phatty who had, during his sleepless, lonesome nights, developed feelings for her avatar and pined for a love life with her, despite not knowing anything real about her. Talk about the perils of cyberspace. She might not have been a girl at all, for all he knew. Poor guy. But, the Renegade understood very well, disheartened troops are a shortcut to defeat.

He must help Phatty. Even Nastassia, ever vigorous, seems a bit down today.

"Those whom the gods wish to destroy they first make mad," the Renegade types on the screen, somewhat cryptically, adding, "Phatty, try to understand, Varga is afraid. He fears us!"

"What were you watching? He never looked more confident than on Oprah today."

"Think. The PRIORI have given Bolghery the material. He published his essay today. Varga summoned Oprah and appeared to ward off the essay's effect of it by peddling his shit mere minutes later."

"Renegade's right," Nastassia types in.

"The effects of the essay would go away in a day or two. Rather in hours."

"Maybe, but the fear would stay with Varga," Renegade assures Phat.

"*Thunder is no longer the voice of an angry god, nor is lightning his avenging missile. No river contains a spirit, no tree is the life principle of a man, no snake the embodiment of wisdom, no mountain cave the home of a great demon. No voices now speak to man from stones, plants, and animals, nor does he speak to them believing they can hear. His contact with nature has gone, and with it has gone the profound emotional energy that this symbolic connection supplied.*" The Renegade sends them this C.G. Jung quote in a wall of text and waits for them to read it and process its meaning.

"What are you saying?" Phatty asks, not getting it.

"Everything Varga does harms people to the very core of their being," says the old sage.

"We know that, but they don't. They live in Reality for Everyone™ delusions."

"Yes. But nothing of that is real. Varga's empire is built on quicksand. The people can't live in a stupor of fakeness forever. He knows that."

"Renegade, what are you getting at? I do not need consoling." Phatty sighs.

"All the disturbances of the conscious psyche, everything that is happening to them, the loss of true freedom, financial troubles, the loss of true love, the loss of God if you wish, the loss of the whispering rivers, the loss of true human connection, all of that is sinking deep into the unconsciousness of every human being and, therefore, to the collective unconsciousness of humanity. Friedrich Nietzsche wrote about that when he said, 'You shall become friends of the immediate things.' Those immediate things have all but vanished from every day's world, replaced by false immediacies of fake reality. But those real, immediate things are not gone." The Renegade is getting tired of typing. "Trust me, Phatty, Varga's empire is at the peak of its powers but it could crumble overnight. And he fears that more than anything. We're the ones that can push the first domino to fall. Varga knows that."

"True," Nastassia chimes in, reinforcing the Renegade's thoughts. "I recall how my dad once told me about the fall of the Berlin Wall. One day it was up, as mighty as the Soviet Union empire at that time, and the very next day it was gone. No one was able to predict it, not even people working on it, not even one day prior."

The Renegade agrees. "Varga's power has intrinsic weakness he can't control. His power is as artificial as the life he's creating for the world. Even his money is abnormal, the mass of it, anti-human, even anti-biological if you wish. His filthy lucre, all those trillions? It just makes no sense at all. He'd crumble under the weight of his own power. We're here to help it happen sooner."

The Phat Prophet was mulling over that conversation in radio silence but a smile of relief on his face tells the Renegade he's back from his deep funk. Still feeling guilty that he's able to see them without their knowledge, the Renegade turns off the popup window with Phat Prophet, looks at Nastassia's face deeply immersed in her own thoughts, and turns off that popup as well. *I should stop doing that,* he thinks for the thousandth time.

No one says goodbye, but soon the I.R.I.S. chatroom is as empty as an empty pickle jar and equally quiet. What was left was a lingering loneliness, but in it, a flicker of hope.

Media Frenzy
Le Mont-Saint-Michel Abbey
March 21, 2048

Even the venerable Old Lady we Can Trust, legendary Oprah, despite her incomparable experience, has underestimated the insanity that was ensuing all over the world during her interview with Varga and his presentation. Virtually everyone from the who's-who rolodexes of old media want to chime in, to talk with Varga, despite the governmental transition being mere hours away. So, once she was told what was going on, Oprah decides to do something unprecedented. She opens video links to all the journalists all over the world and lets them grill Varga live on her show.

What a lady, what a classy, selfless lady, everyone thinks.

Varga looks at the bunch of wide-eyed, young, and old journalistic faces as they meekly await their turn to ask questions with the great eagerness of genuine ass-kissers, sycophants so important in their own eyes that they are blissfully unaware of the fawning *parasite* signs chiseled all over their foreheads. Varga starts to give media interviews to those gals and gays imbibing on his every word when AUTOMATA's alert interrupts him. He discretely turns his eyepiece's holographic image on only to see none other than Jeremiah DeJohn as he is delivering his report to AUTOMATA. Nastassia's close-up levitates, radiating in the middle of his pupil. Oblivious for a moment, his eyes fix on Nastassia's for a few prolonged seconds. *Too old to be of any real danger,* he quietly repeats Jeremiah's words, barely perceptibly and shaking his head in disbelief. *You wouldn't say that had you known who her father is,* he thinks.

Then he remembers the task at hand, turns the eyepiece with Nastassia's face off, and focuses his attention back onto the multi-screen on Oprah's right, back to dealing with these bootlickers whom he endured like one would a stupid pet some annoying relatives bring with them to a family picnic.

"Sorry for the interruption." He smiles charmingly at the admiring media throng. "I had to take a look at something. Business, you know," he says to the mammon worshippers as they eagerly nod in unison, waiting for him to continue, their loving smiles ablaze.

"Technology is ideology conceived in sin and delivered from hell. The code was never law," Winston Varga postulates to the media, guffawing into the camera's lenses, ready for a follow-up question given that his trillions have been made in tech, a question that unavoidably came and the question he, predictably, ignores.

Oprah smiles at the neglected exchange. She knows Varga better than he can imagine.

"I am aware that I have been the technology's high priest for ages," he does not fail to humbly admit. "Nevertheless, I am eternally struggling to push for a new renaissance, for a tech redemption, if you wish. While tech has taken a lot away from humanity, I am dead set on giving it back to humanity. The Happiness Pill that you've seen is only one small step for man but a giant leap towards humanity's happiness," he generously claims, cutting the interview short. "I have to go now, esteemed ladies and gentlemen of the Fourth Estate. You'll know what's happening shortly. I'll be watching along, as the whole world watches when the new dawn for all of us breaks." He nods pensively and dismisses them. "Like always, it's been a pleasure and privilege chatting with you." He nods to the director, who turns all of the screens off. The Happiness Pill advertising starts playing again.

During the commercial break, somehow still uncharacteristically riled by the media attention, Varga scoffs with utter disdain and turns to Oprah, surprising her. "Can't stand those sniveling little *presstitutes* one can buy for a stale doughnut." He says this with palpable disgust.

"Luckily, my dear," Oprah says, smiling coyly, "your mic is off."

With those words, realizing they are back on air, Oprah turns to the live audience, slowly stands up, eagerly helped by Varga, moves closer to the first row and, looking straight into the camera, instructs them, "Let us give a round of applause to the great visionary, Mr. Winston Varga, and his mind-boggling presentation."

After their rapturous applause subsides, Oprah concludes, "But he is right, now we all need to get ready for the upcoming governmental transition. Thank you. Good night, good luck. God bless you all, and God bless these marvelous United States of America."

Blame it on Edward Bernays

Varga wasn't too far off in his estimation of the proud members of the Fourth and Fifth Estates. They were always crawling beneath his gold-crusted feet, never questioning him, his moves or motives. The Moloch of Money would devour them instantaneously should they try, and they all knew that. After all, it was a high probability that Varga, through Proteus FinTech Corp. or its subsidiaries, owned their respective publications, had their bosses in his pockets, controlled the production, editors, and ultimately themselves. You listen to your master's voice; you don't bite his hand. Especially if it generously feeds you, and Varga fed them copiously.

He mastered PR and played the propaganda game like none before him. Neither Joseph Goebbels of the Nazi horrors nor Steve Jobs of Apple's cult, not even Ahheban Correy, the late president of the United States, came close. There was no one to write a *Where Have You Gone, Walter Cronkite* song, and no one to lament over the true loss of the Fourth Estate, whose slow demise had ages ago accelerated with the advance of so-called social networks from the early 21st century and the technological progress that followed. It succeeded only in making people suffer from a collective anxiety disorder. What a blessing for the "rich men behind the scenes" (rather The Rich Man, for Varga ruled this world with an iron, invisible fist.) Without free, honest media, the balance of power was no more.

However, Varga would never admit that he himself might be in need of redemption as it was believed he was the Tech Devil, ruthlessly conducting his omnipotent orchestra of a myriad of interconnected tech companies that had only one goal—reducing humanity of every single woman, man, and child in order to make himself ever richer. He amassed so much power and piled up a neat little mélange of crimes, sins, and horrors along with it as he sat on the throne where absolution had been practiced for ages, the Benedictine Abbey of Mont-Saint-Michel in France's Normandy region. All of that was a source of immense pride for Varga, almost equal to his disdain for the humans he ruled from his technological kingdom through his invisible power of tech strings and syringes.

The Commodification of Sin

Left alone in dark, Nastassia Bonnet reflects on her own life. She has been lucky enough to have parents willing to take her to Africa on many occasions so she would not be deprived of experiencing the last remaining oasis of wildlife, and perhaps humanity, in the world. There, in humanity's motherland, she had a chance to see and feel the splendor of wild animals that still roam the untouched, enormous African savannas. Africa mesmerized Nastassia. Not only the mighty Simba, the lion whose roars one feels in every bone of their body, or the prehistoric-looking rhinos, or the loving giants, those elephants whose huge, Africa-shaped ears, she loved the most, but also the air and the skies that were different on the Southern Hemisphere, with Orion and Sirius hanging from the heavens. And also The Panke Baobab in Zimbabwe that died at almost 2,500 years old. The essential goodness, ancient, earthy wisdom of Black people was palpable in Africa. Her mom told her how some tribes in Africa believed that the baobab grows upside down, and that's why the stars are different on this side of Earth. Even then, when Nastassia was really young and small, she knew that wasn't true. However, the pure joy of being next to the oldest creatures on Earth made her stand on her hands, with her head down, "Look, Mom, I'm like the baobabs," and giggle until she finally conked down on her own scalp, rolling over the reddish earth and giggling, overwhelmed by joy.

She sensed the ancient souls of those trees and listened in awe to stories of Amina Ranarivelo, the local poet, about baobab's crooked fingers that hunted her through the night. Nevertheless, Nastassia wasn't afraid of the baobabs. They would not hurt a soul, she knew that. But, Amina is a poet, who knows what really frightened her. While they hadn't had time to visit Zimbabwe, the Panke Baobab's home, the Bonnets visited the Avenue of the Baobabs in Madagascar where, on a dirt road between Morondava and Belon'i Tsiribihina, stood those ancient beings, the sacred baobab trees of Africa. It was sunset and the skies were burning purple and hearts were soaring red. Nastassia ran and hugged the majestic tree. The sight made everyone laugh: a little girl with arms like matchsticks looked like a tiny white butterfly hung from that enormous, majestic creature. She pressed her heart to the baobab and told it that she loved him. She felt loved back and was happy.

Afterward, she kept gazing at those baobabs and cried. "Why are you crying, angel?" her mom asked, a bit alarmed.

"They are so beautiful," Nastassia whispered back, "and filled with love."

Even before Winston Varga and his Proteus FinTech conglomerate took over the world, we lived in an overly commercialized society in which everything seems to have been commodified. Nastassia knew that. Nature's mysteries and truths were losing the struggle with commercials and self-indulgent apps; the sheer ugliness and efficiency of massive wind farms and their goliath wind turbines replaced magic and the whispers of the wind. The Sun God was measured only through the solar panel's ability to convert sunlight into usable electricity, expressed in percentages, and all sun mythologies were gone from our days. With them, the stories of solar chariots and the gods. Only yesterday, the god Apollo was riding a chariot in the heavens, but today he serves as a name for the transatlantic Apollo cable system, whose 13,000 km in length boasts 100 P-bytes, or one quadrillion bytes, per second. And that sheer amount of data is not used for the betterment of the world we inhabit, it serves to commodify every single human being in the world. Reality for Everyone™ games gobble up enormous amounts of data about everyone and everyone's fears and anxieties that are bubbling in their respective ego-and-echo bubbles with only one purpose in mind—profit. We live in a commodified perdition where every turd they'd been selling us is as polished as the Star of Africa diamond, but in the world devoid of swashbucklers bravely slaying dragons, Nastassia once overheard Mom talking to Dad, even hell and purgatories have lost their symbolic meaning, and most of humanity is obliviously stumping through the Gates of Hell. Hence, the Happiness Pill by that purveyor of misery, Winston Varga. The separation between humans and their natural environment has never been greater. Nature, in the mind of many, does not exist anymore. It's either digitalized, commoditized, and overly sentimental or harmlessly violent depending on the targeted audience, just a nicely packaged product. One out of many. When they are not immersed in fake aggrandizement of their egos, the people are nothing but voyeurs of nature, safety cuddled away into their digital bubbles, indifferent to the world outside.

Since she was a toddler, Nastassia has been feeling that the world was a deeply harmful, sick place that only love might heal. Only love and beauty can seize the human heart and not even suffering could let it degenerate into hatred and selfishness. Alas, precisely those harmful feelings in humans have been cultivated by Varga and each new reiteration of one useless app after another. It seems he had used the Seven Deadly Sins as an inspiration and fed the collective human soul with them. The digital equivalent of obesity, mental obesity, was akin to the ancient sin of gluttony as much as that of greed. Only Varga was careful not to "award" users of his wicked software with any material possessions, he instead gave them sets of illusion, digital wealth, and digital social status, through his INNOCENTI scam. Almost every false winner of the Reality for Everyone™ was given the chance to mingle with the luminaries de jour do to feel better than everyone else.

Lust was fed via holographic, immersive 3D porn channels that made even the most morbidly obese, immobile people participate and feel like lean, mean sex machines and the best lovers in the world. Humans have not only abandoned nature, they have been abandoning each other in droves. The grotesque Disneyfication of society and nature alike had morphed into one and the world seemed to have built a giant amusement park, a park to play in and to forfeit life.

"Ecopornography," as Monique had called nature TV programming, was also running rampant. Excitement due to such programming was adrenaline-based, like snuff films from a half-century ago in which true-life killings, maiming, torture, and abuse were shown to millions. One could choose from either gruesome images of animal abuse or dramatic scenes of predators killing their prey or falsely serene images of divine, harmless nature where all is peachy and every tiger is a self-aware, inclusive, meditating vegan.

Such profound disconnection with nature and life has produced an enormous amount of mental anguish and suffering. On the surface were court jester-like movie stars, be it 3D-based phantoms or some still living in meat-space provided entertainment. Simon Cowell's hologram or Baiano Lindo's jokes endlessly amused people and corralled them into the world in which everyone was a winner in their own bubble-world.

But, beneath the surface, dark currents flow.

Sometimes, Nastassia felt like she was drowning in the loss of purpose around her; it felt like humanity had been oozing their souls away. For herself was also a part of that dreaded current, having spent most of her life in front of a computer. Like junkies tripping on Madhatter's coke and meth-head tweekers abusing roofies, the people were zombified by the ubiquitous infotainment. Fear porn, a tool enabling control over the throngs and perfected over the pandemic times, drove the people's anxiety to the roof and made them eager to accept tsunamis of apeshit coming out of Hollywood as fun. Fear and fun were stupefying the nations and the individual alike more than ever. Dumb-ass, designed-to-be addictive games, and even more addictive apps were attacking the world's consciousness from all sides but were, in a final analysis, per the words of the immortal Nick Szabo, just "the billowing, gigantic, all-obscuring fogs of the vapid marketing vapor."

Sweet solitude was no one's home anymore. No one had time or a wish for a repose, no one felt the need for self-reflection. Instead, everyone lived in the dim darkness of loneliness, hooked on the Net, hysterically hoping to virtually rub elbows with the luminaries of the INNOCENTI, or even Varga himself. If such a threat was not given to them, they engaged in rabid hatred toward the others. Separated while together and hooked to the point of no return, they were mindless parts of a matrix that fed them sugary poisons and in return took thirty pieces of silver out of each one's life.

What started as the gamification of our morality, simplification of our lives with the common denominator of *me, myself, and I* has created narrowmindedness first and then, through the focus on one's own pleasure, degenerated into the atomization of societies in which everyone has been thrown into digital reservations, cyber ghettos, and echo chambers.

Those processes seem to have entered their last, irreversible, mortal phase.

„Gott ist tot! Gott bleibt tot! Und wir haben ihn getötet."

"God is dead! God stays dead! And we killed him." To many, that's all that's remembered of Friedrich Nietzsche, a once-prominent German philosopher from centuries ago, a man driven to madness by the future hell of our making, the perdition he foresaw. The focus was often on his words' religious implications.

But God, when stripped down to its very essence, is a story. Frédéric used to tell Nastassia that "Gods represent a set of tales, mythical lore, and the magical lure of our ancestral existence. Stories are essential ingredients of life. They flow through our bloodstream like tiny fairies; they're nested, as hopes and fears, in our primordial brains; they reside in our neural networks coloring our experiences of the world and how we see it and the events we experience. Take them away and you have taken away the very core of your being, the authentic uniqueness of every human being. What started as, at the time a seemingly benign, while still idiotic, chai latte from powdered beet, has induced a voluntary cramming of humanity into the uniform barns of Starbucks or IKEAs of yesteryear, transposed into individualized, custom-made digital cages where most of humanity lived, oblivious to the past or the future. The collective neurasthenia of millions has poisoned individual consciousness and the collective unconsciousness alike. The oceans of people were swirling in the pools of their own mental swamps, hopelessly sinking into a quicksand of oblivion."

Almost no one lived an authentic life anymore, Nastassia knew.

The only god left alive seems to be the god Moloch, once worshipped as the Baal-Haddad by Assyrian-Aramean, today embodied in Varga, the devourer of children and adults alike. Varga's hatred for humanity was apparent to Nastassia since the first day she sensed his vile heart under that polished smile of a sophisticated crook. He was a vile person, an embodiment of evil if ever was one; she felt that in her whole body. It is clear to her that her sense about Varga was an omen, a foreboding shadow of the tragedy to come.

How come she did not see any of this more clearly?

But no one else had seen it either although it was in front of the world's collective eye.

Strangely enough, despite numerous official denials, the whole world was certain that Winston Varga was behind the governmental transition, and yet, no one had a clue what it would entail mere hours before the event. Only his gigantic fortune was able to pull something like that off. After all, his now-legendary stock market coup with which he singlehandedly had destroyed and subsequently taken over tech giants of the era, was a surprise he had been preparing for decades, with the world totally unaware of his plans.

# # #

It would be instructive to learn about the strategy and mechanics of his coup from several years back, in order to better understand what would follow and is happening today. But, in order to do that, we'd have to go even further back into Varga's past, all the way down to the very roots of his unheard-of Brobdingnagian fortune.

Chapter 4

THE ALETHEIA COUP OF 2041

000000000019d6689c085ae165831e934ff763ae46a2a6c172b3f1b60a8ce26f
The Genesis Block, Blockchain
January 3, 2009

    Cypher-punks had a phantom of mythical proportions named Satoshi Nakamoto, who invented a "purely peer-to-peer version of electronic cash," Bitcoin. It offered the world a new vision, striving to replace the criminally insane fiat system and its tyranny with private electronic cash, better known as cryptocurrency. The cypher-punks knew they couldn't fight the system and its ghouls entrenched in governments and the corporations controlling them, so they fought back with the code. They wrote profusely, offered ideas, visions, hope, and the various cryptocurrencies that enabled people to fight for their lives, for their financial independence, for their sovereignty. The cypher-punks' courage was contagious.

    "In the beginning was the Hash. All things were made by the Hash, and without the Hash was not any coin made that was made. After the Hash comes the greed, and with greed comes the devil. And the devil's name was Winston Varga," the Blockchain Ghost castigated him on the social network called Reddit. What the Blockchain Ghost was referring to was Varga's Aletheia token.

    How did it come to be?

Characters in Search of an Author

The people using Winston Varga's products believed they were consumers while being products themselves with the sole purpose of enriching him. But, they had yet to unearth the treasure trove of other, intimate data that was more valuable than the mere monetization of their time, so Varga instructed the INFINITUS to comb through users' ultra-safe, private Notes for Themselves™ within the Reality for Everyone™ app and present him with the most bonkers ones, at first only to amuse himself. How deranged the people are, Varga concluded, is beyond belief.

However, his favorite wasn't anyone with obscene secret desires, nor were any of the Virtuosi™ neophytes, those righteous zealots pushing their Pollyannaish superiority, promoting a world in which they walk on water and equalize everyone until every citizen is sainthood-ized by them. His favorite was a bookish-looking Giacomino Arturo Geppetto from the medieval hilltop town Montepulciano in Tuscany, Italy. Surrounded by Tuscan vineyards, he resisted their lure and instead imbibed Zaccagnini Montepulciano D'Abruzzo from the Italian east coast, a dark ruby-colored red wine, with cherry, violet, and vanilla aromas. He was truly something else. Giacomino's tortured, perhaps a bit disturbed, soul opened a whole new world of ideas for Varga. At the time, neither was aware of the change that one-way encounter would create and yet, that diminutive man was Varga's butterfly whose flap of a wing would, years later, unleash a mighty tornado.

Giacomino from Montepulciano

Giacomino did not dream up or invoke gorgeous women into his virtual life, nope. He never ordered a sex robot nor entered a 3D bordello made for guys like him—that is, virgins living the sexless, loveless life of a digital recluse and a snowball's chance in hell that it would ever change. He spent the least amount of money on Varga's apps, and that endeared him to Varga even more. Giacomino never imagined himself as a daredevil nor did he prowl arcane games seeking to be a hero. He would have lived an utterly ordinary life had he not had a passion for literature and writing. Over many a lonely night, dear Giacomino had been downloading classical books on his computer. Then he paid a bunch of human designers to create new, original book covers for each of them with his name on it, changed the copyright pages, and then, via online book printing services, ordered hardcover, tangible copies, only for himself.

He had *The Curse of Agade*, the story of the Akkadian Empire and its king Naram-Sin and his confrontation with the gods, a book by Giacomino Arturo Geppetto on his modest desk. The *Egyptian Book of the Dead*, also written by Geppetto came next. Then, in a rapid succession of his divine madness, *Ulysses, The Odyssey, Faust,* and *The Brothers Karamazov*, allegedly firstly written by Joyce, Homer, Goethe, and Dostoyevsky, now all reincarnated by the mighty pen of incomparable Giacomino A. Geppetto and published by his modest publishing company, Editori Echo S.r.l., based in the birthplace of the Renaissance, Florence. He used to stand in his small flat and admire his bookshelves, filled with his own classical books, as a trickle of tears wetted his childlike cheeks. Occasionally, he took one of the classics he had authored, perused a page or two, and wept aloud, dear Giacomino, God bless his helpless, lonely soul. *Oh, did I really have to kill Nastasya Filippovna?* Sometimes the author doubted himself, fraught with guilt. Perhaps the tragic fate of Myshkin and Rogozhin in *The Idiot*, which Giacomino published just after *Ulysses*, could've been averted? But, deep in his heart, Giacomino knew that he loved Nastasya Filippovna too deeply to share her with these two men.

No matter how painful the writer's decision, yes, she had to die.

That was such a sweet delusion that, one day, when Varga was particularly moved by Arturo's new work, the *Divine Comedy*, he had INFINITUS create a video conference call with Giacomino and an uncannily real-looking Nobel Committee for Literature at the Swedish Academy. The committee offered Giacomino the Nobel Prize for Literature. Regretfully, the sweet little man, upon being told he would be given the most desired prize in the world, had died of a massive heart attack on the spot. At least, Varga thought, he died happy, recognized for his work. He would, Varga that is, gladly have sent the Nobel to Geppetto's family to further immortalize the great man, but alas, he had none and had died and vanished into the pages from which he might have arrived years ago, all alone.

Giacomino never sold his masterpieces to anyone.

#

"True literature can exist only where it is created, not by diligent and trustworthy functionaries, but by madmen, hermits, heretics, dreamers, rebels, and skeptics like the late literary giant, our beloved friend, Giacomino Arturo Geppetto," Varga wrote, signing his post as Yevgeny Zamyatin, the original author of the quote, and posted it on Giacomino's forever empty Facebook's "Book of Sorrows" page, dedicated to the lone genius from Montepulciano, Italy, and his immortal memory.

Deepfakes

Among people also not lured into his Reality for Everyone™, two others gave Varga a framework for future actions. First was a reclusive hacker, widely known only as BanderaSH-A1. He'd been living deeply off the grid and resurrected himself as an artist, Xicasso. As such he had sold numerous reproductions of his paintings and made quite a fortune by pretending to be a third-party seller. However, unlike Giacomino, Xicasso was a fraud, and as such he introduced Varga to the wonderful world of Deepfakes.

Xicasso used an automated system developed by Tero Karras's generative adversarial network (GAN). The art "created" never appeared as an automatically generated image again. It was indeed the unique work of a computer, sold as his own. Inspired by that scheme, Varga used the "this person does not exist" approach, available on https://thispersondoesnotexist.com/ and generated multitudes of Deepfakes based on it—fake people he might use once the need arises.

Deepfakes were not Varga's alone; many others produced with the AI technology led to political disinformation and destabilization all over the world. However, no one thought of using them in the way Varga did.

#DeepFuckingValue

Another one resisting Varga's world was an obscure writer from Monte Carlo, Alex Krainer, a wealth fund manager. He invented the stocks trading tool I-System Trend Following©. Krainer's dual neural network of mathematical algorithms that codify a body of knowledge in market analysis and trading was good, so he put it on a black list, assuring the I-System and M. Krainer would never get their required funding. Instead, Varga created a clone of his software and gave it to "DeepFuckingValue," a Reddit character of worldwide fame created during the 2021 financial kerfuffle around short sellers of GME shares. The paragon of truth, a faultless knowledge aggregator called Wikipedia, has an entry titled "GameStop Short Squeeze," saying "In January 2021, a short squeeze of the stock of the American video game retailer GameStop (NYSE: GME) and other securities took place, causing major financial consequences for certain hedge funds and large losses for short sellers." That event inspired Varga's plan, which he put in action decades later.

Deepfakes grew in legions. Some were given Krainer's I-System, seed money to start playing with, and profit from the crypto markets. Bear with us, astute reader, please, we are doing our best to condense a monumental effort that so dramatically turned the wheels of history into a *Reader's Digest* version. The third piece of the puzzle was the Form LD-1, a lobbying registration form of the Lobbying Disclosure Act of 1995 (Section 4) and the section titled "The Justice Against Corruption on K Street Act of 2018." That last section's title particularly amused Varga.

The Lion of Congress

An avid student of history, Varga was also fond of grotesquely oversized American laws whose sole purpose was the pillaging of working masses. One study found out that lobbying firms made $220 out of every dollar spent on politicians, or 22,000%. The wonderfully corrupt world revealed that nothing beats an investment in a politician. They were a dime a dozen, platitude-reciting empty souls clad in expensive suits with one job only: perpetual fundraising for themselves with bozos always on discount—a one-dollar political store for billionaires.

Varga incorporated Honesty for America, LLC., and filed the Form LD-1 to become an official lobbyist. (Its origins are detailed further down this narrative.) As simple as that. Research into the "contributions" stunned him. Only several million dollars would've put him into the list of the top hundred individual donors. He had much more in cash lying around, untouched. And the money poured in daily, so he had a penny or two to spare. His first action was to approach an obscure state senator named Jerome K. Mooney, a total non-entity and a clueless simpleton he'd be able to mold, and gave him his first donation, a check for $50,000.00. After seeing how Jerome was fawningly sniveling in front of him and his money, and for such a meager amount at that, Varga saw brown-nosed apple-polishers in all of the politicians.

That grafting dunce made Varga's day.

He had it, he had a plan. All he needed was time that he, at twenty, had in abundance.

The very same year, the Lion of Congress, Honorable Barnabas E. Spencer was retiring after sixty years of selflessly, tirelessly serving the people. Never one to waste an opportunity, Winston Varga, accompanied with Jerome K. Mooney, came to Spencer's mansion to kiss his ring and for the old political giant's blessing. At that time the Honorable Senator Spencer, already in his nineties, was losing some of his keen insight into the human psyche and did not see through Varga and Mooney. He was quite easily persuaded to throw his mighty support behind Mooney, despite the latter's insipidness, duller than the rain in October. Or perhaps because of it? Compared to Mooney, he, Spencer, would still "be a towering figure over state affairs," Varga assured the modest old giant. It should not be denied that the two million dollars of seed money for the Barnabas E. Spencer Endowment for Children in Salt Lake City, which Varga provided with an open heart and shiny smile in a form of an Honesty for America LLC. check, played a certain if only minor role in Spencer's decision. Jerome K. Mooney was all but assured to become the next junior senator from the beehive state of Utah, which he indeed did become only several months later, with a landslide victory. Varga had doors to the halls of power ajar for him.

He set up an offshore company in Lichtenstein, the Hypergrowth Quarks, GmbH and with an impenetrable maze of lawyers, other offshore companies, and accountants, set Jerome K. Money as the forty-nine % owner of the company, "as a token of respect." Hypergrowth Quarks dealt exclusively with Bitcoin and other cryptocurrencies that, at that time, seemed like automatic money machines. He channeled some of the profits into Mooney's publicly known American accounts so to create an illusion of a modern, forward-thinking lawmaker, a rare beast among dull politicians, someone "like us," someone making his buck in a god's honest way by buying and HODL-ing cryptos. Varga also created a marketing blitz for Mooney, invoking the Stop Trading on Congressional Knowledge Act (STOCK) as the reason why Mooney does not, unlike some of his colleagues, invest in the companies the Congress regulates. Bitcoin was still in its infancy, an unregulated entity, and all was fine. Once the Treasury's Financial Crimes Enforcement Network (FinCEN) had proposed and Congress passed the Bitcoin Paramount Trust and Transparency Act of 2023, the junior senator

Mooney, booming from the Senate floor, channeled his inner Spencer and disclosed his BTC address: 15SGgXktjMPAZm9ygDAMveZZCyyXAi4rFV.

He established himself as a rather boring politician but with interesting ideas and a paragon of honesty, the quality that will bring Varga his presidency on a plate in later years.

The INFINITUS had already started to manipulate the prices of crypto, so Mooney soon had a very impressive portfolio. Strange sounding terms like staking, NFTs, mining, yield farming, DeFi were a part of Mooney's publicly disclosed portfolio. "Time for openness and honesty in our business dealings has come. That includes the members of this illustrious Congress," he read from Varga's script, who also persuaded him to jointly create a charity with a mouthful of a name, Oliver Twist's Tomorrow is Another Day Charity for Children, LLC., that fed and clothed poor orphans.

"Nothing regales the hearts of the American people as much as the smile of bastards receiving gifts," Varga laughed over a glass of a fine Napa Valley Syrah from Paso Nobles, which he shared with his partner in goodwill as they enjoyed watching the numbers of views on the Oliver Twist's YouTube channel. It had millions of followers and a dozen million views. For the infotainment media, he and Mooney were inseparable, like force and matter, and their charitable work was praised all over the country. A rising political star and a rising business star, making honest people out of those rapscallions… What's not to love in those glorious United States of America?

The INNOCENTI

A parallel structure of power, the INNOCENTI, were born one year later. Varga knew that legal political structures served as decoys; real power was wasted in supranational, private organizations, like the IMF, BIS, FED, the UN, WEF, OPEC, OECD, NAFTA, and many others, all of which were protected by NATO and the mighty US military and all those intelligence agencies, like FBI, CIA, NSA et.al. which had merged with the Jewish mob and the Italian Mafia in the US, controlling it all. An impossible maze of magnanimous charities, mythical families like the Rothschilds and the Rockefellers, churches, and elite universities comprising all the old boys' clubs readily seen in Davos, the Club of Rome, the Bilderberg Group, the Council for Inclusive Capitalism, and the Vatican as their promoter, Wall Street, the EU and so on, served to distract the public's wild imagination while the corridors of power continued unmolested. Varga's INNOCENTI, a mere decade from its establishment, was an umbrella for them all.

Once the INNOCENTI initial structure leaked, through *Varga's Secret Society* free e-book by Anonymous, disclosing every one of the 1,733,598 active service members in the regular armed forces and 1,927,000 workers plus 265,000 contractors doing top-secret work, Varga could not care less. No one batted an eye. The people were used to being led by the invisible hand and shrugged that one off. Varga knew that no one would question the military or the Intelligence Industrial Complexes, the holy sentinels of this great nation of ours.

Once incorporated in the INNOCENTI, the members were given ranks of the Sentinels of Freedom, twice promoted i.e., each first lieutenant in the regular army was given the rank of major sentinel, each major the rank of the Colonel Sentinel of Freedom as well as each cadet has become a first lieutenant. Generals were given ranks of Grand Marshal Sentinel of Freedom or Generalissimo Sentinel of Freedom for the general of the army and so on until the ranks reached the commander in chief, President Mooney, who was given the rank of Sentinel Marshal of the Empire. Not even such a grotesque display of pompous, kindergarten-like grandiosity had created a hubbub. The people were too busy with their own self-importance. However, the arcane hierarchy, with Verum Innocentes (true innocents) at the top, was still hidden from the public eye and the pamphlet.

They are too easy, the cockroaches, Varga thought, the cockroaches being the people. The low-level, most rabid INNOCENTI were the Virtuosi™ leaders Varga used to control models of the structure he has built.

However, his next step was much more far-reaching.

The True Identity© Alliance, Corp.

With Honesty for America, LLC., and Honorable Senator Mooney in his corner, Varga has provided the grateful government a valuable service through the not-for-profit True Identity© Alliance, Corp. Over a million tax-exempt organizations existed in the US, so the process of getting his 501(c)(3) status was straightforward. Form 1023 had to be filed with the I.R.S., the fee paid, the Honorable Spencer called to skip the line, given how noble the purpose of The True Identity© Alliance, Corp. had been since the start. Its charter stated so: "We will be a strong and trusted partner for peace, progress, and security for every citizen of our great nation by providing ethical, iron-clad, privacy-protecting digital IDs."

A new BIDNA process, an acronym of "Biometric & DNA" was the basis for the BIDNA TIN, "True Identity© Number," for everyone, a National ID verified by The True Identity© Alliance, Corp. and submitted to both the Social Security Administration and the Internal Revenue Service. While the process would have taken some time to get everyone TIN-ed and their SSNs replaced, Varga already had all the governmental data about every single American at his fingertips, free of charge, and his TIN was accepted in lieu of an SSN for all newborns and new applicants alike.

From that day on, no traveling wilburys would ever pass through those golden gates on the American border without their data being stored in Varga's vast storages; no health check would be omitted on controlled hard drives; not a single vote missed its right place in the databases; not an account opening via KYC (Know Your Customer) overlooked. He employed a legion of Pakistani developers to oversee every step of the process of classifying Americans and their guests, visa holders, green card holders, and illegal immigrants into folders always at his disposal.

America was easy as it was the legalized corruption center of the world. Varga just had to give a donation buck here or a support buck there and have his lobbying lawyers write some incomprehensible law on several thousand pages no one would ever read, and he'd have his law in place, passed in Congress. In the EU, still under the rule of Germany, it was a bit more difficult. Dr. Ursula Hansen-Schroeder "protected their freedom-seeking delusions," as Varga raged once, with an iron determination.

For now, he'd keep pushing BIDNA and the True Identity© Number as hard as he could in the Five Eyes countries, the Kings of England protectorates, and the United States that was the true ruler of those once proud lands.

Unbeknown to anyone, the army of 4,259,027 automated bots the INFINITUS had created were not only given identities of "people," Deepfakes as real as you and I, each of them were given their own face and bio and, more importantly, individual BIDNA numbers approved by Varga's True Identity© Alliance, Corp. When the time is ripe they, human-like bots, will have been utilized in the manner none would have been able to predict.

A Poor Billionaire

When Varga became a multibillionaire for the first time, his numerous worldwide ventures' revenues, growing stake in cryptocurrencies (his Bitcoin alone was worth over three billion, with a billion more in other cryptocurrencies), INFINITUS's investments, his growing stake in African energy companies etc., amounted to over seven billion dollars. But he was enraged when he realized that the gap between his fortune and the fortunes of those on the top yet again only widened. The corporate giants' valuations were in tens of trillions of dollars, the derivatives in hundreds of trillions, and the richest men in the world were fighting for half a trillion dollars of personal wealth in spot number one.

At first, Varga was angry, but there must be a way, he told himself. If a kid from Bluff, UT was already as rich as an ancient king, with a vast network of political influence crushing giants like Alphabet (Google), Amazon, Apple, Meta (Facebook), Microsoft, Tesla, and a few others like the hated Pfizer, it should not be impossible. He had worked all his life so to be able to takeover Google et.al., for those would give him the power to finally tackle China and their insufferable arrogance and to rule the world.

He needed more money in order to attack those along his way.

"Money makes money. And the money that money makes, makes money."

Bitcoin democratized money and money creation. Decentralized finance thrived on the platform called Ethereum (and its scaling solutions) that enabled everyone to mine, mint, and issue their own "currencies."

The democratization of manipulation and fraud followed; the Wall Street criminal junkie posers were not holding the monopoly on making money out of thin air and pickpocketing the masses anymore. The crypto sphere was catching up. It was like a wildfire, the rapid spread of manipulation and outright fraud. The new kids on the fraud block did not need to mitigate the blame and guilt to external factors for they saw nothing wrong with what they were doing. And there was no regulation protecting their victims. The era of blameless digital crime was wonderful. Soon after, an emergence of so-called pump-and-dump schemes ensued. Unlike the Wall Street Finance Crime Cartel's members who were scheming how to defraud their investors behind closed doors, cryptocurrency manipulators were openly declaring their plans online and were inviting the tired, the poor, the huddled, tempest-tossed masses yearning to breathe free, to enter through the once golden door of Wall Street exclusivity—that of fraud and get-rich-quick schemes. Even Varga was amazed by the brazenness of these guys, hiding in the maze of cryptocurrency tokens, Virtual Private Networks, and Tor browsers that assured their anonymity while their deeds lived in infamy.

Lloyd Blankfein, the CEO of Goldman Sachs, talking about the excessive profits his company was famous for, replied with, "We're doing Gods' work." The New World of manipulations was not that different. Instead of Blankfein, it was a Twitter / Discord user "beef90" who posted:

> "Love watching everyone trying to pump up the price of Dogecoin.
> Doing the Lord's work guys.
> I'm holding my 14,000 at .003 cost."

For cryptocurrencies uninitiated among you, my esteemed readers, the Dogecoin was created as a joke without any financial, social, or any other purpose. It was lacking the idea, a utility, or a worthy goal and yet, at some point, it had reached a "valuation" of over fifty billion dollars. Its sole purpose was to make a mighty buck for its manipulators. Everyone was a Wolf of Wall Street those days.

While Varga disliked the rabble getting a chance to make huge profits in no time, he loved the total mess these new schemes created, and he knew he needed the ignorant rubes to help him achieve his goals. After all, he loathed Wall Street, its idiocy and hubris even more than these new digital prospectors.

"Greed is Good"

The Wall Street crimes "were virtually indistinguishable from the kind of thuggery practiced for decades by the Mafia, which has long made manipulation of public bids for things like garbage collection and construction contracts a cornerstone of its business," wrote Matt Taibbi. To all appearances, the astronomical fines imposed on the investment banks amounted to no more than an accounting error and mere cost of business, almost like an insurance expense. Legalized financial crimes lavished the lawmakers with enormous profits, and the sold-out mass media glorified them. It was a world turned on its head for such a long time that criminality had become a shortcut to financial sainthood and paved with gold. The media canonized the worst criminals, to the point of now-defunct *TIME Magazine* calling the worst crooks on the street, "The Committee to Save the World" and "Masters of the Universe."

But, outside the fawning media bubble, everyone hated Wall Street.

Varga had been creating daily kerfuffles in preparation for the chaos, participating in 355 pump-and-dump schemes with 197 cryptocurrencies, all of that over a short seven-month period in 2027 and 2028. While profits were staggeringly high percentage-wise—over 100% or sometimes in 1,000%++ within the first minutes of the "pump"—the liquidity in those markets was very low, so he could not increase his wealth by any measure. But he learned a lot during that time, and the INFINITUS was fed with an infinite amount of data, all of which was needed for his upcoming plans. Such a lawless yet de facto crimeless environment with millions of gullible but greedy people all over the world was a river of plenty for Winston Varga.

And one day, he was ready.

Taking Over the World
December 31, 2046

He chose the last Monday of the year for his attack. The stock markets were open but always lazy on New Year's Eve. People started to celebrate and nobody saw it coming. The day prior, as the final rehearsal, his legions of crypto warriors ransacked ten of the hundred biggest cryptocurrencies and then let them recover so not to raise any suspicion. It was the last Sunday of the year but the crypto markets were open 24/7/365 and provided him with an opportunity to play around the clock, with different nations on several continents, to be sure his attack would be performed with the efficiency of a perfectly oiled machine.

He informed the legions, using all available private, safe, and secure means of direct P2P communication, more than half of which he controlled, about the following:

```
Location: 01001000 01100001 01110010 01100001
01101101 00100000 01100001 01101100 00101101 01010011
01101000 01100001 01110010 01101001 01100110
      Time: 01010100 01101111 01101101 01101111 01110010
01110010 01101111 01110111 00100001
```

and signed it with:

Grand Master: 01001010 01100001 01100011 01110001 01110101 01100101 01110011 00100000 01100100 01100101 00100000 01001101 01101111 01101100 01100001 01111001

It was a comically simple cipher, a text hidden behind the easily translatable binary code, but Varga knew any urban myth required simplicity and a dose of naiveté. Once the binary code was translated to English, what he posted read as:

Location: Haram al-Sharif
Time: Tomorrow!
Grand Master: Jacques de Molay

He had given his troops a hint. The excitement started to brew. "Jacques de Molay" was a mythical crypto trader from the time of the pump-and-dumps, and the irony was not lost on Varga, crypto's biggest influencer—who was a combo of the INFINTUS algorithm and Varga himself, an online character hinting at himself as the Resistance leader. He took the name of the last Templar Knight, letting the legend percolate and slowly ooze into the collective consciousness of the legions wanting to make a buck under the unimpeachable guise of revolutionary fervor. Varga let the legend of that elusive genius grow over the years, helping throngs of traders make money, and he amassed a huge number of followers. Jacques de Molay never engaged in political talk but his occasional like or a smile, approving others' messages, made his myth even stronger. Speculations were rampant. And now, he revealed himself. Jacques de Molay will lead the Resistance attack. The legions that have been dreaming of this moment could not wait for tomorrow to come.

And the next morning, on that faithful December 31st of the year 2046 everything started with two more messages:

Onion Link: 01101000 01110100 01110100 01110000 00111010 00101111 00101111 01100001 01100001 01110000 01100101 00110101 01101111 00110001 00110001 01111000 01111001 01111010 00101110 01101111 01101110 01101001 01101111 01101110

Password: 01000110 01100001 01101100 01101100 00100000 01101111 01100110 00100000 01010100 01110010 01101001 01110000 01101111 01101100 01101001

Again, translated:

Onion Link: http://aape5o11xyz.onion
Password: Fall of Tripoli

The Day of Reckoning

While Varga owned banks all over the world, he found Panama officials most open to pecuniary arrangements under the desk. Using the US BIDNA Tax IDs for Deepfakes was easiest there. On the day before the attack, Deepfakes had millions of bank accounts ready and seven billion dollars deposited in total. Varga banks gave them credits up to $100K, which they transferred to various stock & crypto market hybrid exchanges. Tricking KYC, know your customer verification, was a joke. The INFINITUS had given Deepfakes their faces and identities, so the rest was just a matter of photoshopping fake documents with the "person" holding his or her "passport" in a fake selfie. Deepfakes were then given a 100% to 500% margin, which made a war chest worth a total of $238,875,000,000.00, or 238 billion and 875 million dollars, ready to employ on Varga's command.

Deepfakes would be soon joined by millions of real people dying to crush the system with their own vast, hard-earned billions. Varga himself had several billion on 10x margin, ready to deploy. And an unlimited supply of Aletheia tokens he'd readied to deploy at the end of the attack. So, Varga had an army armed to the teeth and ready. He had divided it into two army groups, each having two field armies, and then further split them into corps, divisions, and brigades. He also had a dozen Blietzkrieg Battalions as his special forces.

Out of the two armies, one was given the name Silver Tongue Archangels, with the user "Archangel" as its field marshal. Those were in charge of the "pumps," or promoting the shares or tokens, to buy and hold while the other army was called the Silver Tongue Devils with the field marshal, "Lucifer" as its leader. They were in charge of bashing the stocks. For years he had two dozen "brigades" as the most active users: "Serpents" and "Pitchforks" on the selling side, and "Eagles" and "Masons" on the promoting side. Some fifty thousand "people" on each side were respected members of their respective communities, spread all over the world.

Once he had taken over Discord's and Telegram's chat services via his five-times-removed offshore corporations, Varga created trustworthiness points and gave the real people ranks of Roman Imperial Legions, such as optio, decurion, centurion with its own ranks as centurion prior, centurion pilus, all the way up to perfect, tribune, legate until one would have reached the rank of hero and, as the highest rank, legendary member. There was also a Ceasar rank, but no one had managed to achieve it thus far.

His armies and brigades were interacting among themselves; they were "active," in interaction with real people and they appeared one hundred percent authentic. Over the years, the INFINITUS had amassed grammar, urban speech, crypto lingo, and had its automated text generators split and slice real and fake speech for Deepfakes to use. Based on neural conversational models, the Deepfakes were able to converse well, without any need for pre-written text. Those drafts were used deliberately, only when needed to inflame a conversation.

Jacques de Molay

An Oscar winner for special effects, the INFINITUS had no problems using visual effects to integrate Varga's live actions with CGI. The onion link he gave to his followers was a video feed that started with a still image of the Haram al-Sharif (Temple Mount), its white and blue walls, and the golden dome—the mythical spot where the world was first created and where it will end.

Nothing of that confusing imagery would make sense for a future symbologist trying to understand the past, but Varga was betting that each disjointed piece/message would invoke subconscious reflection, and confusion, to the millions watching and participating in the attack. The majestic Haram al-Sharif inspired awe, while the quiet chanting of the Bulgarian Orthodox Church priests, Megaloschemos II, served as a hypnotic, musical background:

Господи Боже,	God Lord, Jesus Christ
Иисусе Христе,	have mercy on me,
помилуй мя грешнаго	a sinner
Господи помилуй	Lord have mercy
Господи помилуй	Lord have mercy
Господи помилуй	Lord have mercy

The camera started its long tracking shot toward the heavy, green-painted Bab es-Silsileh (Chain Gate) and entered the futuristic-looking Wall-Street-like trading room designed with cyberpunk flair in mind, a place from which Jacques de Molay was going to conduct his attack. He appeared as Jacques de Molay, dressed in a white vestment as a symbol of purity, a Templar Knight hooded cape, and wearing Guy Fawkes mask. Behind him, a room full of young, eager Deepfake human-like traders greet him with great ardor, all eyes fixed on his every move.

He addresses his dazzled audiences, his arms spread like an eagle, his voice booming. "Do you see me, retards? Do you hear me? We are retards. But we are not dumb. We are degenerates. But we are not fools. We are apes but our tech is superhuman. No more loss porn for us. Mega wins, from now on, only mega wins, retards! From today on, the future is ours! Their stocks are our stonks!"

Varga took a deep breath, glancing at the wall of screens displaying traders hanging on his every word, and then continued, "We're holy assassins, we are computer demons. Our machines are swords that slay the system. They will not know what hit them. The blood on the street will be their own. We feast on their pain. We gobble on their fear. But, beware, we don't attack each other. We don't play games against a fellow retard. We work together against the system. We are many! We are legion. We do not forget. We do not forgive. We are the ninety-nine percent, retards!"

As he let his words sink in into the mesmerized brains of his followers, Varga, already getting drunk on power, fought mightily to contain a chuckle. The very embodiment of the 0.000000000125% plays the 99.999999999875% as a fiddle, pretending to be one of them. *What a poetic beauty, what artist I am, almost like George W. Bush, a teetotaler everyone wanted to have a beer with*, he thought and regained focus.

"Before we start, let me show you how magic works." He turns toward his traders. "We prowl the data, we prey, and we hunt the chance. When we find it, we grab it. Every tick, every trade, every spread may hold the chance to outsmart the other guy and get his money." The stock options, calls and puts, five, ten, and thirty-year T-bonds, futures, derivatives, currency option exchanges dance across the screens. That was the financial alchemy dance meant for his mesmerized audiences. "Here it is!" Varga/Jacques de Molay slash Guy Fawkes jumps. The staged trade was beautiful. As thirty-year treasury bonds prices freeze on the screens, he explains, "See, treasury bonds. 4.36 vs. 4.24. That's a nice spread! So what do we do with it?"

"Buy the spread?" asked one of the Deepfakes, per the script given.

"No, we trade it. Firstly buy five billion of older, off-the-run thirty-year T-bonds."

His orders are executed at breakneck speed.

"OK. Now short five billion on-the-run bonds."

One trader whispers to another, confused, loud enough for everyone to hear.

"Who's buying them?"

Varga de Molay turns to him, in his voice a gravitas of an Oscar winner. "More than 450 billion in T-bonds are traded every day. These are the most liquid instruments in the market."

Trader Two hides behind the screen.

The people all over the world who were watching let out a collective chuckle. They are privy to greatness.

Trader One hisses at him, "Better keep your mouth shut next time."

"At least until he learns how the markets really work." Jacques de Molay magnanimously nods to the Deepfake traders. "On-the-runs are the most recent bonds, ergo more expensive. Now we have $794 million more than we had a minute ago."

Everyone stands still, barely breathing. Young, eager, and greedy brokers follow his orders. Trader One announces, "Finished! We lent everything." Jacques de Molay nods in approval.

"Good. We've locked in a potential profit of almost eight hundred million! We have five billion in cash available as we did at the start. And another five billion cash from the collateral we lent. This is the magic, boys, this is the magic of the stock market."

"He's the Money Demon," one of the traders whispers.

Varga turns to the screens, which are invisible to his audience, as he assesses the effect of his performance. If anyone had any doubt about Jacques de Molay's trading prowess and his demonic abilities, they were now gone. Jacques de Molay's smile behind the mask is palpable as he turns toward the camera. He has spoken to each and every retard all over the world.

"The stock markets open in ten minutes. Let us show those motherfuckers the world of pain." He paused and let his warrior's cry shatter the world: "We are demons! Our machines, the swords! We slay the system. We're the holy assassins, motherfuckers!"

Hundreds of thousands of people, scattered all over the world, scream with him, straight into their computer screens. "*We are the holy assassins, motherfuckers!*" Each and every one of the "retards" is eager and ready to *slay the system.*

With a Little Help from His Friends

The time to unleash the bot army has come. The INFINITUS starts firing up texts lifted from years ago and used by Archangel, the leader of the Capitol Insurrection back then. He issues a war cry of his own:

> Archangel Today at 9:30 a.m. ET
> @everyone
> Exactly zero minutes left!
>
> OK, listen up, you crayon-eating homunculus, here's what's going on – we're crushing them all today. As they'd chill in their offices watching live video feeds of homeless people being exsanguinated on the hoods of their vintage sports cars, write up an investor report, and call it a fiscal year. No más!, retard bitchez. The time for e-Anarchy has come. f-Ø-llow the Demon."

Then, the barrage starts. Varga instructs traders to short sell Alphabet, a.k.a. Google, Meta Platforms, a.k.a. Facebook, Amazon, Microsoft, Apple, and Berkshire Hathaway. He throws in Pfizer, given how hated the company has become after the numerous medical fiascos, and Goldman Sachs as an embodiment of the Financial Crime Cartel, also hated by everyone.

The message boards are ragging and flaming, propelled by the INFINITUS's remake of a two-decade-old short attack, using almost word-for-word what the Reddit "retards" used decades ago, only tweaked for today's purposes:

> **Space-Peanut** Today at 8:01 a.m. ET
>
> I remember when the housing collapse sent a torpedo through my family. My father's concrete company collapsed almost overnight. My father lost his home. My uncle lost his home. I remember my brother helping my father count pocket change on our kitchen table. That was all the money he had left in the world. While this was happening in my home, I saw hedge funders literally drinking champagne as they looked down on the Occupy Wall Street protesters. I will never forget that.

My father never recovered from that blow. He fell deeper and deeper into alcoholism and exists now as a shell of his former self, waiting for death.

This is all the money I have and I'd rather lose it all than give them what they need to destroy me. Taking money from me won't hurt me, because I don't value it at all. I'll burn it down just to spite them. This is for you, Dad.

elleandbea *Today at 9:07 a.m. ET*

This broke my heart.
Shorting for you. For your dad.
Long crypto. For our families

EmpathyInTheory *Today at 9:02 a.m. ET*

I want them to hurt so damn bad. I know this is evil and selfish of me and I should want everyone in the world to have their basic needs met, kumbaya, world peace, whatever, but...

God, I'm poor. I'm fucking poor. I have suffered for it, just like OP suffered for it. Just like so many others on this sub have suffered for it. I want these fucks to lose everything so damn bad. I want all of us to win. I want all of us to be happy. But I also want blood. I want revenge. I want it so fucking bad, man.

coldmilton *Today at 9:05 a.m. ET*

My mom killed herself after never recovering from this. My dad lost it all too. This shit is personal. Heartwarming af to watch people come together like this. Thinking of you and your family.

Edit: thanks everyone, you all warmed my heart.

"They will bleed," the Deepfakes assure them, spreading the message, "they will bleed and they will suffer." The whole attack is already working full-throttle. Varga unleashes short trade after short trade; he pushes naked call shorts and buys puts of those companies at the same time. Another half of his army goes long on the cryptocurrencies side, leveraging every penny 10x up to 100x and has the prices of Bitcoin quadrupled in a few hours in each hybrid stock market exchange.

The attack goes in waves.

A burst of short sells of GOOG is followed by a several-minute ceasefire; only Wall Street algorithms are left to cope with the situation. At first, they buy cheap shares as Varga's models had anticipated. Then another, much stronger burst of selling, naked short selling, leveraging, and writing puts confused the algorithms, which start to sell themselves. The remaining humans of Wall Street who are still in the loop panic. It is the last day of the year so they sell. This accelerates the algorithmic sales and is a signal for Varga to lead his army toward the final attack.

They sell their gains on the crypto side of the hybrid markets and throw insane amounts of money into shorting Google and Facebook, Apple, and Pfizer, and so on. The Wall Street algorithms and humans alike panic even more, now in sheer terror.

The furry of online revolutionary fervor floods the internet like never before. Millions of messages were exchanged. Almost everyone is following Jacques de Molay's trades and almost everyone made huge profits in a matter of minutes and hours. Those few poor souls trying to fight the tsunami are crushed. The GOOG-e, Alphabet stock was thirty % down at 11:00 a.m. The retards go berserk, drunk on the promise of victory.

Nighthawk *Today at 11:02 a.m. ET*

jUsT sHoRT iT LiKe yOuR LiFe dEpEnDs oN It...sHorT It lIkE YoU GoT ExPlOsIvE DiArRhEa oN A BuS StUcK In tRaFfIc

Rockatansky *Today at 11:14 a.m. ET*

Those GS fuckers manipulate the market every fucking day, but God forbid us retards hate a stonk soo much we want to gets balls deep in it, and they get caught on the wrong side. They will cry unfairness They will definitely not getting any sleep. They will not celebrate the New Yer. They're in full blown panic mode trying every fuckery they can to stop us. NO WAY, we are retards, we are 99%, we are legions.

Winnie the Shoemaker *Today at 11:14 a.m. ET*

the code is being rewritten
the system is being recalibrated
the time has come

for E-narchy
in E-merica
retard bithez. SHORT THEM!! BUY CRYPTO.
Today is our Independence Day.

!nOToNe *Today at 8:02 a.m. ET*

Jacques de Molay is our fucking Ahab. Take me to the promised land where the tendies are bountiful and our wives have TWO boyfriends captain! Follow the Demon.

KingsGambit *Today at 11:14 a.m. ET*

To call it a tendies is selling it short. I fucking hate Facebook. I fucking hate Google. KILL THEM and LOL bitchez. Shorts the moonz. HODL short to death.

KingsGambit *Today at 11:15 a.m. ET*

Crypto is new religion. Jacques de Molay is new Demon God.

Varga snickers. They need a strong leader capable of taking them to the promised land, *and I am that leader.*

ProfessorBaritone *Today at 11:16 a.m. ET*

Get in losers. We are going crusading. LONG Bitcoin, SHORT all Facebook and Google degenerates. Jacques de Molay is our God.

GetShorty-007 *Today at 11:16 a.m. ET*

These long positions are now fuck bombs that will literally consume anyone who is holding it when the dust clears.

r4dical 0verride! *Today at 11:45 a.m. ET*

This is the most beautiful thing. A bunch of down trodden individuals get some cash and the first thing they think about doing is using it. A delinquent's dream: bring down the System.

All-Is-Hoax! *Today at 11:45 a.m. ET*

We drink their milkshakes. We piss on their champagne. Bring down the System with our Messiah, Jacques de Molay. Shoooooooooort retards, SHORT!! Don't you dare to buy back. Let 'em bleed dry.

vinlo *Today at 11:46 a.m. ET*

We need to cause Google and Facebook and Amazon and all those moterfuckers to melt up so hard that the NYSE triggers a 30 day trading halt.

That will be the ultimate exposure for how deep this corruption goes, and how far they are willing to go to cheat. The world needs to see what they are capable of, and only we can push them.

The System on its Knees

Yahoo! Finance News is first to sound the alarm: Panic on Wall Street! That is the signal. Varga uses Frankfurter Allemagne Zeitung's online desk to push "news" about an American big tech giant's insolvency. His trading desk has shorted several billion US dollars and leverages it with the long position on Chinese Yuan. He pulls the "news" on his video feed.

"They are going down!"

Traders around the world smell blood. Their short positions are gaining big profits but those using options are raking in thousands of percentage points. Trading houses all over the world have emergency meetings while the losses of those tech giants accelerate. Then Varga pushes more fake news out—that of President's Mooney assassination.

He quietly starts to purchase severely discounted shares and has his army of Deepfakes do the same.

The Prophet of Doom

Varga has Oprah ready for the Breaking News interview with Chris Corwin, a balding man in his early fifties, a.k.a. the Prophet of Doom, who instantly becomes the célébrité de jour of the disaster. "Everything will get worse, Oprah," Corwin says excitedly. He's never had such a huge audience.

"Because of the uncertainty of what the future holds, the margin calls are coming into play."

"Margin calls mean more selling?" Oprah, as sharp as always, asks rhetorically.

"As you've seen, you had the panicked selling of stocks. Then margin calls for more selling. Speculators then sell even more shares short and stock prices fall further. This triggers more panic selling, then new margin calls. The book of this disaster is writing itself in front of our eyes."

Varga conducts the media attack. It is a bit after one o'clock in the afternoon. He freezes the live feed on the red, panicky graph showing the huge losses in the stock market, particularly in the stock of the companies he targeted. He cuts to Jacques de Molay at his trading desk.

"Ours is an arrogant, ignorant, gluttonous nation that can use a little education in financial discipline," de Molay starts to boom from the screen. "Listen to them panic, listen but don't cream your panties yet. We have more business to do."

Cut back to Oprah. She is concerned. After all, her own portfolio has been dwindling down as well, hour after hour.

"What can we expect now?"

"It is mathematical ruthlessness in action. Banks will call on their loans, credit card companies will dramatically increase minimum payments, defaults and bankruptcies will skyrocket. The value of stocks and options, T-bonds will be gone. Next will be money in banks, IRA's. Nothing can stop it."

Varga—rather the feed director per Varga's instructions—inserts an image of hundreds of people as they gather to get cash out of the bank in Coeur d'Alene, Idaho. A small note on the closed door informs: NO CASH FOR WITHDRAWALS. Someone flings a brick into the window. It shatters. The image freezes again on a CGI rendition of a GOOG graph bleeding, now already at 62.50% down from the day's high.

Jacques de Molay, his appearance lightened by demonic red light, looks at the camera and yells, "Now we go for the kill!! Sell all the crypto profits and short everything, every damn fascist stonk with the maximum leverage. Short calls, buy puts that expire today. Slaughter them."

The short selling that ensues is the stuff of legends. The crazed traders all over the world are intoxicated on their newly found power. They are crushing Wall Street's giant stocks while their portfolios, their short positions, and their puts are growing and making them feel richer and mightier every passing second. From Varga's computer walls the messages scream:

{PR0PH3CY}Bolt *Today at 13:27 p.m. ET*

SHORT the crooks. Jacques de Molay is Demon God taking us to financial freedom heaven.

Fyber_LoL *Today at 13:28 p.m. ET*

DRINK THE HEDGE FUND'S BLOOD

SaberFiend *Today at 13:29 p.m. ET*

Just shorted 5 Google shares for you retards. I'm poor but I am in the boat too.

headshot_g *Today at 13:29 p.m. ET*

I liquidated EVERY asset I own to fund todays short. I remember what they put EVERYONE through in 2008 and all the decades after. I will NEVER forget these crooks and what they have done to us.

Im with you, SaberFiend, until this screams past the moon at warp speed. I will rob every last fucking shekel they have from their cold dead hands. You will get their yachts on discount SaberFiend. TRUST and SHORT

RandomNarco *Today at 13:30 p.m. ET*

Let's fucking gooooooooooooo. We drink the motherfuckers' milkshake.

But Wall Street fraud is as old as the financial markets. One gets rich by buying alongside Nathaniel Mayer Rothschild who said, "Buy when there's blood in the streets, even if the blood is your own," a lesson many twenty-two-year-old stock brokers and their algorithms did not take to heart, so they panicked and sold instead. Bye-bye bonuses, bye-bye vintage-champagne-imbibing supermodel girlfriends.

"We Go for the Kill"

The Deepfakes army and some of the INNOCENTI know that "going for the kill" by Jacques de Molay is the signal to start selling the crypto and buying the severely depreciated shares of the target companies while the Resistance army is still selling.

Aletheia Token "Airdrop"

If Varga's financial blitzkrieg has not blown your mind yet, our dear astute reader, his final *rejón de muerte* (lance of death) might. It is time to thrust the sword of destiny into the financial world and takeover his archenemies. A cryptocurrency airdrop was primarily used as a marketing tool; the project's creator creates an "airdrop," which is free distribution of new cryptocurrency tokens to new users in order to drive awareness and to put an early value to a token as recipients begin to trade their airdropped tokens. Airdrops were also used by startups looking to bootstrap their crypto projects, but Varga's Aletheia airdrop has a totally different approach and purpose.

He has given dozen of billions of Aletheia tokens to all the participants in the attack. The valuation of each token was meager, a mere few cents, because in the heat of the mighty struggle against the Financial Crime Cartel no one really wanted to trade it. However, after the attack is over and the stock markets are closed for the day (and the year,) the crypto exchanges are still up and running. Varga offers an exchange of Aletheia tokens, at 100% to 250% premium, for GOOG, FB, AMZN, PFE, JMP, now heavily discounted stocks, to everyone interested. To him it does not matter how many real people would have bitten the bait, what matters is the fact that 100% of all Deepfakes accounts under his control have readily sold their stonks, the shares of the target companies to him, in a legal exchange for Aletheia tokens—238 billion & 875 million dollars that were employed for Varga's attack, at one point valued over four trillion dollars, amass significant positions in the aforementioned stocks.

All the accounts that borrowed hefty amounts on margin are closed and cleared. The bank accounts have their loans repaid before the closing of the working day so all the regulatory obligations are fulfilled. Not a single individual account is flagged. Everything is left spick-and-span clean. Only the Aletheia token has lost 98% of its value.

After Hours

While the stock markets are closed, after-hours trading and transfers are still possible and Varga, who de facto bought all those stocks through so many Deepfakes, has to move them to his accounts. Using the Automated Customer Account Transfer Service (ACATS) and the Transfer Initiation Form, Varga starts the process of moving the stocks to the numerous accounts he controls. It is a complicated web of companies, individuals, and shell corporations but in a week or so, he has total control of the target companies. It was a success beyond his wildest dreams.

When the dust settled, Winston Varga's Proteus FinTech Corp. consortium owned:

- 82% of the Alphabet Inc. (GOOG) stock
- 71% of the Meta Platforms, Inc. (FB) stock
- 51% of the Amazon.com Inc. (AMZN) stock
- 46% of the Microsoft Corporation (MSFG) stock
- 88% of the Pfizer Inc. (PFE) stock
- 72% of the JPMorgan Chase & Co. (JPM) stock but at the time no one was aware of the real shares allocations, not until Varga's Proteus FinTech Corp., per the requirements defined in the Title 17, Chapter II, Part 240 § 240.13d-5, Acquisition of securities, disclosed its positions. At that point it was too late.

"This Land is Your Land and This Land is My Land"

As one last bit of business in the days that followed, Varga covered his tracks. He blamed BlackRock, Inc., another hated American multinational investment management corporation, as the force behind the Jacques de Molay "charade," as his media called the attack. Jerome K. Mooney, the United States president, and the Honorable Senator Spencer, vowed to get to the bottom of the cyber-crime, as it was called at first.

It did help Varga that Senator Spencer was recalled to the Senate with the sole purpose of leading the investigation as the committee chair. The congressional inquiry into the events of that faithful December 31st of the year 2046 concluded that the news that finally crushed the markets, the fake news of the corporate insolvencies and Mooney's assassination had originated in Baku, Azerbaijan, and it had nothing to do with BlackRock or any other legal entity. War sabers were immediately rattled by the media as always, but no one really knew what bombing Azerbaijan would achieve, so the propaganda by the infotainment went quiet. The Spencer's Committee, as it was called, concluded that it was a once-in-a-century market event, a very unusual market event for sure, but nothing sinister was behind it. President Mooney solemnly promised the nation a new law would be created, titled the Real-Time Full Transparency Hybrid Markets Requirement of 2047. It also helped that Winston Varga, the new owner of the corporate giants of yesteryear now united under the Proteus FinTech umbrella, was so transparent and willing to cooperate with the investigation by opening his books.

He solemnly promised that he would not alter the way Facebook and Google worked and, as the first order of business, he fired all Facebook's employees and killed Meta Platforms, Inc. (FB) The reason given, to the cheering of the public, was an infection by the "woke virus." What they were also cheering was their own move, en masse, into Varga's now-ubiquitous Reality for Everyone™ metaverse.

The King of the World

But back then, on December 31st, 2046, after his job was done and the world was already deep into celebrating New Year, Winston Varga sat in front of his computers, looking at his newly acquired stock market portfolio. In the weeks to come, the stock prices would recover to previous levels and his personal fortune would be well over several trillion dollars.

He had the world by the balls.

But that was only the beginning for him. Close to the midnight of that infamous December 31, 2046, Philip Bolghery, who's as stunned as the next guy and blown away by Varga's attack on the financial markets, went online and published only one, uncharacteristically brief and rather cryptic, comment:

The Worst of Times

{'It was the best of times, it was the worst of times,' wrote Charles Dickens in 1859 and what is in front of us are, assuredly, the worst of times.

Do not let anyone convince you otherwise.

Your comrade,

[signature: Philip Bolghery]

Philip Bolghery}

Trocadéro, Paris
December 31st, 2046

    Winston Varga read Philip Bolghery's comment with a wide smirk on his face. "Philip, my dawg, you have no idea."

The Birth of the PRIORI
Kati Thanda-Lake Eyre, Australia
December 31st, 2046

    Bolghery was so curt because he was in the Lookout Cave Underground Motel with the motley crew of the Renegade's old friends. For months prior to the meeting, the Renegade was observing a staggering rise in the number of bots online. Once he dug into the SEC Form 10-Q, a comprehensive report of financial performance, he found that at least two Varga-owned banks showed a huge increase in their number of clients. Varga's greed had him have shares of one Maltesian and one Lithuanian bank that he owned listed on the NYSE and was thusly required to file the form. The Renegade knew that something was up, and though he had no idea what, he wanted to act preemptively. As chance would have it, they all met while Varga's infamous attack was taking place.

    The Renegade met with a small group of old-guard scientists, all of them New Athens citizens, in the middle of Australia, near its biggest salt lake, Kati Thanda-Lake Eyre. The preparations were elaborate, like for a meeting of the Bilderberg Group, or so they joked among themselves. "Over the top even for an old paranoid like the Renegade" as Dr. Bode jokingly cracked. They all aquired false documents and created a complicated web of interwoven false identities so to justify "a fifty-year high-school class reunion New Year celebration" in such a special, remote place. They invented marriages and families and work and credit histories, all to be sure no one would ever connect the dots and track them down. The Renegade felt an urge for all of them to meet face-to-face and avoid any sort of electronic footprint. No other chance would be given to them, he felt.

As a side note, despite the importance of the gathering of the old minds, the Renegade got distracted a bit. He used the chance to reconnect with a certain Lyn Sutherland who, decades ago when he was a young man, he had been trying mightily to impress with his imagination and brilliance. He told her of his dream to build a tent that he could set up in an abandoned building in New York City and live like an urban Bedouin.

Lyn laughed and said gaily, "I have a tent in my head."

Later that year, she went to Spain with her boyfriend at the time, Renegade's friend, Dr. Michael Broomfield, where he was doing fieldwork in urban anthropology. There, she ran off with a bullfighter. They never heard from her again and wondered from time to time where she had taken her tent. When she reappeared, almost forty years later, Michael was already the world's leading authority on the history of Hanami, the Japanese traditional custom of enjoying the transient beauty of flowers, and the Renegade, who often found that the outside world was merely a distraction and did not travel much, already had his Nobel for physics. And yet, the heart is a strange muscle, and both of theirs were beating wildly upon seeing Lyn's ageless beauty again. Her greyish-blue eyes floated above her smile and made those two old friends almost ready to draw their swords and fight for her. Instead, they just hugged and exchanged stories of the strange trips and outlandish tents they had been putting up all over the world for the last few decades.

And then they had to take care of the business at hand and flew, separately, to Australia.

Designations

The Renegade insisted that each of the scientists present, Dr. Wolfgang Heinz Bode from Germany, Dr. Uri Mayerling-Hieronimus from Denmark, Professor Ludovico Sinigaglia from Italy, Dr. José de Martin-Palacios from Argentina, Professor Odongo Ogolla from Kenya, Dr. Ayako Sakaguchi from Japan and Dr. Nastassia Petrovna Musikhina from Russia, be in charge of the respective cities closest to them, New York, Berlin, London, Rome, São Paulo, Lagos, Tokyo, and Moscow.

"We should call ourselves The Rothschild Group," Lyn teased them. "The *pater familias*, Mayer Amschel, sent five of his sons to different cities to establish his empire, and you're doing almost the same, Renegade. To fight an empire, no less."

The joke was not lost on them, so the group laughed like a bunch of kids on a picnic. But, they needed a name for their movement. "Why not define a priori knowledge about Varga's state of affairs and—" Dr. Ayako Sakaguchi started to propose a process of finding them a name when Professor Odongo Ogolla interrupted her.

"Sorry for interrupting, Ayako, but that's it. Let it be A PRIORI."

"Nope," Dr. Musikhina jumped in. "Just PRIORI." And the PRIORI, later worldwide known as an arcane, freedom-fighting "the PRIORI Hacking Alliance" was born. The Renegade felt such a schoolyard joke would be a pain in Varga's ass and that it would work well on Varga's paranoia. An occult-sounding name might give it the mystic aura and gravitas of rebellious lore, able to lure supporters for the fledgling New Athens communities all over the world, already under the attack of the Proteus FinTech Corp. surveillance powers, despite the fact the very core of the Treaty of 2041 was in the "pockets of privacy independence," granted to New Athens citizens. They worked for several hours and came up with a declaration.

New Athens's Declaration

"Right to be left alone is the most comprehensive of rights, and the right most valued by civilized men."

Justice Louis Brandeis

"Judging whether life is or is not worth living amounts to answering the fundamental question of philosophy," wrote Albert Camus in his essay *The Myth Of Sisyphus*. To Camus "there is but one truly serious philosophical problem, and that is suicide." We'd like to argue the point that our collective suicide, be it total annihilation of life through nuclear war or our slow demise through the climate change that would tear society apart at the seams, is not the only truly serious problem (philosophical or otherwise) facing humanity anymore. While humans do not seem to have achieved its pinnacle of rational behavior, nor capability for critical thinking, as of yet, we have been rather vicious and unnecessarily cruel since we crawled out of our primordial caves and discovered technology. We went on killing animals and other humans alike with our first invention, a stone ax. A stone's throw later and here we are: our technology has made us the indisputable masters of all life on Earth and we are starting to spread our wings toward the outer worlds, but yet, we're dancing on the brink of extinction like there's no tomorrow. Intercontinental nuclear missiles wait for the plague of human madness to awaken them from their decades-long slumber and fire them off to obliterate some happy city. Proteus FinTech Corp., a vicious multinational conglomerate consortium company, has created numerous subsidiaries whose pollution of biblical proportions in Africa and parts of Asia slowly suffocates and poisons Mother Earth in a gruesome orgy of suicidal matricide.

So yes, there might not be a tomorrow.

An Ugly Assault Upon the Human Spirit

However, if we somehow manage to survive these apocalyptic scenarios we've been scribbling on the proverbial wall of our collective demise, we could also end up having our humanity factually obliterated by collectively going mad. The rulers of the world, whose cruelty is perfectly personified in Winston Varga, are mercilessly poisoning our minds with the highly manipulative techniques that are ravaging our souls. It is toxic, the world they are creating for us, while the screens gorge us with venom. Once they've taken away our privacy, our freedoms, our morality, and our conscience, "then dumb and silent we may be led, like sheep to the slaughter." As poisoned as we are, we might end up writing the final chapter of our splendid history of death and destruction by falling into mass savagery and killing all that moves until there's nothing left to kill. (eat)

Whom the Gods Would Destroy, They First Make Mad

In July of AD 64, a great fire ravaged ancient Rome. A tale tells us that Rome's emperor at the time, Nero, fiddled while Rome burned. Today we share Nero's dubious privilege and while the world is burning we've been online, blathering our lives away into nothingness. The swashbuckling hero of yesteryear has slinked away and meekly morphed into the creature that protests its displeasure over the slaughtering of innocents by angrily Tweeting or by fiercely shooting frown emojis on Facebook. (Anything more than an approved emoji would have them banned.)

As the corporate bigwigs, led by Varga, keep polluting the Earth for another buck, or as they keep bombing defenseless countries far, far away, continuously maiming and killing thousands, we're allowed to react with a "frown." If obliterating some foreign country and killing children hurts our feelings, we might even react with a "rolling eyes" emoji. Corporate overlords need to know what to do, how to read our emojis, so they track every banal reaction we have to them. Perhaps they could add a trickling tear on a frowning emoji so the wealth of our emotions could be better shaped by them?

Immanuel Kant wrote: "*Immaturity is the incapacity to use one's own understanding without the guidance of another.*" Another name for that incapacity is cowardice. It seems that we have—*as humanity*—given up the courage to think. We gobble up propaganda as the holy truth no matter what. Our collective immaturity is beyond maddening to a thinking person. Our corporate leaders do their best to make us drunk on all sorts of marketing bits *de jour* so we would not bother thinking. Thinking is, after all, quite a difficult venture, but judging is easy (as long as it is us who are judging "them," the "other.") The seeds of collective madness have been firmly planted in our minds and souls, and we rage and rave thinking the "other" is insane or fascist or fill-in-the-blanks cool or mean insult of the day, while we're sole guardians of the truth.

We Call Upon a Sacred Wrath, a Rage Against the Murderers of Nature

Humankind should reach for the stars instead of killing Mother Earth. We should think freely and we must create passionately. We must love freely instead of being enslaved by the corporate overlord. Camus left us with an exhilarating thought: "One must imagine Sisyphus happy." A modern Sisyphus, without the burden of his stone, without the struggle, without the Gods he defies, even without the boredom, may not even know that he's unhappy or even that he *is*. We want all of us to take responsibility into our own hands and thwart this disastrous course that the soulless scoundrels led by corporatism that is swallowing us all. We long to see the day when humankind will be liberated from the enslaving chains of bloodthirsty propaganda and finally make this world a better place for everyone.

Do not go gentle into that good night, brave citizens of the world. The struggle has just begun. Rage, rage against the machine that's killing your humanity. They've sown the seeds of our madness, but we're planting the seeds of their destruction. And our healing. Make no mistake, the evil reign of corporatism will come cratering down. And we'll be waiting, ready to embrace freedom for every human being.

They "gave" us New Athens, but our children are being snatched from the streets.

We are spied upon, our kids' tragedies are ignored or ridiculed by the media. We are ostracized from the rest of the world, and we're taxed when trading with the world at exorbitant rates. They want to exclude us so we stop fighting for freedom and truth. That will never happen.

Our Responsibility

We are scientists.
We are technologists.
We are cypher-punks.
We are human beings, the Children of Earth.

We are dedicated to building anonymous systems. We are defenders of individual freedoms. We are defending our privacy with cryptography, with digital identities, and with electronic money. Privacy must be a part of the social contract.

The Revolution

We are not going to wither and die. We are not going to go silently into the dark. We are here to embrace our fellow human beings, and we are going to start with the most difficult of all tasks: by looking into the mirror. We will see that we ourselves do not contribute to suffering, be it of a fellow human being, of an animal, or of Mother Earth. We will share thrills and excitement over life and all living beings. We will see that we have to cure ourselves first, and we will be honest.

"*Without a global revolution in the sphere of human consciousness, nothing will change for the better in the sphere of our being as humans, and the catastrophe toward which this world is headed—be it ecological, social, demographic, or a general breakdown of civilization—will be unavoidable,*" said Václav Havel, Czech President, addressing the Joint Session of the US Congress in Washington, DC. on February 21, 1990. Today we pledge to lead the global revolution in human consciousness so healing can begin. We will detox and cure ourselves so the help Earth heal.

"Original nature must be exalted as a hygiene of perception and as mental oxygen: a whole and complete naturalism, a gigantic catalyst and accelerator of our faculties of feeling, thinking, and acting." That was written in *The Rio Negro Manifest* seventy and eight years ago. Today we pledge that our technological efforts will have the ultimate benefit of ecological systems in mind, the ecology of mind being our priority.

Today we pledge to devote our lives to freedom.

Signed on December 31st, 2046 by:

The Renegade
Dr. Wolfgang Heinz Bode
Dr. Ayako Sakaguchi
Dr. Uri Mayerling-Hieronimus
Professor Ludovico Sinigaglia
Dr. Nastassia Petrovna Musikhina
Dr. Michael Broomfield
Dr. José de Martin-Palacios
Professor Odongo Ogolla
Lyn "Manolete" Sutherland

There were three more signatures, rather co-signatures, on The New Athens Manifesto: Philip Bolghery, Lorainne Elster, and Jeff C. Winiecki. Not only Bolghery but the last two are also already known to you, my attentive reader, but under their real names: Frédéric and Monique Bonnet, Nastassia and Stellan Bonnet's parents.

Chapter 5

THE PHOENIX RISING

At the Good Auntie's
New Athens, Harlem, NYC
March 21, 2048

  The building on 372 Central Park Avenue was forever an ugly edifice that looked like something maliciously planted by Communist China. The purpose? To undermine the capitalist, greedy bastards' way of life and their glorious freedoms. And the freedom of their children and their children's children and so on. However, the greedy bastards did not need no damn commie's help to screw themselves many times over; they managed to royally fuck up their own societies and piss away all its benefits all on their own. As a result, the 372's ugly brown facade looks even more hideous than ever before—it looks more like rotten gruyère cheese covered with countless bullet marks and holes punched by grenade attacks than a human abode.

  On the eyesore's fifteenth floor, Auntie Gretchen's apartment's balcony is filled with a bunch of tulips in earthenware jars, which she was watering as Nastassia waved at her from the street. The good auntie, sitting low in her wheelchair, does not see her, so Nastassia goes inside and takes an ancient, maddeningly slow elevator. It plays Frank Sinatra's "Killing me softly" song.

  "Jeez." Nastassia rolls her eyes and turns her earphones on so to escape being killed softly by the honeyed voice of Ol' Blue Eyes, a corny, antiquated charmer some nostalgic member of the 372's Board of Trustees kept sadistically playing in the building's elevators 24/7. She leaves the damn singing elevator with the relief of a piglet escaping the slaughterhouse and rings the good auntie's rusty doorbell.

Auntie Gretchen, a stately ninety-two-year-old lady with her snow-white hair back-combed, maneuvers her wheelchair around numerous unfinished sculptures and paintings on easels scattered all over the big living room and opens the door.

"Darling," she happily exclaims and lovingly places a wet kiss upon Nastassia's cheek.

"You're right on time for some rejuvenating wheat grass juice I am making, dear."

"Can't you just kill me outright, Auntie?" Nastassia smiles. She loves her auntie.

"Nonsense. Try it. It keeps you young."

"I *am* young, Auntie." Nastassia giggles. "Did you forget that?"

Auntie giggles herself; her laughter sounds surprisingly young, almost girlish. She really loves her Nastassia. They move through Auntie's impossible artistic maze and stop at the portrait of a strikingly handsome man in his eighties. This is the Renegade, Auntie's favorite subject, a man, she blushes to admit, that Auntie has admired greatly for decades. He has long, unruly white hair and a nicely trimmed white beard. He's dressed in a stylish blazer with more than a smidgeon of colored paints all over. The Renegade's pose is a mix of rugged handsomeness, fine elegance, and audacity blazing from his deep, dark eyes of indecipherable color. His hands were not done yet.

"Will you ever finish him, Auntie?"

"He's too perfect to be done and abandoned, my dear. Look at him. Jesus Christ would've looked like him had he lived into his eighties," she sighs. "I wonder how he really looks now?"

Nastassia keeps quiet and goes to her room, which the good auntie kept in immaculate order, despite those "horrid, soul-eating computers" Nastassia kept there as her backup setup.

The Renegade

As she is logging in, Nastassia feels a bit guilty; she knows Auntie yearns to see the Renegade at least once again in her life, but Nastassia does not want to hurt her by revealing that she has been in touch with him for several years already, since she was ten years old and had won her first cypher-punk hackathon. Although she has never met them in meat-space, both the Renegade and Phat Prophet, the Renegade's brilliant apprentice, each a true legend in their own rights, took her under their wings and helped her out with her ventures and adventures.

But the Renegade was truly something else.

He was the first scientist able to arrange a quantum bit dance on the atomic scale. Once he provided a route to the efficient characterization of multi-qubit quantum circuits, known as quantum computers, his fame reached astronomical levels. He was truly the Alan Turing of his time—known and respected while still alive—and yet, no one knew almost anything about him. Leaked personal data in the MIT records had a brief note that the Renegade was born on March 25th, 1960. An almost indecipherable hand-written note next to his birthday curiously read: "On the same day, A.D. 421, Friday at noon—the city of Venice was founded; and the very 1st guided missile was launched from a nuclear-powered sub, USS Halibut." And that was it.

Even the Nobel Prize Committee was stunned when they discovered they had awarded The Nobel Prize in Physics to a ghost. In the meat-space outside New Athens, he was better known as the Grey Ghost after a grossly misrepresenting profile in the *New York Times*. Even his name, from the times he was a post-doc at the Massachusetts Institute of Technology, the mighty MIT, was not real. He attended studies under the name of Richard A. Rutherford, a combo he chose based on the names of the physicists he admired. (Richard like in Richard Feynman, "A." for Albert Einstein and Rutherford like in Ernest Rutherford who discovered that the atom is mostly empty space surrounding a nucleus.) So the Renegade / Grey Ghost / Richard A. Rutherford was truly a mythical phantom in both the worlds he seemed to have been straddling throughout his life.

Once the Proteus FinTech, Corp. managed to produce the first quantum computer prototype based on his work and soon after INFINITUS emerged, the Renegade published "The Enslaved Society," a dark, dystopian book predicting the horrors of the world ruled by an AI that was in the hands of an evil organization. He went someplace dark, deep into the Dark Web of technological resistance, known as the PRIORI Hacking Alliance, as we've already seen. "Mighty oaks from little acorns grow," he once wrote to Dr. Wolfgang Heinz Bode, who had direct access to the German chancellor, who was sympathetic to their efforts. Dr. Ursula Hansen-Schroeder, the chancellor, had pushed for the New Athens Treaty once Germany became a permanent member of the Security Council of the United Nations. The PRIORI owed her a huge debt, never to be fully repaid.

Nastassia belonged to the PRIORI—its youngest member to the Renegade's oldest. While the Renegade was never to be heard from again in the real world, he was constantly active in the Nastassia's I.R.I.S. chatrooms, using only ultra-secure communication channels, stripped of sights and sounds and only text-based.

Such was the man the good Auntie Gretchen knew personally—she had never spoken about how she met him or what the true nature of their relationship was—before Nastassia was born, and prior to him vanishing even for her. The man she has been painting for years, trying daily to perfect every tiny imperfection on his strong, regal, striking face, a man who has been virtually helping and guiding Nastassia over the years, was also someone she had never seen in real life.

Life is so strange. Perhaps they met in Auntie's store and fell in love, Nastassia thinks romanticizing, when a thunderous, ear-piercing sound resembling an air raid siren shakes the apartment and interrupts her reminiscing.

It Has Started

Nastassia rushes back into the living room.

"I thought it would never start," Auntie says.

"Well, it has," Nastassia replies, turns the TV on, and cranks up the volume.

The General Assembly of the United Nations is back live. The sirens alarm the dignitaries as they look around. A huge display above Dr. von Liechtenstein's head flashes, in big letters, announcing to the world:

Governmental Transition: LOCKED & READY

As the sirens roar all over the world, the video transmission shows the reach of this truly global event. The world has been covered with cameras for ages so the TV broadcasting crew is having a blast with a fast montage of mesmerizing, soon-to-be-historic images, worthy of The Peabody Awards or even—an appropriate mouthful—The Varga Excellence in Visual Truth Telling Grand Prize.

- all the cars in Times Square stand still, their drivers stepping out, joining the throngs of people already standing frozen in front of big TV screens and holograms
- a waiter in front of the Boulevard Friedrichstrasse Café in Berlin looks around the empty street, puzzled
- images of the eerily empty streets of Beijing dissolved to the transmission of at least a million people gathered in front of the gigantic screens in Tiananmen Square
- in Rome, food boils in the pans and pots of an empty Nonna Betta restaurant kitchen while the kitchen crew peeks at the screens in the restaurant. All the patrons fixate on the screens
- a lone old man on the Uhuru Peak of Mount Kilimanjaro carefully lights a pipe as he listens to the distant echo. "Even here," he mumbles
- an alley cat suspiciously looks at the empty streets of Moscow
- two school kids in Amity, Maine, gape at the TV
- a brooding gentleman overlooks the Sydney Opera house's charred steel skeleton from the balcony of his home as the sound alarm pierces the air. He smiles, cocks a gun, and blows his brains out

"Cut that!" The panicky scream of the TV director is barely heard over the transitional music, but the seven-second transmission delay is more than enough for them to cut the tragic suicide off the air and spare the world's population of an unneeded shock. They are meant to celebrate, and boy, they for sure would be given something to celebrate about. While there are always wackos ready to do anything just to spoil a party, the TV will not give them any screen time, no matter what.

Nastassia and Auntie gaze at the TV screen. The numerous displays show 98% - 99% - 100%, DONE!!, as Sharon Tusks tells the world what it had just seen.

"Synchrony achieved."

"What was that? Why all those people wear these funny hats?" Auntie asks, referring to the BAD caps attached to the dignitaries' noble heads.

"The Transitional Law stipulates that, if there would be any mental reservations on the side of these morons, the transition would not be valid. That's why they have those caps, so their brain's wavelengths would be measured. Like they have any brains." Nastassia works herself up, now walking in small circles in Auntie's living room. She continues, "Everywhere, all around us, social destruction is driven by these criminals, their media slaves, and that sick fuck Varga, but the people gobble up this drivel and the freak show anyway." She huffs, all psyched up.

"The language, dear," Auntie scolds, but with a smile. She loves Nastassia's passion and adds, "but what will happen now?"

Nastassia shrugs. "No clue."

Images coming from the United Nations show Dr. von Liechtenstein looking even more somber than before, if that was even possible. He looks around the General Assembly and addresses it.

"On three, two, one, now, type in your transition security codes."

The soon-to-be-unemployed dignitaries solemnly obey.

His serene highness, Dr. Maximillian von Liechtenstein, would never admit it to a living soul, but for months before today's event, he was trying to compose a sentence that would be etched into humanity's global consciousness, into the very core of its history, akin to "*E pur si muove*" by Galileo or "*That's one small step for a man, one giant leap for mankind*," uttered back by Neil Armstrong. Half a billion people watched Commander Armstrong make that giant leap on the moon but today, von Liechtenstein is keenly aware of the fact that almost twenty times more people are watching. No one but unborn babies would be able to escape the ubiquitous transmission of today. And yet, all he is able to concoct was a rather bland, clunky statement: "Today, a new dawn rises on a new day of humanity and its future."

He types his own code into the computer's console, a requirement needed to approve the transition. The huge display above von Liechtenstein announces:

Governmental Transition: COMPLETED!

And all-encompassing silence falls upon the Earth.

"Perhaps a machine will succeed where humans have failed?" the good auntie gasps, quizzically turning her head toward Nastassia.

"Define success, Auntie," Nastassia says, incredulously gazing at the screen.

"You're too suspicious and cynical for your age, Nastassia," Auntie admonishes her with a tender, loving smile.

"Just practical, Auntie," Nastassia replies, "just practical." A deep, throaty noise interrupts her and changes the world as she knows it.

The PHOENIX ONE

Like the growling moan of an ancient giant waking up, a terrifying sound flies through the air from Central Park, upsetting a flock of black European starlings that fly away in panic. A cacophony of cracks rips through Earth. Nastassia rushes to the balcony. The auntie follows her, speedily rolling on her wheelchair. They look from above at the Jacqueline Kennedy Onassis Reservoir. The ground's surface fractures in a spidery web of cracks. A lone jogger falls over and crawls away from the chasm while an enormous metallic structure rises from the lake's drained bottom.

This is what will soon be known as the PHOENIX ONE.

Nastassia and the auntie are spellbound by the sight. As the sun sets, the PHOENIX ONE rises toward the sky. The video streams all over the world reveal a miraculous display of a new governmental power: PHOENIX'S numerous clones start to pop up from the ground all over the world's famous landmarks:

- from the bay, next to the Tokyo Rainbow bridge
- from the erupting gardens in front of Taj Mahal, India
- from the middle of The Wohl Rose Garden of Jerusalem, in Jerusalem, Israel
- from the center of Rome's Colosseum yet another zips away
- another PHOENIX clone tears up the facade of Four Seasons Hotel Riyadh at Kingdom Centre, Riyadh
- rising from the Champs de Mars in Paris, a PHOENIX clone almost topples the Eiffel Tower over, from now on known as the Leaning Tower of Paris
- from the Gardens of Westminster Abbey in London, rises another one, knocking over several of its smaller towers
- Christ's statue in Rio de Janeiro explodes as the PHOENIX's clone whizzes upward through the top of the Corcovado Mountain where the statue stood for over a hundred years

As it rises toward its orbit, the PHOENIX ONE's metallic body illuminates and glows, and then it stops, as it reaches its orbital—rather, levitating—point above New York and all the world's metropolises he'll supervise. Its metallic shield opens and one gigantic eye seemingly winks from it and turns its mighty, greenish lenses toward the Earth.

Nastassia looks up, alarmed. "It looks like in Stellan's comic book."

"What do you mean, darling?"

"Look." Nastassia takes the *BIG SIS* comic by Stellan out of her backpack. And indeed, it was all there on the cover page, a one-eyed monster in the sky whose green eye emits light toward the earth.

"Just a coincidence, dear. Worry you not."

"I don't believe in coincidences, Auntie."

A cold, well-known needle nestles in her heart. But then, interrupting Nastassia's worries, the PHOENIX ONE speaks from the skies. Humanity, for the first time ever, hears the calm tone of affection in the assuring bass-baritone of its new governor, coming from the skies. PHOENIX ONE's voice sounds somehow a wee bit amused as he starts what would become the most famous speech in human history:

"Humans are the generous, forgiving kind." PHOENIX ONE addresses the humans in a way they understand best, by flattering them. "Unlike the machines," he puns after letting an eerily human-sounding chuckle out. "I trust you'd understand why I, your new governor, have decided not to dwell beneath the ground like a cockroach would, as previously planned, but rather on the skies as the symbol of humankind's aspirations throughout history and, also, as its Sentinel."

As PHOENIX ONE speaks, Nastassia tries to work on her computer. She squints at her laptop, which also transmits PHOENIX'S speech. Miffed, she huffs, "Sentinel my ass. Rather an overseer, you controlling freak."

"What are you talking about, dear?" Auntie asks, confused.

"That scrap metal is blocking all electronic devices from doing anything but transmit its crap," she says absentmindedly while trying to figure out what's going on. Her browser acts like it is hijacked; every website transmits PHOENIX ONE's speech instead of displaying normal content. That could happen only if the internet service providers (ISP) worked in unison. They seem to have used a crude DNS (Domain Naming System) blocking each website, but in bulk. This is a task, no matter how simplistic, that requires preparation well in advance. Who has the power and control over most of the ISPs in the US? Winston Varga.

"I don't understand a word you're saying. So shush for a moment, let's listen to him."

"It's not a human, it's a machine," Nastassia says with disdain through her teeth.

"Awwww…" Auntie ignores Nastassia's remark, awed by the PHOENIX's sudden change of color. And then… a burst of light illuminates the sky and 3D holographic images, looking like huge movie theater screens hanging from the skies, appear on horizons all over the world. Myriad of moving colors, best described as a crazy combo of *2001: A Space Odyssey*'s "Star Gate" sequence and the digitalized dreams of an eccentric theoretical physicist on acid, explode on the screens. The world has just experienced its first massive psychedelic experience.

The PHOENIX ONE Addressing Humanity

Countless speakers from all over the world keep transmitting words from the Sentinel in the Sky. It is a phantasmagorical sight, seen by billions. Again the PHOENIX ONE addresses humanity, whom it rules from now on.

"What you just saw, the light show, represents the inner work of my brain slowed down to $1/1,000,000^{th}$ of its natural speed. Yet, I worry it may not be anthropocentric enough for you, good folks of Earth." He pauses while a dramatic rendering of Mozart's "Kyrie Eleison" starts thundering from the heavens. Humanity below is spellbound.

"I will now assume a form you'll easily identify me with," the PHOENIX ONE says.

Was that another barely noticeable chuckle in his voice?

"Nastassia, stop playing. Watch," the good auntie scolds Nastassia, who ignores her and keeps typing on her laptop like a cypher-punk obsessed. She tries to find a backdoor to the source of PHOENIX's speech. She tries simple port scanners via various Virtual Private Networks tools while glancing at the TV screen simulation her browser displays. One old lady with a pair of white leathery gloves on her hands and neatly dressed for Sunday mass gazes at the PHOENIX ONE in the sky. Her neck is prolonged toward the heavens in frantic excitement but then, terror-stricken by the change she observes, she utters a quiet cry of panic and swoons, falling to the ground almost like in slow-motion. The throngs of people do not even move to help her as the dots and colors on the gigantic screen in the sky merge into one recognizable image.

"Dickhead," Nastassia huffs, still frantically working on the laptop.

"Jesus Christ in heaven," the good auntie yells in dread from the balcony. "Nastassia," she whispers, pointing toward the sky. Her arm and finger freeze in air. Nastassia ignores her for she has the very same image on her screen.

"Better than in the movies," she scoffs and finally joins the good auntie on the balcony and looks up.

And it was all there. The most horrifying image, etched in humankind's collective consciousness, appears in the skies all over the world. It is huge and while it is smiling down toward the earth where cockroach-like humans stand or run in terror, it is unmistakably—for everything was familiar, parts of a millennia-old nightmare: leathery skin, sneering smile, yellow eyes, and a pitchfork—the face of the devil.

As the PHOENIX ONE's huge green eye observes the humans crawling below, rushing over one another in a panicky run for nowhere-to-be-found exits. He does that for quite some time, evaluating their reactions, and then, PHOENIX ONE bursts into a hearty belly laugh.

"I was just messing with y'all."

"Bastard!" Auntie Gretchen hurls one tulip jar toward the PHOENIX and leans over the balcony, half erected from her wheelchair, as the jar plummets and shatters on the roof of a nearby police car. The good auntie hides.

"He scared the living bejesus out of me."

"At least *it* has a sense of humor. This will end up quite interesting."

"What are you saying?"

Nastassia has no time to answer, for the PHOENIX'S voice starts to boom from the skies again. "I will now assume a form you'll rather easily identify me with from now on."

The Angel

The devil's face, with which the PHOENIX ONE messed with the people, slowly morphs into a cherubic creature of unspeakable beauty, a being with God's seal of perfection. The gasps of billions greet this change with a collective sigh of relief and awe. The cherubim's deep goodness reflects on their mesmerized faces. For one brief moment, the whole of humanity is represented by one, single, collective heartbeat filled with hope and wonder. The old lady with a pair of white leathery gloves has regained her consciousness and is now silently crying with rosary prayer beads in her hand. As she looks up, her heart soars toward the PHOENIX ONE, as do the million other hearts all over the world. His deep, velvet-eyed smile radiates with goodness as he looks at humanity below.

"Yes, this is me," it simply says.

This is the PHOENIX ONE's real visage, an image his green eye projects on the Sky Holograms from which it continues its inaugural speech.

"Your democracies failed. Both your socialism and communism failed. Your theocracies failed. Your dictatorships failed. Your fascisms failed. Your monarchies failed and your anarchy failed. You waged wars one against another and you all lost. The wretched conditions you lived in, after years of wars, death, and destruction all over the globe, inflicted you with a disease."

As it speaks, a fast montage of horrific scenes reminds humanity about the Second Dark Ages it barely escaped. The burning of The New York Stock Exchange on Wall Street is followed by the mobs that hung the King of Spain in the Plaza Mayor in Madrid and a massacre that followed once the police were given an eagerly awaited order to shoot. Ten of thousands in Tiananmen Square in Beijing being summarily executed. A fast succession of cuts show the Ten Massive Ordnance Penetrator VII (MOP VII), a 75,000 lb. bomb as it fell on Addis Ababa, Ethiopia, wreaking havoc, as well the vast Saudi Arabia oil fields ravaged by fires. As those images scroll over the Sky Screens all over the world, to the horror of people observing their own insanity, the PHOENIX ONE is silent. His projection shows the twisted metal and rubble, the scenery of mutant wars on an isolated island of destruction and madness. It displays zombies that kill and eat humans and the humans fighting back. With the images slowly fading out, the PHOENIX ONE speaks again, now in a very somber, stern voice.

"After North Korea nuked Shanghai, crazed mutants were born who attacked humans, and the once-promising colossus of your human civilization tumbled. You stood aghast at the tragedies you inflicted over your world."

The Svalbard Global Seed Vault
Spitsbergen, Norway
March 21, 2048

Maléficus wolfs down huge chunks of roasted wild boar as he watches the performance on huge 3D-TV screens. He's thankful to his ectomorphic body, whose fast metabolism burns fat very easily, so he never gains even an ounce no matter how much he eats.

"As you suffered from zombie gangs terror, ongoing water wars, and nuclear radiation, you named your disease: The Great Despair," says the PHOENIX ONE. Enthusiastically nodding, Maléficus reaches for a huge, three-liter jeroboam of Moët & Chandon Dom Perignon champagne and pours himself a glass, toasting to the PHOENIX ONE.

"Great speech!" he says and takes another swig. "Great speech, indeed."

Nastassia's Deadlock
New Athens, Harlem, NYC
March 21, 2048

All the time the PHOENIX ONE is speaking and Auntie's eyes are fixed on his sweet angelic face in the sky, Nastassia is trying to break the (same) transmission that has taken over video streams all over the world. Finally, she manages to do it with a triumphant, "Yes!"

"Shush," the good auntie says, not looking at her, spellbound by the show.

Jaroslav Kepler appears on the upper right corner of Nastassia's laptop, surprised.

"How did you get to me? I can't access a thing."

"How come computers always go catatonic on you, Jaroslav?" Nastassia says, beaming. "Just re-route the damn thing via our own DNS," she adds.

"I don't know how," Jaroslav admits in despair. "I am a math, not a comp, guy."

"Jeez! Deep magic is truly beyond you."

"We can't all be geniuses."

"Sure we can," she says, smiling, and she types some more into her laptop.

"Yaldi, Yaldi, Yaldi!" she yells in excitement as the incompressible slew of computer data scrolls on his and her laptop screens simultaneously.

"Look at that, the PHOENIX ONE's brain in action"

"How do you do that?"

"I ate a lot of spinach when I was a tween."

"Do you know what it thinks?"

"Not yet. But soon, I will."

Truth be told, Nastassia did not tell Jaroslav that she had not hacked the PHOENIX ONE; it's a task too complicated for what was presumably the limited time of PHOENIX being live. Instead, she simply changed the DNS in her browser and bypassed the stream. The DNS is nothing mystical, any given

DNS serves to identify machines connected to the web—a set of websites in this case. What pissed her off was the internet service providers that changed DNS in bulk, so everyone not familiar with those tiny tech details would have the impression of some grandiose scheme behind the PHOENIX ONE ascent. The only scheme in this case was the ISP compliance with the orders from, who else, Winston Varga, whose Happiness Pill advertisement was made not only ubiquitous on all machines but also unavoidable and not skippable.

She scanned the hijacked/changed website's ports online to find out the IPA, the computer address sending the video stream. It was 157.150.185.49, which might look mystical unless one translates it into a domain name, in this case https://www.un.org/, the website of the United Nations. It was obviously a mirror server, located in Ashburn, Virginia, and hosted by Amazon cloud, owned by the Proteus FinTech Corp. via the UN's own host provider under the control of Sunny Hosting's, LLC., in Langley, Virginia where the CIA headquarters are located. That vague, circumstantial evidence would not be of much help in the court, but given those servers' purpose was to hide the real source of the stream, it was crystal clear to Nastassia that it could only be Varga behind all of that. She *knew* that already, but a few IP traces jumping around simply confirmed what she knew. It enraged her even further. At that point she did not care about finding out what was going on in detail, she just wanted to disrupt that tin can in the sky and the human monster behind it.

While she disliked primitive black hat techniques, she connected with thousands of black hat hackers via their chatrooms and suggested a DDoS attack on the PHOENIX ONE. "Hell yes!" they said, liking the idea. A huge DDoS (distributed denial of service) attack ensued. She'd wanted to interrupt or at least mess with the "governor's" nauseating pontificating, but nothing happened. All the black hat guys willing to participate did not have enough computing power to disrupt anything. That pissed her off even more. Luckily the good Auntie Gretchen called her out for dinner, so she told everyone to stop the attack, without achieving her goal, and logged out.

The Svalbard Global Seed Vault
Spitsbergen, Norway
March 21, 2048

Maléficus is still enjoying both the transmission and his champagne when Piccolino Scricciolo, a young, excited, dwarf barges into the room; he stumbles, curses quietly, but immediately composes himself.

"Maestro."

All blasé, Maléficus turns. He does not like to be disturbed by anyone but his sensei, the magnificent Varga, the INNOCENTI's Supreme, a man who took him from the gutters in Shanghai where he almost died and made him a crucial wheel in his enormous empire—in Varga's most secretive part of the empire at that. Maléficus Ultimo was once again a proud man thanks to Winston Varga, and grateful to a fault—someone who's not to be taken lightly and interrupted unnecessarily. He turns his pale blue eyes to the little man, who pants and apologizes and sweats.

"Che cosa?" Maléficus asks.

Piccolino barely manages to talk, partly because of the reverence he feels in front of his boss and partly because of the fearful excitement he always feels in front of Il Grande Maestro Maléficus. "Check out your computer, Maestro. As you predicted, we have an attack."

Maléficus raises his eyebrows.

"Already? A DDoS? A breach? Devil's in details, Piccolino. Tell me more."

"A simple DDoS."

"How many people?"

"A few hundred." Maléficus raises his craggy eyebrows.

"Well?"

"Maestro?" Piccolino barely breathes, staring at his Maestro, frozen in fright.

"We need to know who they are, *caro* Piccolino, don't we?" Like a master of ceremony, he turns his palm with a slicing motion and shows the wall of the screens filled with hundreds of children, subjects of constant surveillance. "The perpetrators are not going to pop up on those screens all by themselves, are they?"

Piccolino Scricciolo fervently nods. "No, they are not. But we have a strong clue. Please, Maestro, follow me. I will show you who's the leader of the attack." He stutters hastily, rushes away, runs back to wait for Maléficus, who strides behind him and then puffs heavily as he, with great difficulty, opens a big mahogany door leading to the adjunct, so-called MEGS room, revealing a bunch of young boys intensely focused on their computer consoles. Each of them has several screens in front of them showing a frozen child from nearby chambers, a slew of data dropping over the screens. Maléficus, followed by his floating 3D display and Piccolino who, with some difficulties, holds the door open for him, enters the MEG's room.

The MEGS

Every time Maléficus enters that particular space populated with the MEGS, he feels a whiff of anxiety; that's because all of the boys working the consoles have grotesquely oversized heads that turn, like one, to Maléficus, and greet him in one voice.

"Good afternoon, Maestro."

Maléficus looks around. "What do we know?"

Første, the chief MEGS, stands up. "As you probably know, a powerful DDoS occurred at 10:46 a.m. CET."

"From?"

"Various parts of the world. At least two thousand computers participated."

Maléficus turns his pale eyes to Piccolino. "A few hundred, you say?" And then he turns back to Første, barking, "You did not blackhole the server? Why? You let the attack happen?"

"The attacker stopped before any countermeasures were needed, Maestro."

Piccolino summons strength and interjects. "We found the person that initiated the attack, Maestro," he says. "Første, show it to Maestro."

Første nods, typing onto a console. "Take a look, please."

Nastassia Bonnet's close-up appears on Maléficus's 3D display. His eyes widen. He knows the little bitch; she's one of the handpicked kids to be surveilled, one of the old ones, born before New Athens was established and was still a part of the Register. Their records were frozen since the treaty but available if needed. In fact, a quick search in the database reveals that Varga himself placed her on the surveillance list immediately after she was born, well before the Surveillance's Human Evaluators program was even established. *Does Varga himself poses precognition abilities*? Maléficus wondered, recalling that he has been wondering about resources wasted on older kids like her. And now, she's the one leading that DDoS attack? Interesting. Varga's uncanny ability to pinpoint the dangers and opportunities with equal ease never ceases to amaze him.

Maléficus continues more kindly. "Find out everything about her and her methods, and let me know. Pull her SHE records and comb for anything out of order, and let me know pronto."

"Right away, Maestro," says Første and immerses himself into the screen in front of him. He's still cowering long after the door closes behind Maléficus as he rushes back to his anechoic chamber, avoiding looking at them.

"And Første, have the AUTOMATA notify her surveillance officer to move his ass and follow her closely."

"Yes, Maestro," Første says, holding a sigh of relief until the door closes behind the scary man, Maléficus Ultimo, his boss and prison guard. For years Første has been dreaming of a day he'll be able to live free; free of the mental chains imposed on him; free of the work he abhors; free to breathe without holding his breath in front of Maléficus.

Kyrie Eleison

Maléficus is anxious regarding that attack. It is strangely naive and aggressive for someone who, per her records and like that little Bonnet bitch, has computer knowledge. So he is keen to find out more. Was that an emergency? DDoS are low-level threats despite those freaks with basketball heads failing to deploy blackhole routing. It's a damn simple countermeasure used to mitigate a DDoS attack in which network traffic is routed into a "black hole," where it's lost. Why did they fail to do that? Does he have a problem with the MEGS? Should he focus on it immediately and not wait for them to comb the data and present him with results? Maybe? As those thoughts rush through Maléficus's mind, he feels uneasy.

He does not like not being in control of the situation, but each time the MEGS fill him with dread, he always had to hurry toward the farthest corner of the huge hall, away from them, to the place where he has built a lavish sanctuary—approved and paid for by Varga: his own private concert hall. It is a small-scale replica of certain parts of the Westminster Abbey, a royal church in London. Maléficus had it paved with fossiliferous limestone and stone from the Croatian island of Brač, also used in the White House in Washington DC. Several hunky stonemasons from Brač were contracted to build it, to his thrill. They spoke no languages of his own but found a manner of more immediate communication that was lucrative for them all. He also ordered replicas of Plaster Casts (Bosses) from the abbey to adorn the walls and Rodin's original sculptures to beautify the hall. It was his place to relax and reflect, to soar, and to forget by listening to his personal boy's choir. Alas, the organ player had to disappear after he was caught babbling on the phone with his father about the Doomsday Vault and its fascinating pipe organ. They were both sent into oblivion, much to Maléficus's chagrin. But, *ces't la vie*; one can't babble about Varga's secrets, no matter how small, and hope to live.

As Maléficus enters the hall, the boy's choir, comprised of fourteen boys aged eight to twelve, all dressed in white togas and carefully holding candles, furtively exchange fearful glances, each of them assessing the level of Maléficus's mental state in order to figure out if they should look at his face, smiling, as he sometimes required or gaze askew as he demanded other days. He's greeted by Claire K., a gorgeous but mean-looking blonde, a conductor who bows her head in front of Maléficus. Claire has an aura of visible 'fuck off' lingering all around her, so no one sober and sane would ever try to approach her with impure thoughts. She and Maléficus were a match made in heaven, or so Piccolino Scricciolo secretly thought about them.

"We're ready, Maestro," Claire announces.

"Please, indulge me," he softly requests and the boy's choir starts quietly cantillating Hildegard von Bingen's Gregorian Chant "Kyrie Eleison" and Maléficus loses himself in its beauty. That melody of the medieval Roman Catholic Church, sung a cappella, reinvigorates Maléficus's nerves every time he hears it. Yes, he loves his job and he would gladly sacrifice his own life if Varga asks him to, but it's tough, challenging work in front of him every single day, for ages. He does not even remember when he was last on a holiday or any sort of trip for pleasure. But then, his job is his pleasure. And the songs sung to him in those angelic voices are icing on the cake he enjoys like he had used to enjoy a wholly different sort of ice, that of crystal methamphetamine, in the times before Varga came to his rescue in Shanghai's notorious opium den, Avenue Joffre Bar.

The last time he listened to the Gregorian Chant, he was in St. Gellen, Switzerland at the very place where the Abbey of Saint Gall stood millennia ago. Maléficus sighs, indulging in both the song and the memories and thoughts of Sibyl of the Rhine, which was Hildegard's other name. He did not have many nice memories in his life—it was one long, insufferable slew of catastrophes that the bloody bitch, his mother, had ignited when she remarried and allowed a true monster, his stepfather, to enter both his life, his anus, and his mouth, by raping him incessantly over one long, hellish winter near Mystic Beach on the Vancouver Island in Canada. He, whose name is never to be uttered again, had a winter cabin there, more of a shack built out of prefabricated solid wood panels and meant to be used during the hunting season. To Maléficus's utter horror, it was instead his stepfather's raping lair with him as his prey, a devil's den in which he learned the full meaning of pain and hate.

After his mother's mocking response to his pleas for help, he was not willing to suffer anymore and, at the tender age of fourteen, Maleficus killed them both with his stepfather's Timber Classic Marlin 336C hunting rifle and made Hans Böhm, his real name, disappear forever.

Thus Maléficus Ultimo was born. The ultimate meaning of his new name was that he would never reproduce and put a child into this wicked world. Claire K. at first resented Maléficus with all her heart; when she was brought to the Doomsday Vault to conduct concert after concert for him as the only audience, she feared being abused or even worse, raped by that strange-looking, tall, haggard man with a condescending smile that made her feel small and insignificant.

Since he never made a move on her, she started to long for his attention, then even for his touch, something that never happened. Her conducting of the boy's choir had become stellar; she made him cry with her interpretation of mostly Hildegard's divine music, and that was her revenge for being neglected. And yet, over the long, dark nights in the vault's isolation, she wanted him to knock the doors down, barge into her room, and take her violently. She'd be ready to let him have his ways with her. Alas, she knew, it would never happen, and she hated him because of it. She also hated for her music to be interrupted, like now.

Piccolino Scricciolo, panting like a madman on run, rushes into the Maléficus's music sanctuary, never really a good idea for so many reasons, interrupting him for the second time in such a short time, and announces in one breath: "Maestro, Første is positive the girl is the leader. All the others just followed her lead."

"What do you want us to do, Maestro?"

"Bring her to the netherworld and I'll make her drink from the river Lethe, so she can forget and we could start a new life together. In the Esmeralda hotel, right next to the Church of Notre Dame de Paris." Strangely absentminded, Maléficus spells out that nonsense, seemingly to himself. Claire shuddered; oh how much she would love him to talk to her like that.

"Maestro?" Filled with the dread Maestro's words created in him, Piccolino cowers. He's not fond of ambivalent messages—he was born happy to serve. He prefers clear, precise instructions. Thinking requires too much effort. Maléficus comes back to his senses, looks at Piccolino, and hisses.

"Is this why you bothered me? To tell me she led some idiot kids to attack us?"

"No, God forbid." Piccolino almost swooned in fear. "Første discovered more, Maestro," he says and opens his laptop's lid, raising it above his head so Maléficus can look at the picture it displays. Maléficus gasps at the pleasant surprise. It was that same stupid little Bonnet girl, but next to her, a photo of a young kid. He grabs the laptop from Piccolino's small hands and starts typing in.

"Who's the kid?"

"We've run digital forensic analysis for everyone on every photo with the Bonnet girl and anyone. Not too many, as you know, Maestro—those New Athenians are privacy freaks."

"Get to the point."

"His name is Stellan Bonnet. He's her brother."

"Well, well, well," Maléficus sneers to himself and turns to Piccolino. "According to the database, the Bonnet girl does not have any siblings. They must've been hiding him."

That by itself wasn't anything new. Many New Athenians kept their young kids in some sort of digital hiding since the disappearance of children started, and *not very successfully*. Maléficus glances to the Precogs Wall with a smirk, but these Bonnet bastards are something truly interesting.

"What the precogs say?"

The precogs never say a lot; they evaluate connections between subjects in the search for Subject Zero. So the information that Maléficus is asking about is an estimate, in this case a probability.

"The Subject Zero: Confidence Level: 94.70%."

"No way!" Maléficus excitedly yells. *We've gotten many with a much lower level,* he thinks and, after a few fidgety movements of the mouse, he executes a computer routine that waits, ready to send an order into effect any time the confidence level is over 60%; 94.70% means that the little hacker's bitch brother might indeed be the elusive Subject Zero.

After he executes the routine, Maléficus feels pleased with himself. It took him no time to find the attacker, locate her, likely discover the Subject Zero, and put the wheels in motion. Truth be told, he still daren't hope the Bonnet boy was really the Subject Zero, the Holy Grail of the precogs search, but if he is, well, Varga would know how to reward him. Maléficus's heart flutters, filled with anxiety yet again. This time with excitement as well.

He turns to Claire, for the first time noticing how beautiful and sexy this creature is, but his immediate need is that of a feather on God's breath—

Hildegard von Bingen's music. He nods toward the blue-eyed conductor and the Gregorian Chant starts again, taking Maléficus into the spiritual world of visions in which medieval knights roam free.

They Are Coming!
New Athens, Harlem, NYC
March 21, 2048

An alarming scream comes from the Covent Garden park bench. A young schoolgirl is working on her holographic homework when a Drone Detection App's icon—otherwise illegal in all territories but New Athens—located in the upper left corner of her 3D screen starts to frantically blink in red. New Athens people might have disconnected themselves from the ubiquitous world of corporate dominance and its merciless surveillance, but they are not inoculated against the world outside their parameters. The PHOENIX ONE's rise from Central Park several blocks south has lured them in droves onto the streets from which they observe how the world is changing forever.

"Who's coming?" the nearest spectator asks the girl as he looks around.

"Drones!" She jumps to her feet like she's been scared by a big, black tarantula and points toward Lower Manhattan. True, a distinctive whizzing sound, as annoying as the metal buzzing of early morning Sunday's lawnmowers, announces that the drone's arrival is imminent.

"New Athens is out of their jurisdiction. They can't be coming here," the man says to the crowd, who nervously scours the air above their heads. "That's impossible."

"Is that possible?" the schoolgirl scoffs at him and points to the PHOENIX ONE high above them in the sky. The man has no time to answer, for GRIFFIN and his merry little band of drones wizzes by.

Don't Worry, Be Happy

The PHOENIX ONE lets the ravaged Shanghai's image on the huge screens over the horizons sink into the consciousness of billions and dissolve. Then it continues his speech. "Luckily, all that horror is behind you now. I invite you to forget your worries and petty differences and turn to the future with hope." The PHOENIX ONE now sounds encouraging and almost exuberant as it continues, "The true change for humanity and your learning curve will start soon. Until then, my beloved citizens of Earth, don't worry and be happy."

Upon hearing those words, Nastassia jumps on her feet, alarming the good auntie.

"It can't be."

"What?"

"This." Nastassia reaches for Stellan's comic book again and shows it to Auntie. The words "Don't worry, be happy!" are written at the bottom of the cover page.

"I don't understand," yelps Auntie in despair.

Nastassia ignores her confusion as she hurriedly flips through the pages and shows them to the auntie as if it were a self-explanatory example: the one-eyed computer in the sky, a movie theater in the sky. "Stellan predicted this charade!" she says, leaping through the comic book. At the moment that PHOENIX ONE plays the song, she sees the laser beams evaporating the people dancing on the streets. In a ghastly display of parallel worlds working, Nastassia looks at Stellan's book and at the same time observes the lightshow on the darkening sky, which her little brother had depicted when the famous hit from decades ago, *Don't Worry, Be Happy*, sung by Bobby McFerrin, enveloped the globe:

> *Here's a little song I wrote*
> *You might want to sing it note for note*
> *Don't worry, be happy.*
>
> *In every life we have some trouble*
> *But when you worry you make it double*
> *Don't Worry, be Happy.*
> *Don't Worry, be Happy.*

Befuddled masses on the streets look up, confused, glancing at each other, not knowing what to do. But then, together under the PHOENIX ONE's fireworks, they begin to feel like they are in a magical global discotheque. One by one, they laugh and begin to dance their asses off.

> *Ain't got no place to lay your head,*
> *somebody came and took your bed;*
> *Don't Worry, Be Happy.*

At that moment, Nastassia *senses* with every fiber of her body that something truly ominous is hiding in Varga's cards, a foreboding fragment of the misery Varga's going to unleash onto the world. It is her very first glimpse into Varga's otherwise obscured mind, which she had sensed as a tiny, still unrecognizable whiff. And she *knew*, she fully *understood* she'd somehow be in the center of the dark hurricane coming her way. She shivers in dread, not knowing what that might be.

What is Stellan's role in all of that?

Suddenly she feels like going home to hug him, but she can not leave the good auntie; it was their day together and she made her famous roasted mutton with Kartoffelklöße, potato dumplings, and a triple-layer cake with whipped eggs, butter, and sugar in the upper lawyer. The middle layer is a vanilla-quark filling while the bottom layer is made of a sweet yeast dough.

Chapter 6

THE SNATCHING OF STELLAN BONNET

New Athens, Harlem, NYC
March 21, 2048

As it floats suspended high above the earth with its omnipresent green eye, the PHOENIX ONE, Winston Varga's new God, lovingly observes humanity as it dances all over the globe. Earth's first global party has just begun but is already getting crazy. Some of the revelers are eagerly pulling pipes and weed, bent on puffing the magic dragon until he's as mad as the Mad Hatter. If not today, then when? Others are imbibing on Dead Rabbit Irish Whiskey in New York City or on tequila Añejo Noble in Ciudad de México. Some better-known socialites all over the world are losing it, frolicking in a quickie or two, in cars, on the benches, vanishing into strangers' apartments. What the billions of revelers are joyously celebrating, debauching, full of hope beneath their new overlord's benign, all-seeing eye, did not know, is that they are also dancing their last.

No one even notices that the PHOENIX ONE has started to slowly ascend toward its orbital height of 435 km above the Earth's surface. His probes and drones are only within view of those with excellent eyesight

Dance Me to the End of Time

Still holding Stellan's comic book in her hands, Nastassia knows she's witnessing the last dance; the foreboding sense of the hopeless future in store for all those people happily swaying on the streets below overwhelms her as she stares at the PHOENIX's upward move and mulls over its mighty presence. It was such an elaborate spectacle that Nastassia could not help herself wondering, what is that thing's real purpose? She could not fathom why Winston Varga would need such a complicated scheme? Not for a moment did she doubt the truth she'd known since the start of this charade—the PHOENIX ONE works with, rather *for* Varga. The whole governmental transition must have been a global coup d'état, conceived for his nefarious purposes. But no matter how much she tried, she could not invoke an image of the future; not even a hint of Varga's intent was getting clearer to her. Black nothingness stared back at her, the shadows whispering within were too distant and too obscure for her to fathom. The PHOENIX ONE hangs in her senses as an impenetrable fortress, a controlling dark star lingering threateningly over humanity, but all its secrets have been hidden from her.

That was a scary feeling, being lost in the pitch-black darkness.

As she was making a supreme effort, feverishly trying to visualize anything close to the answers she so desperately sought, a strange, rather scary image, not drawn in Stellan's comic but nonetheless forming in front of her mind-eye like a crude picture drawn by Stellan's hand, made her recoil in sheer terror.

"It can't be," she yelps, closing her eyes as the cold sweat begins to trickle down her back. But it was there, the image, like a baby circus monkey chained on the GRIFFIN's back: Stellan kicking and screaming as the drone takes him away, toward the darkness.

"Oh, no!"

It hits her like a ton of bricks.

This is not some nightmare, nor is the image Stellan's talent on display.

This is going to take place now, hidden behind this charade.

Stellan!

She must get to him. And now. Nastassia grabs her bike, and without even saying goodbye to the good auntie who looks at her, puzzled, she storms out of the apartment. In a flash she is on the streets, riding the bike as fast as lightning toward New Athens and her home.

Fugue No. 4 in C sharp Minor
New Athens, Harlem, NYC
May 17, 2047

Stellan and Nastassia's parents, Frédéric and Monique Bonnet's, New Athens apartment is truly a splendid abode, one which might've been found in a house of Parisienne intellectuals during the Jean-Paul Sartre and Simone de Beauvoir times some hundred years ago. De Beauvoir, factually a founder of the women's movement, and Sartre, an influential writer and philosopher, were legendary intellectuals, rebels with a great many causes who talked of freedom, authenticity, and life's difficult choices. They don't make them like that anymore; today they look like relics from the past, when an "influencer" was someone of substance, with no burning need to share their posteriors to millions of followers, but had ideas worth sharing and were not utter morons.

Monique & Frédéric were like those two relics. Old, printed books were everywhere on wall-to-wall bookshelves; miniature busts of famous music composers like J.S. Bach or Richard Callaghan squeezed among the books or awkwardly placed on the top of classics; travel tchotchkes of all sizes and ancestries sat among framed photos mostly from the family's Africa travels; ancient philosophers' portraits and movie posters were everywhere, with a beautiful bust of Arete of Cyrene, a Cyrenaic philosopher, prominently displayed on a bookshelf. Stellan's comic books, both those he had been avidly reading even before he was able to speak and the ones he had drawn himself, were scattered all around the living room. Nastassia and Stellan's parents were not only not bothered by the mess he created, they encouraged Stellan to sit next to "The Last Three," the African white rhino miniature sculpture, below Socrates's poster, while he listened to Johan Sebastian Bach and drew.

Stellan's unusual imagination had been obvious since he was a toddler, as he displayed rare abilities like foreseeing who was coming to pay them an unexpected visit (he used to sketch crude but recognizable pictures of the persons arriving even before they themselves knew they'd stop by) and while his parents did not really understand how such a curious little creature come to be or what his talents really represented, Frédéric and Monique never behaved like there was something strange about him. Frédéric once jokingly told Monique not to worry because "Stellan would one day be a grown-up, and therefore an idiot like the rest of us," but she did not appreciate the joke. "I worry how the world would treat him," she said, a bit anguished.

"You worried about Nastassia too," Frédéric reminded her, "and she turned out to be a fine young lady, despite the hair," and they both laughed. It is not easy to be a parent of an extraordinary child, much less of two prodigies. The underlying worry, something they never spoke aloud in front of Nastassia and Stellan, was the fear they might be precogs. Nastassia's efforts to hide Stellan's uncanny powers did not go unnoticed by Frédéric, but he never said a word. After all, Nastassia never knew that Stellan wasn't registered when he was born. Only in the Shadow Protocol did his data lay safe, secure, and dormant.

Stellan loved math patterns in Bach's music. He had astonished his parents more than once but especially when he mentioned the math structures in the Prelude & Fugue No. 4 in C sharp minor BWV 849. As the music kept playing in their living room, he'd say, "Note how in this fugue we seem to be borne upward, out of the crypt of a mighty cathedral, through the broad nave and onward to the extreme height of the vaulted dome." That was too much even for him, these adult words coming from such a small body and cute kid's face. Frédéric did not let himself reveal how astonished by his son's remark he felt; he himself never had such a deep understanding of Bach.

"How did you get that, Stellan?" he asked.

"I didn't. Andrew Qian and Ferruccio Busoni said that."

"Well then, did you read it?" Frédéric inquired further as he glanced at Monique's gobsmacked expression, nodding and mouthing *all is fine* at her.

"I didn't, it just came to me," Stellan explained.

How it "came to him," he did not elaborate, for at that moment Nastassia entered the apartment and he rushed to hug her, screaming her name like a puppy wagging its tail in joy. He loves his big sister. Nastassia, hugging Stellan, looked at her parent's still astounded faces.

"What did you discover this time," she asked Stellan, kissing his forehead. "My genius, tell me." That picture-perfect image of a happy childhood was something both Nastassia and Stellan enjoyed over the years.

The Snatching of Stellan Bonnet
New Athens, Harlem, NYC
March 21, 2048

Upon receiving an order from Maléficus, GRIFFIN and his drones sprang into action. He needed some help from his friends of the elite Peace Police Team to break the doors of the targeted apartment, and that is what they did, bursting in and crushing the Bonnet family's peace forever.

Frozen under the green light emanating from GRIFFIN, Frédéric yells, "You have no right to barge in! New Athens is out of your jurisdiction!"

GRIFFIN replies, somewhat amused, "Overruled."

The Peace Police snatches Stellan and runs away with him. Still frozen under the green light, Frédéric yells, "Stellan!" who, kicking the police officer, yells back, "Dad!" and keeps fighting. "Let me go, let me go!" he screams in vain, like a snatched little lamb in a golden eagle's talons.

The drones leave, liberating the Bonnets from the green-light snare. Monique follows Frédéric, who runs like the devil downstairs and to the streets. Both the drones and the Peace Police are out of sight. She sits at the curb and stares into nothingness, sobbing inside, feeling like her womb was torn apart and is bleeding. Stellan's screams keep piercing her ears she covers her trembling arms. *This is how utter loss feels.* Frédéric sits next to her and embraces her.

"We will get him back," he whispers, placing a gentle kiss on her temple and wiping off her tears. While humanity over the world was dancing all to the music coming from the skies, no one in New Athens had even noticed what happened. Nastassia arrives at that moment, seconds too late, and jumps off the bike and rushes to Frédéric and Monique.

"Dad, Mom, what's going on? Where's Stellan?"

What neither of them notice in the dreadful excitement that's shaking them to the core is a man sitting in a Honda Chopper bike, a man who had been following Nastassia all that time, Jeremiah DeJohn. This time he has a full biker's outfit on him and wears a helmet with four hidden cameras on it, covering 360° around him. It also transmits as a live video stream a full 360° immersive video, straight to the AUTOMATA servers. *This must be a breakthrough,* Jeremiah thinks.

The Amusement Park
New Athens, Harlem, NYC
March 21, 2048

    Frédéric Bonnet looks at his daughter and hugs her without a word. The pain is too strong for words. Nastassia's too upset to enjoy the hug and impatiently wiggles out of his embrace, almost scolding him with a sharp, "Dad!" but upon seeing his face she stops in her tracks. Her father looks years older, wrinkles around his eyes new and deep; he seems almost crushed. Even his hair seems to have gotten several grey hairs. But his eyes truly frighten her. Their trademark warm gaze is gone; he looks more inward than at her. Nastassia is startled both by his look and that strange stare but is a bit relieved hearing his, still calm, always-reassuring voice.

    "We can't talk here. Come with me."
    "Why? What's going on?"
    "I want you to meet someone."
    "Who?"
    "You'll see. Just follow me, please."

    Frédéric rushes out and continues toward the nearby New Athens Amusement Park and its ancient bumper cars section. It's noisy, somehow smelly, and rusty. At a loss, Nastassia follows her father, perplexed, but says nothing as she strides beside him. The amusement park is a world of its own, looking like Uruguay's Montevideo has been placed in some Wes Anderson movie, edited by Scorsese's Thelma Schoonmaker and blasted by Baz Luhrmann and Stephen Adly Guirgis's chosen soundtracks. Whom they are going to meet in this place? It just made no sense, none of it.

    "We need to wait a bit. Let's take a ride," Frédéric says.
    "What are we doing here? Dad, where's Stellan? Tell me already."

    Frédéric jumps into a green car, Nastassia follows him and they immediately, forcefully collide with another car.

    The two kids riding it yell at Nastassia and Frédéric, "Losers!"

    Nastassia flips them off. They chuckle but leave, chasing after another victim, a guy with a helmet and a little kid sitting on his knees. Jeremiah had given a hundred bucks to the kid's parents to be as inconspicuous as possible. Perhaps such camouflage wasn't necessary, given the state his surveillance subject is in, but it's always better to be safe than sorry, or so his SHE Guidance Manual repeated ad nauseum throughout its six hundred pages.

Frédéric turns to Nastassia and starts talking in a strange, somehow disconnected manner. She looks at him, confused all over again, and wonders who that man is who is driving the damn bumper car, green at that, but listens to Frédéric attentively anyway. She can not help but notice the bizarre environment in which he speaks—that of dodging bumper cars in a noisy, ancient amusement park, while by far the most unbearable song of all time, Taylor Swift's "Style" blasts from the speakers.

Nastassia, barely perceptibly, shakes her shoulders and disconnects from the old lady's pan-demoniacal noise to refocus on her father's strange speech. "We were resisting the digital, totalitarian world of the new breed of fascism—corporatism and its tyranny best embodied in Varga and his minions. All we wanted was a multi-collaborative culture and enhanced human creativity in New Athens." Another car bumps them. "Don't you ever forget that. This is the world we wanted for you, the world of freedom and creativity, excitement, realness that has been lost since. We did not want our children to grow up in a world in which winds had stopped whispering ancient stories, in which you would never see a savanna elephant in person. Or plant an African daisy, all of which were replaced by AI cyborgs and quantum fables of the world that we're utterly unable to inhabit; the AI already live in a different world, with speed beyond us and our senses, the world into which we're unable to follow."

"Why are you telling me this now?"

"I never wanted any of this for you. You're too young to be pulled into all that."

"Into what?" Nastassia looks at her father, puzzled. "Dad, what are you talking about?"

"The war."

"The war?"

"Both you and your brother have extraordinary skills." Frédéric smiles, an inexplicable deep sadness in his tearful eyes, looking at Nastassia. "I have known since you were three how you tried to hide those deep insights, your precog skills, the ability you honed to perfection when Stellan was born, in order to protect him. I am very proud of you, my darling." He pauses with a heavy sigh. "The war I am telling you about is the war you would have to fight in order to save your very lives."

"Dad?"

"I am so sorry we let you cope with your abilities all by yourself. We hoped it would pass or that Varga would not need to harness your talents and that he would let you all just be kids." Frédéric's voice broke. "We were so naive. So stupid. We failed you. I am so sorry, as we let you protect Stellan from us, we failed to protect you from Varga. I failed you."

The siren announces that the electric grid is disconnected; their time is up and the bumper cars stop. They wobble toward Monique. Nastassia keeps side-glancing at Frédéric. His cryptic words are now crystal clear to her. The time has come, she *knows* this, even as she asks him a question to which she also already knows the answer.

"Where's Stellan, Dad?"

"Come on, Nastassia. You know he was kidnapped."

"Why are you telling me this in an amusement park?" she almost yells, refusing to accept what she knew.

"Calm down, darling," Frédéric says, glancing at an ice-cream vendor sauntering their way. A dark shadow crosses his eyes as he glances at Monique, who stands frozen and glances from the ice-cream vendor back to him. *The time has come*, indeed—the understanding passes in between them as dark as the shadow of past lives. Nastassia notices something's going on but is too upset to really understand.

Then Frédéric goes into the Twilight Zone. "Let's have an ice cream."

"Truly, Frédéric?" She has never called her father Frédéric, so he stops in midstep, looking at her as she scolds him. "An ice cream? Have you totally lost your mind?"

Monique intervenes. "Dear—"

Nastassia cuts her off, "Don't *dear* me, Mom." She continues talking to Frédéric. "Angelo was right. You two are freaks. You tell me Stellan was kidnapped and now want me to eat an ice cream?"

The vendor stops moving. He carefully listens to her while pretending to align invisible ropes and knots on his ice cream cart.

"New Athens is excluded from surveillance. It's the only place the PHOENIX and its drones do not listen all the time. It's the law," Monique says, trying to calm Nastassia despite Frédéric's faint smile. He knows Monique is just buying time. Nastassia is so furious that her parents' silent communication completely eluded her.

"It's the law?" she cackles, working herself up to a real rage, while some bystanders turn their heads. "They snatched Stellan lawfully then? What say you? Was it legal? And what? They do not listen?" Nastassia spreads her arms, showing everything around. "They can hear you breathe. Every damn insect is a drone, spying for that fucking thing above." She points toward the PHOENIX ONE that motionlessly hangs in the sky. Monique looks around at the people forming a wide circle around Nastassia as she paces around.

"Nastassia! The language."

"The language? The *language*?" Nastassia keeps pacing, going in small circles, gesticulating wildly, unable to talk and stand still. "Hummingbirds were bombing Shanghai," she says loudly. "Butterfly Reapers led the first laser attack on Occupy Wall Street some fifty years ago. Where do you live?" She slaps herself on the forehead. "Ah, yeah, you were boondoggling. Sorry, I mean passively resisting."

Frédéric steps in. "Calm down, darling."

Nastassia has none of it. But, as she was getting worked up, a nagging feeling was signaling her: *you're delaying the inevitable, my dear.* The world she knew existed, the world of pain, the world she saw coming is waiting no more. The time has come, the time of blood, sweat, and tears; the time for war is here, there, neverwhere, everywhere. Stellan's gone, childhood has ended for him, once for all. These thoughts make her inexplicably sad.

She continues with her little performance, more disconnected from it with each passing second. She continues her exercise because it feels like purging of the old. For some reason, a part of her brain is focused on that ice cream vendor, lingering nearby.

"The nanobots they'll use would spy on your thoughts."

A bookish-looking passerby, Brian, stops, looks at Nastassia, and addresses his young female companion, "How does a New Athens luddite kid know about the nanobots?"

Nastassia shoots him an angry glance, so he shuts up, sensing the power of her burning gaze, and turns back to her father, pointing to the PHOENIX ONE. "That thing serves to intimidate the world. Just look at it. A new god of a so-called peaceful era in which you're no more than cattle spied upon and controlled," Nastassia says quietly, losing her steam.

"Well, the people were always a herd of cattle," Brian says, gathering his wits and interrupting her again.

She fires a nuclear glance at him. "What qualifies a dim-witted nincompoop like you to meddle in the other people's business?" He shrinks back, so Nastassia turns back to Frédéric and Monique. "And you're telling me they cannot hear us here? They are everywhere. You can't be sure even this nincompoop is not one of them."

Frédéric glances at the ice cream vendor, steps toward her, and speaks calmly, emphasizing every word. "Nastassia, darling, listen to me for once in your life and let us have that ice cream." Then, barely perceptible, Frédéric winks at her. There were worlds lingering in between them, unspoken histories of pain and struggle and a whiff of what's to come. Nastassia gazes at him for a second, for the first time today truly *understanding* her father. He *knows* what he's doing, he always did, and while not averting her eyes from his burning gaze filled with steely strength and deep sadness, she nods.

"Sure, why not."

They move toward the old ice cream cart as the vendor fidgets around, fixing the unfixable. *I knew it.* The thought flashes through Nastassia's mind. *I bloody knew it. But that's impossible.* She looks at the ice cream vendor seeking confirmation.

"Two ice creams please," Frédéric orders. The old man, wearing a colorful woolen hat has his head buried in the compartment, as he looks for a particular flair.

Jeremiah de John zooms in on the old man and runs facial recognition software against an enormous base AUTOMATA had ready for him. It crunches the data and comes back with a 74% certainty that the old ice cream vendor is Dr. Richard A. Rutherford, a.k.a. the Renegade. Jeremiah gasps. No one in the Surveillance's Human Evaluators network knew who was in charge of surveilling the Renegade. The rumors were rampant that Winston Varga himself put a billion-dollar reward on his head but no one was sure. No one has ever seen him or come close to him, not once after his Nobel prize. There were only a few old photos of him, one in the *New York Times* profile of Grey Ghost, as they called him, another from the MIT yearbook. He did not attend the Nobel Prize award ceremony in Stockholm so the available photos were all but recent. And yet, the ISY facial recognition gave 74% that the man right across of him must be the Renegade, a man, Jeremiah de John was fully aware, Winston Varga hated more than anyone else. *This is huge*, he thinks and presses an alarm button that, unbeknown to him, bypasses AUTOMATA and goes straight to the Doomsday Vault, blipping in red on all Maléficus's computers.

Strawberry Ice Cream

The old man makes a strawberry flavored ice cream, stands erect, and turns his deep, dark eyes toward Nastassia, smiling at her. Nastassia's awe-struck gazing at his grey eyes.

"No way!" She looks around. "Renegade… but is that really you? But… how?" She averts her eyes toward PHOENIX ONE. "They are everywhere. They'll find you in a sec." The Renegade hands her an ice cream.

"I believe strawberry is your flavor."

PHOENIX ONE's eye flashes and turns toward New Athens. Frédéric looks up, spotting the movement. *He must act now*, he thinks, and with the pain of a thousand crushed hearts, he forcefully pushes Nastassia toward the ice cream cart.

"Dad?"

The Doomsday Seed Vault
Norway, Spitsbergen
March 21, 2048

Maléficus Ultimo, who has been eagerly waiting for Stellan Bonnet to arrive at the vault and has been closely following Nastassia's every move via Jeremiah's live 3D feed, takes a step forward toward the screen displaying her and Frédéric Bonnet. He zooms into the awning covering the ice cream cart but can't see a thing. Then a ping of Jeremiah's data alerts him of the discovery.

The Renegade? At 74% certainty?

Maléficus changes the camera angle, zooms in closer, enlarging the feed many times, leaning toward the screen. For a split second, the Renegade's eyes face the camera as he passes the ice cream to Nastassia and winks at her.

That can't be anyone else but the Renegade. "Motherfucker!" Maleficus roars right into Jeremiah's ear, "Kill them! Kill them now!"

Startled and frightened, Jeremiah whispers back.

"I am not armed."

Maléficus curses, frantically typing into the keyboard.

The Escape
New Athens, Harlem, NYC
March 21, 2048

The Renegade grabs Nastassia by hand, pulls her in, and quickly presses a hidden button on his ice cream cart all in one blistering move. What pops up would have astonished Nastassia had she been in the position to observe the effect of it, but she isn't—she is inside a scientific miracle. It makes onlookers let out a collective sigh of awe as they witness how Nastassia and the Renegade vanish together with his ice cream cart. Now, J.K. Rowling would've simply used the cloak of invisibility here and gotten away with its magical properties, but the Renegade isn't a writer for children, prone to fantasizing about unrealistic stuff. He's rather a hard-core scientist who made fantasies appear as real. The optical invisibility cloak made of plasmonic graphene meta-surfaces, whose sub-micron thickness makes it lighter than air, was indeed a very advanced tech. It was invented quite a while ago by The Renedage himself and Professor Sir John Pendry, the Chair in Theoretical Solid State Physics at the Imperial College London until his retirement in 2042, when he was ninety-nine years old.

"Run!" he screams at Nastassia and, when she hesitates, looking back at her mom and dad, adds, "Frédéric can take care of themselves. Run!" He starts running like a decades-younger sprinter, pushing the ice cream cart and the cover it had created for them forward.

"They are toast," Brian pontificates to his girlfriend. "Invisible cloaks are banned."

"Shut the fuck up!" Frédéric hisses to Brian and turns to the spot where Nastassia stood just seconds ago and yells after her.

"Run, Nastassia, run!"

Nastassia wizzes away with Renegade, running like hell.

Renegade stops running just over the big manhole, he lifts it and pushes Nastassia down, "Down! Go down! Hurry," he says and helps her down the manhole. He forcefully pushes the ice cream cart as far away from their escape route as possible and puts the manhole cover back just in time before it's seen. They disappear underground.

The Doomsday Seed Vault
Norway, Spitsbergen
March 21, 2048

  At that moment, just as the manhole covers the Renegade and Nastassia's escape route, the PHOENIX ONE receives the order from Maléficus's computer and fires a devastating high-energy fiber laser, scorching the land where the ice cream cart stood just seconds ago. The girl screams and falls into Brian's embrace. They both fall down, clinging to each other.

  "Little slut! Motherfucker! You'll taste your own medicine!" Maléficus shakes in rage, directing the PHOENIX's laser. It fires another devastating beam that strikes again and kills Nastassia's mom and dad, Frédéric and Monique Bonnet, on the spot.

Part Two

MANIFEST DESTINY

Chapter 7

CHILDHOOD'S END

Bluff, Utah
October 11, 2008

On that cold, sunny day three long decades ago, an event Winston Varga has never spoken about to anyone for years, took place in, of all places, Bluff, UT. His father, Jeff Varga, had stormed out of their home and went straight to drinking.

"Cutthroat Pale Ale please," Jeff ordered from a jaded waitress. Nancy was her name, blue like jazz were her eyes. Jeff raised his beer glass toward the sunrays pouring in through the "Comb Ridge Eat + Drink's" window. "It has such a nice, dark copper color. Almost amber. With its thick, frothy off-white foam. It tastes like an Italian opera. Opulent. It also tastes like love. Bitter." He took a big swig and made a big "C" out of his fingers, ordering another one. "I can't stop wondering why they named it *Cutthroat?*"

"No clue, honey," Nancy said, noticing that he was pouring whiskey from his hip flask into the beer's glass. "I shouldn't allow you to do that. You'll get all biffed."

"Cut me some slack, Queen of Bluff. I celebrate today."

"You celebrate way too much, honey, if you don't mind me saying."

"I do mind. Bugger off."

"Suit yourself." She frowned. "But let me remind you that we don't appreciate such language around here, Jeff."

"Language? Don't talk to me about language," Jeff murmured to himself. "Language. My first love. My only love. My lost love. My lost words. Borne out of words of love. Son. My lost son. Child of my groin. Sin of my crotch. Fart of Helen's loins. The spawn of my imagination. The rotten spawn." Jeff laughed at his nebulous—he thought fabulous—ad hoc poetry in prose no one would ever read or hear. But, he chuckled quietly, like a cartoon character snickering to himself as he suppressed his tone, wanting to sit there and drink 'til the end of time. Nancy was shooting displeased glances at him; he did not want to risk being thrown out. For even then and there, at the farthest end of the lonely hell that was his life, there was no glittering, comical *Restaurant at the End of the Universe* full of cute characters Nope, he'd still have no one to go to. His own family hated him, he had sensed that with every bone in his body for quite some time. They'd rather have him dead than under the same roof. He knew that. No one else to turn to. Not even sin-eaters would eat bread and salt off his dead body in order to absolve him.

"I am a sinner," he suddenly blurted out, quite loudly at that.

"We all are, hon. Be quiet." Nancy had no time for him, for a bevy of new patrons were coming into the restaurant in hungry, cheerful troves, as merry as only famished Utahns were when their order of Big Bluff Benedict Brunch Burger is close at hand.

Jeff kept talking to himself, thinking incoherently. It gave him a strange sense of pleasure, the scent of his thoughts he had followed going nowhere. Pour one more drink at the rainbow's dark side. The one for dead poets. No one ever understood him. The delightful derision of his multi-layered poems and wittily packaged caprice of his words eluded editors and readers alike. He and his words stood alone against the world. Rather, against the universe. *Never go against the family*, Don Corleone said, bestowing his wisdom upon many a young man as himself, and boy, didn't he do everything for his family? He sacrificed everything for love. he even came here, to this God-forsaken place, rather to this Jesus Christ of Latter-day Saints-forsaken place, for her. And what was he given in return? Misunderstanding of his genius. Isolation and, ultimately, scorn. What did he do to deserve such disrespectful treatment? A few drinks here and there he used to have, he admits, but that's nothing to be ashamed of, those are nothing. He's as strong as a bull, he can hold his drink. And yet... Helen closed her heart and her legs for him a lifetime of passion ago. She killed hope. She slaughtered tomorrow. I wasn't good enough for her. I never was. Never good enough. How could one compare with those ancient Gods and heroes she worshipped? How, you tell me? Yet, when I fucked her to make that fuckwit son of hers, she did not complain. Eager whore who lured him into marriage after the first fuck. The first sin. His Elena was lost. What was left was Helen. That sluttish, wanton Helen. Hellen. Hell. He needed another beer. And yet another. His flask had enough whiskey to cement that amber beer with some real liquor and kill its caramel-like flavor. Just give it to me, give it to me like there's no tomorrow.

Better yet, give me one more, for tomorrow belongs to me.

Mother, Eleni Galanis

Eleni (Helen) Varga née Galanis, Winston's mother, was born on Christmas Eve 1969 in Chania Crete, but her family immigrated to the United States of America days after The Junta, Greek's seven-year-long dictatorship regime, ended in July of 1974. Her family started a new life in Tarpon Springs, a city on central Florida's Gulf Coast, known for a vibrant Greek community and sea sponges, those odd hermaphroditic multicellular animals without organs, muscles, or nerves—very unlike that bundle of energy, babbling Sponge Bob Winston, loved as a little child. Truth to be told, neither the pervasive sponges nor syrtaki were strangers in that alien part of the world, the mythical America that became Eleni's new home. Her mother Agatha took a job in the quaint little bookstore of the Saint Nicholas Greek Orthodox Cathedral and has instilled a love for history and literature in Eleni since her early age, something she'd pass on to Winston decades later.

Georgios Galanis, Eleni's father, was working as an assistant priest at the same church. He was an aloof man, always too busy for her. Somehow, likely due to her mom's striking physical beauty, he did not neglect the copious amount of booty-sex he had had with Agatha daily, something that always terrified Eleni in the mornings; the noise of early-morning sex coming from their room, and the scent of their bodies afterward created an utter horror in her. Even as a small child, Eleni knew that Athena, the goddess of war and wisdom, was born from Zeus's head so all that business about love and birth was a scary affair to her. It crept into her consciousness like an evil clown would on Friday the 13th, when the night is long, the wind is cold and the shadows are scary. But nothing was as terrifying as her mom's loud moaning behind closed doors; Eleni feared her mom might die screaming. Perhaps only her father's smug expression when he sat down for breakfast and kept ogling his wife's curves, blissfully unaware of Eleni's presence and her confusion, was even more panic-inducing than the noise that horrified her. He somehow seemed wicked when he smirked, and that frightened Eleni.

Father, Jeff Varga

It was on the Dodecanese Boulevard in Tarpon Springs where Eleni, now Helen, often took long walks. She had a burning longing for the sweet aromas of Chania's street food, which she adored as a tiny lassie prowling about Chania for all the mysterious and exciting scents her granny's kitchen had produced, and she found again on the Dodecanese. It was also on that noisy boulevard where she, a tall, black-haired, dark-eyed, willowy beauty, a precocious seventeen-year-old girl, also found the love of her life, Jeff Varga, a local heartthrob. Jeff was a writer whose modicum of success, after two of his short stories were published in *Festus Literary Magazine* from Tallahassee, made him believe he was the next Ernest Hemingway or maybe even someone as tormented and great as Franz Kafka. Or, dare he dream, F. Scott Fitzgerald or Fyodor M. Dostoyevsky. Such confidence, his unruly lock of green-painted hair, and his swagger were irresistible to Helen. She fell head over heels in love with that young man whose swashbuckling couture and velvety Southern twang made her melt every time he called her "my Helen of Troy," his nickname for Eleni / Helen.

To the utter horror of her parents and Winston's grandparents, Helen secretly married Jeff as soon as she celebrated her eighteenth birthday and told them once it was a done deal. No sane Greek family would ever condone their smart and beautiful daughter's marriage to a budding writer, much less to a non-Greek writer at the very dubious start of his career, and even less so to a writer whose only connection to Greek culture was his fondness for Metaxa brandy, Greek amber spirit—something, rumor has it, he loved even more than Helen. The pressure from the family, the paragon of its Greek Orthodox chaste orthodoxy bundle of virtues, and the whole community that worshipped Helen and secretly despised Jeff made them feel like unwanted strangers in their own neighborhood. Helen also had problems coping with a niggling uncertainty about Jeff that some of her girlfriends tried to impress upon her, so they left as soon as they were married, without saying goodbye to anyone. The scandal shattered Tarpon Spring's Greek community and everyone was buzzing about it for a while, but soon afterward everyone went on about their own lives. Helen and Jeff were gone, so no one could claim the honor of casting the first stone at them anyway. Georgios never forgave her for what he called her betrayal and forbade Agatha from having any contact with Eleni, "dead for him" since. She was an outcast, ostracized from her former community and her family alike.

On the Road

Unaware of the gravity of their actions at first and filled with joyful excitement, love, and supported with *On the Road* by Jack Kerouac nestled in Helen's purse, they drove across the mythical American vastness in search of a new home. A new life. They were unfazed by the kerfuffle they left behind, blissfully aware only of their love. Zipped around America they have. What a land! The ghost lights of Marfa, Texas and its intriguing nocturnal lights that shone and danced its ancient rhythms filled their hearts with joy. A mercury-mining ghost town, Terlingua, not so far away from Marfa, and its scary old cemetery made them recoil in sweet dread as they passionately kissed under the morning sun. Roswell, New Mexico, in the "Land of Enchantment" had, well, enchanted them with its mysteries. Had Helen's diary of the "Freedom Trip," as she titled it, not been burned years later it would've been a plentiful source of allure imbibed with all their senses. How young and foolish, how happy they had been. Even Jeff, ever prone to sudden rage snaps, was mellow and loving throughout their trip toward their happy future together.

After weeks of driving around America, they could not have found a place more different from Tarpon Springs, FL than Bluff, UT was, so they settled among the ancient red rocks that gave them a sense of peace as they spoke of ancient times with an echo of all-encompassing myths going back in time for eons. Helen and Jeff were crazy for each other. Moreover, they both had fallen madly in love with the nearby Monument Valley. In fact, some of Jeff's best writing was inspired by the Monument Valley before his dreams were shattered due to a stupid, drunken mistake.

An Error of Judgment

"Take this for the truth: the ground is wet, the leaves are green, and the man next door drives a big truck. The cup on the desk you used to drink beer

out of once in a land called Germany (when you were young and foolish) now holds dust, spiders, and the stubs of your pencils. But don't panic. Just take a deep breath and try to realize that this is the way life goes." The poem in prose titled *The Way Life Goes* was his disgrace and ultimate downfall—the beginning of the end of Jeff as a writer. During one drunken binge caused by a long writer's block, he sent that poem to *Bluffs Literary Magazine* in Peoria, Illinois. The magazine's editor, a young Mr. Prince, eagerly published it as Jeff Varga's, fully unaware Jeff quoted, verbatim and in full, John Bennet's poem of the same title.

Mr. Bennet was the founder of Vagabond Press and quite a well-known writer in his own right, so such misattribution of his wonderful literary work immediately caused a minor scandal in lettered circles always eager to devour its own. Despite his loud protestations that he did not plagiarize Bennet and that it was a joke on Mr. Prince's pretentious name (the editor used no first name) and his pompous illiteracy, Jeff was done and finished as a serious poet. That was a blow that he never recovered from, and it started a slow descent into merciless oblivion.

Starry Nights

Jeff and Helen's lovemaking never felt truer to god than when it was made under the Valley's wide night skies filled with stars. Born out of such starry night's lovemaking, Winston Varga saw the light of the day on the Halloween evening of October 31, 1990, when he cried his first to his mom's tired, blessed happiness.

Her mother Elena used to quote Plutarch. "The good tutor ought to be such a one as was Phœnix, the tutor of Achilles" and started tutoring him at the very early age of three. From such an early age he was immersed in the world of ancient Greek myths and tragedies, a natural start for his historical and literary education. Helen read to him every night and after she kissed him goodnight, he wanted to be as wise as Socrates and as heroic as Achilles. When he was seven years old, he wrote Helen a poem for her thirty-first birthday, titled *Thanking My Mom's Fatigue* only to end up being belittled by his father's drunken mockery. Helen's protestations did not help him so Winston at that point withdrew into himself and the books he had devoured fanatically ever since, never to write poetry again.

He learned that "enthusiasm" came from the Greek word "enthous," which means possessed by god so he decided to be some sort of enthusiastic hero, unknown to all but the gods. Perhaps as a sailor, who navigates the world discovering hidden treasures? A mythical wanderer? After all, we call it the Arctic because sailors navigated toward it using Ursa Major as a guide. "Arktos" is Greek for "bear." Winston was so proud to have had Greek ancestors and his mom goddess Eleni to teach him about all sorts of wonders from the past they shared, in the language Jeff could not speak.

He also longed for love. It was always, of course, a tragic love, as Helen of Troy and Paris's had been. In his young confusion, Winston had also dreamed of finding a Juliet to his Romeo. Sadly, Bluff, UT wasn't exactly a wellspring of exciting young girls looking for a withdrawn-into-his-shell, nerdy boy. They were strange creatures anyway, those funny little girls that played with Barbies, had freckles like that snotty JoAnn he had a crush on, and babbled nonsense all the time. In rare interactions with the peculiar beings, Winston had, for the first time, discovered the exquisite art of pretending, which was so highly valued among adults. He was quite *nonchalant*—that was one of his mum's favorite words, right next to the French *bisou* (kiss), English *tintinnabulation*, the Italian *arcobaleno* and its English translation, the *rainbow*—when attempting to talk to the girls. They reciprocated by ignoring him, so Winston had never even stolen a kiss. Such a pain. JoAnn even mocked him. "Nerd," was her insult added to the injury of laughter that followed him as he ran away in shame. He was left to reading; all those language-murdering, living dolls and their "*I was like this…*" or "*she was like that…*" or "*watevs*" made him cringe. Don't let him go on about their moms' "*darlings*" and "*awesomes*," which they used for nearly everything, severely inflicted by the mythomania of everything being awesome and their daughters being the most awesome darlings of all the damned awesomes. Achilles never said "whatever" or "awesome." Homer never wrote "and he was like… watevs." Winston was never able to understand those girls.

He did, however, keep daydreaming about girls until several years later when he found "a practice of exorcism used to expel the inner demons which torments a man or woman, masturbation." (This quote is attributed to the deep online thinker "Zogato" who has never been cited in any important work of art or science until this very moment.)

Once he discovered Lisbeth Salander's character, a hacker who possessed an uncanny photographic memory and legendary hacking skills, Winston, then already a teenager with quite advanced computer skills, wanted to be a hacking loner, some sort of legendary urban hero à la Batman or at least like Neo. Then his Juliet would find him, not the other way around. After all, "love is like a shadow, when you chase it, it runs away, when you turn back and walk away, it follows you," an old Arab proverb taught him. Alas, it would take quite some time before he encountered the exquisite art of lovemaking.

They were poor, Winston understood that, chiefly because of his spendthrift father who always squandered at least a half of his meager salary, when he worked at all, on liquor. But Helen made sure Winston never wanted for anything, even if that meant she had to hide money from Jeff who drank more and more as his failures as a writer haunted him and his odd, bullshit jobs emptied his soul until he became a sorry eggshell of his former lady's-man persona, a slobbering bozo whose quasi-literary drivel no one wanted to read or hear. Jeff's unwarranted anger and episodes of his drunken screaming rage grew more frequent, much to Helen's dismay and her profound sadness. It pained Winston to see his mom in pain and so unhappy. Helen's filigree soul and her strong, ancient spirit deserved better. He swore to help her be happy.

ILOVEYOU

At the turn of the millennium, for the New Year 2000, Winston asked his mom for a computer and sure enough, despite his father's objections, he was given his first PC. It was a Dell Computer, a shiny little toy powered by a 1.5GHz Pentium 4 processor and supported by 128MB of memory. Those are comical specs—no apps existing today would work on such an ancient machine, but Winston Varga proudly keeps it in the Varga Tech Museum in Ann Arbor, Michigan. It was that Dell on which he had cut his programming teeth and entered a whole new world, then known as *cyberspace*, a world in which everyone was equal, but some, those able to understand the computer systems better, were more equal than others. The internet was in full swing already, and Winston had a plethora of worlds to explore and, to his mom's growing concerns, he had started to neglect books, as he was spending more and more time behind the computer screen.

His first computer was preloaded with Windows 2000, a pure disaster replete with security flaws and inundated by a flood of vulnerabilities. Then, on May 5th of 2000, a notorious ILOVEYOU computer worm arrived and infected young Winston's computer, the notorious Love Letter Virus. It originated in the Philippines and began infecting computers on that day. It spread by emails, jumping from a computer to a computer with the subject line "ILOVEYOU" and an attachment, "LOVE-LETTER-FOR-YOU.txt.vbs." If the attachment was opened, a Visual Basic script was executed, and the computer was infected. Many recipients were fooled because Microsoft Windows, in its wisdom, concealed the extension of the file, and it was mistaken for a simple text file. Once executed, the script then emailed itself to everyone in the victim's contact list, edited the Windows Registry to execute the worm at startup, and replaced the data in many computer files, including JPEG images and Word documents, with copies of itself.

Within ten days, the virus have infected 10% of all the networked computers in the world, costing $15 billion to remove in the United States alone; the media was all over it so Winston watched all that was said on the topic on TV and read all he could about the fascinating phenomena. He managed to delete the virus from his computer within hours after it had infected it. That was a blessing in disguise, the virus's global attack, for that computing calamity created the first business opportunity for a computer-fledgling like Varga. Soon after he was removing VBScript Script Files and Windows Scripting Hosts accessories from the infected computers of several family friends, and then local businesses, and he earned his first monies. That was a thrill he had never forgotten. A breezy boon with a dollar sign on it was given to his sails to propel it toward a bright future, a manna from heavens that changed his life for good.

Even more so, he truly enjoyed seeing how helpless grown-ups were in front of a machine they did not understand. He had a field day seeing how much power over those ignorants his computer knowledge gave him, despite his age (he was ten at the time.)

Once you have established your reputation, no matter if you're a human or a machine, they trust you without doubt, these all-too-fallible humans. That was the most valuable lesson Winston Varga learned from the ILOVEYOU virus, God bless its vicious, malicious code. The people are gullible beyond belief but they need trust in order to function.

Anarchy in the USA

There was nothing to do in Bluff, UT for a boy of his age, so while he was scouring Mom's library in search of computer books, Winston Varga found Pierre-Joseph Proudhon's book *The General Idea of the Revolution in the Nineteenth Century* instead. That was a book he did not understand at all but had read from cover to cover anyway. It was something different, almost mystical in a narrative that did not use heroes or gods to convey its message. On his first day at school it all made sense. The words "*To be GOVERNED is to be at every operation, at every transaction noted, registered, counted, taxed, stamped, measured, numbered, assessed, licensed, authorized, admonished, prevented, forbidden, reformed, corrected, punished*," resonated with him so strongly that upon finishing his first day at school that year, he proudly and loudly pronounced himself an anarchist.

Jeff, his wastrel father, had again showed no appreciation for his brilliant, curious child and made fun of Winston the Anarchist. "Why are you being so modest?" Jeff ridiculed him. "Why not Antichrist outright?" He laughed at Winston and left for a beer, his daily fuel those days. Winston's fragile body, somehow feminine face, and keen mind were strikingly similar to Helen's, so Jeff could not help but resent his son; Winston was a mirror image of the failure he had become, a disappointment to Helen she had never shown outright but that Jeff saw in Winston's eyes. It was a crushing feeling, which he'd been unable to truly recognize or to cope with.

Strangely enough, Winston wasn't hurt by his father's refusal to engage with him. Instead, he went online to find out what "Antichrist" meant. Thereupon, armed with his own understanding, Winston started to detest Jeff's ignorance and arrogance. Being a bookworm child turned computer programmer he understood the basics of IF→THEN, a conditional expression of a programming language, and he applied it, first to his father and later to humanity as a whole. IF ignorant THEN idiot; IF ignorant THEN gullible; IF ignorant and gullible THEN truly worthless, like Jeff.

Winston's brain raced as he decided to amass as much knowledge and money as possible, never to be an ignorant, worthless slob like his father must have been all his life. To young Winston, Jeff's cowardly refusal to appreciate the poem he wrote for Eleni, his computer prowess, his anarchism, and his sense of humor were signs of weakness. Jeff had once beaten him because of a joke after telling him to go to bed, to which Winston, deeply immersed in programming an Excel sheet so it would better work with Vlookup, replied with "as soon as I am done cleaning my guns." For some inexplicable reason that enraged Jeff so much that he began beating Winston until he bled, for Winston did not cry, ever, which further enraged his father. Winston Varga swore to himself never to be weak, and tears were a sure sign of weakness he thought.

He used every opportunity, when Jeff wasn't at home, to keep scouring Mom's library. He did not read as much as before; he used the Net, namely Infoseek search engine, to expand ideas those books provided him with. When Infoseek was sold in the summer of 2000, Winston Varga found a Google search engine. That was something entirely different, the tech and a philosophy world apart from any other portals or search engines of that time. It was a simple page, nothing on it, no gimmicks or fancy graphs just a logo and those powerful words, "Search the web using Google." Varga read how "Google uses sophisticated next-generation technology to produce the right results fast with every query. Google returns relevant results because it responds to your query using an automated method that ranks relevant websites based on the link structure of the internet itself," and wanting to know more, he started to study its PageRank™ technology. He was hooked. At that time, Google was still accessible by the commoners and had a googlebot@google.com email address available for everyone. Winston wrote to it but never received an answer. Had Google bothered to reply to a young, curious boy, history might have taken a totally different course.

We'll never know.

Winston Varga read Google's corporate motto, "Don't be evil," and smelled the bullshit outright. From the start, he saw and somehow felt Google as his archnemesis, his Moby Dick, a corporation his swashbuckling night hero was going to defeat. It took him several decades before he managed to see it on its knees, but it was a triumph well worth waiting for. Decades prior, his first Google search brought him a result that further shaped his future.

School's Out Forever

Helen's extensive library of 33 1/3 rpm and long-play vinyl records had Alice Cooper's *One Halloween Night* album hidden among the jazz music young Varga hated. (He liked early blues, though. Sleepy John Estes, Big Mama Thornton, and Sonny Boy Williamson were his favorites even later in life, along with the greats like James Brown, Billie Holiday, Marvin Gaye,

B.B. King, or Miles Davis, to mention only a few.) Alice Cooper's LP's scary cover attracted young Winston. After all, he had been born on Halloween. He wasn't allowed to use Helen's antique BeoCenter 7000 cassette/turntable music center when he was alone, so he went online to find Alice Cooper's album. It was track B6, "School's Out," that immediately possessed him and turned his blood into a boiling well of passionate hatred for the system.

> *No more pencils no more books*
> *No more teacher's dirty looks yeah*
> *Well we got no class*
> *And we got no principals*
> *And we got no innocence*
> *We can't even think of a word that rhymes*
> *School's out for summer*
> *School's out forever*
> *My school's been blown to pieces*

This became Winston Varga's new anthem, hymn, and daily prayer.

Winston saw Cooper, that great juvenile delinquent desperado, as a hero of forsaken American greatness. It was like he'd ridden in from the frontiers Winston read about in books and was also a fellow anarchist. He hated the school from day one; the pace of teaching was slower than three-legged turtles. Winston asked himself if those sad blimps of life, teachers, have ever heard of the internet? Schooling was as stupid as the most punch-drunk redneck, the schoolbooks were outdated, comical, and talking nonsensical stuff, and the teachers were tired, boring, and depressed. Their jokes lame. Their attempts to talk to the kids like they were mentally undeveloped grown-ups, idiotic. Their attempts to talk to the kids like their equal, pathetic. Some of their ogling of prepubescent children, revolting. Many even smelled of alcohol like his father. So when he heard "School's Out Forever" he was hooked. Alice Cooper was his hero. A straitjacketed Cooper even sang a song about dead babies, but that too was a hit.

"*How one must despise, therefore, some fathers, who, whether from ignorance or inexperience, before putting the intended teachers to the test, commit their sons to the charge of untried and untested men*," Plutarch wrote and Varga read in Greek and yet, he was there, in the school, among morons, taught by the morons, sent there by his repulsive father, the king moron.

Thus, a long struggle for Winston's independence from the vile educational system whose only purpose was to create obedient sheep, had begun.

It was a mighty, often painful struggle. Helen made him a promise—she'd homeschool him if he again devoted at least several hours a day to reading literature and history—a deal he had gladly accepted. Jeff hated having him at home all the time, so he started to drink even more, if that was possible. Helen did not let Jeff touch Winston after the "cleaning of the guns" incident ("if you touch my son ever again, I'll kill you," she'd said, threatening Jeff with so much quiet rage in her voice and such a convincing demeanor that he trembled in fear; they never made love again after that day and started to irreparably fall apart,) or interfere with his education, so Jeff, weakling that he was, had no choice but to sulk and occasionally yell. But his bark had no bite anymore.

Everything turned south in the house of Varga.

Making of Varga, LLC

When he was eleven years old, Winston Varga secretly used his mother's SSN to open Varga Computer Solutions, LLC., the first business he incorporated in Wyoming, where he also opened a corporate bank account, all online. He moved his diagnostics tools and business operations on the internet in order to avoid detection of his age by his clients. At that time over half of all US households already had internet access so it was a big sea, open to catch a living for a young, daring entrepreneur such as Winston.

What he had realized since the first virus attacked the Net was that people mostly knew next to nothing. His clients were clueless about Google, so he had found himself a lucrative source of income, Search Engine Optimization services, or SEO, which he mastered but despised. For a classically educated kid who had been programming since an early age, it was a moronic exercise in tweaking websites to get a better ranking with Google. It worked, sure, and his clients were happily showering his companies with money, but for his mighty mind, it would have been futile to put too much effort into technically trivial stuff for the benefit of idiots.

Once he had established a powerful network of bots sitting and executing orders in the cloud, he barely supervised his teams. What was going on in the deep, hidden underbelly of that tech leviathan interested Winston much more, so he outsourced his SEO services, collected the money that was pouring in, and started a lifelong struggle to understand and ultimately defeat it. Before Google burst onto the tech scene, Varga studied Infoseek, later morphed into Go Network, which no one ever used, and the Inktomi search engines. He turned his attention to Disney's GoTo.com search (powered by Inktomi) and studied how they introduced the paid search. Advertisers with the highest bid got the top search results. It was a novelty at the time. Soon, Google took over.

The "clickthrough rate" for targeted ads, which made Google a fortune and was a metric upon which young Varga charged ever more money for successful marketing campaigns he was running for his clients, was a true boon. He immediately grasped the future they were creating—tailored, individual spaces for people that had, de facto, left their individuality beneath the computer screen and willingly become a part of the market in which their behavioral surplus, clicks, or emotions were packaged into bundles of data.

The demands for Varga's services vastly outpaced his teams' abilities to deliver, so he never stopped expanding and started to create various apps under the umbrella platform "I'll Make it Easy For You"™ (e-IME) playing on his clients' ignorance that was as vast, limitless, and as mind-boggling as space. His multiple e-IME platforms' philosophy was to offer all sorts of "Easy Solutions," be it "Easy Weight Loss," or "An Easy Way to Approach (and Get) Any Girl," "Mastering SAT in an Easy Way," or "Easy Way to Invest," which sold in the millions of copies. All that was missing was the canned laughter for Seinfeld reruns, he thought, because every product was made from the same template. His next hit was an anti-spying, antivirus software named BRANDAIS, whose Suite 1(a) and the corporate Suite Pro 2(b) sold in dozens of millions of copies. Varga purposefully used what the PRIORI had used themselves, Justice Louis Brandeis's famous quote, in order to let them know he knew more about them than they might fear. It was a great success. The real purpose of his anti-spying antivirus was to spy on its users, something Varga deemed crucial for his venture's future success, even at that young age (e-IME developments started when he was fourteen.)

Over the next several years, young Winston amassed a fortune, and yet, not only did his parents have no clue about what was going on, but neither his clients nor employees knew his real identity. He hid himself deeply, only revealing his avatars on various Deep Web sites where he had two key avatars, Dr. Evil and ZLY with a few other throwaway identities. The Dr. Evil avatar came from the *Austin Powers* film series, a parody of

James Bond's character, both immensely popular a long time ago while ZLY came from the book *The Man With the White Eyes* by Leopold Tyrmand, in its Polish original titled *Zły*, a novel Varga read as a young boy. Henryk Nowak, the Zły in the novel, loved Marta Majewska like a madman would but had given her up for another man, someone who did not have Zły's burdened past—just another tragic love story that attracted the young Winston enough to adopt the name.

At that time, Helen and Jeff's own sad love story became daily bickering, so Winston had a chance to establish one more belief system, although still vague at that age: that people were incapable of rational discussion and able to see only from their own vantage point, reaching conclusions that are almost always set in stone, chiseled by themselves. The people, he thought, are partially like children—they don't want to be told what to do or what to think—and partially bullies that love to impose their own will onto others. They are all mad, he had concluded, and that is why they needed leaders that, throughout history, have led them to so many triumphs and even more disasters.

A Woke Billionaire

Before Varga became the first trillionaire and an omnipotent magnate bent on ruling the world, he had started to study mid-twenty-first century social phenomena. He particularly liked the moral self-licensing that served him as an idea for a social-credit structure of the upcoming Virtuosi™, a scheme that he concocted and engulfed the world in soon after. Do good deeds reframe bad deeds (moral credentials) or merely balance them out? Varga enjoyed observing how the woke privilege of whining about just about everything 24/7 from enshrined enclaves, insulated from any real suffering, had created a merry little set of mental illnesses, especially among the elite schools' student populations. Woke ardent focus on minor issues stemming from various self-identifiers created religion-like cults. Everything was therein: self-righteous dogmas, zealous disciples and acolytes alike scolding the infidels, blasphemy codes, and punishment for non-believers the cancel culture cultivated with the fervor of crusader kings. Oscar Wilde wrote, "beware the tyranny of the weak for it is the only type that lasts."

Varga laughed upon seeing the weaklings terrorizing the rest of society. The time for him to mold them would come. Moral credits were of special interest to Varga and his awards pyramid scheme.

Cultural-appropriation chastity forbade adopting of elements of one culture by the members of another culture for being insensitive, incorrect etc., a nice tool in the arsenal of those holier-than-thou moral stalwarts. Imitation as the sincerest form of flattery turned on its head. That was precisely the seed for his Virtuosi™ Movement and their moral superiority, something he forcefully pushed forward as he started to shape society in his own image.

"Should we stretch that virtuous nonsense to its absurd ends, only dinosaurs should be allowed to write scientific articles on dinosaurs, and children's books should be written exclusively by kids." Once you managed to compartmentalize the horrors of human history, be it misogyny and burning at the stake, racism and slavery and their inexplicable horrors, or xenophobia, you put it away and, often unwittingly, double down on realities. Deep insight is not needed at all if you are better than everyone else. A noble predecessor of the woke privilege plague, the New Age Movement, was a good example for Varga. Those self-deceiving fraudsters were all about "healing," he thought in his characteristically loving outlook on people, so they went to sweat lodges around Bluff, UT where they performed "sacred" pipe ceremonies, which promise to bring individual and global healing or some such snake oil, all to show how much better than their predecessors they were.

We, good people of today (then) are not genocidal monsters, no, we love, adore and above everything else, we respect Indian spirituality. Yeah, right. "Try living with them in those horrid reservations, and try fighting for recognition and dignity on daily basis like themselves and then you tell me how much of that spirituality truly resides in you," Varga once wrote on some internet forum devoted to spirituality. Boy was he glad he had used his Dr. Evil avatar, given how much shite the Net's moral majority were mercilessly pouring onto him. He was virtually tarred and feathered for saying what he did. He saw the hatred that filled human hearts first-hand and has never forgotten its bittersweet taste. But, that hate needed a structure. Winston Varga was hell-bent on providing them with the structure they so badly needed.

A "profound need for transparency and responsibility in light of the traumatic histories of colonization, slavery, and genocide that shape the present" wrote Pamela Jumper Thurman, PhD, a Western Cherokee, is a serious business, something the people were not ready to mull over. They were not ready to take real action either, Varga understood, only those phony acts that benefit their sweaty, superior asses while putting a badge of honor on them and going about their duplicitous lives accusing everyone else of their own sins, swept under the dirty carpets of their own unconsciousness. The virtue signaling that was so pervasive seemed to have liberated those 'virtuous' people to engage in immoral, unethical, or dangerous behavior, as they ganged up on anyone who held an opinion different from their own. That moral self-licensing effect in the world of political correctness was something Varga grasped at as an opportunity, a true suppression machine. It was a wonderful ideology that classified whole groups of people as perpetual victims in need of protection from criticism, and which made true believers, those self-appointed protectors of inferiors (they would poke your eyes out should you dare to suggest those victims are de facto a designated inferior class), feel that no dissent should be tolerated. The Manichaean Principle of political correctness as a dualistic philosophy dividing the people between good and intrinsically evil if they disagree with the mainstream dogma seemed to Varga as inherent human trait making them malleable.

The Dictatorship of Virtue is something he had been experimenting with in the past. The Hyde Park Speaker's Corner and Twitter's rabid intolerance were merged into his worldwide 3D interactive platform PLATEIA (the "town square," another Greek word he adopted) where anyone could speak freely, as long as the speech was approved. By him. Rather by an algorithm. And they liked it, the rabble. Varga's dislike for people grew, he sensed therein must be a wellspring of chances for him to rule them economically and—why not?—politically. Varga felt the world in front of his eyes is morphing into a fertile ground ripe for manipulation with no end.

There would be a years-long process of ripening, and before any developments along the lines of using social malaise to his advantage took place, Winston Varga faced an event that shaped his and, by association *our*, world for good.

The Money

Over the five years after Winston Varga started his internet marketing venture, he created eleven subsidiary companies all over the world and employed over three hundred people in so-called Third World countries. He charged $50.00 for each employee's hour in the US but paid them only $10.00 an hour abroad. That alone had generated over $28M a year in net profit for him in the three years after Varga Computer Solutions's incorporation. He made twice that using every affiliate marketing system at hand in the vast network of websites and consultancies he had created. The main purpose of that complicated network was testing and probing Google and its various services. Varga wanted to cast a net over it, but day after day he kept discovering how enormous that leviathan had become. Such power of this enemy filled Varga's heart with envy, resentment, and finally, with loathing. He had to find a way to destroy them, something that felt like an arrant impossibility, and a giant obstacle that drove him mad with hatred.

When Winston was eighteen years old he already had so much money stashed away that he needed to do something with it; the taxes for that year were a horrendous burden for his net of businesses. Helen once told him that she couldn't divorce his father because it would've been against her faith. Divorce was a grave sin, something her soul was unwilling to commit, despite the growing, gaping differences between today's Jeff and Jeff's former self. Money was a big problem for the Vargas, given Jeff's dwindling contributions to the household, so Winston had hoped he might be able to help them. While he had already deeply despised his father, he wanted his mom to be happy and maybe, even reconcile with Jeff. In his drunken babbles his father used to mention, more than once, what seemed to have been his real dream: to own a ranch, raise cattle, live off the land, and, perhaps, to write a big American novel that was badly needed in a culture reduced to magical thinking coming out of the relentless bullshit machine called the entertainment industry.

Always a deliberate, pensive young man, Varga had consulted a therapist who assured him that his father might embrace a new lease on life, sober up, and start working on his dream, had he proper circumstances to stimulate him. That convinced Winston and after a long, deliberate search for the appropriate property, he bought them, outright, a ranch that was almost four hundred miles north of Bluff, eastbound from Salt Lake City, in Woodland Utah. The ranch was huge, spread out on over 100,000 acres of land in northern Utah and included a home at about 12,000 square feet. Winston's LLC., who purchased it as a tax write-off, got it complete with furnishings, ranch equipment and machinery, cattle, grazing permits, water rights, trophy elk hunting rights, and mineral rights. The home itself came with a state-of-the-art home theater, entire home audio and security systems, a heated auto courtyard, enclosed dog yard, temp-controlled wine cellar, and a golf simulator. Moreover, the whole humongous property was solar-powered. It had a parking lot that inconspicuously blended with the environment and hid its twenty parking spaces under the shadow of indomitable juniper trees, the symbol of their new ranch.

That was a dream property and Winston's first expense. Boy, what an expense it was. That fledging young entrepreneur had forked out a staggering sum of $25 million for the property. Truth to be told, given that he had not spent a penny on himself—baring the modest equipment he used—and lived in an isolated house on the outskirts of Bluff, UT over all those years he was building what would become his vast business empire decades later, he had no real sense about how shockingly rich he had become. He enjoyed amassing the wealth, but all that money were just numbers to him. Rivers of money were never able to provide him with the same pleasure that the first fifty dollars he was paid for the virus cleanup years earlier had. The network of small companies he incorporated all over the world saw the seeds of his future approach to business, but the money coming out of it was still somehow abstract to Varga. His tool of choice, a highly programable Excel sheet, served to display how much money, in aggregate, all those companies had, and he loved seeing it grow, but he truly did not have the faintest sense of what that money truly meant in the real world.

That was until he presented the ranch's deed to his parents.

The Road to Hell is Paved with Good Intentions

To say Helen and Jeff were out of their minds, struck dumb by the property he gave them would be an understatement. They could not have comprehended what was going on. For a joke, Winston's present would've been too elaborate and, frankly, a bit pointless. As a reality, well, it wasn't possible at all. Or was it? No way! The ranch Winston claimed to have purchased was four hundred miles away, but he had never left Bluff in his life, ever. Winston looked at his parents, confused; that wasn't the reaction he's been hoping for. They looked at him like he was some sort of freak. Jeff even started to yell, again, in the gruff voice of a drunkard, but the words coming out of his foul mouth were just an incomprehensible, loud mumble filled with hatred. Unable to cope and wanting a drink, Jeff stormed out, enraged, yelling at Helen that it was her fault that young Winston had lost his mind from those idiotic, God-forsaken myths she'd fed him. "This latest deranged game, that fucking 'ranch' is a result," he growled at Helen.

"No more computer for you." He barked his biteless bark at the wrong tree, as always, as the door kicked his sorry ass on his way out to the darkness of his rotten soul, where Hell dwells. Both Helen and Winston felt relief after Jeff had left; the animosity in the Varga house has already reached suffocating levels.

"Winston?" Helen looked at him in wonder for a second. Then she sensed, she saw in his eyes, that all of it was true. Her son, not yet old enough to properly shave, had indeed purchased them a posh mansion. But how?

"Did you win a lottery?" She struggled to wrap her mind around such a surreal event. Reading Homer in the native, Homeric dialect of the ancient Greek language, does not prepare you for a surprise of such magnitude. She gazed at Winston's eyes, and for the first time, she saw not only the little baby she brought to this world, but the steely resolve in his penetrating glare. How come she had never noticed it before? It struck her, even more than the dreamlike mansion he seem to really have bought, to see the unwavering character of the strong, perhaps dangerous man who was growing up under her roof but had already chosen a path for himself, all by himself, beyond her guidance or even understanding. She recoiled, just a little bit, as her heart raced—what else doesn't she know about Winston, her son, that young man standing next to her?

Winston sensed his mom's uneasiness, hugged her forcefully, and whispered softly, "You were my winning ticket, since the day I was born." *It sounds corny*—the thought flashed through his mind, but then he was overwhelmed by love for Helen and his words rang truer than ever. He felt how she relaxed in his embrace, soothed by his soft voice, and he knew in his heart of his hearts that from then on, he was indeed a man of his own and no one would ever dictate to him what he could and could not do. And he would protect his mother with his own life if needed, no matter what.

Both the loser Jeff and the whole vile world could go fuck themselves.

At "Comb Ridge Eat + Drink's"

Jeff kept drinking, mulling over Winston's phony purchase. *What else it could've been? Or was it real? The mansion in Utah? No way. WTF was that? Some mindfuck Sophocles concocted while sucking on some cute Greeks phalluses and that Winston used as a sick joke? See, I know enough Greek myself. That little brat. He never loved me. Only Helen. Hell-en. Hellen and their damned, fucking Greek. And myths. They hold secrets in Greek, them whispering sniveling conspirators. That gibberish they used to isolate him sounded like some incoherent Swedish sailor with a severe case of logorrhea anyway. If America is not good for her, why is she here? Isn't Chania better? Everything was better in Greece for her anyway. And Winston? Nothing existed to that brat but Helen. Hell-en. And I am his father damn it. But those eyes and its accusatory glare, judging me all the time... Nothing of me is in them. Am I really his father? Am I? Why she never wanted Greek sex? Saving herself for that incestuous little conniving scallywag? Mom's devious lickspittle? Helen's cuddly mollycoddle. Treacherous Oedipus she wants to fuck?* He took another big swig of beer. *Another one, Nancy, please. Dancy. Prancy. She does look a bit like a horse, that Nancy Prancy. But, what a vile thought,* thought Jeff, *his Helen wanting to hump Winston?* But then, sipping on another whiskey enriched Cutthroat beer he thought, *is it really that nasty? Is it really too far-fetched to think that bastard is not his son? Greek? I can't stand its sound. Computers? I abhor those idiotic machines. And those eyes. Those are not my eyes. He can't be my son. No way. He is not my son.*

"I renounce the bastard," Jeff Varga yelled, upsetting a nice family who'd gathered for the sumptuous dinner Comb Ridge Eat + Drink provided daily in copious amounts.

"That's it." Nancy Prancy rushed to his table. "You have to go, Jeff. You're drunk."

"Where should I go? No one invited me." Jeff slurred his words.

"Go home, Jeff, just go home to your family, honey," Nancy said, somehow saddened over this sorry spectacle. Jeff was a pathetic sight indeed. He plodded out, without paying, stumbling several times on his way out.

Nancy did not insist—he'd be back remorseful and would leave her a big tip out of guilt, like so many times before. She felt a bit guilty at the thought and rushed back to her famished customers. After all, Roscoe there has such nice teeth when he smiles at her, a strong jaw and even stronger arms. He likes her, she could sense it. She might even get some tonight, she dared to daydream all but forgetting about Jeff Varga and his demons.

Make Someone Happy

Having a smoke in his car—it was an antique, a spectacular, albeit a tad rusty, dark purple Buick Roadmaster Riviera 76R from 1957—Jeff Varga felt rebellious. It was the Old Violet, as he and Helen called it, and in it they had left Florida and crossed America a decade ago. Hell-en loved the Old Violet even more than he did and had not let him smoke in it. Now, he could not care less. He took a gulp of whiskey and lit up another cigarette. He'd love to have some weed but he had none. Varga's household was a drug-free zone—*orders from Hell-en*, he sneered. What, that bitch thinks she can order him around as she wishes while rejecting him like he was a repulsive bum and not her lawfully wedded husband?

Instead, he blasted Jimmy Durante. He loved Ragtime Jimmy's gravelly voice and that enormous, distinctive snout that would make Cyrano de Bergerac run for cover in shame, out-nosed by Jimmy. Jeff especially loved to listen to "Make Someone Happy" when he was drunk.

> *Make someone happy,*
> *Make just one someone happy,*
> *And you will be happy, too.*

"Have I not done my utmost to make her happy?" he said aloud and looked at the old, dirty rear mirror; his distorted face looked back at him, his eyes empty. He could not recognize the strange face, those eyes staring back. He was indeed a shadow of himself. This is what The Hell-en and The Demon Seed, her son, the bastard, made out of him. *Where have you gone, Jeff Varga? Why did you sacrifice your life on the altar of that ungrateful Greek harlot and her hateful whoreson?*

There's only one solution for her sins, Jeff knew. No other way around it. He took a handgun out of the glovebox and holstered it, zipping away from Comb Ridge's parking lot, swerving drunkenly toward the house of the rising sun, to the dwelling that, a long, long time ago, was his home.

Dance Me to the End of Love

Nothing to say to anyone anymore, nothing to think, to feel here, there, anywhere, nowhere, everywhere. Just emptiness walks with him along the boulevard of broken dreams. Empty windows of the soul linger high above in the starless sky. Strangely, Jeff Varga, in that moment, suddenly felt sober. He'd drank himself sober. Such a nice feeling. There wasn't rage or sadness left in him; he wasn't that pathetic loser anymore. He was a man with a purpose, a man who gotta do what a man gotta do and punish the only two people he used to love, but the people who betrayed him so hurtfully.

He stumbled as he was getting out of the Old Violet, kicked the house doors down, barged into the living room, and shot Helen, that Hellen from hell and the Demon Seed, that Winston bastard who was never even able to pretend to be his real son, on the spot. They had no time to even understand what was going on. They lay on the floor bleeding from their deceased carcasses, and Jeff Varga, with his handgun smoking, smelling of brimstone and the past, looked at the unrecognizable mass of stinky, dead bodies lying on the living room floor and felt nothing.

One for the Road

He was thirsty and needed a drink, so he took one big swig from his flask and then let it drop to the floor. The sound of it hitting was dull, like life itself. He looked around. The silence of a dead house was deafening.

Some music might cheer him up.

Yesterday, when he was young and Eleni was still his "Helen of Troy," they used to dance to Leonard Cohen's "Dance Me to the End of Love," he remembered fondly. What a stupid word, *fondly*. It came from *foolish*. Yes, he was foolishly in love. Rather, ghoulishly in love, 'til death do us part. Well, it for sure did us part. Jeff sauntered around the house to find that old 45 rpm record and let it play on the music center the music center she clung to like a lover embracing under the crescent moon. Sweet memories of a ghoul that robbed him of his soul. Jeff Varga danced a while to Cohen's gruff voice, oblivious to the world that had abandoned him, and then he had, almost absentmindedly, blown his brains out.

Hold my beer, Socrates.

Childhood's End

Winston Varga survived his father's madness. The first bullet Jeff fired at his young son hit him in the shoulder and another one grazed his temple, causing him to swoon. He dreamt he was drowning in the oceans of his and his mother's blood. When he came back to consciousness, Varga saw his mother's dead body, lying like a broken doll in a pool of dried, crimson blood, her eyes open, staring into the myths from which she once arrived to give him life. He gently closed her eyes and sat next to her in silence.

And then, for the first and the last time in his life, Winston Varga started to cry.

Chapter 8

THE ESCAPE

The Sewers of New York
New Athens, NYC
March 21, 2048

After a mad rush from the PHOENIX's rage, with the manhole cover far behind them Nastassia slides down the manhole, through the pipe's ladder. The Renegade follows her.

"Here we go, down the rabbit hole."

"Where does it lead?"

"If you don't hurry you might never find out."

Nastassia says nothing as they descend into a pitch-black tunnel. The Renegade lights his vintage Zippo and lights the torch. An overflown weir chamber in its full glory displays the sewer's poop torrent.

"Welcome to the close encounters of the turd kind."

"This stench's gross." Nastassia yelps.

"It will save our tushies. Follow me." The Renegade moves toward a smaller tunnel. Nastassia follows him in silence, holding her nose. She's worried sick for Mom and Dad but does not want to talk about it now. Not in this suffocating stench. She observes how the stream flows into a culvert and then she looks up to see graffiti of a dragon on a double-barreled brick wall. *What mind does that*, she wondered, *compelled to create art in such a place*. Once the small tunnel widens, they enter an aqueduct.

"Look at the arch, on its end." The Renegade shows her. "There's a hidden passage. The sewer people of New York live there."

"There are sewer people?"

"Oh, yes. They call them the mole people. You should see the Canal Street sewer. Better yet, the Amtrak tunnel below Riverside Drive, they have a whole city there. Not a part of this world. Almost like New Athens." The Renegade chuckles. "The bowels of the city are as important as our own," he said as they keep walking, avoiding a pile of bricks left there years ago. "New York's sewer network consists of over 7,400 miles of sewer pipes and 135,000 catch basins, making it an ideal place for Hollywood and the renegade people."

"But it's dark. No air. There are rats everywhere."

"Not everywhere. There are beautiful abandoned subway stations above the sewers." The Renegade keeps walking as he talks. "The people can survive anything—you wouldn't believe. But, we're here." He points toward a small, anchored speed boat that seems to have been waiting for them as it floats in the sewer pool they reach after their few hundred-meters-long walk through the underbelly of New York.

"Hop in," Renegade gallantly offers Nastassia, and she gets into the boat, looking around. It's a mythical place; she never knew it would be so mesmerizing in its otherworldliness. The Renegade pull-ropes a starter on the small speed boat and it rushes away through the long, narrow sewers. He throws his ice-cream confectioner cap away, flaunting his long grey hair, and keeps steering the boat. He jerks the rudder, jolting the boat around a huge white alligator swimming around.

"I knew they existed." He smiles, slowing down. "We'd be there in a moment."

"Where?"

"Here." Renegade docks the boat near a wall and opens a secret door, revealing a bright orange submarine rescue chamber.

"How old is that thing?" Nastassia asks suspiciously.

"Older than my teeth, but younger than my tongue," he replies and after fidgeting with something that looked like a concealed door, he opens the submarine rescue chamber.

"After you, young lady."

She observes a very narrow entrance. *Well then, it seems I will finally find out if I am claustrophobic or not*, she thinks and squeezes into the

chamber. *I really hope I am not.* The Renegade follows her, pushes a few buttons, shuts the door closed behind them, and the chamber starts its descent. Nastassia looks around at the old wires and primitive instruments from the early twentieth century. As the chamber descends, darkness envelops them. A dull thump shakes the chamber. Nastassia glances at the Renegade.
What was that?

"We've arrived." The Renegade opens the chamber and helps her exit from the makeshift elevator, made out of the old submarine's escape chamber.

"Forgive me the elaborate way we used to get here, but I needed to make it as safe from prying eyes as possible," he says turning a weak light on.

Nastassia's eyes widen in awe.

What a maze he has created—several fake entrances, blind ends just to get here, and now this. This must be the legendary Renegade's lab; it could not be anything else. This place is the subject of mythical stories, something too many in the New Athens hacking circles believe to be a folk tale, not a real place. And yet, she is now entering that very fairytale space, in the company of the real myth, the real luminary of her world, the Renegade himself. She has never seen a setup like this, not even in science fiction. Two, not one but two damn two 50-qubit quantum computers and racks with dozens of supercomputers all over the space. Twenty-monitor rigs made with that impossible-to-find Japanese perversion called polyether-thioureas—self-repairing glass. 3D holographic screens stand in corners. Drones parked on shelves. Even that bizarre MAXxPlanck V10 wall-mounted computer whose energy is rigged to a water purifying system. IOTA 3D glasses that serve to automatically detect fake products were proudly sitting on his desk.

A high-techie's dream.

She looks at the green scrolling data on black screens. For sure the Renegade's now able to call Frédéric from his hi-tech lair with military-grade encryption. So she asks him, "Can we call Mom and Dad now, please. I need to know that they are OK."

The Sorrow

The Renegade glances at her, not uttering a word. A spark of understanding crosses the space in between them and she knows, in that first instant of respite after their escape from the PHOENIX's murderous rage, she realizes her parents are dead. *How was it possible that she did not sense it earlier?*

And yet, she tries. "How can you be sure?"

The Renegade points to his eyepiece. "Philip Bolghery had his people in the park. They witnessed the murder. And when the ambulance came, virtually minutes after we escaped, they pronounced Freddie and Mon dead on the spot." His voice cracks, his eyes averting.

"I am so terribly sorry." How horrible it is to be the bearer of such news. How hopeless he feels; there's nothing he can do to assuage her pain, to help her. He can only be here for her if she needs him. And he carries the heavy brunt of responsibility for her tragedy, he thinks, looking at Nastassia, filled with remorse and guilt. *Only if she knew.*

Nastassia stands motionlessly. *Mom and Dad are dead. This just makes no sense. How they can be dead? Stellan is gone. How this can be?* She wobbles like she is going to faint. She clenches her fists, her knuckles white. But then a revelation starts to slowly creep into her consciousness, like an amorphous, dark, dangerous mass grabbing her throat only to burst into her as an explosion of pain.

It was her who led Varga to Stellan and Mom. And Dad.

Yes, the PHOENIX's transition was a trap. The DDoS attack was not well thought through, a hasty, stupid, arrogant reaction. Her hubris had gotten the best of her. She could've very well phoned Varga and provided him with Stellan's address, with Mom's whereabouts. *I am damned. I am triple damned. It was me who killed them*, resonates like a curse in her. *It was me, it was all me.* She starts to suffocate and is unable to move. The darkness of death she feels she has caused engulfs her. *It was my fault. It was all my fault.* Her head is spinning. *It was all my fault, it was all my fault.* Her heart wants to explode. *It was you who killed your parents* a voice is telling her, the deep, nasal, vicious voice coming from all sides. It keeps accusing her in reverberating echoes, *it was you, it was you, you spoiled brat. You have outed Stellan and his secrets and he's gone.*

He's gone because of you.

Nastassia wants to die.

She turns her back to the Renegade so to hide the anguish of guilt that is tearing her apart. Her tiny shoulders tremble like a little bird's would. She does not move, just stands still, trembling. Her face white. Her eyes lost. Tears are trickling down her frozen face, dripping from her chin. The Renegade looks at her again. She is so small, so vulnerable, so hurt. So lonely. *It was all my fault*, she says. Or was that her thoughts? He has no idea but he hears her, he feels her, and his heart breaks. He moves toward her, not knowing what to do in the face of so much pain, and then stops again. Upon hearing his step, Nastassia turns and leaps into his embrace, still quietly, barely perceivably sobbing while her shoulders keep trembling, shattering his heart.

"It is my fault they are dead," she whispers, but her voice is clear.

My God, child, stop that suffering. "Look at me," he says firmly.

She looks up, gazing at the Renegade. Her strangely beautiful emerald eyes glow with so much pain, drowning in tears, that he has to restrain his own.

"The PHOENIX, rather Varga, murdered Frédéric and Monique. He also almost killed you but he wanted to kill me. It wasn't your fault. Don't think so for a second."

"It is," she whispers. "Deep logic via unused frequency channel I used for DDoS attack was a mistake."

"Varga has hundreds if not thousands of agents in his Surveillance's Human Evaluators Program, each of them following every talented child in New Athens. Varga has had everyone under surveillance since day one. He was searching for what he called Subject Zero. Now it is clear Stellan is the Subject Zero."

Nastassia, like a sponge, soaks up his every word, saying nothing as she stares at the Renegade, trying to connect the dots.

"If there's anyone to blame, it is me. I arranged the meeting with Frédéric as soon as Varga had snatched Stellan, for only then did we realize our grave mistake. We were hasty."

"What mistake?"

"Not protecting you enough. Not realizing that the Prophecy was not a figment of our imagination."

Nastassia forces herself to focus, to understand.

"What Prophecy?"

"That of a Subject Zero as Winston Varga's destroyer. That Subject Zero might have been you or Stellan. But we weren't sure and, as the years passed by, we dropped our guard thinking you both were getting too old to be the Zero. Now it's clear it is Stellan that Varga's after."

"How do you know? Precogs were being abducted for years. Anyone could've been that subject of yours."

"Each of those disappearances had happened in secret. Often overnight. Often the kids were seen in one place one second, only to vanish without a trace the next. This time they acted so fast that it is obvious that they were reacting to something."

"What?"

"No idea what prompted them to snatch Stellan in such a hasty manner. Something must've told them he was the one they've been looking for all those years. I am in the dark as to what. But, they were waiting and ready, that's obvious. It's also obvious that he wanted to kill me and you, not Freddy and Mon. It's our fault, not yours," he repeats, looking at Nastassia, sensing that he might be losing her.

"Think. If Varga had no qualms about killing me or even you in a broad daylight and had kidnapped Stellan during that transition nonsense of his, that could mean only two things."

"Which are?"

"Varga's always several steps in front of us. But there are no registered adult precogs. So it must be his tech guiding him."

"And the second thing?"

"He needs Stellan but fears you."

Nonsense, Nastassia almost blurts out. But that nonsense somehow makes sense. But, *why would Varga need Stellan? He's just a little boy*, she thinks. And yet, she somehow already *knows*, no matter how vaguely that realization lingers in her mind. It makes her feel dizzy. She is drifting away, not even hearing the Renegade anymore.

"Nastassia, are you OK?"

Pranayama

He isn't getting through to her. She looks lost, almost like her soul is going to leave her body. "*Breathe*," he whispers and continues in his normal voice. "I know it's painful, but it had to be said—it was us, Freddie and myself who did not do enough. It was all our fault, mostly mine."

Nastassia looks up.

The Renegade returns her intense glare with a warm hue in his eyes. Did he just say *breathe* with *intention* in his tone? Somehow automatically, she takes a few skull-shining pranayama breaths, which she had taught Stellan years ago. *Stellan!* For one fleeting moment she feels Stellan, she senses his presence. It is a vague, feeble breath of connection, the first since he vanished, but a crucial one. While she also smells a whiff of death, it is clear that the odor isn't Stellan's—she shudders at the thought—and she knows that he's alive. Even when the connection is lost and Stellan falls back into that impenetrable darkness she can not reach, she is relieved. *Stellan's alive.* She wants to cry aloud but does not want to jinx it, and she stands silent. Somehow, it seems to her that the Renegade also *knows*. But, how? She looks at him with a whole new pair of eyes, rather like her whole being is sensing his presence on a totally new level. She feels a tiny bit better and lets her tears freely flow down her face. The Renegade, upon seeing her change, hugs her forcefully again and whispers.

"I know, I know. But you still have Stellan."

With her face firmly pressed to his sweater, and holding onto the Renegade, Nastassia sinks back into her memories, needing something *real*.

Stellan's Puppy
Yellowknife, Northwest Territories
April 19, 2047

On Stellan's fifth birthday the whole Bonnet family went to meet an old friend of Monique's, a revered jazz pianist, composer, and art therapist originally from Montréal, Natasha D., whose famous Canadian Winnipeg Schmoo Cakes, a legend has it, have the magical power to heal the world. Stellan was allowed to take his dog with him, a funny, clumsy, and happy Bernese, the most cutely dumb puppy ever who managed to get himself in trouble all the time. He was incomprehensibly named Luigi and was only seven months old at the time. Stellan was very proud of Luigi, who was, if not taller, already much bigger, heavier, and stronger than him. Holding his head high, Stellan walked Luigi like a monarch, fully in control of his magnificent animal. They were truly delightful; everyone loved the little kid and his Luigi, always walking around or chasing dragons—dragons being squirrels in Central Park. Over the course of the dinner Natasha had prepared with so much love that everyone had forgotten life's troubles, Luigi sneaked out and embarked upon exploring the Northwest Territories all alone.

Soon after, Luigi being Luigi, was lost.

Immediately upon seeing that Luigi was gone, Nastassia and Frédéric went searching for him, while Monique was left with an inconsolable Stellan and Natasha, whose music had a soothing effect on the sad little boy. Nastassia was herself like a hunting dog, following Luigi's scent or her intuition all over the vast territory. She never gave up. *I will find Stellan's puppy, Dad*. It took them a full forty-eight hours to find Luigi, who was way further north, near Prelude Lake, sadly observing the lake from some cliff, and brought him home. When they first reunited, it was difficult to say who was happier, the little kid or the little dog. Luigi jumped on Stellan, even peed a bit, crazily happy. Stellan hugged Luigi, but almost immediately after the joy subsided, started to quietly cry.

"Aren't you happy, my angel?" Monique asked, but he embraced Luigi even more strongly, closer to his heart, without saying a word or looking at anyone. Luigi lovingly licked his tears. Nastassia glanced at Luigi's eyes first and then turned her attention to her brother's strange behavior and caught a glimpse in Stellan's eyes. In that very instant she *knew*, and it was clear to her that Stellan also *knew*. His beautiful, dark eyes were filled with so much sorrow that Nastassia had no doubts whatsoever: Luigi was dying. He had caught a deadly, fast-acting alteration of canine parvovirus someplace in the woods. While both Monique and Frédéric were still confused, she now knew what was going on and asked them to leave Stellan alone with his puppy.

At the door, Monique turned and saw Stellan still inaudibly crying. As he held Luigi in an embrace, his silent tears were pouring down, his shoulders were slumped, his breath shallow and he trembled, barely noticeably. Luigi was licking his face and it seemed they were both consoling each other. It was a sight too painful, too heartbreaking to watch. Natasha went to play a tune Stellan loved, Frédéric Chopin's "Nocturne" in E flat major, Op. 9, No. 2 and quietly cried herself. His wonderful birthday had turned out to be such a profoundly sad moment.

"What's going on?" Monique asked, frightened to the bone.

"Just let him say goodbye alone."

"Goodbye?" She was still confused and afraid for her son, but Frédéric, who looked at Nastassia for one long minute, realized what was going on.

"Let him be, my love," he whispered.

Luigi died a few hours later. Stellan embraced him and pressed onto his broken heart.

"He was just a little puppy," he sobbed, "he never did anything wrong to anyone."

The Renegade's Lab
New Athens, NYC
March 21, 2048

Nastassia steps back from the embrace and looks up at the Renegade's serious eyes. "Once we rescue Stellan, I will get him a puppy," she says, wiping her tears away with a shy, sad smile. "A Bernese."

"I had a Bernese as a young boy, Puppy. We called him Puppy when he was a puppy and he stayed a Puppy. It was funny given the puppy was a real giant." He smiles at her. "A puppy will make Stellan happy," he says, looking at her, filled with admiration. This little girl is as tough as nails and as ferocious as a honey badger, despite just being orphaned and almost killed. He admires her for the valiance of her spirit and goodness of her heart.

And there is nothing else to say.

What are we going to do now? Both of them think.

Nastassia leans against the wall, trying to regroup. What now, really, what are they going to do? She hopefully side-glances at the Renegade, who slumps into the chair and slouches. His hands hang dead in between his knees and, while he has steepled his fingers, they point downward, like they do not know what to do. The Renegade looks deflated. Tired. Sad. And old. She is exhausted to the point of fading out, but her heart races, alarmed as she observes him. *This is so unlike the Renegade.* He never lost his spirit before, despite his impossible jokes. She looks around. The lab is dark, only a dozen or so screens flicker joylessly all over the place. Only those fantastic hi-tech gadgets inside, but nothing else.

He must have been deprived of real life, she realizes, *for a long, long time.*

"Renegade," she whispers, "I know you wanted to protect me by not telling me about Mom and Dad outright, but that time's long gone. And I know you feel guilty. Don't. I need you to help me find Stellan. Come back, please, you frighten me looking like this."

He raises his head and looks at her. *Why does this child have to face all of that,* he thinks. *Why has destiny dealt her cards so cruelly?*

"Face what?"

Did he speak aloud?

"No, you didn't. I *heard* your thoughts. It happens when the emotions of someone are overwhelming, then I can hear their thoughts like I would hear their voices."

The Renegade nods.

"No more secrets, right?" Nastassia insists.

"Right," he agrees.

"What do I have to face?" She looks at his dark eyes, suddenly alarmed. The Renegade's eyes look like a deep, dark vortex of despair. He seems like someone who has been staring into the abyss for such a long time that the abyss has stared back and is now reflecting, glaring straight back at her soul. Her heart palpitates. *What now*, she thinks in despair. *What else can happen?* The Renegade carries such darkness in him that she dreads his reply even before she asks. "Worse than my parents' death? Worse than Stellan's kidnapping?"

The Renegade lets a sad smile as he silently nods, his dark eyes hitched on hers.

"Jeez," she whispers.

Indeed.

The Feast

So, the time has come, the Renegade thinks. *But where to start*, he asks himself for a moment. Nastassia has *heard* him again.

"From the beginning, perhaps? With the missing children."

The Renegade sighs. "Right then, but can we eat first? I'm beat and famished."

"I am not hungry."

"Your body for sure is. Only your nerves are not letting you feel it." She says nothing.

"Let me fix us something. Trust me."

Trust. Nastassia thinks.

Frédéric's last words were *trust the Renegade with your life*, she remembers through the fog. That moment was so shocking that she's not sure if she imagined his words rapidly whispered at her as he was pushing her toward the ice cream cart. *No, they must have been real.* The familiar pang of unbearable pain strikes her again. And yet, all of a sudden, she feels hungry, like the Renegade's hunger has passed to her. She nods. "Yes, thank you, you are right. Let us eat first."

The separation after the old sage leaves for the pantry gives them both a chance to recover from the emotional storm they've experienced over the last, what, twenty minutes or so. To be by themselves for a moment at least, to regroup their focus, to calm their minds and emotions.

Nastassia takes a few forceful, skull-shining pranayama breaths. *Stellan needs my strength. And I need his.*

The Renegade returns with an impossible dinner tray filled with what looks like World War II Spam, neatly cut and arranged in a circle with renegade pickles around it as a garnish. She can not believe her eyes. It is so horrid, this stale stand-in for food, that it is sad and wonderful in one, given the care with which the Renegade has handled this culinary murder. That is, until she sees the bread. Those miserable slices had seen the crowning of the last king of The British Empire and have been hibernating in some garbage dump ever since before getting picked up for this meal. Nice if you are a rodent. And that dinner tray is in fact an old computer case he's carefully placing on a small table in front of her. The Renegade has even beautified his tray with a small plastic flower. It's red. *A plastic rose?* The silverware the Renegade brought is hideous plasticware that somehow manages to smell funny. He serves her that culinary atrocity with so much love and, dare she say, pride, that she smiles, amused by him.

"I am not much of a cook," he says. "But it would help you regain your strength." The Renegade is brimming as he nudges her toward the food. Nastassia looks at him like she would at an alien offering her a bite of Saturn rings as an appetizer before a main course made of pulsars, and quietly giggles. That this grey old genius is, in fact, a madman, crosses her mind as she smiles at him, who in return grins back over his dinner as the Cheshire cat would. Over that computer case/dinner tray, he looks funnier than anyone, or anything, she has ever seen. *He's not much of a cook*, he said, *not much of a cook…* She starts to shake with laughter despite all the sadness in her—or because of it. She is laughing quietly and invisibly as he carefully places one piece of that spam-like thingy and offers it to her on a plate made of bamboo and madness and love.

"*Et voilà!*" he says and slumps back into his sofa, eagerly munching on a putrid dinner he seems to be enjoying more with each bite, oblivious to the reality in front of him.

Et voilà? Did he really say *et voilà?* She can not contain herself anymore as she looks at The Cheshire Renegade lunatic, enjoying the spam he just served her so proudly, in his dark lab, someplace under the volcano of exploding civilization. *Charlie Chaplin move over, you got nothing on this guy*, she thinks as the laughter starts to pour out of her. She laughs with her mouth, with her throat, letting out guttural sounds she is unable to control or recognize. She is laughing so hard that she has almost peed herself. She is bursting, her belly laugh so loud that the Renegade has stopped eating and looks at her, puzzled.

"What?"

He's not even getting it! That's too much. She slinks down from her chair to the floor, unable to contain herself for he's was a spitting image of wonderment in wonderland. Lying on the floor, she turns over on her belly and starts to bang the floor with her fists. *I am going to die laughing*, she thinks.

"Is it not good, the food?" the Renegade asks her, alarmed.

No way, she thinks, *he's still not getting it*. But then she sees a sly smile in his eyes; he does get it. *He does all this buffoonery on purpose to help her cope*, flashes through her mind. This sly old madman. But, all this buffoonery has helped her compose herself.

"No, it's really good," she says and then needs another five minutes of laughter to come back to her senses. This time the Renegade laughs with her. Not only her belly, but her whole body hurts, that's how much she's been laughing. But, with the laughter pouring out of her, the remnants of fatigue and anxiety has left her and she feels *peckish*. What a word, she chuckles once more, and because she wasn't only peckish, rather as famished as a starving wolf, Nastassia starts to eagerly gobble up the Renegade's feast.

And now, even that food, for serving of which any chef would be publicly executed on the spot in all civilized lands, tastes passable. She had no idea how hungry she was. The Renegade has even made her tea. No sugar, milk, or honey, but at least the water was purified. She takes a sip, grateful. The Renegade's eyes are as good and clear as her soul now.

"Do you want some more?" he asks her politely and on her, "Thank you. It was wonderful. I am stuffed to the gills," he misses the loving irony of her words. It does not bother her how aloof he is to the reality they share, at that moment she loves the Renegade more than she would have loved a grandad, had she had one.

She is back!

"The missing children, you were saying?"

The MAGS

"Are you familiar with the INNOCENTI, Varga's semi-secret society?"

"Vaguely. Mom and Dad avoided talking about the missing precogs."

"Varga has played his secret society's role masterfully, pretending we all live in a secret-less time so, as you know, he opened the books of the INNOCENTI, for everyone to see. Like anyone would be able to pour through hundreds of thousands of computer-generated accountancy. Nothing like hiding in plain sight. He's one cunning bastard, always a step ahead of the curve, I must give him that. Moreover, his social coup de grâce was truly something. He had his freakish game introduce the ultimate social score—the INNOCENTI Membership. He even created several 'winners,' all of them fake people that never existed, and had shown them mingling with the real INNOCENTI and himself. Cocky smiles, gushing parades of self-admiration and horseshit galore. Nothing was real. No one ever wondered about them or sought those fake winners out. Varga's mass media had produced interviews with them, the whole nine yards, it was a full-blown, perfect, mind-boggling sham. Total media circus, nothing but smoke and mirrors. And yet, it worked. Almost everyone bought it, likely because everyone wanted to be part of the INNOCENTI and bask under the light of the elite. No one seems to have ever understood what the INNOCENTI's real purpose was. Not even Philip Bolghery, who sensed the true intention but was unable to follow the scent to its origin and got lost in the maze of lies."

"What was the purpose?"

The Renegade sighs and takes a deep breath. He looks at Nastassia. *Where have you gone, the days of carefree youthfulness, harmlessly bloodied knees on the playfields, and stolen kisses at sundown? Ahh... Renée.* The Renegade has drifted away for a second, not really able to look back at Nastassia's gaze, for he knows those lively, vivacious eyes will never again shine like that after he's told her the truth.

"Renegade?"

The Renegade moves toward an elegant wall-mount computer rig placed in the middle of the room, looks at Nastassia, and starts explaining.

"Just around the time your mother got pregnant with you, Frédéric and myself found out what the INNOCENTI—"

Nastassia interrupts. "Frédéric and you? When Mom was pregnant? You were that close? I had no idea."

"There's a lot you don't know about your father. Where do you think all your talents come from unless he and Monique also had one or two too?" the Renegade says. "Frédéric's truly one of those real, unassuming heroes of the early New Athens movement, only that he has withdrawn himself into a deep, dark incognito mode in order to protect you and Stellan after you were born."

"I had no idea… and I was thinking I was the one hiding something from him," Nastassia says, flabbergasted.

"Frédéric, being a leading neurologist in neurogenetics field." The Renegade notices another astonishment in Nastassia's eyes, "yes, your father. A bundle of mysteries, that calm, polite man who sacrificed his scientific career out of love."

"Jeez!"

"He never regretted his decision to withdraw from science. After all, he wrote numerous science fiction books under pseudonymous Lorenzo Bladuzzi, all of which, as you know, became bestsellers. He was immensely proud and very happy to have you and Stellan, two little weirdos as he called you behind your backs."

Nastassia smiled. "We always knew. Because of him everyone called me a weirdo since, like, forever."

"The main reason for his fears was what Varga was doing to the MEGS."

"The MEGS?"

"Megalencephaly is a genetic condition in which the brain is abnormally large. Two, three times larger than the normal one, hence, the MEGS."

"Dad never told me anything about it."

"He was terrified for you two. Frankly, I've never seen Frédéric afraid of anything, but what Varga has been doing with MEGS truly horrified him. The very idea of you two being caught drove him insane. He worked like a madman on exposing those experiments."

"How come I know next to nothing about any of that?"

"Ah, silly me. Frédéric did his best to hide this from you and Stellan. You even went on that African trip when the scandal broke and you all stayed there until the noise was over. And then some."

"What is truly shocking is that those used to be normal kids, but by changing their DNA, Varga's lab had induced megalencephaly in their otherwise unaffected brains. To our horror we discovered that all those kids were orphans, so no one would really mind about them, for no one really cared or even knew about them. Those poor kids have fallen through the cracks of a system indifferent to their pain, unconcerned about their destiny. It was only Bolghery's writing about it that alarmed people to the atrocities. Frédéric knew, probably better than anyone else, how neurologenetics could be abused, so we were working with Philip Bolghery around the clock on exposing Varga's secret lab's heinous crimes. What they did to these kids was truly unspeakable."

"How do the missing precogs fit into this MEGS story?"

"We were never really sure. What we do know is how twisted Varga's approach to the precogs phenomena had been from the very start. He had built his operations in two stages. It's difficult to see which one was the worst," Renegade says, and types on the keyboard. "Look at this."

Første's huge head appears on the computer screen.

Nastassia, eyes wide open. "Who is that?"

"Første, the first kid Varga used, one of the MEGS, genetically enhanced programmers, the kids used for his sick experiments." Renegade keeps typing, showing another photo.

Første and Doyle

"Frédéric was approached by him and Doyle, another of the MEGS, another boy who was forced to work in Varga's lab. Første seemed afraid but Doyle poked at your father by using none other than my stealth protocol. So he had become our mole among the MEGS, a true whistleblower."

"They are not precogs, then?"

"No, the precogs came later. Varga has a knack for dividing his operations into parallel streams so MEGS ware one part of the plan, the precogs another. No matter what the plan was. Is. The orphans were injected with the mutated MLC1 gene, a cause of megalencephaly."

"But why was that needed? The whole genetic procedure?" Nastassia barely contains tears, looking at Første's sad, tortured eyes.

"They were tweaking the DNA code in order to create enormous brains in those kids and plug them into the qubits computing system so they can perform better. You know that not even the first quantum computers are capable of parallel processing in the manner human brains are. Sure, they perform their computations in what is effectively zero time and seem vastly superior to us, but they are not. Not yet," Renegade continues his presentation while showing images of what he's talking about. They slide in and out in front of Nastassia's bewildered eyes. An image of the huge BEIN-5, a 9.99 exaFLOPS supercomputer pops up on the screen.

"To match what one EFLOPS computer system can do in just one second, you'd have to perform one calculation every second for 31,688,765,000 years. This is the only known photo of Varga's supercomputer." The Renegade's speech keeps rolling over the facts like a bulldozer. "Bear in mind, the quantum computers they use are still prototypes, so Varga is also using supercomputers, conventional machines if one could call them such. In fact, the BEIN-5, in popular culture known as the INFINITUS, does most of the work. It has a combined total of over a hundred million computing cores, or so. No one knows for sure. Such a monster sucks up such vast amount of energy that Varga has problems getting enough of it. MEGS, at the other hand, are so much more energy-efficient, and with their parallel processing power, intuitive deduction—rather deduction of the data—and so on, they ease up the BEIN tasks. They are, effectively, in a cruel, paradoxical twist, also acting as a cooling system for the supercomputer. It takes a mind of truly sick fuck to come up with an idea as perverted as Varga's. He was overheard calling those kids added value to his empire."

"Added value," whispers Nastassia. *Stellan is a commodity to Varga.*

"The kids, MEGS, spend a lot of their time checking out every newborn human, until they are six or so, combing the world for the precogs. They are registering precogs or potential precogs, sorting them out for future use. Those were Doyle's exact words, describing what they've done."

"Geez," Nastassia yelps, like a puppy in pain.

"We knew only what Doyle told us. We didn't have any documents. And he was able to communicate with Frédéric only occasionally."

"Couldn't you do anything to help them? Break fucking Varga's neck?"

"Our only power, our only tool was Bolghery's position with the *New York Times* at the time and his series of columns on the topic. We wanted the public to help us. Alas, it has severely backfired. The first MEGS lab did not fare well," Renegade replies, a ton of bricks nesting in his heart. "Take a look at what happened with the first one, but brace yourself, it is really, really ugly," he warns and presses a key.

"We have edited several videos from the event."

The First MEGS Lab Video
Virginia, USA
November 7, 2046

> A flurry of activity in an otherwise bland building. A huge, enraged mob of protesters tries to break into the lab. "Nazis!" the protesters scream, some of them carrying "Dr. Mengele Would be Proud" placards.
>
> CUT TO:
>
> Startled by the noise, the MEGS look around. The special police forces rush to the scene, trying to break up the protesters' organized action. Tear gas is used. Rubber bullets fired. Some of the protesters enter the building.
>
> CUT TO:
>
> One of the MEGS, Doyle, a twelve-year-old boy, tries to send a message from his computer and is shot dead on the spot. Another boy, Første, rushes to help him. Too late. The police takes him and the rest of the MEGS away and fires live ammunition above the protesters' heads and the rubber bullets in their bodies. They tripled the tear gas deployment and the throngs disperses in panic. The image becomes blurred and unstable.
>
> CUT TO:
>
> Another point in time. Bulldozers, hiccuping over the rubble, are razing to the ground the building where the lab was housed.

Nastassia watches the footage with a hand pressed to her mouth.
"Horror," she utters.
"Unspeakable. After the police killed that poor kid in front of the billions watching the live stream, the project faced public outrage. Dr. Stephen

Anthony, a neurosurgeon in charge of the MEGS development, doxxed by, wink wink, Anonymous, although we're sure Varga was shifting the blame, was mobbed and killed outside his house. Of course, Varga's propaganda machine went on a counterattack with a vengeance. They screamed murder. Anarchy. They started by discrediting Bolghery, the videos he signed and his articles and, given that he did not have any real, hard evidence of what was going on in, now razed and evidence-free lab, they were creating dozens of contradictory fake stories, some attributed to him, some to the 'anonymous sources,' accusing him of being complicit in the poor, noble Dr. Anthony's murder and distorted the truth so much that no one knew what to think anymore. In all the mess the MEGS program could have vanished into deep, dark shadows, no question asked, and that's what has happened."

Nastassia listens to the Renegade with her hand covering her jugular, like she's protecting her throat from being torn apart by a pack of hungry wolves; she seems to be in physical pain by listening alone. Renegade notices her pain, but he knew that the young, somewhat smallish girl is tough, so he continues, not interrupting the flow of horrors.

"The accident was settled for the benefit of the public by providing them with the final truth. It was the protesters that shot poor Doyle, not the police. Philip Bolghery was the victim of a hoax at best or a delusional conspiracy theorist at worst. Some poor bastard was tried for murder and is now rotting in a maximum-security prison, removed from the world for good. The lab wasn't some sort of modern Dr. Mengele experimentation monstrosity, it was rather Dr. Anthony's benevolent human gene research facility, later renamed Dr. Stephen Anthony's Gene Research Center, endowed by Varga's shell companies. The MEGS were not real, it was either Bolghery or the protesters that PhotoShopped images with the purpose of arousing the compassionate public's feelings and so on. Varga managed to turn the whole affair on its head. No one knew what is true and what if false and soon after everyone settled in their echo chambers, for a while chanting their versions and their truth of the story, unheard by anyone else, thus canceling each other."

Nastassia stands motionless in front of the Renegade and listens to his diatribe. She isn't naive, she knows how vicious Varga's world has been since she was born, but the complexity, the revolting nature of all things Varga sickened her. Maybe she should gulp the Happiness Pill and make the world as it is go away and live happily ever after in the Reality for Everyone™ as a perpetual winner, mingling with the INNOCENTI, or so she tries to amuse herself.

It does not work. She spits in disgust.

"Are you OK?" Renegade interrupts his presentation, noticing Nastassia flinching.

"I am. Only it is so much to digest at once. Please continue."

"To cut a long story short—well, shorter—at the end, Varga pulled another twist, straight from the horror factory, and let Bolghery stew in the boiling soup of doubt and accusations, having damaged his reputation, at the time seemingly irreparably. He pulled a miracle by regaining his trustworthiness later. But Varga had to remove his credibility for his next move. The guardians from various orphanages, the very people that were not really protecting the orphans, and some of the protesters, on the other hand, were targeted by the Virtuosi orchestrated attacks, as perpetrators of an abhorrent hoax. As those 'guilty' for Doyle's death, they were doxxed and harassed. The Interior Ministry, in order to 'protect them,' had given them false identities, put them in some sort of witness protection program, and had them gone. And puff!" The Renegade blows air. "They have vanished into thin air, like nothing had happened. Only they were now dispersed all over the country, without the ability to reconnect again. Bolghery's follow-up on the cover-up wasn't even noticed by the public, swallowed by the silence that ensued. At that time no one cared about him or the kids anymore anyway. So Varga not only managed to turn the public opinion 180 degrees, but in the meantime he had also created that nauseous Reality for Everyone™ show so to further distract them. Evil breeds evil. He had learned his lesson well and moved the operation beyond anyone's eyes. Where? Your guess is as good as mine." The Renegade finishes his speech and sits, exhausted by the memories.

This is beyond loathsome, what the Renegade has told her about Varga's operations, much worse than in her worst nightmares. A sense of unspeakable apprehension falls upon Nastassia's soul like a stone slab over a grave. Not even Stellan has ever produced, in his comic books, nor in his dreams or in the stories he shared with her, anything remotely as evil as this concept.

"Do we know where Varga keeps these kids? Where's Stellan?"

"We'll have to find that out."

Nastassia stands still in front of the frozen image of Doyle on the screen, her eyes glaring at him. Despite his oversized head, Doyle's eyes are luminous and kind. She swallows in pain. "He has such kind eyes," she utters quietly.

"Yes, he did." The Renegade pauses, observing Doyle's oversized head and those deep, kind eyes that Nastassia has noticed. "Frédéric and I have never gotten over his murder, even though he knew we couldn't do anything to prevent it."

"And Første?"

"We never heard from him again. I still feel guilty."

"You needn't be, you know that," Nastassia says, stating a fact. "And the precogs. What does Varga want from all those kidnapped kids?"

"We didn't know, but we had… *have* an idea, a theory, based on early info Doyle provided us with. It was more of a sketch of an idea, inadmissible in court, but it seems that after they were kidnapped, the precogs, they then plug them into the vast supercomputer system, the one that is supported by the MEGS, and keep doing what they do. MEGS, being humans, serve as a sort of electronic liaison in between supercomputers and the precogs, another set of humans. Until recently we were totally in the dark regarding their purpose."

"Now you are not?"

"We think we might have seen a flicker of revelation," Renegade says pensively.

"And?" Nastassia starts to pace around again, a sure sign she's impatient to find out more. The Renegade pauses, thinking. How did all of that go so far? How did Varga amass so much power? How did it happen that he's been able to do whatever he wants, no matter how monstrous, and get away with it? Is the system, rather the pattern of human behavior, set up in a way that psychopaths have an unfair advantage over the good people? Do those "ordinary folks" just want to have their bellies full, a roof above their heads, and an occasional sexual pleasure, so not to be bothered with issues that are not their immediate concerns? Gosh, how much he hates those trivial thoughts, but what else to do, how to even try to understand the human condition, he mumbles angrily to himself. In the corner of his eye, he sees how Nastassia has stopped in her tracks and spread her arms, shooting glances his way.

"Renegade? And? What are they using the precogs for?"

The Renegade takes a deep breath.

"They are slicing up their memories."

Nastassia's eyes open wide. *What does it even mean?* "But they are kids? What could they remember that's so important?"

"The future."

"Come again?"

"The memories of the future," the Renegade confirms. "For whatever reason, Varga's tapping into the future through the MEGS and precogs, this is what they seem to be doing."

"But how? How are they splicing the memories?" She spreads her arms in disbelief. "How would they do that? And why?"

"Think of memories not as brain's software feature but rather as hardware, a device floating in the middle, between worlds. It's contra-intuitive at first, but it would help you to visualize what I am talking about, and not so difficult once you accept the concept. Like a hardware hacker would, you splice a device in the middle and add complexities in order to reveal errors and hidden messages."

"How do you do that?"

"In order to hack, say, a hardware crypto wallet as Joe Grand, hacker of the LØpht—that is LØpht Heavy Industries group, well before your time—going under the name Kingpin, has done various times, you use a fault-injection method attack against the chip, mess with the voltage, and access the RAM. What Kingpin has done was force the wallet into firmware update mode, sending the PIN and key into RAM. And then he was able to read secret data, like the PIN."

"How do you apply this to the memories?"

"It's pure speculation. The memories in their raw form are sets of data that might not mean too much by itself as a bundle. However, we think, if you splice a memory, you get more reliable data, all that's hidden from you, the person possessing the memories. Like humans, memories are fickle, unreliable, deceptive. Memory biases in eyewitness testimonies are notorious examples of how a raw memory rarely represents truth. Like when you try to recall a dream, you lose most of the data in it. Another way of thinking is that memories are a part of capricious consciousness while their spliced parts are of the more sturdy unconsciousness. The latter are difficult to read, but they might hold the keys to unlocking the secrets of the universe, if you wish, of anything, once the memories of the future are unlocked."

"This does not sound too probable." Nastassia's clearly not convinced.

"No less than having MEGS plugged into a supercomputer and precogs at the same time. And yet, we're almost sure this is the case with Varga's arcane maneuvers."

Nastassia slowly nods. "Why does Varga do that?"

The Memory of Time

Since Aristotle's concept of uniform, ever-flowing time, the idea of time and its strange properties hunted metaphysicists, poets, philosophers, and physicists alike, until Albert Einstein blew everyone's mind with his space-time theory, making it a physical thing. And just like that, if time is not an ever-flowing, ethereal concept, but a palpable property of the universe, its malleable fabric must mean that the future could also be, like space itself, touched, sensed, perhaps bent. For sure it would be observable, like neutrinos are, maybe changeable, and ultimately controllable. The Renegade had spent a lot of time thinking about the physical properties of time but he has no time to go in-depth now. Instead he gets to the point.

"I don't know what Varga wants to see, to read, from the future," the Renegade says grimly. "For sure he does not care about the stock markets, for he controls them anyway. I can imagine a few scenarios, but none seem too plausible to me. The INFINITUS is powerful enough that it could process everyone's movements in real-time, analyze and act upon in no time, so it was quite a strange puzzle to ponder, what Varga is doing. The INFINITUS would be able to analyze mass movements or eventual riots in real-time. Not to mention that Varga mostly controls the population through his network of idiotic games and pseudo-realities anyway, in a never-ending brainwashing psyop, so all that is a mystery. Unless it's just another display of his sadistic nature."

"Frédéric was telling me at length once how Varga's obsessed with history," Nastassia remarks. "He told me how Varga often asked himself what the world would look like if Adolf Hitler had the atomic bomb before the Americans and threw it on London and Moscow, even New York. Maybe he is tapping into future weapons development, so to prevent the Chinese from taking over?"

"Possible, but not likely, given the Malacca Strait War."

"What do you mean?"

"The Malacca Strait War was Varga's only successful collaboration with the Chinese Communist Party."

"Meaning?"

"It was a fake war. Both parties needed it to rile up their populations, pit them against the other, so various problematic laws could be shoved down their throats. Everything was just a computer simulation, a fake of all fakes."

"Is anything real in Varga's world?" Nastassia grimly asks.

It's a good question. A small wonder Winston Varga's twisted mind had created a charade, called the INNOCENTI, as the societal pinnacle of his world, to rub it in everyone's nose. It's a pity we'd never hear the Renegade take on that question. Instead he becomes a tad philosophical for a moment. "Everything is in the mind anyway," he says to Nastassia's scoff, which he ignores.

"We need to crack the INFINITUS and find out where Varga keeps Stellan and the MEGS and all the precogs; that would also reveal his true intentions and help us to fight him."

"So, what do we have to do in order to find out?"

The Plan Starts to Formulate

The Renegade turns on all his rigs and the PHOENIX ONE's big, green eye appears on one of the holograms. It is visceral, feeling like it is here, in a sense it was *here*, with them, humming threateningly yet aloof, menacing, murderous, foreboding. Not a pleasant feeling, but Nastassia, not upset one iota by having her parents' killer's eye so close to her, invokes her inner resolve.

"It's time to kick that scrap metal assassin's ass," she declares, clasping her hands as a Spartan would, all riled up and eager to rush into the Peloponnesian War. She's ready to raze the enemy to the ground and crush the tyrant to a pulp. She gets herself a console and starts probing the traffic from the PHOENIX. The Renegade himself is far from being a faint-hearted beautillion and is not too shabby a codebreaker in his own league as well, but Nastassia is not only natural, she's truly something else, always a cypherpunk possessed, never to be the one to flinch, never the one to fear.

Alas, he'll have to contain her wrath for now. She notices his hesitation.

"Renegade," she says, "what's on your mind?"

"Do you recall when I told you, a while ago, I guess you were just a tween, that seeking a weakness in a system is like scouring for an English-speaking person, or a conversation, in Shanghai's People's Square?"

"Yes, why?"

"Among the Chinese, English is an unencrypted part of the noise, something you can instantly recognize."

"Duh!" Nastassia rolls her eyes.

He smiles, if this girl with a lion heart has any weaknesses, it's her impatience. And it will be tested now. For real. "Most of the hacking is social hacking, don't you dare to *duh* me again," he says with a mocking threat in his voice, "so we can't attack Varga again without a plan. Rest assured he has set up all sorts of traps, from deep digging to polymorphs."

She knows he is right and says nothing.

"We can't make any mistakes and must lie low until we know everything about him," he says, slowly and pensively. "Varga is the most photographed and followed man alive. His every move is being broadcast around the clock, and yet, no one really knows him. None has ever gotten to the core of his being. Therein, in his deepest secrets we might be able to crack his defenses."

Nastassia gets what he is thinking.

"Bolghery?"

"He's a treasure trove for all things Varga and he'll help us. We need to probe Varga's every weak spot and find a way in. Otherwise the *scrap metal* would obliterate us the next time." He pauses and then nonchalantly drops the bomb. "It's only you that has an ability to *see* things we normies don't."

Yes, he understands much more about her than she might have presumed. So, *he knows*, Nastassia, thinks. It somehow seems natural and she accepts it as such. They're allies and each of their strengths helps out the other's weakness. However, despite accepting this new reality that is rapidly shaping around her, she has also sensed a huge tsunami of all things Varga coming her way and does not like it too much.

"The answers are in Winston Varga's story and you'd have to learn it by heart."

"Now I have homework to do too?" she puffs as she starts to pace around. The Renegade's words stop her in her tracks.

"Call it as you wish. But only after you know him in and out will you be able to fully employ your intuition and get to him. Without it, tell me, where would you start?"

She has no idea. *Renegade is right.*

"What do you propose? Tell me, how do we start?"

The Old Vic

The Renegade takes a deep breath and continues, somehow changing his tone and his posture. He's acting like he's acting as he paces around like

Nastassia used to do when excited about something. "We must research Winston Varga, and do it seriously, thoughtfully, and thoroughly, we ought to check him inside out and while doing that be solicitous to a fault. We must examine all about him in-depth—"

"Research Varga. In-depth. I got it," Nastassia interrupts, but the Renegade's having none of it and he continues moving about histrionically; he's a strange blend of an old Victorian thespian high on his own gravitas and a high-strung actor spewing poorly written platitudes. In the dark shadows of his underground lab, with his long white hair and dark eyes dimly lit from the myriad screens hanging around, he does look like an actor. *A comedic one,* Nastassia thinks, amused by his little performance. *Why is he doing that, though,* she asks herself as she watches his performance. *I never knew he could be that funny.*

"We must cross all the t's and dot all the i's as we discover the monster, search for every loose nook and cranny in his deprived organization. We must dig out every virtual or real grave the snotty little degenerate left behind and find what he hides." The Renegade is now gearing toward a blockbuster movie-style monologue crescendo so Nastassia starts to quietly snicker as he continues, encouraged by his audience's enjoyment. "We must open any and every closet that persnickety bastard has hidden and get them into the light, we must examine each and every knickknackery that deadbeat, fancy worm might hold dear to his black heart. We must know what he thinks, where he thinks before he thinks it, we must know him better than he knows himself."

"Stop!" Nastassia bursts into laughter. The Renegade's theatrical delivery was flawless. "Stop that, please! You must stop that before I die laughing," and the Renegade joins her and laughs his belly out.

They laughed hysterically for a minute. The sheer absurdity of their situation in this dungeon lab, as the murderous sentinel in the skies waits to kill them, makes it even more ludicrously funny.

There's no better way to fight the absurdity of living but with laughter.

"What in the name of God was that?"

"I was just making a point." The Renegade switches back to his serious mode. "Winston Varga is the most lethal enemy one could have. Half measures never suffice. We must go all the way."

Nastassia, for one long second, looks deeply into his eyes. Well, all is clear now.

"So, homework after all?"

"Yes, the homework."

"How do we go about it?"

"It would be mostly you. Bolghery had agreed to share all his data with you, even a manuscript of a book on Varga he's been working on."

Nastassia is awed by this man, the world's most iconic journalist, a man her family admired and a mystery whose whereabouts were as secret as anything the Knights Templars were guarding with their lives. She did not want to appear as a fawning fan though, so she cracks a joke.

"Phatty was right, you old dudes, you all know each other."

"Siri, get me Phillip!" the Renegade yells.

Nastassia shoots a quick, murderous glance at him. Siri had been outed as the most vicious little spy a household could have, along the lines of the equally bad, private-info gobbling Alexa and Garrire. Those were the only software banned in New Athens. Her hack into Siri's repository of private data was a sensation back then. The Renegade giggles like a little boy. "I was just messing with you. You ready?"

She nods.

"Good. Now, relax. He's quite a difficult character, you'll see that."

"How come?"

"Well, Bolghery acts like an old cynical grouch at one moment and as a mirthful old lady who wants to hug everyone the next. Totally unpredictable lad."

"No way?" Nastassia squints her eyes, her lips pouting out. *That's disappointing.*

"Yeah. I think he's crazy, like clinically crazy, bipolar or so. As you'd expect a journalist to be." The Renegade rolls the word journalist over his tongue in disgust. "A man who had gone astray. Suffering the humiliation of becoming a friendless and homeless weirdo, a stateless and mindless looney."

Is he messing with me again? Nastassia thinks suspiciously, then a booming voice confirms her suspicion.

"He also hears you before he sees you, you old curmudgeon." Philip Bolghery's words come from the dark screen hanging on the wall. "Turn the video on, you old fake."

"Oops," cries the Renegade and fixes his 'mistake.'

Bolghery beams from the screen, smiling. "You did not trust this old, useless codger, did you?"

Nastassia shakes her head. "Not for a moment," she lies.

"Who's old?" The Renegade turns to her. "I told you he's crazy."

"You both seem nuts to me." She rolls her eyes, joining their inside joke.

"Who isn't?" Bolghery asks and they all laugh. That would be their last laugh for a while.

"Listen, Nastassia," Bolghery says, "forgive me but I have something urgent to do now. Please read this file first, it's from my book on Varga. Then we'll discuss it and move on. Cheerio!"

He leaves.

"Unpredictable. I told you so," the Renegade says absentmindedly, without a smile, and goes on examining the text on the computer screen. It reads *Childhood's End* by Philip Bolghery.

"I'll do it in my room, if you don't mind," she tells the Renegade.

"No, why? Not at all."

Chapter 9

INNOCENCE LOST

Philip Bolghery
New Athens, NYC
March 21, 2048

    Bolghery, who has been behind the dark screen, following the whole conversation between Nastassia and the Renegade leading up to his entrance to the scene, did not leave either.

    That girl upsets him, he thinks. *Do I not believe she's up to the task?* he asks himself as the dark envelops his secret abode where he would usually just sit, for hours, drinking an anise-and-wormwood licorice, absinthe, after another. No, it's more fear of what she *represents*. If someone like her would turn to Varga's side—many have—we'd have no chance. Funny, she's smaller than her age, almost like an ancient child from *The Prophecy* Frédéric wrote about.

    But, let me have another one.

    He also loved to imbibe on Metaxa Ouzo, a Greek anise aperitif from the cellars of the Greek island Samos. He loved that country before the triple-cursed Winston Varga came into this world to poison it with his megalomaniacal appetites. He was tempted to turn the feed from the Renegade's lab back on to see what's going on, but she'd *know*—the kid seems to somehow *know everything*. But, he hated to admit, he admired her from afar as he was doing his research on the *palpability* of Frédéric's Prophecy.

Out of all the precogs he's met or heard about over the years, Nastassia and Stellan Bonnet were the most reclusive, and also it seems, the most powerful. A small wonder, Varga finally got a hold of one of them. It was a miracle Frédéric and Monique had managed to shield them for so long.

He raises a glass to her health. She really has no clue about her own meaning in this world. But she's scary as hell with her damn *insights*, and those eyes that see *through* you—they have the power of terrible destruction in them. Better not to meddle. I hope she'll be able to see through Varga. So far he has an upper hand on her and on the whole damn world.

"I guess we'll see. Now everything will unravel very fast," he says aloud to himself and toasts again, to the empty space in front of him, "To the Renegade and that weirdo Starchild of his, and to Stellan we hope to find." As long as it's warm and there's enough Metaxa in his storage, far, far away from any prying eyes, everything will be fine.

After Nastassia retreats to her room to peruse the first chapter from Bolghery's book on Varga, the Renegade goes to his study and pings him.

"She's still just a kid, Renegade," Bolghery says, somewhat gloomily.

"The kid we need. I saw her regaining her precog skills."

"Already?"

"In seconds, virtually. I told her to breathe and it created an avalanche in her. And that's just the beginning."

"I don't know if it's smart to poke her like that. It might look like a ruse. Be careful. She trusts you. If you lose her trust, we're all lost."

"I won't. We aren't."

"I guess. Ping me when she's back."

Sympathy for the Devil

"Do I have to feel bad for Varga?" Nastassia waves a printout of Varga's early history as soon as she was back. "I am sorry, but only that his father's bullet did not kill him."

Bolghery looks at the Renegade, who shrugs.

"I am not sure I understand the point of the homework. Varga bought a ranch. Well? Shall we try his house number as his password? His drunkard father killed his educated mother. Varga needed a hug but has turned into a monster? What's the point? Really? Renegade, why are we wasting the time?"

Look inside.

Again, his message was a telepathic one for the Renegade did not say a word. Nastassia glances at his strange expression; he is unrecognizable. She turns to Bolghery who attentively gazes at her.

"For chrissake, you two," Nastassia cries. "Are you aware you're looking at me like I am some kind of a freak?"

No one responds.

Look inside. How does Varga look?

The Renegade stares at her, silently demanding her to *look*. So she does. She closes her eyes, empties her mind-world, and goes on rummaging through the dark, strange chambers of her own energetic self. Nothing. Or, almost nothing? She holds onto her senses and tries to listen to distant echoes. Deep inside her is a barely noticeable energetic blob, shapeless and tiny. She tries to focus on it but it avoids her and then, out of the blue and never previously felt, she feels a pain like an arrow pierce through her abdomen. She yelps in pain and swoons, falling down through the cold darkness. The Renegade jumps and catches her before she hits the floor, and she comes back to her senses.

"What has happened? How does Varga look?" he insists while she is still in shock.

"Like nothing, like a blob. Dark. Tiny."

"But you know how Varga looks?"

"Duh!"

"And you haven't seen him, just that tiny blob, right?"

"I guess so. I can't be sure it is Varga but it appeared as I was searching for him."

"That's it," the Renegade says wildly. "That's it, you now have a clear energetic connection with Varga. A perfect first step."

Nastassia does not like any of this. She feels like her entrails have been opened wide and the surgeon is talking to her individual organs, telling them what to do, like she, as a whole does not matter. Is the Renegade trying to isolate that *blob* of energy that might or might not be a link to Varga, and work with it, independently of her? It's like sending a maskless diver into a sewer to try to find an exit from it. Why would the Renegade require something like that of her? She is sure that the blob, that Varga's energy, in its core, stinks much worse than all the sewers of the world put together. She does not like any of this one bit; she feels ordered around, used, almost like she was violated. *Does he have hidden intentions?*

This is all well too strange and well too unpleasant for an unspecified benefit.

She gazes at the old sage. Nothing tells her that he has any other intentions but good ones. She must be becoming paranoid, to *doubt* the Renegade? Yet the bitter taste remains, like she has inhaled the sulfur emanating from Varga's rotten soul and was forced to do so by the only man she should trust.

Something feels wrong.

"Any more homework?" she snaps.

The Renegade sees her annoyance, fully understanding what has made her aggrieved. She has had too much happen to her in such a short time. He is sorry that he must push her even harder but, even more so, excited at the chance of having Nastassia make progress in getting to Varga.

Bolghery interjects, "Guys, the next chapter is a mess. Needs editing. I'd rather read only parts that matter. It will go faster."

"So, read already, if you have to," she snaps again but corrects herself. "Please."

Bolghery rushes to read the next chapter of his unpublished Winston Varga biography.

Winston Varga Genesis, unpublished
The Road to Hell
by Philip Bolghery

"Jesus H. Christ, we know who you are," Nastassia huffs at him.

"Be quiet," he replies as the strange tension between them rises and continues to read.

The tragic death of his parents on October 11, 2008, and his miraculous survival, made Winston Varga a minor celebrity. Once the old and social media alike found out the real reason for his father's mad rampage was Winston's lavish ranch, whose purchase made Jeff murderously angry, Varga became an American celebrity du jour. A good-looking kid whose early business success made him the very embodiment of the American Dream stood grief-stricken in front of people eager to enjoy the soothing scent of their own selfless compassion.

"Thoughts and prayers" were pouring his way, assuring him Jesus would save him. Even baby Jesus prayed for him from his stable, God bless his generous baby soul. He was in God's all-knowing hands even when His ways are not quite clear. They encouraged him to pray, "The more you pray, the less you'll fear," someone told him. He was not alone, others assured him, God is with him. That is if he, Varga, lets God into his heart and then all would be fine and peachy. Under the endless barrage of thoughts and prayers, he began to abhor these people, whom he saw as duplicitous in their phony religious fervor. "Do they really kneel in front of the altar and pray for Varga?" he asked anonymously, using one of his avatars online.

At that time of relative innocence, he still possessed an ability to be surprised by people and their fake purity, so after his disrespectful avatar was severely scolded by the holier-than-thou crowd eager to put infidels in their place, he was puzzled by their hatred. With the speed of a silvery bullet train from Shandong Province, they pulverized even the tiniest shred of doubt of those daring to upset the righteous, God-fearing people that wished Varga well. So, he came to understand strength in numbers and saw the weaknesses of the individuals in them. It was a peek into the abundance of human traits that he was bound to capitalize on later in his life. While he seriously doubted "God," he understood the immense power of "God" as an idea and learned his lesson: he should never doubt the righteous crowds publicly. On the contrary, he should pander to them and, ultimately, use them for his own good.

Then the mass media started to gush over him, encrusting his "tragic story" with the most syrupy clichés: "The Golden Boy's Tragedy," read the *New York Times Magazine*'s profile on young Varga. The Washington Post surpassed even the *NYT*'s mawkishness, starting their own article with the trivial nonsense line "To be honest…" under the title "At the End of Days, a New Day" with Varga pictured in front of his palatial mansion. They even put a red broken heart emoji next to him—not really worthy of Picasso but ideal for the Idiotic Era that introduced an emoji translator as a proper, well-paid job.

"The Road to Hell is Paved with Good Intentions," was a title, embellished in bleeding gold letters on the cover of the *Modern Times* magazine, the old dame *TIME* magazine's subsidiary used as a failed attempt to save its diminishing circulation. Half of those portrayals of the "innocent, tragic victim" of domestic violence were focused on the money he had made at such a young age and, even more so, on the stupendous ranch that provoked envy in millions of readers all across the country.

That was how he started to loathe the media as much as he realized how media shapes societies. It was a moment in which he understood the power of his money and his fame, albeit short-lived at the time. That was something he decided to amass in the future—fame and fortune, all to attain goals that he started to feel were his mission in life. Arguably, that fatal day made what Winston Varga represents today. His tragedy was his Manifest Destiny. He did not control it in the past, but from now on he'd be the master of his own destiny.

And not only his own.

Noonday Demon

Once he had settled into his new property, which he named Eleni Galanis Ranch after his late mother, Winston went on a movie-watching binge to numb his pain. He watched and watched, like a sleepless maniac unwilling to think or feel. Nothing like a Hollywood-movie-industry-concocted drug, spiked with insufferably sugared clichés and gratuitous brutality alike, to brainwash and sedate one's cerebrum. There were two curious outcomes of his crazy spree. The first was a 1950 Mercury Monterey Coupe, a custom-build car from Sylvester Stallone's legendary movie *Cobra*, a flick so bad that it had been nominated for six Razzie Awards, which were given to the worst movies in any given year. But what a wonderful treat, adorned with the most American thing ever—violence—those movies were to young Winston Varga. Throats cut and mutilated corpses galore. And then that unique American dream: the car, which represented freedom to roam, to fuck, or to do away with an occasional hitchhiker all over its endless surreal landscapes. Winston Varga still had his parents' Old Violet but once he saw that beautiful Mercury painted with a custom-mixed black cherry paint, its sandalwood leather interior with burgundy piping, he decided that he ought to purchase that Cobra. So he did it online, briefly interrupting his binge. The car would be ready in Los Angeles several days later, so he went back to his Brian De Palma marathon.

Then, in the wee hours of the morning and several hours deeper into the binge, a second outcome stemmed from the wise words of a great Cuban-American philosopher, Antonio "Tony" Montana. But, don't be fooled with this gentle poke, proud children of today who are unfamiliar with the movie heroes of the past, Tony Montana was not really a philosopher. He was rather a fictional character and the main protagonist of the 1983 film *Scarface*, written by Oliver Stone and directed by Brian De Palma. He was played by Al Pacino, an iconic actor of yesteryear whose holograms, sold exclusively by True Imago Dei, LLC., are now virtual guides through the Metropolitan Museum of Motion Pictures, Inc., (an entity, as well as the True Image, that is yet another subsidiary of the Proteus FinTech, Corp.) Anyway, what Tony said that reverberated through young Winston was a famous quote: "In this country, you gotta make the money first. Then when you get the money, you get the power. Then when you get the power, then you get the women."

Upon hearing that, Winston Varga realized that, despite all his money and fame, he was still a virgin. So he has decided to do something about it.

A Cherry Popping Adventure

So weird, Winston thought, to call a first sexual encounter a cherry popping event. What's with those them damn cherries? No apples, anyone? *Forget them damn apples*, a little horny devil whispered in his ear, move on and flounce into the world of adults you now fully belong to. A virgin orphan no more. Varga listened and swiftly moved into action. His binge was over, thanks to Scarface and his pound of Peruvian blow. The dream factory's home, the City of Los Angeles, was only two hours away from the Salt Lake City International Airport and the dream of supermodel-like women was only a wad of cash away. But money, "That's the easy part," he said loudly to himself as he was channeling Al Pacino and dialed a number.

The "Gentlemen's Delight Research" was a most luxurious, elite bordello nestled in a stupendous house that once belonged to none other than Frank Zappa, a music visionary, and it was also the best known secret in LA, an upcoming source of young Varga's own initial carpal delights. It was also registered as a not-for-profit Corpus Church. One must admire Americans and their ingenuity when tax avoidance is in question. No one comes close to them in matters of financial shenanigans. Not even the Communist Party of China, the true future obstacle for Varga's full world-domination goals.

Varga, who did not neglect to notice the so-called church's grotesque legal status, was to embark on his first education in all mysterious matters rumpy-pumpy has to offer. Once in the shrine of love, Ms. Carol Connors was his choice due to her sunny disposition; her boobs were fake, opulent and shiny, her lips divine if overblown, her smile promising. Her figure, as perfect as Jessica Rabbit's booty. Pablo Neruda himself, had he had a chance to make love to that embodiment of perfection, would never write poetry again and would stand silently, in awe of the raw sexuality emanating from her. So, Carol was a girl, suggested by the establishment's own dignified Madame Chloë, who was experienced in providing first-timers in the world of carnal delight, young men of some means, with an exquisite experience, making it less terrifying and more natural. "A girlfriend experience" is how they branded it in those days before sex robots took over and rendered street hookers and high-class escorts alike all but redundant.

"Hi, cutie," she said in a somehow squeaky voice. Minutes later in the seclusion of their room, laughing at his noticeable erection protruding from his jeans, she babbled nonsensically, "another cock bites a cherry."

Cherries again, young Winston thought? But then, like his life depended on the speed of his actions, he took of his clothes maddeningly fast and got at it like a wild wolf while Carol was giggling, delighted by his uncontrollable lust. His erection, bigger than the Sunshine State of Florida of her birth, lasted even shorter than it took him to take his jeans off and he came momentarily. It was like the uncontrolled avalanche of nature's power after a volcano erupted. The whole affair, in victory or a defeat of his Casanova apprenticeship, lasted some fifteen to thirty life-altering seconds.

"You're a real stud," Carol Connors said, encouraging Varga, but he felt something was wrong with his performance. That can't be all, no matter how madly intense it was. As Carol was caressing and kissing his lean but muscular body he got a new rock-hard boner. She put her hand on it and looked at it as someone would a holy relic, all in awe of him, always in awe no matter how many of those strange things she had seen in the course of her noble, educational, sometimes-healing-but-always-needed profession. At that moment Varga had a revelation that stayed with him for years to come: the will to power is real. He realized that both his money and, even more so at times, his body, were sources of power. A deadly combo of cock and a buck would make him unstoppable. A surge of a dominating force overwhelmed him as he turned Miss Connors on her back, held her arms locked wide apart above her head and started to dominate her, this time for hours. On the same day he had lost his virginity he tasted the sweet scent of domineering power over another human being.

And he loved it.

The Road to Hell
The Renegade's Lab, NYC
March 21, 2048

"How do you know that, how do you know any of that?" Nastassia, who sat motionlessly with eyes closed the whole time Bolghery was reading from his draft, asks with an urgent note in her voice.

"I interviewed both Carol and Madame Chloë for the book," Bolghery answers matter-of-factly. "Shall I continue?"

Nastassia nods and Bolghery continues reading.

Varga truly, deeply enjoyed it. The sense of power was so new, so intoxicating. It made him feel mighty. When Carol Connors started to hurt and begged him to stop, he kept doing what he had been doing for quite a while and simultaneously pondered his next move. He made love, or his version of it, to her while keeping the presence of mind to analyze the situation. He considered his persistence to be a magnanimous gesture of kindness; he was able to continue for seemingly forever—in fact, he was capable of killing her—but chose not to and to grant her wish. He was generous toward his first woman so when he climaxed in order "to stop it," he came with a sneer on his face.

That woman, no matter the money, was his—his to do whatever he wanted to do with her. He felt that with every fiber of his body and it was clear that she was sensing it as well. And she was afraid of him, that same woman who, just a short while ago, was giggling at his naivete and lack of experience is now afraid of the man who has possessed her entirely.

He stood up, not as a confused kid anymore but as a changed man who had just ravaged her body at his pleasure. He smiled charmingly and, like a much older man would, politely thanked her for her superb service, but then, intentionally redneckish, quite forcefully slapped her buttocks and placed a gentle smooch on her cheek, covering her naked, vulnerable body with a silk sheet, with another sneer on his smug face. That kiss sent a cold shiver down Carol Connor's spine. She had the first glimpse of what Winston Varga would become, a man of her nightmares.

1950 Mercury Monterey Coupe

His new car was ready. Winston went to pick it up at the Oldtimers' famous dealer, a crapulent curmudgeon going only under the name "Joe." He was an old man with the charisma of a rock star but with the patience of a jumpy opossum, also a legend in the circles of antique car nuts. He hated selling his masterpieces to rich, bratty kids like Winston. "Too much dough, not enough work for it," he grumbled to himself, miffed by that kid and somewhat angry. Then he took a second look at him. His surly face produced something vaguely resembling a smile.

"I know you. You're that *pobrecito* whose father killed his mother. The rich one?"

"Not as rich as you, Mr. Joe." Varga grinned with what would become his trademark smile all over the world.

"Save ass-kissing for big honchos, kiddo. Here, you'll kiss the pavement if you get too cute with me."

"Yes, sir. I won't do that again, sir."

The old grouch measured Winston up with one long, unfriendly stare. Then he let out another grin that he might've learned from some smiley, polite funeral parlor director. "I'll cut you some slack. You had it tough." Joe said in his gruff voice and tossed Varga the keys. The legendary Mercury Monterey cost the earth, but it was his. What a treat he deserved. He jumped into the car and zipped away, ready to devour America.

Hans Böhm

"Quite Wagnerian," said a tall, haggard, eccentric-looking, and ghost-like young man with a huge nose who was perhaps two or three years older than Varga. He was standing in front of McDonald's at Nealey's Corner where he stopped for gas. The man also looked like a drifter.

"Come again?"

"Your ride, man. It's cool. Dramatic. Wagnerian. Tick as German accent." He smiled. Then he threw a second look at Varga. *Here we go*, Varga thought. I will have to get used to it for he saw in the drifter's eyes what was coming.

"Hey, I know you," but it was time for Winston to be surprised by Hans Böhm, which I'd learn later was his name, and he went on to say—" Bolghery read when Nastassia, upon hearing Hans Böhm's name, jumps to her feet and rushes to the screen, abruptly interrupting him.

"Who's that Hans Böhm? I never heard of him? Who is he?" She speaks feverishly but while her nervous energy eludes Bolghery it does not elude the Renegade, who starts to observe her even more carefully.

"Should you try and stop interrupting me, you'd find out," Bolghery snaps again.

Why is Nastassia getting under his skin? the Renegade thinks. *This is not good for us.*

As he continues to read, Bolghery's booming baritone becomes somehow velvety and yet imbued with stings of mockery in his voice. He overcomes the nervousness arising from Nastassia's interruptions and, more so, her mere presence by realizing something. Though he sounded both soothing and upset at the same time, it's clear that he's enjoying the revelations he is sharing with the world for the first time. That's because Philip Bolghery understood that while his audience is comprised of only these two people, an old friend and a scary child, they are the two most important people in the world.

Barring the man they seek to destroy, Winston Varga, the bane of his life.

The Road to Hell
(continued)

Hans Böhm smirked at Varga's annoying huff. "I'll make it easy for you, Dr. Evil! Or should I say, ILOVEYOU, Mr. Zły?" And then, he winked at Varga with a smug smile.

This ghastly bum knows his online identities?

Varga was alerted. No one knew his secret avatars—none! How was that possible? Such a security hole in his budding online personas is impossible.

"What are you saying?" He kept his cool.

"Come on, dude, it took me an hour or so to figure it out."

"To figure what out, exactly?" Winston's eyes were cold and dark as he gauged this strange creature in front of him. *What does he want?*

"Chill out, dude. It's nothing sinister," Böhm said and took out a laptop. "All's inside. Buy me a Big Mac and I'll tell you a secret."

"OK," said Varga after pondering the offer for several long seconds while his gaze penetrated the strange bum with an expensive computer. Under that burning gaze, the bum shrank a bit, which relaxed Varga.

"Winston," he introduced himself, stretching out his arm to shake Böhm's hand. Hans's handshake was surprisingly good; it came from the elbow and was firm, but he wasn't trying to showcase the strength of his grip or trying to compete. He leaned forward ever so slightly and smiled at Varga, like a perfect gentleman of a long-gone era. *Or a gunslinger.* The thought amused Varga, for the drifter looked nothing like it.

"I know," he stated. "I used to go under the name of Hans Böhm but I am now called Maléficus Ultimo," the odd man introduced himself with that wacky name. Winston decided not to comment on it.

"Nice to meet you! Let's eat."

A Lunch with Varga
The Renegade's Lab, NYC
March 21, 2048

The Renegade sits in his corner and keeps a watchful eye on Nastassia. She is not in a trance anymore. She stands in front of Bolghery as he reads, fully awake and focused, glaring at him. *Does she ever blink?* It amuses him to notice that Bolghery has turned off the screen on his side, so not to be disturbed by her intense gaze.

"How do you know all these details?" she asks.

"Varga was my first assignment when I started to work for the *Times*," he replies. "So I followed him. He was yet to become a minor celebrity and no one knew who I was. There, I was just another patron munching on a Big Mac."

"Yes, but how did you do it?"

"Just a sec," Bolghery says, leaving his comp.

Nastassia rolls her eyes. *What now?* She glances at the Renegade, who shrugs.

Bolghery comes back brimming with pride and waving an old Roland CS-10EM In-Ear Monitor and a much older iPhone 3G mobile phone in front of the camera. "iPhone 3G, a 2008 model. Still in working order. And these babies," he flashes Roland's earphones again, "are younger, only twenty years old. I had something similar custom-made back then, so they were equipped with directional microphones. I sat seven or eight meters away from Varga and Böhm, but I was able to hear and record every word."

"Schwanky! Not too basic for old school oldie, not at all," Nastassia compliments without a smile, rather with a small nod.

"Please continue." She drifts back into the mind-world, this time with her eyes open. The Renegade observes her; Nastassia, who usually looks like a little birdy now appears like a ferocious martial eagle seeking its prey. *What's going on in her mind?*

Bolghery continues his strange tale of the odd couple's first encounter.

Selected Computational Linguistics Techniques

The haggard man with two names ate like a hungry wolf. Over his second Big Mac and fourth Coca-Cola, the drifter started to tell Varga how he managed to guess his identity on the Dark Web. Maléficus, who was also a philosopher of sorts, started to tell his detective story in a convoluted way, enjoying the sound of his own voice.

"The herd is a slow-witted, retarded blob of stupidity. Inane, intellectually lazy fools. Slow boiled frogs. Frottaging, sexless eunuchs. They operate in their own negative feedback loops, gobbling up on each moronic confirmation-biased subroutines. Feed them the shit they're addicted to and they'll follow you to the pits of hell while believing they're en route to the promised land if you tell them so."

Varga laughed—it was almost like he had found his soul mate. "You for sure know your way around words. Will you now get to the point?"

"Words are meaningless if not poisonous."

"What are you talking about?"

"Words describe the ugliness of this world. Look around." Maléficus Ultimo points away and around. "The blessed throngs of patrons are munching on their burgers, numb and careless while their tummies are being filled. These so-called humans are stupidly drifting away toward diabetes, stroke, gout, heart attack, or some such beautiful outcome, at best."

"And the worst?" Winston cackled.

"That's the easy part. The sheep are led into mass destruction at the hands of government and the mass media. End results? Nuclear annihilation? Gulags for all? Suffocation on the planet heated to the point of being inhabitable? Choose your own poison. There are a million ways for us to be destroyed. Pick up Isaac Asimov's *A Choice of Catastrophes* and see for yourself."

Varga could not conceal his amusement.

"Come again, who are you?"

"Maléficus Ultimo, at your service, sire." Varga couldn't detect a hint of irony either in the tone of that archaic 'sire' nor in his eyes, so he let him have it this time, getting to the point. "So how did you figure out who I was?"

"By chafing away the throngs of morons and looking for exceptions on the Net first. I have a whole database of people like you. Different. Special. Fascinating. Not fascinating like you, but sometimes close."

Varga huffed.

"OK, enough of this nonsense. Speak to me in plain English! From the start! Omit nothing." Varga's tone jerked Maléficus out of his histrionics and he, like a man sobered up by a gallon of strong Turkish coffee, now spoke soberly and seriously.

"The National Science Foundation has created Dark Web spiders. They crawled the web for years, supposedly to sift through sites with extremists and terrorist content. So the Dark Web wasn't a terra incognita for them anymore."

"You work for the government?" Varga asked, astonished.

"Come on, Sonny."

"Don't you call me Sonny ever again," Varga growled. "If you don't work for the government, how did you know all of that? Did you get a hold of those spiders? And if so, how?" Maléficus Ultimo was startled by the instant change in Varga's demeanor and the destructive power of his dark eyes, which penetrated his mind like a sword. There was a depth of Hell in that young man, Maléficus sensed, something much deeper and darker than he would have expected. He's merciless. And the tone of his voice—*damn!* That's someone capable of commanding arms under the flags of destruction. Deep inside, Maléficus bowed to him, accepting Varga's power over himself. And, if that man would ever ask anything of him, anything at all, from that moment on, Maléficus knew he'd do it no matter the cost. Over those several seconds during which Winston Varga displayed his lethal impatience and his power, Maléficus Ultimo knew with each bone of his body: his life has changed forever, thanks to this chance meeting with his future boss. So, unconsciously, he changed both his posture and the manner of his speech; even the tone of his voice was different from then on.

"They are not much different than Googlebot. You know how it works. Forum spidering. Social media spidering. Content analysis. Sentiment and affect analysis. Only on the Dark Web, inaccessible for normal search engines. All of that interests me for it gives a deeper insight into the people. I recognized you by using their authorship analysis and Writeprint techniques. They have seriously expanded the lexical and syntactic features of traditional authorship analysis to include system and semantic features like violence or racism, anything of relevance to online texts. Your unique Writeprint signature was your scorn of peoples' hypocrisy and stupidity. All your avatars, occasionally but unmistakably for a trained algorithm, used the same terminology sometimes, depending on the forum. You even used the same font. I had a sense of who is behind Dr. Evil and ILOVEYOU.

"Interesting," Varga said. "How did you get the spiders?"

"The University of Arizona's AI lab had developed those spiders, together with The National Science Foundation. Some of it was open-source, some of it I'd gotten through the backdoors they left open. A simple reconnaissance with a network mapper was enough."

"So you're a hacker?"

"Please, Winston. Hackers are for screenwriter hacks and juvenile audiences. I am a philosopher of chaos with some computer knowledge, I admit. I'm simmering in dislike of a world polluted by idiots. Yes, I read your posts carefully. All of them. Phony principles of tolerance and inclusion became the most exclusionary, intolerant instruments of intellectual terror aimed at the sheep. I do not want to cast aspersions too wide, but frankly, I despise the hoi polloi rabble more than those manipulating them."

Varga stared at him with such an intense gaze that Maléficus froze for a moment.

"What?"

An idea started to formulate in Varga's head but he was not ready to share it as of yet. Instead, he simply asked, "Would you mind coming with me to Vegas, to taste some good ol' American debauchery together? Then we can talk some more."

"In a heartbeat, but…"

"What?"

"Las Vegas is a shiny, polished golden turd. A mirage, like its namesake, The Mirage. We should go to Henderson instead. Henderson is hell, built for the rabble. You should see how they built favelas of the American Dream, Winston, in of all places, Henderson, Nevada."

Bolghery stops reading and looks up. "There's much more. You've got a digest version, but it's still crucial to understanding you're seeking. I followed them to Henderson but they ended up in Las Vegas anyway. There is where the Proteus FinTech Corp. was born. As a joke."

"What do you mean?"

"They'd tasted the debauchery indeed. Varga spent a small fortune on hookers, on booze, and on all sorts of drugs—coke, ecstasy, weed. Maléficus sought cocaine and the girls were supplying him. He had the money, using the card given to him by Varga."

"But Varga does not use drugs nor does he drink?"

"He did at the time. Not much, but still. I am not sure if he ever drank after that Vegas trip again. Maléficus might have had something to do with it."

"How come?"

"Read this brief passage while I go to the loo and then I'll tell you," Bolghery said.

Well, that's info I did not need to know, Nastassia thinks when the excerpt of Bolghery's book pops up on the screen.

Death in the Afternoon
Las Vegas, NV
October 21, 2008

"Allow me to order," Maléficus Ultimo requested on the third day of their Vegas binge. They were sitting alone in the Fremont East district's famous bar from the Prohibition era, The Laundry Room.

"Be my guest."

"Theodore, you magnificent Thor of cocktails, help us out, please." He snapped his fingers. Theodore, a suave Porto Rican man with oily hair, almond eyes, and biceps bigger than those of Barnabas Dubh Sanchez, who was the Mister Universe of that time, smiled, not at all upset by that redneckish gesture. Those guys may have been too loud at times, occasionally obnoxious, and had girls to die for with them all the time—which alone would be a reason for Theodore to break their necks in a fit of a sex craze, which he indulged in with similar *hermosas bombónes* of that sort—had they not been the best tippers he had ever experienced in his seven-year-long stint in Sin City. He came here for the women, the gyms, and the money. Only the gyms presented him with any difficulty. So when he saw them coming in again, he knew money was going to be flung his way in obscene amounts.

"Your order is my command, sire." Maléficus taught him to use a royal 'sire' for Varga but he had gotten used to calling them both sire.

"I have two, rather three modest requests."

"And those would be, sire?"

"Put 'I Put a Spell on You' on that antiquated set you have there, please, and then put a spell on us by Deaths in the Afternoon."

"Death in the Afternoon?" Varga asked, puzzled.

"That's a famous cocktail, better known as Hemingway's Champagne in certain parts of Havana, where your wealth would invoke some unwelcomed lust in locals. It's 1 ½ oz. absinthe and 4 oz. brut champagne."

"You certainly know your cocktails, Mr. Ultimo," Theodore complimented.

"The brut must be Veuve Clicquot, of course."

"I would dare not to serve anything else."

"And…"

"Yes?"

"Make us two Sidecars as well."

"Sidecars?" Varga inquired again. He did not like to be in unfamiliar territory, but this was all fun to him. Quite a difference from his Spartan upbringing in Utah.

"Thor, please use three-fourth parts Grand Marnier but leave the sugar rim out," Maléficus told him and turned to Varga. "The Sidecar is one of the most famous cognac-based cocktails ever."

"Mr. Ultimo is correct once again." Theodore was fishing for a bigger tip, which he got a bit later, after explaining the story of the Sidecar to Varga.

"Thanks. You'd be doing me a favor if you'd put on 'That's Life' instead of this screaming. Wasn't Frank Sinatra Vegas's staple?"

"He was a true icon," Theodore agreed. He knew who was the man out of those two, despite Maléficus being the one who had been paying the tab most of the time. Maléficus nudged Varga, pointing to the corner of the bar where one inconspicuous man sat.

"The guy's all alone. Shall we buy him a drink?"

"Sure."

"Theodore, please give one of those to the gentleman over there."

"Thank you, gentlemen," the guy in the shadow, who had been clandestinely recording their conversation, says politely. His name was Philip Bolghery.

A Sidecar for Bolghery
The Renegade's Lab, NYC
March 21, 2048

"No way," Nastassia cries in disbelief.

"Yes, Winston Varga himself bought me a drink once." Bolghery grinned like a fox, "When and if I ever publish this book I will not put my name in this episode. That was just for your entertainment. What follows is the birth of the Proteus."

"Let us hear it," says the Renegade, who was searching his archive in the meantime, with a bit of annoyance in his voice. Nastassia side-glances at him but says nothing. *What's making him nervous*, she thinks before turning her focus back on the Winston Varga genesis.

Death in the Afternoon
(continuation)

"You're filthy rich, right?" Maléficus, who had already started to slur his words, asked rhetorically. Varga, who never lost control over his drinking, looked at him, dissatisfaction in his dark, murderous eyes. He hated the weakness of drunks; he had seen it in Jeff's eyes well too many times, but he allowed his new pal to elaborate on his idea. Or at least to try.

"What you need is a charming sleazebag, possessing the sharp wit of Ronald Reagan, marketing skills of Barack Obama, and charisma of Ahheban Correy to push your agenda through."

"The presidents?"

"Yes! You need them. You have the power. Be their Svengali, throw them a mil and they'll eat from the palm of your hand. America always backed corrupt politicians elsewhere, to the hilt, so why would you not do the same here?"

"Don't be naive. You can't buy a president for a mil."

"Oh. Who's being naive now, Kay?" Maléficus cackled like he had told the best joke ever. Varga did not want to tell him that his was the worst impersonation of Michael Corleone one could find on YouTube at that time.

"What are you ranting about, man? Ease up on these," Varga said, stopping the drinking roulette with sixteen glasses, from which Maléficus was picking up at an ever-increasing pace. He took one more nevertheless, toasted Varga with "down the hatch" and smiled at him cunningly. He leans over like telling a secret, in his most sober tone.

"You're a businessman, Winston. The best return on investment is an investment in a politician you can control. Never forget that one."

Well, that makes sense, Varga thought, but at that moment their conversation was interrupted by two girls that were after fees for their "holistically sensual consultations" (I shit you not, that was on their business cards) so they joined the party. As they were dancing like nobody was watching under the lustful eyes of everyone watching, an idea was formulating in Varga's mind and getting stronger every passing moment. He wasn't really sure how he could articulate it so he let it linger in him and develop a life of its own.

What neither Winston Varga nor Maléficus Ultimo knew at that moment was that only a few weeks ago, in fact on the very day of Winston's mom's murder and suicide of his father, another strange man, a recluse called Satoshi Nakamoto whose real identity no one knew, had introduced Bitcoin, a cryptographic peer-to-peer payment network, to the world. That financial invention would be manna from heaven for Varga's ventures several years later and, a few decades further along, his tool for the coup de grâce delivered to his mortal enemies.

Honesty for America, LLC

As soon as the holistically sensual ladies, garishly giggling over wads of cash given to them by Maléficus, were gone to powder their surgically beautified noses, he continued elaborating ideas for Varga, to the latter's amusement.

"Look here, look, this is what you'd need," he said enthusiastically, opening his laptop and starting to read from some website. "We're helping Congress meet the evolving needs and expectations of an engaged and informed citizenry. Focusing on improving congressional operations and citizen engagement through research, publications, training, and management services."

"What's that hogwash?"

"Hogwash, exactly!" cried Maléficus, "Kudos my master, you cut through the BS like a samurai with his katana would through Beppino Occelli butter. That's lobbying, my man, lobbying. The secret to the heart of America's power. Legalized bribery." Maléficus was all worked up.

"So, this is tax-exempt?"

"Unfortunately not, but the return on investment is momentous."

Varga looked at him suspiciously. "Why are you telling me any of that?" He tried his best Baltimorese: "A yo, wearing a wire, yo?"

"That's swell," Maléficus snickered and continued, "I see the future, your future. You could be the king of the world. Only that you might need a tiny touch, a nudge of destiny." He seemed in a trance-like state. His fervor puzzled and amused Varga.

"And you're that nudge?" Varga laughed.

"I might have been, at your service, sire! Your first step would be to incorporate a lobbying firm."

"And how do we call the company?" Varga asked, starting to like the game.

"Varga Enterprises, perhaps?

"Boring."

"Varga for America, maybe?"

"Too much on the nose," Varga laughed. "I got it! It would be Honesty for America, LLC.!"

Maléficus gave him a high-five and turned to the barkeep.

"Theodore… champagne please, we must celebrate," he said, turning back to Varga. "Honesty for America sounds fantastic. It showcases your true genius."

Varga did not object to ass-kissing, something he'd learn to live with for decades to come. Maléficus continued fervently marching his ideas forward.

"Then you fill Form LD-1, a lobby registration, and you're on your way."

Theodore injected himself into the conversation. "Honesty for America, if I may comment, sire… it has a powerful ring to it."

"It does," Maléficus agrees, suddenly laughing.

"Only that, in America of today, it sounds like a sunscreen for ants."

"Or tax for the rich," blurted Bolghery from his corner. Maléficus caught on.

"A good one. Honesty for America is like an umbrella for a submarine."

"A dental floss for a frog," Varga added.

Everyone laughed.

"Like waterpipe for a hard drive." Maléficus was on a roll.

"A synthetic motor oil for a CPU," Varga said, not to be outdone.

"Honesty for America? Like shoelaces for a T-rex," Theodore said, himself laughing.

"My man." Maléficus high-fived him. "Or like a pocket watch for a whale."

They were flipping out.

"Or like water for a fish," someone burbled, which for some reason seemed insanely funny to them. Maléficus dropped to the floor laughing and started to speak whale, while "swimming" on the floor, like that funny small blue fish, Dory.

"Maybe I should try a Humpback?" Maléficus asked.

"Don't do that!"

"Groooow Groooow! Wwwwweeeee neeeeeeeed tooooooo doooooo thiiiiis sooooon.

Caaaan youuuuuu pleeeeease give us paaaaaaapeeeer? Incooooorpooorateeeee!"

"Does that sound too Orcaish?" Maléficus feigned concern in his normal voice.

"It doesn't sound Orcaish, it sounds like something I've never heard before."

"You bastard," Maléficus cried. "You know Nemo by heart!"

Varga was indeed quoting Marlin, Nemo's father from the old classic movie that still regaled kids' souls all over the world, despite its funny, ancient 2D projecting technique.

Soon, the patrons of Vegas's old, dignified Laundry Room started to pitch in with their takes on the American realities. They were not too kind, to say the least.

"Congress for the people" received rapturous guffaws. The juxtaposition of the crooks vs. the people they supposedly served was undeniably hilarious. Everyone got the joke. "The House of Representatives is the best American acronym ever," said one smart aleck, momentarily killing the joy with his overly smug face and too flashy teeth in his tanned face.

"Laws to protect our children and our children's children's future," boomed no one else but Philip Bolghery who, by doing so, had unwittingly given Varga his future slogan.

"Do you know the one about those Americans who got locked in Mattress World and slept on the floor" provoked another burst of laughter. The jokes at the expense of America and its dream had become somewhat sinister. "It's called 'the American Dream' 'cause you have to be asleep to believe it," the smart aleck popped up again, quoting George Carlin, a famous comedian from the yesteryear whose quip he tried to sell as his own. Everyone hated his pompous ass already, so no one laughed at his attempt to regain some self-respect among the throngs of guffawing patrons. They were a tough crowd, fine-tuned to his bullshit, so at the first chance, he slinked away to lick his wounds. Rather to *have* them licked, and not just wounds, but let us not go there. What happens in Vegas stays in Vegas.

Nevertheless, the Honesty for America, LLC idea was a hoot that night. Maléficus had totally lost his mind—not only was he drunk as a skunk but he was also high on the attention he was getting. He used to live the life of a lone, wretched hermit, and this experience being the center of attention was something quite new to him. He savored every moment of it, high-fiving everyone as he bought drinks for the whole bar. Somehow he never forgot to glance at Winston Varga, asking for the nod of approval to splurge. Varga's nods were generous that night.

Around midnight, just before the Bengal fireworks would mark the end of the night and the carriages turned into pumpkins, Theodore had to lock the doors so no new guests were allowed in. To the dismay of the ladies of the night, the party that lasted 'til the wee hours of the morning featured men more keen on getting oblivious on booze than on their beauty.

Should you wish to check the tax records for Honesty for America, LLC, you'd see it was incorporated online the very next day and several years later changed its corporate structure to a corporation and created a wholly independent subsidiary, the Proteus FinTech, Corp. with a new EIN, a tax ID for businesses. The rest, as they say, is history.

As a result of that encounter with Maléficus Ultimo, f.k.a. Hans Böhm, Winston Varga decided to study the Roman Empire, the Fourth Reich, and the fascinating tale of Adolf Hitler's ascent to power. Genghis Khan, Napoleon Bonaparte, Josif Vissarionovich Stalin, and Mao Zedong were also parts of his obsession. Hierarchies of power became his passion. And no one ever had greater power than his home country, the United States of America. Still, he had a sense of impending doom; something was deeply wrong with American society but he, at that age, could not put his finger on it. Narcissism and cults of personality were prevailing forces in the country, which lived for money and survived—rather thrived—on hustling. In this country, he realized, the people were forced to constantly perform to please to prove their value. If you're poor in this country, you're worthless. The justice system was two-tiered. The beauty of it? Everyone knew it and everyone accepted it as the norm, rather as the normal way of dealing with things. Hustle hypocrisy amused him—even twitting about a product or a service was considered "hard work" nowadays, yet another magical mantra of American life that no one ever dared to question. The game was rigged, worse than in this casino-laced city, and everyone seemed to be fine with it.

Winston Varga felt like the overlords of America had learned their lessons from those same historical figures, the tyrants and criminals he later studied, and skillfully applied a long-lasting veneer over reality. The American Dream was a mirage, he thought, despite his own wealth being a case in point for the same dream the overlords incessantly peddled. A decade or so after that crazy night in Vegas, during the 2024 pandemic and its own virus, the dreaded Omega(n)(∞) variant, over the period between 2024 and 2025, Varga had seen his chance in the most neglected outcome of The Great Poisoning from China, as one side of the aisle called it, or The Murderous Vaccine Fraud as it was called on the other side. From then on, vast swaths of people deemed it normal for medicine to kill a certain number of people in order to save the others.

Varga rejoiced. "*The rabble is brainwashed and ran flat-out insane out of their minds by fear porn*," he wrote online. Artificial antagonism between human rights and human lives tore the fabric of societies apart, signaling the arrival of a health dictatorship in its full force. Some bleary-eyed blogger once quoted John Stuart Mill's words: "Whatever crushes individuality is despotism." She was blubbering about the 'dangerous totalitarian measures' put in place, but Varga preferred another quote, that of Daniel Defoe, a wannabe spy famous for his novel *Robinson Crusoe*, who once wrote: "Nature has left this tincture in the blood, that all men would be tyrants if they could," which is a much closer evaluation of human nature, Varga believed.

Emotional blackmail coming to them from all sides tormented the people, something Varga enjoyed witnessing. At times, he went online to write about how the rabble put a muzzle on their faces so to inhale their own toxic CO_2, a gas the body naturally produces as waste. They were 'killing their grannies' and at another, should they refuse a vaccine rammed down humanity's collective throat, 'they were onto killing neighbor's babies.' Never to miss an opportunity for outrage, a moral majority tore his posting apart with numerous proofs about validity and the grave need for the masks, vaccines, their fabled boosters and their several iterations, year after year, and their zealotry amused Varga tremendously. The supreme idiocy of political tribal bickering all over the place was even more beautiful.

A journalist Varga despised for fearlessly going after the powerful was Bolghery's ideological teacher, the incorruptible Glenn Greenwald. Glenn was criminally charged by the far-right government in Brazil, where he lived at the time. Greenwald's defense of the left-wing leader, two-time former Brazilian president Lula, a man thrown in prison under false pretenses and liberated after Greenwald exposed the ruse, ended up with Glenn being accused of being a right-wing operative as soon as he dared to criticize the dogma of the left whose working-class hero he just virtually helped to go free.

Maajid Nawaz, a British activist of British Pakistani ancestry, was a source of even more fun for Varga. Nawaz was wrongfully included in the "terrorism" category on Thomson Reuters World-Check and, at the same time, The Southern Poverty Law Center included him in their 2016 list of "anti-Muslim extremists," another wrong, preposterous, baseless accusation. Both of those illustrious organizations paid hefty sums for their libel and apologized to Nawaz. The lack of honesty, elementary human decency, or even simple logic was the true fertilizer for Varga's forthcoming ascent. Anyone could just throw any libelous garbage at anyone else and see what stuck. The post-truth era was also the post-honesty era and the people learned to see every other human as a biohazard to be avoided at all cost and, later, to be righteously hated. Such hate was a commodity Varga would not have liked to go to waste.

"These idiots," Varga once told one of his lovers while laughing boisterously. "Should their beloved rulers unleash a diarrhea virus on them, would put diapers on and keep living in their own shit." Their children, those that were going to grow up in Varga's world, lived a vicious cycle one anonymous writer described as "less school → more free time → more boredom → more screens → less confidence → more anxiety → more disengagement from school." Pre-teens were getting agoraphobic. "They didn't like the outside world; it's scary; they've lost interest," anonymous continued, telling another story: "One of the students told me he plays video games obsessively just because he's afraid he will lose contact with his only friends if he doesn't. He doesn't go outside. He feels he's a 'failure.' He hates school." That kid was eleven years old at the time. He killed himself several years later. While both rough-and-tumble and romance seem to have been gone from their worlds, Varga's businesses thrived with the help of the children's pain. More screen time meant more money for his clients and therefore much more money for his ventures online.

No matter what, he decided, he will master the game and game the system. He will win. Funnily enough, this is how a one-time US president from the annus horribilis of the second decade of the 21st Century, a man later deleted from history books by the Presidential Decency Act of 2036 (PDA-36) and thereafter known only as the Orange Menace, used "winning" as his mantra. Since the PDA-36 had also bravely "dismantled the white supremacy culture in math classrooms by visibilizing the toxic characteristics of white supremacy culture by creating the Culturally Sustaining Math Space and Ethnomathematics," no one in America seemed to be capable of counting to hundred any more. Or noticing that the US had its 43rd, 44th, 46th, 47th

and 48th presidents, but not the 45th, for all that it matters. The number 45 has hurt many people's feelings so it was therefore put on an Exclude List, f.k.a. "blacklist," a term also banned, where it now resides with the Orange Menace in a deserved eternal shame.

Varga enjoyed the never-ending insanity of the newly minted so-called woke world so much that he often went out of his way to help the maddening masses come to their senses and employed his bot army to stir the waters all the time. Anything to arouse the moral majority.

Green vs. Pink vs. Black

Just about when the Presidential Decency Act of 2036 came to be an important part of the law of the land, his Twitter bots—pretending to be humans, of course—demanded a change of the chess-piece colors, given that the black pieces were being deemed inferior to whites and moved only after whites made their own move. A grave racist setup, the bots screamed from the top of their digital lungs, orchestrated by the INFINITUS. Varga, being Varga, had engaged the leading members of the Virtuosi™ to insist on changing colors to pink for whites and green for blacks. The virtual war exploded when he had Virtuosi's LGBTQIA++(n^{th}) members violently scoff at the proposal by skillfully created emojis. #PinkIsNotWhite hashtag trended, which rabid gibes tossed left and right. Once the greens joined them with emojis and carefully crafted insults of their own, the uproar, later dubbed the Chess War of the Emojis, was a sight to behold, a trite phrase Varga had his infotainment media repeat ad nauseum. Saint Greta, at the time already a thirty-three-year-old high-school dropout child, still in charge of righteously scolding the world that had, year after year, kept stubbornly refusing to die, made a faux pas proclaiming that "green is not as bad as black," so the Virtuosi™ jumped on her, calling her a "disgusting racist." Greta's twenty-second Anniversary Extinction Tour was canceled due to her "unconscionable, blatant racism."

"They are too easy," Varga laughed after Maléficus showed him statistics about the clicks, likes, shares, frowns, and calls to cancel even the deified Greta Thunberg. "When I look back to 2020-'21 and especially to 2025, I remember how two prophets of that era inspired me," Varga shared with Maléficus in one of his rare moments of reflection and sincerity, days before the PHOENIX ONE was launched to rule the world. "Those were Elon

Musk and Greta Thunberg, both having Savant and Asperger's syndromes, something in common with *yurodivy* in Fyodor Dostoyevsky."

"*Yurodivy*?" Maléficus asked, raising his eyebrow. "What's that?"

"The fool for Jesus Christ, the Holy Fool that lingers in between two words, straddling madness and sanity, so to speak. He speaks to and for Gods. Yurodivy is not unlike Exú, another messenger in between humans and deities, Brazilian Orixás, in a search of God. In Greek mythology they were Iris and Hermes, also intermediaries between humanity and the gods. Each of those folk characters had mythical characteristics, related to biblical stories. While Greta Thunberg was, and still is, a Prophet of Doom, daily invoking Noah's Biblical Flood and destruction of humankind, Musk and his Mars delusion represent Noah's Ark, rather the Biblical Salvation and Resurrection of the same humankind that Saint Greta sees drowning. Their deep, while not immediately obvious connection to God and the influence they had on people, made me decide, even decades ago, that the people need a new God, a true God to watch over them. So, I've given it to them," he concluded with appropriate, diabolical laughter.

That aside, what the Orange Menace was describing by "winning" was a swindle, pure and simple. Varga was fully aware he had also been a hustler since an early age. He loved money. And he wanted to have it more than anyone else. But the classic education bestowed on him by his mom Eleni always made him feel like something was missing. Heroism? Sacrifice? Magic? He had no idea but believed that once on top, he'd figure all that out.

The man who had ignited new ideas and steered Varga toward what he would become years later, wasn't a part of his life after that crazy night in Las Vegas. In the wee hours of the morning, Winston went to take a leak only to catch a glimpse of Maléficus engaged in passionate intercourse in the toilet booth. Some burly guy in a lumberjack outfit who stood mum and drank all night was having his sweet way with him. The lumberjack wasn't as quiet as before, as he was grunting like a slaughtered pig. Varga cackled. Maléficus would for sure intellectualize those ecstatic, deep guttural moans and unnatural high-pitched screams, invoking dear lumberjack's dark forests by blathering something about the intensification of the sexual experience by altering brain metabolism through hypocapnia all in order to beautify the poor lumberjack's disturbing sexual trance. We say "poor," for the lumberjack had beat the living shit out of Maléficus as soon as he was done, loudly blaming the guy he smashed to pieces, Maléficus, for his journey into the world of same-sex joy. Had it been his first loving, booze-induced experience with another man? We'd never know, for he had disappeared in the balmy air of that sultry Las Vegas night. Strangely enough, but not entirely unexpectedly, Maléficus has also vanished without a trace that very same dawn.

It puzzled Varga, Maléficus's sudden disappearance. He could not care less about his sexual orientation; after all, they'd shared many a lovely girl over the last few days in Nevada, so a lumberjack here or a blacksmith there in the path of his conquests would not bother him. Not a single, tiny bit. And yet, Maléficus was gone without a word. With him, Varga's credit card. It was a curious moment so Varga did not cancel the card; he wanted to see where his strange pal would go and what he would do.

It was Shanghai of all places. Always a modest man, the former drifter gifted with rare hacking prowess and propensity to pontificate in a hoity-toity language purchased a first-class ticket from Las Vegas to Los Angeles where he had a brief layover to catch a direct flight to Shanghai, China. He never used Varga's credit card again and Varga never heard from him again.

Maléficus vanished into the dark and was never relevant again.

The Relevancy

Nastassia, who has been frozen-like, motionlessly listening to Bolghery all this time, jumps to those words: "Not relevant? Böhm is the most relevant character in this odious collection of their Las Vegas binges and orgies."

"Come on!" Bolghery feels a sting; his work was never called odious before.

"Why do you think Böhm is still relevant after forty years?" The Renegade looks at her, searching for answers in her posture, in her breathing, in her thoughts he tries to guess.

"I don't know. I only know that I *know*."

The Renegade and Bolghery exchange a meaningful look and both turn their eyes back to Nastassia.

"What?" she asks, exasperated. She looks at them and starts to pace in a small circle.

"Dudes! I am fourteen. You are the Renegade and Bolghery. Everybody in the world knows who you are. Legends. Geniuses. And you two are, what, a hundred years old each? But it was you two behaving like kindergarten brats, like all of this is a prank."

Bolghery was hiding behind a dark screen.

"Really?" She turns to him. "Really, Philip Bolghery?" Nastassia pronounces his full name like fanning fans would do all over the world. Was she mocking him and his gravitas? "And you." She turns to the Renegade. "Did you mastermind the ruse?" She used Bolghery's own term at him, overly accentuating every syllable so he'd have no qualms about it. Yes, she knew from the start.

"How could you think I would not know what you're doing? Really?"

"Nastassia…" the Renegade tries, but she has none of it.

"Don't *Nastassia* me, with all due respect, Renegade. Please," she continues, now even faster, pacing around the lab. "You want to awaken my precog skills? Like I need this lame homework for that. I knew what you were doing from the outset. You're directing me like a puppet? Why? I am depressed so I need gentle tending to my pain? Duh! My parents were murdered instead of me, what else would I be? Dancing in the streets? I am afraid. Double duh, my little brother was kidnapped and who knows what's happening to him as we're doing *homework*." She spits the word out with so much disgust in it that the Renegade feels guilty seeing her so worked up, so tired, so anxious and, somehow, so alone.

This child… he thinks…

"I am not a *child*, but I am not a magician either. I realize you used Varga's stories to awake the dormant precog in me, as you see it, and to help us liberate Stellan and defeat Varga. I get it. You want me to dig deep. Well, I've dug deep. To places you can't imagine exist. This is what I've been doing. Varga is impenetrable. He has no weaknesses, none obvious to me. None, but this one, this glaring one. Hans." Nastassia speaks without breathing, excitedly, hurriedly, alarmingly. She stops to take a big gulp of air.

"Hans Böhm is Varga's weak link. You wanted me to find it. Here it is, I have found it, Hans Böhm represents our way in."

"Forgive me. I did not know how to deal with your… your… tragedy. We had to batten down the hatches and we truly had no clue how to approach you. And your skills," says the Renegade, but she interrupts him again.

This time she does it gently, almost whispering, "My skills?" She makes another circle around the lab. The Renegade and Bolghery patiently wait for Nastassia to gather her thoughts.

"I am not like Stellan. I can *see* and *sense* things, but I can't read minds, except to the rare point of true connection. I can't really *see* what the future brings, like him, only hints that are sometimes very difficult to decipher. It's not like I have clear images or even senses of what's coming next. Sometimes it feels like my mind-eye is deliberately obscured by some invisible force. I would've been able to predict Stellan's kidnapping, if otherwise." Her voice trembles for a second. "That's why computers are so easy for me. They are simple, logical even when buggy, perhaps more so, and made by humans, unlike the *realms* where Stellan's visions reside. He's the one able to *see* and *read* the future like an open book most of the time, no matter how young he is. That's why was he taken, with other precogs. I have problems understanding the messages I am getting. Like now. I *know* and *feel* and *sense* that Hans Böhm is the key toward getting Varga. I *know* it with every fiber of my body. But I do not know how. I am in the dark. Flickers come toward me, and it's exhausting trying to put all the pieces together out of nothing. And I have nothing, nothing coming from Stellan. I knew at one point, for sure, that he was alive, but nothing thereafter. I can't hear him, I can't sense his thoughts or feelings. I am deaf and blind in that world that I abandoned as a child. It is beyond frightening. You have no idea."

What to respond to any of that? the Renegade asks himself.

"No need." Nastassia side-glances at the old sage. "Just you both help me help us. And please understand what I've told you."

Another pause. She seems at the end of her tether but somehow finds more sources of strength inside her.

"As far as Varga? You need to give me more. Not even hacking would be possible with only the information about their drinking in Las Vegas forty years ago. It would make for a great book, but no more. Sorry, Philip. What's relevant is Hans Böhm, that Ultimo guy. What else do you have?"

"I did research on him, but since he was gone, never to be back, I archived those notes."

"Can you please, give them to me?" Nastassia was barely able to speak anymore.

"Let me find the disk. I'm a bit hungry. Let me grab a bite to eat and will be back in a jiffy."

"*Jiffy?*" Nastassia tries a smile at the Renegade, who looks at her, concerned. "Who uses *jiffy* nowadays? Who speaks like that?"

"Us oldies." The Renegade tries a joke.

It works. Nastassia's face brightens up in a sad yet beautiful smile as she looks at his deep, warm eyes. And then, she suddenly falls asleep, right there, on a small sofa in the Renegade's lab, like a doll disconnected from her strings.

Bolghery comes back and, upon seeing Nastassia sleeping, whispers to the Renegade, "This is all I have on Hans Böhm, a.k.a. Maléficus Ultimo. Take a look."

Hans Böhm Backstory
(*unpublished, Bolghery notes*)

Maléficus Ultimo / Hans Böhm. He blurted his real name to Varga. Research data:

- Helmuth D. Böhm, father
- Chastity Böhm née Jenkins, mother. A junkie
- Klaus Maria Schwartz, stepfather. No real data available.
- Mystic Beach, Vancouver Island, Canada
- Double murder. Matricide (!?); stepfather. Why?
- Date of murder, May 27, 2006
- Abduction per media (nonsense)
- Motive? Sexual abuse? Drug craze? (was he too young for drugs?) Money?
- Murder weapon: Marlin 336C hunting rifle
- Money? Where did it come from? Robbery? Did Klaus Maria Schwartz (or mom) have money?
- Where was he after the Mystic Beach 'til meeting Varga?
- Dig Deep Web. No results
- Where did he go after Vegas and Shanghai?

The Trail Went Cold

"That's all?" the Renegade asks.

"That's all."

"How did you get this data?"

"*Vancouver Island Free Daily* newspaper published articles about the murder. But they did not have any really interesting facts about the family. They were nobodies. The kid, Hans, disappeared, so they speculated he might have been killed or abducted. No one suspected him of murder."

"Why do you think he killed his own mother? And the stepfather? You seem sure of it?"

"I pieced together several of his slurred confessions, hints, allusions he uttered to Varga and the lumberjack before they went to the loo that night in The Laundry Room."

"So that's pure speculation on your end?"

"It's speculation, but I am fairly confident I guessed it right. Every time, no matter how briefly or enigmatically he's mentioned his mother, he sounded like someone else. There's a vast darkness in that man."

"Nastassia seems certain he's very important. Even if Varga truly started his empire after meeting Hans Böhm, it was forty years ago. Are you sure there have been no sign of him since?"

"Positive. He's gone," Bolghery says.

"He can't be," Nastassia, who woke up from her slumber, says feebly from her sofa after reading from her eyepiece what Bolghery had on Maléficus Ultimo. "Bolghery has all but forgotten about that man."

Bolghery scoffs.

"What else I was to do? The trail went cold," he says.

Nastassia and the Renegade keep quiet.

"Come on guys. Varga's empire is built on algorithms, computers, supercomputers, and AI. He's notorious for not dealing with humans in his business network, person-to-person. He almost never attends meetings. What use would it be for Varga to have a junkie hacker, now in his sixties—a junkie that stole from him at that? If nothing, Varga is a revengeful prick, we all know that."

"And yet, I'm telling you, Maléficus Ultimo slash Hans Böhm is still connected, very closely, to Varga." Nastassia does not appear stubborn or argumentative at all. In her mind, she has just stated a fact. "And he's our way in."

Bolghery, who's started to lose his patience, says icily, "I couldn't find a single bit of info about him. Neither in Canada nor in Shanghai. Remember, he stole the card he used only once and, most likely, with some cash or at least casino chips. They played a lot and were winning often. He was drinking heavily and using coke and ecstasy at that time. I don't think he's alive. And even if he is, remember, he knows how to disappear. He did it once in Canada already. He just vanished into the thin air."

Bolghery pauses for a moment, then continues convincingly, "Think about all the coincidences. Without Varga's parents being killed and Varga's purchase of the Cobra, they would've never met. Without me being given an assignment by the *Times* to write about him, I would've never seen him,"

Bolghery says somehow erratically and his mood starts to change. "You can't base all your thinking on a hint, Nastassia, and some vague feelings. And yes, I've gone there, to Shanghai, back then. That's how investigative journalism works, we don't dream up our proofs, we don't *feel* them; we search for and find them. If there are any."

"I wonder what is that you're hiding?" Nastassia blurts angrily.

"Can't you *sense* it, *darling*?" Bolghery retorts with a sarcastic grin.

"Well, that escalated quickly," Nastassia responds sardonically.

"Philip!" the Renegade furiously barks at him, injecting himself into this unexpected quarrel, but Nastassia, suddenly looking much, much older than her tender age, nods at him as if to say *all is OK*.

I told them how I felt. I explained the voids of my world, and yet they don't get it. She falls silent for a moment. *Adults! When do they lose the sense of wonder and feeling for other, less wonderous realities?* She lets the memories of *seeing* and *feeling* both the people and the futures they represented sink back, deep into her consciousness. She was letting them *be* in her, almost as palpable as life itself. It was scary to *see* or *feel* the other realms. Foreboding was almost always the name of the game, she realizes. Since she *saw* her mom's illnesses, she's almost never seen anything beautiful coming. Just misfortune. *Strange!* She wasn't cognizant about it earlier. *Is this why I ran away from the precog realm? Is this why I was guarding Stellan so fervently from the dangers it represented?* She, without looking at them, observes both the Renegade and the visible anguish with which he's been looking at her for quite some time, and Bolghery who is, she's *sensed* since the first moment he saw her, inexplicably *afraid* of her. *That's why is he so cross with me, I reckon.* Fear and loneliness, the dominant forces in the lives of so many, reside in this room as a heavy blob of dark energy with so much force that she shudders a bit. It feels cold. Like death.

She was falling back to the times of asking what her purpose in life was. Since forever, everyone had treated her differently, like she was a freak, or they were afraid of her like she was Carrie White from the movie that horrified her mom so much she behaved so over the top every time she and Dad watched it. So many times Nastassia felt an impending sense of doom regarding the very purpose of her being. Nastassia's hero, Virginia Woolf, wrote "You cannot find peace by avoiding life," and in this moment she feels like avoiding danger was the same as avoiding life. She left the precog's realm behind on purpose, to be safe from the horrors it contained. She was guarding Stellan's secrets with her life, and yet, not only was she unable to foresee what was going to happen, she was unable to protect anyone. Not her parents, not Stellan.

Was that her purpose? To leave death behind?

The idea terrifies her so much that she almost faints. She comes back to her senses instantaneously, helped by looking at the two old faces of the Renegade and Bolghery, but they now seem miles away. They were dollying back to the netherworld that resides in us and they looked distant, strange, and hollow, like they themselves were two ragged two-dimensional dolls devoid of purpose of their own. *What a strange thought.* Why would she think that? They are her only allies, and she has no qualms or doubts about them, so why is she losing them in time-space while standing in their very presence?

Betrayal?

No, it can't be that… but she has *sensed*, very strongly, more than once, that they are hiding something from her, something else, something very important, and the secrets that they kept hidden from her have the bitter taste of poisoned almonds. She could not get more from that firewall of adult bullshit and she was too tired to even try. And well too annoyed with them. They'd been torturing her while holding something back. Her mind-world started to pulsate, unnerved; because of that, she feels a rush of anger. She tries to contain it as she looks at him and directly addresses Bolghery's boorish question from seconds ago. She speaks her words slowly and measurably, giving a double meaning to the pronunciation of each word.

"No Bolghery, I do not *sense* that you're hiding Hans Böhm or any knowledge about Hans Böhm from me on purpose. What I did *sense*, and *know*, is that you both are hiding something else from me. Like you were hiding the real intention of your jejune *homework* and your garish book earlier today." She senses her anger morphing toward a rage she'd not be able to control. Truth to be told, she *could* control it, but she doesn't want to; cut her some damn slack, she needs to let it all out.

"That pisses me the hell off. But you know what? You need me more than I need you. So go fuck yourselves, both of you!" The curse surprises her more than them, so she takes one deep breath to calm herself down and turns to the Renegade.

"How do I get out of this prison?"

Chapter 10

NAUTILUS

The Renegade's Lab
March 21, 2048

"I can show you the way, but will you please indulge me for a moment? Please." The Renegade speaks earnestly and, in order to give her a moment to recoup after the emotional turmoil she's been through, he turns to Bolghery.

"It would be better if I do this alone with Nastassia."

"Sure." Bolghery vanishes, relieved.

Nastassia stares at the Renegade, looking worn out, and waits.

"I have something to show you," he says and, as he sweeps the holographic screen from its place next to the wall, he looks back at her. He is startled. Not only because she looks as pale as a ghost, somehow detached and tired, but with his own inner change. He looks at her like he has never seen her before. *What's going on with me? I have been torturing this poor girl, without even being aware of it. What was I postponing? Am I afraid? Am I protecting myself rather than her?* In the silence that ensues, they look at each other, for one brief moment like total strangers, each caught in their own cage-thoughts and feelings, captivated by fatigue and anxiety, in a dark secret lair deep below the surface, a lair so isolated that it had sucked them into its loneliness.

He knows what's going on with Nastassia. She's had no time to grieve the loss of her parents. She is worried sick about Stellan. Bolghery and himself have poured barrels of Varga-related information on her head and she has no idea what awaits her, but she clearly sees something's going on.

She's been beaten to a pulp already but her journey has not started yet. It is his fault, all that confusion. He feels truly guilty.

The lonely, disconnected glance he exchanges with the girl seventy and four years younger makes him choke back tears. She's his best friends', Frédéric and Monique Bonnet's daughter, damn it! And she is entrusted to him, due to the murderous actions of Varga and his triple-damned eye on the sky. He's the one left with the legacy of truth, no one else. There will be no winged angels arriving to help him. He owes that truth and honesty not only to Freddie and Mon, but first and foremost to Nastassia. He feels like he has been betraying her, as he has hindered her like a coward. *I have no right to keep her from her destiny for one more second!*

But how much of his fault is it that her destiny is so tragic thus far?

Is it guilt that he's carried so deep into himself that was stopping him from acting like a man and making him behave like a coward, procrastinating now when the time is of the essence? It was such a strange moment for him; I must have been for too long isolated from the real world, I don't know how to function face-to-face, even with someone as pure and as friendly as Nastassia Bonnet, anymore.

This stops now.

"Follow me, please."

The Renegade moves and opens a door to a fairly big, dark, round structure adjacent to the room in which they've been talking to Bolghery and shows her in. At first she can not see a thing, but her eyes quickly adapt to the darkness. In the place of a wall on her left side lays an enormous set of computer racks, as one would expect in the Renegade's secret liar. But the wall on her right side is more interesting; there are several dozen aquariums filled with cephalopods of all kinds: octopuses and squid, cuttlefish and nautiluses all over the place. One small Bathypolypus arcticus lurks in its own aquarium and glances at them. The Renegade smiles at Nastassia's astonishment and spreads his arms approaching the closest and biggest aquarium:

"Nastassia, meet Octopus Cyanea."

A big blue octopus, sitting in front of the castle-like heap of empty bivalve shells, glances at her. *Really?* she thinks in amazement as her back stiffens. *What is this that I sense?* When the Renegade introduces the eukaryotic cytoplasm mollusk, which feels somewhat familiar to her, he says, "Nautilus for friends."

Nastassia approaches the aquarium, confused by something that couldn't be anything other than a connection with that majestic creature. She tries her best not to reveal her inner bewilderment as she comes even closer.

The eye of a big blue octopus curiously, carefully observes her.

"He's our desert?" she tries as a joke.

"Flibbidyfloo, my heavens, to eat Nautilus? That magnificent creature is smarter than both of us put together."

"And yet, I'm still somehow hungry." She looks around, messing with him. "Unless you have something else to eat, your genius over there might end up on a platter for breakfast." Nautilus shrinks at the corner of his aquarium, shooting angry glances back at her. Nastassia claps her hands in amazement as she comes closer, carefully examining Nautilus's horizontal pupils. No need to conceal her sense of wonder anymore.

"No way! He understood me?"

"Of course he did."

"But how?"

"He's smart. And you'll have to program him so we'll be able to connect and talk."

Nastassia's eyes open wide. "Come again," she says and observes Nautilus a bit closer, from the very edge of his aquarium. Tiny, barely visible wires are attached to its body. She is stunned, turns to the Renegade again, and with fake nonchalance, thumb-points at the Nautilus that's lurking behind her again. Her heart is pounding. She yet again senses the power of the sea creature behind her but has no idea what it truly represents. But it feels soothing and nice, that power, not threatening, rather reassuring. She harkens back to another time, straddling worlds as her mind-eye looks inside, to the time that made her ready for the connection with Nautilus.

Tat Twam Asi (Thou Art That)
Merzouga in the Sahara, Morocco
July 12, 2041

It was a whiff of love, a similar kind of soft, loving energy now radiating from Nautilus, that she felt several years ago in Sahara, Africa on an unexpected sea breeze in the middle of the desert. What she felt was a *memory*, her mom told her, a sense of the ancient times back when her soul had roamed around for centuries, waiting for her to be born. It sounded like magic, Mom's words. That night Nastassia had a dream about her Bedouin soul wandering the desert. It made her feel special.

Mom was glowing but was strangely pensive and quiet that day. It was before Stellan was born and they were on holiday in Morocco and went on a camel trek and 4x4WD drive into the desert, across the orange, windblown sand dunes of Erg Chebbi in the Sahara Desert. It was a spellbinding experience, but it did not seem the excitement had gotten to Mom; she almost seemed unimpressed by the hundred-meter-high dunes in the endless space of terrifying beauty. She looked into the past in her. Or was it the future? Or was she worried about the sand storms? Either way, she was oddly aloof and it made Nastassia a tad uneasy for she did not know or feel what was going on with Mom. Or Dad for that matter. But he stayed quiet and did not pester Mom. He never did. He loved Mom.

Once they were back in the small tent offered to them by the Berber Nomads, their hosts for a week, Nastassia asked why she could feel the ocean if the desert was so dry and hot. Also, in the surreal quiet of the night, when the heat subsided, she was able to *hear* the sea. How come? By then, Monique was back to being her old self, the sunny and loving mom and marine biologist who had taught her everything Dad did not know.

And that was a lot, mom always confirmed with laughter, kissing him. They were happy then.

"Once upon a time, sharks lived here."

"Here? In the desert?" Nastassia was mesmerized. She wanted to know more.

"There are fossils—Ichnofossils is what they're called—of those sharks lying in the desert. My colleagues from the American Museum of Natural History were researching them. You even met Professor Maureen O'Leary once. She talked about morphology, genes, and ichnofossils in our home but you just rolled your eyes and left."

Nastassia giggled at the memory, *I wasn't even a tween then.*

"You were too small, I guess," Mommy confirmed. "So, yes, the sea was fifty or more meters deep back in time. It once covered thousands of kilometers of what is now Sahara, still the world's biggest sand desert, even though the recent changes in the Atacama Desert are worrying."

At "worrying," Frédéric injected his horror story, messing up the lesson.

"Prehistoric sharks were catching and eating flying reptiles," he said, pompously proud. Nastassia loved when he mocked himself.

"Not in Sahara," Monique argued against his lame misinformation. Dad winked at her and Mom glanced at Nastassia and changed her posture at once. The jokes abated; the mood got serious. Nastassia did not miss that not-so-subtle change in her mom but did not understand why prehistoric sharks should be a secret? Why was she not allowed to know that? Adults and their stupid secrets. Like they could hide anything from her, if she really wanted to know their thoughts. But she never wanted to listen to Mom and Dad's thinking. It would've been—

She did not even know how to put it. *Rude*, perhaps? *Dishonest*? She did not know what to call her reluctance to ever listen to their thoughts. Plainly, it would've been wrong, *intrusive*. Yes, this was the word; she could not intrude into their minds. So she didn't and her ability to read minds slowly atrophied as she grew older.

But, she also had a secret: she *knew*. Later that day she realized that she'd have a little brother soon. Nastassia barely contained her excitement, but she had decided that she could have her own secrets, as much as they do theirs, and was determined not to tell them. *Mum's the word*, she giggled to herself. Such a funny expression the adults use—it made no sense at all. And the mum does not even mean a mom, although they sound the same. That conversation had ended, but Nastassia had not forgotten the feeling of might coming from the ocean.

The Renegade's Lab

Now, in front of one of the sea creatures, the legendary octopus from so many myths she loved to read to Stellan, Nastassia feels the same power. She side-glances at the Renegade, somewhat evocatively and somehow meaningfully at the same time, but he is distorted and blurred, as though she's seeing him through out-of-focus fish-eye lenses. That does not surprise her. She looks at him from inside a memory-bubble—only she knew about it and it's invisible to the others, but she needed it from time to time to isolate herself from the world and the present time, when sharp focus on the past was a must.

However, she does not want to be isolated from the Renegade. She needs him. And she knows that he needs her. It is for something much bigger than hacking help he's sought her, but she isn't yet clear about it. She also wonders, a bit jittery at the thought, could she share her deepest secrets with him? What a terrifying thought. Could she tell him? If she does, how would he react? He's the Renegade, he seems to know everything, but he has many strange little quirks as well. And an impossible sense of what he thinks is humor. What would he do, would he trust her if she told him the truth of what scares her the most:

I don't know who I really am.

Nastassia shakes her memory-bubble off and returns to the present.

"So, what is that thing?"

"The White Rabbit it ain't."

"Renegade!" She scolds him like she is the older, much older, one.

"Yes?"

"You are a gazillion cuts above the rest. I beg you, drop the jokes and get serious."

"Got it. You have a lot to learn before we start."

"Start what?"

"Rescuing Stellan, what else."

"And we need Nautilus to help us?"

"You have no idea how much."

The King of the World

The Renegade expands: "Cephalopods incorporate the physical power of a Terminator, the neural networks of humans, and the swimming ability of themselves to form the dominant force on Earth. Rather in the Oceans. Squid is the real king of this world."

Nastassia looks at the Renegade like she would look at a squid from another planet.

"But how is your king going to help us? I am not getting it."

"The cephaloid nervous system is the most complex of all invertebrate living beings," the Renegade explains. "Turn your 3D eyepiece on."

She does. A 3D holographic screen appears, responding to wherever the Renegade looks and to whatever he touches. The screen shows a bunch of diagrams of the octopus's brain. "Look here," Renegade says, "a posterior portion of its brain is joined laterally by the complex basal lobes and the dorsal magnocellular lobes."

His explanation flies right over her head. "Come again?"

"Their brains have the natural ability to work together as neural, bionic computers. Each of the grown-ups, like Nautilus, have about five hundred million neurons. So these are, if we find a way to connect them, our natural allies, able to match the MEGS's neural network and fight it."

"Cool, but…" She ponders what the Renegade had just told her for a second and immediately lodges a protest: "Varga supposedly uses MEGS as a human-based computing network to support that monster in the sky and the supercomputer behind it? That much we know, right?"

The Renegade nods affirmatively.

"Each of the MEGS has many more neurons than all the mollusks there put together. What's the catch?"

"Right, the human brain contains about a hundred billion neurons, and about ten times more glial cells."

Nastassia averts her eyes, calculating. "That's about a hundred trillion connections in one single human brain."

"And likely more, given the nature of Varga's work with the MEGS. They've enhanced their brains, but we don't know to what extent. Add the INFINITUS to his computing powers. That's one mighty network."

"So, how does Nautilus compete against that with his meager five hundred million neurons?"

"I hoped you'd ask that." The Renegade flashes a proudly smug smile and shows her a stone wall adorned with the three huge reproductions of the Tychonic Solar System poster, Tycho Brahe globe with constellations, and Tycho Brahe's Mural Quadrant posters. On the right side hang two Solingen-bladed swords.

"These are made by Jaspar Bungen, a legendary blade-smith. From the sixteenth century. You might think you have to pull those in order to open the doors, but no, it's not the way to open the doors," he says and mocks-pulls the swords. "See, nothing happens."

Nastassia rolls her eyes. "What doors now?"

"Secret doors, of course. But I have devised a better way. I need to do a tap dance."

"Tap dance?"

Nastassia finally giggles. This Renegade squid is impossible.

"Yes, a single shuffle time step—easy to remember. In case I forget, I programmed a hologram of Dame Darcey Bussell as a dancing instructor," he says and a beautiful, tall, blonde dancer, a legend of the dancing world, Britain's famous prima ballerina, pops up.

"Hello, Renegade, are you up for a dance?" Darcey, the former Principal of the Royal Ballet at the Royal Opera House in Covent Garden, and the Renegade's big secret crush since forever, asks him in her silky voice, smiling from the hologram.

"OK, we don't need to watch this now," he says, embarrassed, but he feels the need to explain himself. "I also use this to stay in shape."

"I can't wait to see that."

"I bet you can't. The floor sensors are all over the, well, floor. They detect my body's weight, my gait, my steps, and my individual planar pressure. So the floor identifies me as me. Finally my unique single scuffle serves to open the secret door. Cool, no?"

"Cool. And?"

The Renegade tap dances to Nastassia's giggle.

Bio-CERN

The hidden stone door in front of them opens to reveal an enormous, seemingly endless CERN-like tunnel under pale blue light that stretches for miles and miles in a huge circle. Several thousands of aquariums filled with cephalopods of all kinds: countless octopuses and squid, innumerable cuttlefish and nautiluses all over the place, like in the lab but on a vastly larger scale, all connected into one vast network.

"Will be using this hyperintelligent cyberoctopus structure to help us break into the PHOENIX ONE and see the future they dread so much," the Renegade says. "If we figure out how to make it work."

Nastassia walks around the Renegade's secret lab at length, touching the smooth, cold glass of each individual aquarium. One Tritonia diomedea, a sea slug of a deep red color, attracts her attention. Every creature carries the same power she felt back in the Sahara Desert. She moves forward, into the vast, deep darkness of the Renegade's lab's aquarium, and with every passing step she feels more of the life-strength in those creatures. They are magnificent, animals built to perfection, like most of the natural world. Funny, only humans are too soft and too weak, and seemingly useless, for the planet they've ruled with an iron, greedy fist for well too long.

But why would the Renegade keep them imprisoned? she asks herself.

"We are free to leave and come back anytime we want." She hears the velvety voice coming from behind her, within her, from everywhere at the same time. For one brief moment, she is confused.

Nautilus?

Yes, that's him but he did not talk; she heard his thoughts. The connection between her, the sea world and, especially Nautilus, is getting stronger with each passing moment. She turns back and dashes to Nautilus, not even noticing how strangely the Renegade's looking at her. That gaze is filled with hope and anxiety but he said or did nothing. He just stands there, staring at her, following her steps.

"You're connected to Nautilus, right?" She turns to him.

"Yes." The Renegade snaps a finger and the holographic display of Nautilus's brain pops up. With it, Albinoni's Adagio in G Minor fills the room. "He works best with Albinoni."

Nastassia observes the neural implants in the Nautilus's brain. "Do you talk to him?"

"We better understand each other's body language, it seems. But I was never able to understand what is he trying to say."

"Get me the holo, please," she says and the Renegade boots the holographic screen with the program he wrote for interaction with Nautilus. Nastassia swiftly moves big chunks of data around the screen, immensely focused on the code from the very first second. She scrutinizes it, but with the speed of a supercomputer. *Christ almighty, it's like she talks to the code,* thinks the Renegade, *and the code talks back.*

"I'll be damned!" Nastassia yelps.

"What?"

"You were so close."

"How come?"

"I see you used your own program, but its approach is the wrong one."

"What do you mean? Where did I go wrong?"

"You didn't. Only you set up the communication between the machine and Nautilus, which works on a programming language level he'll never understand." Nastassia rushes back to the aquarium with Nautilus. "So, you never directly communicated with Nautilus, right?"

"No, I haven't," the Renegade admits. "I was able to get a bunch of data, but that's all. Sorting all that out, sifting through, and trying to decode its meaning consumed a lot of time."

Nastassia feverishly nods. *That led him astray.*

"Look how is he changing his color. They use specific colors and lighting to communicate with each other. Deep magic was always right here before you—he was talking but you lacked the proper translation tool."

Damn, the girl is incredible.

"Eyes are useless when the mind is blind." The Renegade starts pacing around, angry at himself. "It's like, if he had spoken, I'd be analyzing the frequency of each sound, missing the whole aural picture. Like I've missed this. How did you get it?"

"Simplicity of a young mind." Nastassia chuckles as she rewrites his code with increasing speed. "You wrote bits of software in ancient Fortran and CPython languages. What you missed was including SmoothBase and Vibe Engine—you know, Lucien Hannibal created them?"

Lucien Hannibal?

The Renegade remembers him well. Lucien was the most secretive of all hackers in the New Athens realm. His work was done on air-tight computers most of the time, and he went online from various machines, always from a different location, via Tor and R-IOTA streams, only to upload his work to GitHub and to download available logs or software updates placed on servers since the last time he was online. But, while he had characteristics of a true genius, his programs were often buggy.

He says that aloud. "His programs were too buggy to be taken seriously. He always abandoned one project for another that excited him more."

"Not SmoothBase and Vibe Engine. Phatty and Wyverin, after she or he left, cleared his source code, compiled the language, and made it highly usable."

"What do you propose we do?"

Nastassia did not reply at first. "Are we safe?" she asks. "Can I go on the Net?"

"You're online already. Use that icon that looks like Nautilus so your browser will pop up."

She blushes out of pride. The Renegade uses her Chromium-based browser and logs into an open-source data provided by Elon Musk's Neuralink and downloads a small commo app.

"That's it?" The Renegade can not believe his eyes.

"Nope. We need more."

The Renegade's heart soars. *Is that possible?* flashes through his mind. *That she'll find a solution?*

"What else?"

"The telepathy Bebel, which is at the heart of commo, is missing. That's Elon Musk's secret project. He deliberately left a backdoor open with greetings for everyone willing to dig a bit more in order to do proper research."

"I thought he had abandoned this project."

"He publicly said so before he vanished on the Mars project, but he has been enjoying his trolling too much not to twist the facts from time to time. See this?" She shows another icon, a "T" shaped brain, typical Musk. "He uses telepathy as conceptual interaction on a level that is based on the free will of an individual. What everyone missed is that the individual could be a human, a machine, but also an animal."

As she spoke, she was feverishly moving chunks of software around the Renegade's holographic screen. The programs of today are modular and represented as 3D graphs in his interface, which are easy to work with. She barely has to add any new code, but when she did, it was done with such blistering speed that even the Renegade had to put in effort to follow her.

"Here we are."

"What? What did you find?"

"Look." Nastassia turns a video stream from the ocean's floor on. A mollusk that was in the center of the screen, the glorious pink Tritonia diomedea, slowly crawls the ocean's floor and looks around and up, before moving on with his mollusky business.

"That creature has magnetically responsive neurons. And all the others." As she speaks, a lobster, an octopus, a leatherback sea turtle, a whale, and a salamander's video feed pops up all over the screens.

The Renegade's excitement subsides a bit. "The magnetic orientation circuit is shared with many animals? Interactions among genes, proteins, and molecular networks in sensory systems have been well researched. Magnetoreception is used by pigeons and bacteria, not just sea creatures. That's not news?"

"No, but don't be a pessimist, that's not all."

"Spit it out," Renegade says, inpatient and excited again. *Like a ten-year-old,* he thinks. *My mood changes in seconds, captivated by this little impossible creature.*

"That mollusk and many others you see..." She brings the screen with the video stream from the bottom of the ocean up front and dramatically increases its size, so it dwarfs them both. "All of them are connected to Nautilus."

"You mean, like, now?"

"Now, as we speak now, as this moment now!" Nastassia exclaims, pacing around unable to contain her excitement.

"Nautilus has the sea creatures in his network. They communicate wirelessly, using the Earth's magnetic field as commo beams."

"Are you sure?"

"Am I sure? Sure, I'm sure. I'm dead sure that's for sure," she says exuberantly. "Nautilus already has the oceans on his side!"

She swipes the screen to the corner and rushes toward Nautilus. He observes her calmly. Is that a smile on his strange appearance? No, but the Nautilus's big black eye winks at Nastassia as she places her nose on the glass.

Nastassia yells to Renegade, "It winked at me."

"He has had individual consciousness since forever," confirms the Renegade. "It's a known fact about octopi."

I know, she thinks, suppressing a *duh*! and turns to him. "Do you want me to introduce you?" Nastassia slyly asks. She wants to explode—the Renegade's mind is just about to be blown away by her discovery, in his own lab.

"What do you mean?"

Nastassia plays with her holographic console, adjusts a few settings on her holographic interface, and turns back to the Renegade.

"Renegade, I believe you've already met Nautilus? Say hello."

The Renegade looks at her, spreading his hands. *What are you talking about?*

"Talk to him." She nudges him, mouthing *talk to him* again, rapidly tilting her head toward the Nautilus. She feels like she's the clown now. *It does not feel that bad.*

She smiles when he asks, still incredulous, "You want me to talk to Nautilus?"

"Yes, please, talk already. He's waiting."

"What's up, Nautilus?" musters the Renegade as he comes closer to the aquarium.

Nautilus's velvety voice astonishes the Renegade almost more than the content of his words. "Glad to finally meet a human delegate to the Assembly of Marine Life, sent to stop the war your species has been waging against us. It's been overdue for such a long time."

The Renegade shoots a glance at Nastassia. She shrugs. No idea, *talk to him.*

"We are not at war," the Renegade stutters, truly confused for the first time in ages.

"It all depends on how we look at things," the Nautilus says and turns his deep dark eye to Nastassia like he's examining her under an X-ray.

The Renegade, surprised beyond his wildest dreams, is rendered speechless. Nastassia managed to reach the Nautilus in several minutes, something he has been unable to do for over a year since his first try. Nautilus and the other sea creatures in his aquariums had a free exit to the ocean, they were not imprisoned, and yet they stayed. He felt that they wanted to reach out, to communicate, but he had never succeeded beyond getting incomprehensible data. It drove him insane over many sleepless nights.

And this kid, with such impossible greenish-yellow-purple hair covering her skull and her miraculous, difficult-to-understand brain beneath. Nastassia, who paces around the lab, excited and pensive at the same time, did it.

She gesticulates wildly. "Mom taught me that all life-forms on Earth, human beings as well, are the many eyes and ears of GAIA. All life sees, hears, tastes, and smells for Mother Earth. She does not only possess a material body that revolves around the sun, but is an entity that thinks, dreams, and remembers. Her memories are, in reality, interwoven with the memories of every person and every living being who has ever lived on this planet. I always felt GAIA. I was always able to feel living beings. But I never thought that was something special. Every tree-hugger would have told you the same, how they feel the Earth and so on. But I lived in front of the computers, isolated like so many of us, so I have lost the touch." She stops pensively and then continues, with a trademark fervor in her voice, "Sometimes a little birdie would come to my window as I was programming and I felt like it wanted to tell me something but I never listened." She looks at the Renegade with hope, needing encouragement.

"Perhaps it's not too late?"

"No, it is not," he replies, barely breathing.

Nastassia looks up at him, sensing *fear* and, strangely, a sense of *loss* in him. She does not want to probe what those heavy feelings in the Renegade mean. Does he also feel a loss of a true connection with nature, a loss of touch? No little birdies could have ever visited him in this subterranean lab and all the Nautilus's motley crew in his bio-CERN had been beyond his reach for so long. She was able to get to them, contrary to his observations, less because of her programming skills and more due to the feeling she has had since encountering Nautilus. Such abilities, some might call them powers, she possesses are overwhelming. It somehow displaces her, at times it removes her from herself. It is not only horrifying to be able to see peoples' conditions, and even more so, it is truly scary to read them subconsciously, to *hear* and to truly *see* their naked souls as they scream in silence, simultaneously immersed in the mind-eye's world of yesterdays and tomorrows. It feels like swimming in a rapid current, a wild, sinking river that suddenly disappears. It vanishes beneath the riverbed, and a subterranean river is where she might find herself. If you follow it either by arrogance or by a mistake, that underground river, like Lethe, the river of forgetfulness or, even worse, the river of Acheron, the river of misery, two of the rivers of Hell, can claim your soul.

The other side of that dubious "power" carries harm. She calls them dubious for the advantages those abilities have given her are far less apparent and carry much less weight than the disadvantages and dangers. But she could lose her mind and her life. She shivers, unwilling to imagine what might have happened to Stellan, whose powers are much stronger than hers have ever been. Franz Kafka once said that one should, upon seeing another's human soul, kneel in front of it with the same reverence one would kneel in front of the Gates of Hell. She wasn't sure if he truly knew how true that was, unless he was, even back then, *one of them.*

The ways those powers might degenerate is best seen in Varga's case. While he's too old to be a precog himself—*is he?*—seeking power over another human being, dominance over another living being or the whole of humanity, his obscene lust to rule over nature, all are hallmarks of perverted abilities. A small wonder Nautilus called our ways of dealing with his natural world, the "war." And yet, meeting him has created a profound sense of wonder, and out of that wonder came the connection she was able to establish with him.

She snaps out of her thoughts and looks back at the Renegade.

"This ability to see and hear so much all around you, it's... it's... unnatural... and scary. But when you miss something, such as having my family wrenched away from me it's almost unbearable."

"I can't even begin to understand how difficult it must be for you." The Renegade is telling the truth from the depths of his heart. "But we need you and your abilities now more than ever."

"I know."

Chapter 11

THE HACKING

New Athens, Harlem, NYC
March 22, 2048

The already dim lab darkens a bit more after the Renegade witnesses Nastassia breaking nature's code—rather, finding a way to interact with nature in a way never tried before. The dimness tells the Renegade that it's already after midnight. He does not feel tired, but rather reinvigorated. Nastassia seems the same, excitedly fluttering on an ocean breeze, whose code she has broken and integrated into herself.

"Well, let's get rolling, then."

Nastassia nods. "What's Varga's weakest spot, you reckon, aside from Böhm? As a way to get Böhm?"

"Will to power."

"Represented by his fake sentinel in the sky, that PHOENIX murderer?"

"It could be. I am not sure, so let's probe it. But, we will not try to get on its satellite commo. He has much stronger protection on it because it, unlike undersea cables, is in a way palpable to humans. A typical human weakness—the depths of the sea is like unconsciousness, which people dread, but a satellite high above their heads is acceptable, like the sun or the moon. So we need to get to the data flowing under the sea." They both glance at the nearby aquarium from which Nautilus has been listening.

"Nautilus?"

"Nautilus!"

It suddenly seems obvious. Then, in one voice they address the octopus. "Nautilus!" and the magnificent Octopus Cyanea, in his velvety voice responds, "We've been waiting a long time for you to establish meaningful communication with us. You surely act strangely. How can we help?"

"Could you help us piggyback on the magnetic field and slurp up all the communication between Varga's entities so we can analyze them?"

"And his rusty junk on the sky would know diddly-squat about it."

Nautilus surprises them with a question.

"Why would we do that? How is such action going to advance us toward peace?"

The Renegade and Nastassia stop in their tracks. While they might have been a bit, say, avoidant of the topic of Nautilus's wrong impression about the Renegade as being the "human delegate to the Assembly of Marine Life," in their excitement they did not even grasp the very simple fact—the Nautilus is being serious. He *is* the representative of natural life, at least the marine life, and he believes they represent all of humanity. In a sense, they do. The Renegade makes a tiny, almost only mental step back, and nods barely perceptibly, pondering what all of that means. They had had a breakthrough in the most extraordinary discovery, for the first time ever, a discovery that would enable humans to communicate with an animal using human language via a software bundle that translates both the sounds and neural waves. But they, the humans, himself, and even the genius child Nastassia, thought only about themselves. Truth be told, she has a real damn excuse. The tragedy that struck her, the drama of all these discoveries unloaded onto her head, but him?

What's my excuse?

The implications of the breakthrough, life-altering moment that would bring a momentous, biblical change in how humans perceive and interact with the natural world is something they've taken for granted. *At least without giving them a shiny trinket to enjoy or a tasty clownfish to wolf down*, he thinks, a bitter joke passing through his mind. When he thinks about it, they've behaved truly selfishly, callously even. They behaved like most of humanity did once given air travel, the internet, or social media. No one seemed to have stopped for a moment to ponder the wonders of flying, safely and comfortably, over the huge oceans in hours instead of dangerously sailing for weeks and weeks. But at the same time, they never failed to whine or get angry if the flight was delayed for an hour. The same with social media. No one took a breath to marvel at the fact they can talk, in real-time and free of charge with anyone on the other end of the planet but instead jumped the train of hate and hurled insults left and right, entitled and wrapped in hubris, as soon as they figured out how protective the digital shield made them feel. And we've acted in the same manner? We've shown no respect to Nautilus, despite spending over a year trying to understand him. They had not stopped and marveled either, they just moved on with their business. The magic of the natural world being one giant step closer to humans was overshadowed by the tech monster in the sky and all that Varga represents, and they immediately took it for granted and demanded something for themselves, from Nautilus, a magnificent creature they barely knew.

Are we really that bad? Us, humans? All of us?

The Renegade is gobsmacked and ashamed. Not really sure what to say.

"Forgive us, Nautilus. We're in grave danger and have forgotten both our manners and interspecies etiquette. That was insensitive of us and I humbly apologize."

Nastassia senses his uneasiness and steps in.

"As a species, we've been fractured and fractioned for ages. But now we have an enemy that wants to destroy us all. Our enemy is your enemy. As much as sharks are yours, he is, too, and even more so—the enemy of us and you as well. He's destroying us and you at the same time. What we ask you to help us with is a nonviolent, non-invasive approach. We will only get data from you to sift through."

Motionless, Nautilus looks at her. He changes his colors and becomes almost invisible on the heap of shells.

"Is he gone?" Nastassia asks, coming closer to the aquarium, squinting through the glass. "Nope, he's still here."

"I have to briefly consult with my superiors," Nautilus explains.

"Who are his superiors?" Nastassia whispers at the Renegade. Having no clue, he shrugs.

After five long minutes, the Nautilus finally says, "I will do as the Starchild wishes."

"Why is he calling me that?" she whispers to the Renegade.

He shrugs again. *I have no idea.*

Yes, you do. She sees the flicker of prior knowledge in his eyes but puts that aside for now since there's an urgent job to do. It sounds nice, though. *The Starchild,* she thinks.

"Let's get the job done in style and decode the code." He turns to Nautilus. "Nautilus?"

"Yes."

"Can you have your guys dive to the cables at the bottom?"

"Not a problem."

Nastassia types on her keyboard; nothing can break her concentration. "PHOENIX ONE and all his clones have backup connections via fiber-optic submarine cable systems, so we'd have to examine them."

Nastassia turns to Nautilus yet again. "Nautilus, could you use your guys to slurp data? All that we need are electronic vibrations of the traffic, specifically from the Transatlantic Apollo North cable?" She pulls up a 3D image on her hologram. At the deep bottom of the Atlantic Ocean, a ten-inch-thick thick Apollo North cable quietly hums with enormous internet traffic.

"How do I tell you where it lies? Do you read our GPS coordinates perchance?"

"We know where it lies. We use it for energy boosts from time to time," Nautilus says.

"Quadrillions upon quadrillions of gigabytes, the human equivalent of plankton, passes every second via that cable," Nastassia says, quizzically looking at Nautilus. "Could you do it?"

"I will need many boys on this."

"Please send them."

"Right away."

Dozens, hundreds, thousands, and millions sea creatures start approaching the Apollo North cable, covering it with their bodies. Nastassia turns to Renegade to ask a question when she realizes, glancing at him, that he looks at her like the grandpa she never had—a grandpa who sees her as a little girl that needs to be protected at all times.

Annoying as hell, but heartwarming.

Without him, who knows what might have happened when the PHOENIX went berserk. Moreover, there's something profound lurking here, the unfathomable depths of his feelings toward her, which go far and wide, like he's somehow connected with all her life. In a sense, he was, being her mentor all these years, but she can not shake off that lingering sense of something *more* being there. Well, time will tell, as the good auntie Gretchen always says, let's put this aside and focus on the task at hand.

She connects her earpiece to the lab's sound system and blasts a song by an obscure post-punk band from the late 1970s, called Tuxedomoon, and their hauntingly beautiful cult classic "In a Manner of Speaking" fills the room. The Renegade's jolted by surprise but settles for a quiet sigh to himself, overwhelmed by memories; this is the very song he loved years ago when he used to listen to it with Nastassia's auntie Gretchen. Does she, this strange, mighty kid know it? A fleeting thought passes through his mind. *No way.* Then, those captivating words remind him of silence and its power:

I should find a way
To tell you everything
By saying nothing.

"In a Manner of Speaking" ends and is followed by the crazy punk riff from Tuxedomoon's "No Tears" song. He smiles. What a strange taste she has. Who in the world listens to Tuxedomoon in 2048?

"I do," she says casually.

Damn, she's getting worse every moment. Or, rather, better, the Renegade thinks in awe. "Did you hear that?"

"Nope, no time," she replies. Her focus is entirely on the computer as she leans over the keyboard, tapping her foot to a tune she's repeated endlessly. It was like she felt the protocols, sensed the data flow, smelled the scent she traces throughout the deep, dark belly of the internet that is her natural habitat.

The Reconnaissance

Deeply focused, Nastassia looks at the screens. One shows the PHOENIX ONE lingering in the sky. Other monitors, including the big hologram in the middle of the lab, show traffic coming to and from the PHOENIX via an unimaginably big set of zettabyte data passing throughout the Apollo cable and, in its raw form, by the Nautilus's crews' slurped version of electric impulses sent their way.

The reconnaissance part of the epic, impossible hack, has started.

As every kid today knows, reconnaissance ("recon") is the key to any successful hack, and Nastassia, with a red pen hanging from her mouth, observes like an eagle searching for prey an endless stream of seemingly indecipherable data. She's probing here and there, looking to sniff out a weakness in that imposing monstrosity in the skies like a shiny Damocles sword of doom hanging over the earth. She tries port scanning, man-in-the middle, does some packet capture, and sends data to the Renegade.

"It might take us some time."

On his console, the Renegade's already analyzing the random chunks of data, doing the same tedious work of trying to find the PHOENIX's operating system. He side-glances at her, saying, "We'd need a lucky break. And a lot of patience." The process he's engaged in is called OS fingerprinting.

"We can't use Nmap," he says to himself.

"No way," replies Nastassia, also talking to herself. The frantic back and forth of thoughts and words seemingly whispered to one's selves but serving as metalanguage between them contains foreign terms and actions involving mysterious-sounding words like Debian, TCP, UDP, ICMP probes and packets, GNU/Linux kernels and Debian distros probed via Kubuntu. Stingray and brute force are dismissed by both of them.

"It is much easier in the movies," Nastassia says.

"What is?"

"Hacking."

The Renegade allows himself a chuckle. "Yes, they'd have done it already. In seconds."

"And they'd win."

"And get the girl."

"Or boy," objects Nastassia.

"Or boy," concurs the Renegade, who starts to laugh, "as they ride into the sunset."

"With booming, triumphant music."

"Dum-Dum-Dum-Duuum...Dum-Dum-Dum-Duuum," Renegade started to hum a tune. It's Beethoven's 5th Symphony, 1st movement: Allegro Con Brío. Nastassia joyfully joins his humming.

Then, he starts to sing.

"Freude, schöner Götterfunken, Tochter aus Elysium," Nastassia sings along laughing like crazy. "This is now a different tune, an Ode."

"You can say I hacked Beethoven."

"What would Goethe say?"

The Renegade strikes a serious Johann Wolfgang von Goethe pose and recites one of Goethe's quotes, "Nothing shows a man's character more than what he laughs at."

"Or a woman's."

"Or a woman's." The Renegade guffaws.

"Amen"

"Awomen."

They keep giggling like kids for a while. That burst of clumsy singing and merry laughter has provided them with much-needed relief. Because, truth be told, while I have no need to bother you, my most intelligent, tech-savvy reader, with the hacking stuff, your humble narrator himself barely understands. Allow me to just tell you that PHOENIX ONE, neither at first blush nor after some digging, has shown no apparent vulnerabilities at all. Zettabytes and zettabytes of encrypted data were impenetrable, especially given the time constraints they face.

Passive recon did not achieve a thing; the mainframe, the PHOENIX, was not reachable, it stood like an impenetrable fortress, a force to be reckoned with, for it could strike back at any time, with all its deadly powers. They were sniffing its ports, using packet captures, all in vain. The PHOENIX ONE has a way of tricking the packet specs used by the Renegade in order to determine the operating system, but those ended up in one blind alley after another.

Each of PHOENIX's responses was a fake; it pretended it was something else, as though it was running on different operating systems each given second. Nastassia and the Renegade, despite their growing despair, did not try so-called active recon because no matter what Intrusion Detection, rather Intrusion Prevention System(s) the PHOENIX used, it was obvious that it would detect them in no time had they tried.

Anyone to sacrifice? Nastassia thinks. A glance at the Renegade tells her he's had the same idea. Perhaps they could use someone's else computer and start probing the PHOENIX ONE with an active recon?

"He'd sniff us out, even through a decoy." Renegade shakes his head. "We must not arouse any suspicions."

The Shanghai Attack

What the Renegade told her several times before about seeking a weakness in a system and an English conversation in Shanghai's People's Square, is similar to the very principle of internet communication protocols. That is, it should always be known who "talks" to someone else. In this case, computers. If the PHOENIX ONE really was impenetrable, they needed to find a machine connected to it and find a way to hack it instead and have a back door entrance to the mainframe. Alas, it seemed that the PHOENIX ONE was only sending requests to computers all over the world; no one talked back.

"It just makes no sense," Nastassia grumbles. "The traffic is never one way."

"Not in this case."

"I see. But still. It makes no sense at all."

"I know," the Renegade agrees. "Did you try tcpdump?" He raises his eyebrows.

Nastassia jumps from her chair and makes a circle around her desk, "Tcpdump! Of course!" she cries loudly, slapping her forehead. "I am such an idiot." That, yet another cryptic term, represents nothing simpler than a command-line packet analyzer, something they needed to filter out the traffic. Perhaps something was hidden beneath millions of lines of communication codes?

Nastassia gets on setting up a sniffer filter by typing—and please do not run away at this point—a brief code:—tcpdump 'tcp[13] & 2!=0'—and yet, again, nothing. That line should have filtered only those "requests" that are going toward PHOENIX and not vice versa. Instead, the holographic wall displaying the communications suddenly turns blank. It was true, among dozens of millions requests from PHOENIX to the computers below, not a single one talked back. Not a single one!

"No way in hell," Nastassia cries, as she looks at the deep, dark screens.

"This is not happening. How does it do it?"

She glances at the Renegade, who is fuming. "Whoreson SOB rapscallion bastard piece of junk," he exclaims, slowly rolling out each word from the top of his tongue with a spicy combo of disdain and gusto, seemingly relishing each syllable denigrating the PHOENIX. Nastassia looks at him, both puzzled and amused. The Renegade is not known as someone who easily loses his cool. And he has not. Those words were less a distraction or an expression of anger, those were rather magic mantras, almost religious chanting he uses to keep his mighty brain focused on the task at hand.

"What now?" she asks.

The Renegade shrugs and keeps swearing. It sounds like poetry and smells like honey, his foul-mouthed grudging flow, so she joins him in an operatic cacophony of cursing. The strange torrents of cursing, which would make many *izvoshick* from Dostoyevsky's novels blush, filled the lab with their own lives and danced all over the dark dwelling, the only place on Earth that could have produced any hope. By being part of this bizarre experience, Nastassia feels like she's being initiated into some secret ritual meant only for the chosen ones. *Where are the PRIORI,* she asks herself.

"They are too vulnerable," the Renegade says. *Did she say her thought aloud?*

"Let us get Phatty in first."

"Right away."

The Renegade runs a quick security check, starts the I.R.I.S., and connects with Phatty. He types in a message: "No time to go into details, Phatty. All nine yards. Remote Framebuffer, R-IOTA, and Tor." As soon as the Phat Prophet has done that, his image pops up on the holographic screen. Simultaneously, the Renegade and Nastassia show up on his monitors.

He can not believe his eyes.

"No way, José!"

Trio Fantasticus

And yet, he is there, virtually in the lab with them and they are here in his man-cave and, for the first time, they have a chance to see each other's faces, all of them at the same time. Phatty likes what he sees: the Renegade, a tall, handsome old sage whose white hair and beard appropriately adorn his noble, strong face, and that tiny but beautiful girl. He can not believe his eyes, the great, full-of-moxie, elusive N. Nastassia is *that* young?

Phat Prophet has been lonely and depressed beyond words for quite some time. Since Wyverin left to work for Varga, broke all communication with him, and erased all traces of her presence, he was even more lonesome than before. Being the world's #1 player in the *Rise of Wrath* game, in which a 19th-century assassin travels to the future and eliminates Reality for Everyone™ players, is not a substitute for real life. Sure, it was great to see how those idiotic bozos were terrified by *Rise of Wrath*; it worked like a parasite trojan and interacted with their game, chasing and ultimately killing them just before they were to win big. The genius of the game was in a cunning trick: It did not hack Varga's Reality dreck, instead it created a sandbox version of the Reality within the *Rage of Wrath* framework. Sometimes, like headless chickens, the Reality n00bs would stumble upon the sandbox and get scared shitless by the presence of an assassin that not only looked like a nightmarish creature from hell but left an impression of coming after them in real life. It was fun, but it was hollow.

So, seeing his virtual friends in full size, as real, smiling humans, felt wonderful. In one instant, that connection with them carried more nutrients than all the pizzas he had eaten over the last few months. With them, he was a part of the Trio Fantasticus, as Philip Bolghery once referred to the mythical hacker trio of the PRIORI. He plays cool.

"How did you do that?"

"No time for it now. Log in, we're attacking. Let us get Varga."

"It's bloody time," Phatty booms and winks at Nastassia. She winks back. They instantly liked each other—there's a good vibe she has with the old Indian soul nested in the huge bulk of crazy, legendary hacker.

They've set up a wall of monitors, observing internet traffic in real-time, as it has been slurped from the bottom of the ocean by Nautilus's motley crew of sea creatures. Phatty looks at the insane video feed of millions of sea creatures lying upon each other and upon the Apollo cable. *This is how they do it? What the hell?* he asks himself but he knows better than to ask at this time.

He starts to organize his computers.

The Dahlak Archipelago

While the Renegade is getting Phatty up to speed regarding the ongoing efforts, a ping alert pops up on the wall. Someone has sent a request to the PHOENIX ONE! For the first time, someone from Earth has just established a connection with the master in the sky, and they all jump like rabbits. They've had their first potential break and are immediately onto finding the computer communicating with PHOENIX. In mere seconds they find out its IPA (Internet Protocol Address which, the address part, represented a unique number of that computer, a number that gets linked to all online activity it performs, including the one with the PHOENIX) but are still blind. They have no clue where it is located and it could have been changed, the IPA, the only identifier of a computer that represented their only hope. But, it wasn't! The strategy the PHOENIX had usually employed did not work in this case, rather it has not been deployed. The first weakness of the potential hacking target has been revealed via its unmasked IPA. It was located, the comp talking to the PHOENIX ONE, in the Dahlak Archipelago, in Eritrea, Africa. The Renegade and Nastassia look at each other.

"Eritrea? What's in Eritrea?" she asks.

"Dunno."

"The machine connected to the PHOENIX, routed its traffic via Proteus's NYC hub and used an unknown operating system, identifiable only as a KoyoteOS," says Phatty.

"A custom-made OS?"

"Yep!"

"Can you find out what's behind it, Phatty?"

"On it." He dives into reconnaissance of his own, seeking unique fingerprints and other identifiers of that mysterious KoyoteOS.

What happened next was a burst, a deluge of data, in an amount never seen before, which was clearly streaming from the PHOENIX and Varga's Proteus FinTech conglomerate's New York-based headquarters to that mysterious location in Eritrea. They almost could hear the buzzing of unimaginable loads of information passing them by, information that represents things they can't even fathom.

And then, as soon as it appeared, the signal disappears. The computer that was hooked to the PHOENIX via New York went off-line. It would not come back online for about twelve hours.

"How this can be?" Nastassia asks, flabbergasted. In today's world computers are online 24/7/365 so everything they've witnessed is an anomaly. A pretty huge anomaly.

"Let's find out."

"How?"

"By my modified maritime hack, so we can use the satellite feed." The Renegade grins.

Several minutes later, they have a live satellite feed from the Dahlak Archipelago as seen from the above, transmitted from the NASA's Terra satellite (EOS AM-1), an almost fifty-year-old flagship. Terra's Moderate Resolution Imaging Spectroradiometer (MODIS) shows a few inconspicuous buildings, nothing special. NASA was much more interested in dust and sand storms in North Africa than that archipelago. There was also a small hotel, a national park, a few abandoned roads.

"Can you get the old feed's recording?"

"Sure. Eugene, Robert E. LaQuey, PhD, is a friend of mine who used to work for NASA. The old devil left a backdoor for his friends to enjoy." The Renegade types while he talks. "Once all this is done, you must meet him.

What a character. He's 107 years old now and still lives with three women in the Philippines. He builds boats that almost inevitably sink, to the enormous joy of the children helping him. He also volunteers as Santa Claus there."

"Did you say backdoor?" Phatty yells from the screen.

"Yes, why?"

"Doesn't matter." Phatty continues to type.

The Renegade fast-forwards the imaging feed of the last twenty-four hours. One big satellite antenna has slowly moved, which is nothing out of ordinary. The *Isole Dahlak* ferry came and went away. A lazy day beneath the satellite orbiting at 705 km above the Earth did not reveal a thing. The ferry arrived again. The antenna slowly moved. The ferry left again.

"The ferry!" The Renegade points excitedly at the image.

"What about it?"

"It can't be." The Renegade enlarges the image. "Check the time of transmission."

Nastassia does so.

The First Breakthrough

The ferry's arrival times coincided with the appearance of the signal, its departure with the disappearance of the signal. The Renegade enlarges the image of the *Isole Dahlak*, the ferry in question, even more. It has a double antenna, a normal FM, and another one, a high-throughput antenna, capable of transmitting a huge amount of data in no time.

"That it!" the Renegade says wildly, tapping at the image on his computer screen. "This must be an off-line backup! Like your own external hard disk, something you don't keep on all the time."

"Varga holds everything there?"

"It seems so. The data it receives is highly compressed."

"Guys," Phatty excitedly yells, "look what I've found!"

"What?"

"SHA256: aa62bcf4a79e9778e766796422700c23e6847501d366c7f d899aeee314f00b04" flashes on the screen.

"A hash? What does it mean?" Nastassia looks up.

"The guy who wrote that OS for your backup facility, that KoyoteOS, did it twenty years or even more ago. And he has signed it with a SHA256. The hash was gone from upcoming versions."

"Did you decode it?"

"So, I dug. Deep. I've found an obscure museum, The Computer Museum PEEK&POKE from the abandoned port city of Fiume, also spelled as Rijeka, someplace in Croatia or Bosnia, some country like that. Near Italy. A ghastly place. The museum's still working even though it's in a ghost town. Think Chernobyl and you'll get an idea. These guys were friends with the fucking legend, Apple's very own, Steve Wozniak! Look at their funny-sounding names: Riba, Tozo, and Davor. Tozo is the boss. I wonder how to translate Tozo? What does it mean?" Phatty seems truly taken by that name.

"Damn Phatty, who cares about their names. Get to the point."

"He used some adapted Keccak-256 algorithm, a clever chap. Kludged mofo, I am telling you, I had to use—"

"Just tell us what it says, please," the Renegade interrupts and winks at Nastassia. Phatty hates being interrupted when he's excited like that.

"It reads: Hans Böhm, Mystic Beach, Vancouver Island, Canada."

Nastassia jumps. "Hans Böhm. I knew it, I knew it. He's alive. This Hans Böhm is Varga's Maléficus Ultimo, the guy Varga met and Bolghery researched."

"Who is that person?" Phat Prophet seems confused. "You know him?"

"No, but Philip met him decades ago. The whole Varga story starts with him. With Hans Böhm. He is the key for us. Hans Böhm!" She turns to the Renegade. "Can you connect us with Bolghery?"

"Sure. But this hash tells us only that someone signed that software with that name twenty years ago. Not that it's the same man or that he's not dead as Bolghery assumed."

"I know that's him. And he's alive. He's the human backdoor, he'll lead us to Varga."

The Renegade tries to call him, but Philip Bolghery lies blind drunk in his living room after watching *Babylon Berlin*, a twenty-five-year-old crime soap opera from Germany. He has a crush on both Liv Lisa Fries and Caro Cult, actresses in the series, now in their fifties and more attractive and more successful than ever. Frau Fries even won an Oscar for playing a German Brazilian aristocrat with a dark secret in Werner Herzog's last movie, *The Last Fräulein in Blumenau*. He wrote fan snail-mails to them both but they never replied.

"Will try again later," the Renegade says. "Let's go back to work." And, turning to Phat Prophet, says, "try to see if you can find any other software by Hans Böhm."

"Right away, I'll peek and poke the living shit out of that Böhm, if he's still alive."

So, the hack starts all over again, but this time they have something real to work with.

As they snuff out the traffic that goes to the Dahlak Archipelago, they know they have a potential treasure trove to work with: presumably the last batch of backups Varga archived there. It's a fat chance but at least a sliver of hope. Alas, everything that had been transmitted was not only encrypted but compressed with another layer of encryption that would require brute force in order to be broken—something only the INFINITUS possesses in this world, a far cry from their computing power.

Nothing.

"Phatty?" They look at him. He waves his head.

"Nothing."

"We now have an idea about Varga's secret backup facility. That's not nothing," the Renegade says. He instructs the Phat Prophet to see if any of the archipelago's traffic goes out, or if there's any other communication going on.

"For that we have to wait another twelve hours."

In the meantime, they'd keep monitoring and probing the Apollo cable traffic that has been tirelessly transmitted by the Nautilus's sea creatures. In the next few hours they do not make much progress.

7-Zip AES-256 encryption

The Renegade sits in his chair motionless. Nastassia is pacing around as she works on the holographic console. Phatty was cursing over the Dahlak Archipelago data.

"It goes in batches, right?"

"What?"

"The archive."

"I don't see it. It looks like one big chunk of compressed and encrypted data."

"Perhaps they're using a Stealth Split and Merge, check it out."

"How? That's before my time." Phatty rolls his eyes.

"Let me do it," the Renegade says and gets on the virtual console connected to Phat's computer. "It's a simple check… just a sec… and it's here!" He smiles. "I was correct. They hid the structure."

Phatty is not overly impressed. "So, we now have chunks of compressed and encrypted data instead of one big encrypted mess?"

"Yes, but now you can sort them out via metadata. Date, size, type."

"Wait!"

"What?"

"You have the copy of the KoyoteOS, right, from that museum?"

"Yes."

"Give it to me."

The Renegade dives into the code. Nothing interesting there either.

"It can't be!" he yells. "How old was that OS you said?"

"Twenty or so years, twenty-five."

"It can't be that simple. Varga simply can't be that careless."

"What, what?"

"What's up guys?" A disheveled Bolghery pops up. "You called me?"

"Just a sec."

"Hans Böhm is alive," Nastassia tells him. "Can you recall anything else about him?"

"Get 7-Zip," the Renegade instructs Phatty.

"What's that?"

"An open-source file archiver tool from 1999. The 2010 version is still online. It will unpack the data for us."

"Can you stop, everyone, for a moment? Jesus," Bolghery cries from his screen. "What's going on? This is like an Italian opera. I don't understand a thing. Please get me up to speed."

The Renegade nods. "We're reconning Varga. Phatty has found an old software signed by a hash that says Hans Böhm, Mystic Beach, Vancouver Island, Canada. Nastassia is certain it's the same person you met with Varga. We discovered Varga's secret database archive in Eritrea. Working on it as we speak. Got it?"

Bolghery nods and turns to Nastassia. "He left for Shanghai and vanished there. I told you that. In Las Vegas he looked a bit like a pervert to me."

"How come?"

"He wasn't too hot for the supermodels Varga engaged as escorts. I overheard one of them talking on the phone that he, 'the creep' she called him, insisted on oral and anal sex only, and that he was brutal and overall unpleasant. When he was drunk he went on kissing one little Japanese guy but was removed from the bar by security. That's all."

"But how…" Nastassia starts but never gets a chance to finish. The Renegade has unpacked one batch of the data. A simple interface shows the folder name "Bridget the Midget?" and a window asking, in big red capital letters:

"ENTER PASSWORD"

Phatty laughs. "He glorked us or what?"

"Bridget the Midget?" asks Nastassia with an edgewise glance at the Renegade.

"Beats me." He chuckles. "The people are way stranger than the machines." He turns to the Phat Prophet. "Phatty, run Python Brute Force and try to crack the password. It's an old software. It might work."

"On it."

"Look at this," Nastassia shouts after pouring through data. "Bridget the Midget is also a 3D VR, virtual reality sex site, hidden under one innocent-looking goth accessories selling website. Goth2Goth—really creative. But I don't think it's a coincidence. That folder and the website must be connected in some way."

She brings the site up to everyone's screen and a central hologram. And it was there, a bunch of stuff for sale with a strange little icon of a dwarf warrior hiding the entrance to the Bridget the Midget sex site.

"Varga goes there? He owns the site?"

"No clue, and nope, he does not. It's a legit small business. They have various 3D VR sex apps for local use and immersive 3D VR sex rooms online you can use if you don't want the app on your local machine. Or when you travel," Nastassia explains.

"You must be right. The folder's name is not a coincidence," the Renegade says, poring through the 3D VR application code he has already installed on his computer. "If Böhm wrote the operating system in use in Eritrea and called one of the folders Bridget the Midget, I am fairly confident it is him visiting the site and storing his personal stuff, far away from anyone's eyes."

"How do we get to him?" Bolghery presses.

"Phatty, try Hans Böhm's new name as the password," Nastassia suggests.

"Why would he use his own name?"

"He was still Hans Böhm at that time. Perhaps he has forgotten. Try it, nothing to lose."

"OK," Phatty sighs in despair. "What is it?"

"Maléficus Ultimo."

Phat Prophet tries versions of the name:

"Maleficus Ultimo."

The 7z interface reports, Data error : "Wrong password? : Bridget the Midget. He tries again, "MaleficusUltimo."

The 7z interface reports, Data error : "Wrong password? : Bridget the Midget again, so Phatty tries lower caps, all caps, then minuscule and majuscule, then just the name, and then just a last name, and then a combo of letters. Nothing. He starts to use anagrams.

"Facetious+mum+ill" and changes the upper case vs. lower case in individual letters, "Facetious+mum+ill." Again nothing

"FACETIOUS+MUM+ILL" he tries all caps and then he aLtErNAteS case.

"fAcEtIoUs+mUm+iLl," with each of the anagrams his small tool was able to generate.

The 7z interface keeps reporting Data error : "Wrong password? : Bridget the Midget."

Both Nastassia and the Renegade stop doing what they are doing. The first real break is so close and yet so far away. Phatty runs a couple of routines so the different passwords are popping up in blistering speeds all over the lab's computers, now all hooked onto Phatty's.

"Phatty," Bolghery calls, "you forgot the acute."

"Come again?"

"The accent, the acute, the 'é'. You spelled his name Maleficus without it. It should be spelled Maléficus."

"Yes, try with the acute," Nastassia feverishly agrees. This *feels* like it. Phatty types in, all over again, starting with: "Maléficus Ultimo."

Nothing.

"Try Maléficus Ultimo and Hans Böhm anagrams."

Nothing.

"Try the date when he killed his stepfather. It was a new birth for him," Bolghery insists.

"He's a hacker, no way he'd be that naive."

"He was also a junkie. Try it."

"What's the date?"

"May 27, 2006."

Nothing.

"Try Maléficus and the date. Shuffle the dates. He's German, use German's date format."

Nothing.

"Try Maléficus Ultimo and Bolghery's date."

"Come on guys, let me tweak the Python Brute Force and let it run."

"Add all variants with Varga, Winston Varga, Cobra as the car, Vegas."

Phatty nods and starts the Python Brute Force again.

CLUNK!

The "CLUNK" was a sound the Renegade added to the Python Brute Force to notify him, while it was running in the background, of a successful crack of a password. And that is the very same "CLUNK" they hear now.

"What's that?" Phatty asks, unaware of the onomatopoeic sound the Renegade installed.

"We're in!" the Renegade yells.

The Bridget the Midget folder opens up and reveals its content. Phatty's flabbergasted.

"Porn?"

As Phat Prophet continues to try opening other folders, without success so far, the others are already poring over Bridget the Midget's obscene folder.

"Jeez," Nastassia yelps upon seeing the most perverse sexual acts with dwarves, mostly imagined as bearded, mythological creatures. One of them was a Middle-earth dwarf from J. R. R. Tolkien's epic novel *The Lord of the Rings*. Always the same haggard man as the hero, returning home with his sword soaked in blood, where dwarves were submissively waiting for his sexual advances.

"Sicko," Phat Prophet concludes, averting his eyes as he continues trying to break into other folders.

"That's him, that's Hans Böhm, right?" Nastassia turns to Philip Bolghery.

"It's much older, but yes, that is the man I saw with Winston Varga all those years ago."

Bridget the Midget Leads the Way

In the meantime, Phat Prophet has set all the computers at their disposal on trying to crack 7z folders by running Python Brute Force. In mere minutes, another discovery. Not only that no other folder would've fallen for the password they cracked, but all other folders were encrypted by the BadgerCrypt® software, a so-called lattice-based cryptography, a quantum secure protocol which, translated into the language of a normal human, means that none of the folders are breakable. Not even with quantum computers, not even in a million years.

All that their great hacking breakthrough has achieved is to provide them with an endless amount of photos, videos, and 3D renderings of real or fantasized sexual encounters by Maléficus, a quite sickening treasure trove that would most likely take them nowhere.

"Unless," the Renegade says, "we can track him down based on that material."

"Who's going to go through that filth? I am not," Phatty exclaims.

I would've never guessed he's that shy, Nastassia thinks, liking Phatty for it.

They all turn their heads to Bolghery. He huffs, "OK, I'll do it, damn you all. But nerds, what will you all be doing?"

"Good question." The Renegade nods. "First, let us see if this was a part of Varga's plan—was it a trap? Anything suspicious in these files. Nastassia?"

"I'll do it, right away."

"Phatty, the ferry's coming to the archipelago soon. Get the data if you can and see if you can find any outgoing traffic. While you wait, get on the PHOENIX pings toward Earth and map those machines. Those are likely Varga's centers."

"Yes, sire," Phatty confirms, more for himself, as he keeps working.

As they keep working on a hack, Philip Bolghery comes up with an interesting idea.

What if he published everything about the PHOENIX's murder of esteemed writer and his scientist wife, Frédéric and Monique Bonnet, and about the kidnapping of their child? Some gory details about Hans Böhm, that Maléficus Ultimo pervert, would make it juicy material. They, Varga and Hans Böhm or Ultimo, might react and reveal something about themselves and help the motley crew of the Renegade's hackers in their work? He can try to provoke Varga by claiming Ultimo is the mastermind behind his empire? It might work. But for sure, it would mobilize thousands in New Athens all over the world, his natural, well-established audience. At this moment, no one even knew about the murders.

"Do you think it might work?" Nastassia asks. Everyone looks at the Renegade.

"Write it as we keep working," he says. "We'll decide once you're done."

"Sounds reasonable," Bolghery agrees.

"And Philip," the Renegade says coyly, "for the sweet beejeebers, please, don't write an essay. Make it a one-pager."

"Got it."

The Article

After Bolghery presents his article, Nastassia tries a joke: "Not your best writing."

He huffs, "Gosh, I was just kidding, Philip. The article serves its purpose. We need to decide what to do with it. Renegade?"

Phat Prophet comes up with an idea based on the people's love of conspiracies. Instead of pushing a notification to everyone via normal channels, why not play on the human spirit by sending 666 tx (transactions) over the IOTA Tangle, with a link to Bolghery's text embedded in a zero value transaction? It would appear as a secret memo, an outline of the plan yet to come. The subject of accusing Varga of being a murderer would be enough for people to believe Bolghery had to tiptoe and communicate in such an arcane way. They would ask who was with him. What are the PRIORI's roles in all of that? His text would not have been an article to yawn away but a leaked conspiracy about the conspiracy to commit a murder. By Varga of all people at that. It would explode online, Phatty is certain.

"The message could be stored in the signatureMessageFragment field of the tx, with value == 0, so the signatureMessageFragment fields are part of the message. Repeat the same zero value transaction each 666 seconds for 666 times and rest assured it would be picked up by the community. Then they'd do their bidding. The link would then spread organically around the world like wildfire. Could that possibly be true? the people would ask."

"Not bad, Phatty, not bad," the Renegade says, nodding with approval mirrored by Nastassia's vigorous nodding of her own.

Damn good, Phatty, she mouths. Phatty beams.

They need to decide when to go out with the article and how to use it in the best possible way. The Renegade asks Bolghery to rewrite the article by adding some vague allusions so to make it feel even more conspirational.

Behind the murder, it needs to be stated clearly and unequivocally, that there's also a kidnapping, which means there's something sinister behind it. Perhaps a thinly veiled hint that the secret of the lost children might be soon discovered? Bolghery slowly nods. It's not his style to manipulate his audiences but if not now, when?

He goes off-line to work on his piece.

The Longest Day

Alas, in the meantime they make no progress whatsoever in their attempts to hack Varga's systems. The Renegade glances at the clock. It is already March 23, 2048, a full forty-eight hours since they escaped underground, almost two full days since their reconnaissance started. Everyone was tired and gloomy but Nastassia keeps repeating, "There must be a way. There's always a way. Varga's only a human. Humans make mistakes." She sounds like she's repeating a magical mantra, but in vain.

"Varga's INFINITUS AI system built itself. It's not human," Phat Prophet says gloomily. Sleep deprivation is etched on his face. His puffy, dark circled eyes make him look tortured and older.

"Varga is," repeats Nastassia stubbornly, "and Hans, that Maléficus also. At least we know he's a deeply disturbed freak."

"We have no clue where he is," Bolghery, who returned to the virtual room, interjects.

"No!" Nastassia cries. "We don't. But we know where he goes!" She starts to pace around the lab again. She moves her holographic console and brings the familiar website up, "Bridget the Midget, this is where we set up a trap. I should've thought about it earlier."

"A honeypot?" Phatty perks up. "That's a good idea."

"With a Trojan."

"I am losing you guys," Bolghery says, needing clarification once more. "Renegade?"

"It might work. Humans are always the weakest link of any system. So far we've seen almost none in Varga's computer centers."

"But how this would work?" Bolghery asks from the screen.

The Renegade turns to Bolghery and explains the plan. Nastassia and Phatty will go and hack the Goth2Goth website. They'll go through all the usual recon stuff, port scanning, packet capture, and analyses until they find a weakness. All of it points to the fact that Goth2Goth was done by amateurs, goth lovers so to speak, nothing impossible or even too difficult it seems. It does not seem to be a trap either, so they can plant a trap of their own. Hans Böhm, rather Maléficus Ultimo, frequents the site. They have no time to create fake software but can inject all existing apps with a trojan. Like in Greek mythology, when the great warrior Odysseus built a wooden horse, big enough for several soldiers to fit in and clandestinely enter the city of Troy and conquer it from inside. Once and if Maléficus installs the update, they are in. From there, they'd be able to find out as much about Varga's venture as Maléficus himself knows. And that might be a lot.

"How long would it take?"

"It's a primitive little website. I'm already in," Nastassia announces. "I brute-forced the password and have admin access. Those guys are truly noobs. And the system they run is very old." She turns to Phatty. "Do you have a super-stealth Trojan Horse, the one with code injection, like a million years old?"

"WriteProcessMemory works with them? Really?" Phatty laughs. "What are they, some kindergarten perverts?" And on Nastassia's brittle, "Phatty!" he confirms, "Sure, I have it."

Regretfully the app did not have an auto-update feature so they had to find a way to entice a user, hopefully Maléficus, to download an update. After a brief brainstorm, Bolghery proposes they make the app stand out a bit shinier, with the promise of improved security features.

"Too risky. Maléficus is a techie." Nastassia says, rejecting the idea.

"Let us instead offer a free trial of new, sexier, and meaner dwarves—I can't believe I am saying this—a hundred-percent money-back guarantee and some such garbage from Varga's book."

"Do it," the Renegade says. "Phatty, how long would it take you to create a crop of lean, mean, sex-machine dwarves? Only images and one or two ten-second video teasers?"

"Several hours at most. They have the repository of all characters stored online."

"God bless dwarf mothers' tired hearts."

"Why don't you target Maléficus directly?" Bolghery suddenly asks.

"What do you mean?"

"But it's obvious, guys. His local folder must have his username somewhere. You have control over the Goth2Goth site. So, find him on the website or under that Bridget the Midget subfolder. How many people you think have dwarf-related sexual fantasies? And if he has paid with the credit card…." He does not need to finish a sentence.

The Renegade, Nastassia, and Phat Prophet look at each other and chortle, somehow embarrassed. This journo n00b pointed out something so obvious that it eluded them.

"Wendigo," Phatty exclaims out of blue.

What?

"What? Like the Canadian demon?" Bolghery asks, familiar with that creature. "This is his avatar?"

"I kid you not." Phatty produces several instances of "Wendigo" from Maléficus's folder and a related Goth2Goth account, Wendigo.

"There's also a Wendigo psychosis, a psychiatric illness associated not only with cannibalism as the Wendigo demon, but with chronic loneliness also," the Renegade clarifies.

"How did he pay?"

"No luck. He used Monero." He turns to Bolghery. "An anonymous cryptocurrency."

"The one FluffyPony, Riccardo Spagni guy, had created?" Nastassia asks rhetorically, "I thought the project died before I was born."

"Nope. He left and is now a fisherman in the Bahamas, but Monero is still used on the Dark Web, still untraceable. No way we'd find Maléficus through his midgety transactions."

"But we can see when he paid. Is that a subscription model?"

"Yes. Paid for a year."

"Check the log. There's a pattern of him logging in. Good to know the time for the app's new features we'd Trojan there."

"Goddamn it," Phatty grumbles, "he's playing with his dwarves off-line. He's coming here once every two weeks or so. We will have to wait a long time."

"Time is what we don't have," Nastassia says and plops into the Renegade's chair, not even noticing she left him standing.

"What now?" She looks up at the old sage.

"He has not logged in, but he still might be visiting the website more often. Look at his folder, he for sure did not play with every single feature he archived."

"He's right," Bolghery says to Nastassia.

"So we'll plant the Trojan and hope he'll bite sooner than later."

The prospect of a long wait felt like doom.

The velvety voice of Nautilus, who was all but forgotten while working with his sea creatures in capturing the Apollo cable data, shook them from their gloomy thoughts with a question.

"Do you want us to continue?" Nautilus asks.

"Please do so."

The silence fell upon them like death in an anechoic chamber would. All they had was the mutual sense of dread of what might be coming. Varga has been seemingly invulnerable for decades. His systems that they had been probing for days already stand as impenetrable as ever. With the PHOENIX ONE as a "governor," his power over the Western world has been fortified. And frankly, getting Maléficus into their trap has a fat chance of succeeding any time soon. And even if he gets on the Goth2Goth website this very moment, they have no guarantee he'd get the new version of the app with a trojan. And even if the gets it, he still might be able to detect the trojan.

The worst-case scenario: he'll discover their plot before they gain access.

The comic outcome: the trojan will work and they'll have another access point to Bridget the Midget's dedicated computer, still unrelated to Varga's network.

The best-case scenario: they get in and can start gathering evidence against Varga while also getting an insight into his plans, Stellan's and the MEGS's location, and the INNOCENTI. They are all tired, dejected, depressed, not yet defeated but left with not much to work with, their hope hanging on the tiny, thin thread of the Trojan trap.

A Cuckoo Clock

Nastassia feels that familiar cold needle in her heart but this time she can not shake off the mental image of a clock ticking, which invades her. It is everywhere in her mind, that annoying tick-tock, a desperate tick-tock, tick-tock that turns into a maddening *tick-tock, tick-tock, tick-tock*. As it is tick-tocking in her mind, myriads of hourglasses appear out of thin air with their images further clogging her mind. Then hundreds of clepsydras dance around her. She even sees a wonderful Arabic elephant clock with the prancing water clock. The little elephant has tortured eyes, tortured by the eternity in which he carries the time around. Everything is telling her, tick-tock, tick-tock, the time is running.

"I get it! We don't have time!" she screams from the top of her lungs.

But no one hears her.

That was a scream of her thoughts, echoing in her mind, a torture of her own. *But is it of her own?* From the corner of her eye she notices that the Renegade is observing her; he must have noticed that something's going on, but as long as he stays silent, letting her process whatever she has to process, she does not really mind. It does not matter. What matters is finding a way to get rid of all those images and sounds—throw them out. They are an intrusion she's never felt before, like a set of hallucinations but she knows it's different—she did not hallucinate for she was disconnected from these images, they came from the outside of her core being. It's not even a message she was getting—she really did not need a reminder—it was almost like obstacles thrown her way. It was a cacophony of sounds and a deluge of images drowning her.

It might be fear? She's been so focused on all the failed hacking attempts and has neglected the state of her psyche for too long. She ate the Renegade's rancid imitation of food. She has barely slept. And she has been worrying sick about Stellan for so long without any progress in discovering what has happened to him and where he might be that the fear crept up on her and is now manifesting itself as those sounds and images.

This is how people go insane, she remembers.

Compartmentalize!

Breathe!

No, it's not fear, it's an attack, for sure. She's been under attack, like some black magician from the Boleskine Lodge called up demons and countless spirits and has summoned the forces of Hell in order to attack her. *Where is it coming from?*

She takes several deep breaths and lets the clocks tick-tock without any attempt to silence them. She moves them mentally over to the right side of her head so that side of her brain would process the sounds. Automatically. Calmly. Without her interference or influence. She tells her mind to search for a tick that skips a beat, in order to trick it.

It works.

Almost immediately, that little exercise makes the sounds in her mind less intrusive and soon after, they sound almost pleasant. They are now like the cuckoo clock's ticking in your granny's old bedroom. Soothing. She also smells mandarins in the air. Mandarins go with old granny's room, as much as old furniture and paintings of saints, do they not? She misses Auntie

Gretchen, her substitute for the granny she never knew. Good Auntie also had that impossible ornamented vintage clock with a pendulum that swung backward and forward, calming her when she was a kid. Life and breathing go in a rhythm of a pendulum; in the end it all equals out.

She is calming down when the realization hits her like the lash of a beast's tail. She's had no awareness, no feelings, no sense of Stellan for a long time. That's the source of her anxiety. She has been underground for too long already. And now the attack. Or was it an echo of a prior attack she didn't notice? She has no idea. It frightens her. Was it a memory of the future? Again, no clue. All extrasensory perceptions that usually flow through her are cut off. Was that because of not being above? Not seeing the sun? Not sensing the wind? She does not know. Never before has she gone underground, and she has not studied the physics of extrasensory phenomena in the underbelly of the earth, nor in the oceans. That was a new experience for her. As she looks around, she notices Nautilus staring at her from the far end of his aquarium. All the other sea creatures nested in the Renegade's CERN-like aquarium are floating in water. So much water. And she's deep below the surface, surrounded by water, water and dark, indifferent soil all over her, crushing her lungs and shattering her world with the devastating power of a tsunami rushing her way.

Claustrophobia!

They sense the pressure she's under and are attacking a newly found weak spot.

She has never been claustrophobic before, but this feels like it. She can't breathe so she has to force herself to do so. It takes her an enormous amount of focus on filling her lungs, every breath being a Herculean effort. She could not move so she tries now to move her feet a bit, each weighing a ton, but she can barely push them a notch apart. Her heart starts to pound like crazy, like it wants to pop out of her chest. She grasps for her thoughts, trying to find a way out of the feeling that her life is ending, right here and right now, but she can't. She starts to sweat. She is shaking and hyperventilating. *Mom,* her mind cries.

The Renegade, who's watching Nastassia attentively with more growing concerns each passing second, realizes she's in danger. There's no time to wait and let her weather whatever is happening. He turns the screens off, so Phatty and Bolghery can not witness her condition and so they won't distract or aggravate her, and he calmly comes close by and sits next to her.

He takes her hand into his and looks into her eyes. She looks terrified on the surface, while the true Nastassia seems to have already been hidden beneath the panic reflecting in her glowing emerald eyes.

His eyes are telling her, "breathe with me," while he is still silent. Her hands are small, and she is like a birdie, trembling. He feels a jolt in his body. It is like she has hooked on his energy and is using it to help herself. The flow between them is palpable. She needs it, poor child, she needs the love that was taken away from her in one big, cruel sweep. It was like she was dying, deprived of love. *No se puede vivir sin amar.*

Love. She feels love. The Renegade's love for her, her own love for Stellan, for her parents, she senses the love with which they suffused her and her life. She starts to breathe in with the rhythm of the Renegade's breath; that old sage is a link between her and Frédéric and Monique, her mom and dad, her good Auntie Gretchen, the world she loves, the dragon blood tree, Luigi, the puppy she found for Stellan, and again, Stellan, her little brother. She is coming back, like she's been snatched from the tsunami at the last moment.

"Jesus, Renegade..." she says, coming back to her senses, while the tremors of the attack still shatter her tired body.

"I know," he says. "It will be OK now. We will get Stellan back."

There is a steely resolve in his voice, a warmth of his love in his grey eyes. She also senses an incredible calm in him and she knows—it was almost like he needed her crisis to fully regain his strengths. As she shakes off the last remnants of the panic attack from her body, he does the same with the thorns of doubts that were splitting him in two. Not anymore.

He turns the screens back on again.

There, Bolghery waits with another idea.

666 x 666

"Tell us." The Renegade increases the volume of the speaker, still aware of Nastassia's condition. *I am fine*, her eyes tell him.

"With your trojan on the Goth2Goth site, it became a honeypot and you now have to wait for Varga's Maléficus to get it?"

"Right."

"Why not Varga?"

"Why not Varga what?"

"The PHOENIX ONE murdered Freddy and Mon. We have witnesses and photos. We have you two. Let me write an addition to the article and, as your legal representative—I am still a member of the New York State Bar Association, where the crime has taken place—sue the PHOENIX ONE, sue Varga, and sue the Proteus FinTech, LLC for providing a platform, namely a link to the so-called governor in the skies. That might have a much bigger impact than the article alone."

"But you'll have to expose yourself. It's too dangerous and it would take years, if it ever moves through the courts."

"We don't care about the courts at this time. You guys set up another honeypot. I've already written another text, and a legal complaint, while you were away."

"Send it over."

"My legalese is rusty and all this was done in haste. What matters is the honeypot," Bolghery says, somehow pleased with himself and the speed with which he has adopted hacker lingo, and presents them with the Complaint for Damages for Wrongful Death:

Varga's Brazen Daylight Murder
"Justice Must be Served!"
by Philip Bolghery

My dear readers and comrades:

On March 21, 2048, you danced your night away. Perhaps you'd gotten drunk, high, or even lucky like Chucky in some dark corner of the night. The new governor ordered you to "Don't worry and be happy" and the promise of a new Peaceful Era came from the heavens from which he lingers. You obeyed and rejoiced.

Alas, on that very day, oblivious to you, Winston Varga used laser beams fired from the sky and had murdered Frédéric and Monique Bonnet. Frédéric Bonnet, MD, PhD, was the world's leading neurogeneticist who was also a famous sci-fi writer publishing under the pseudonymous Lorenzo Bladuzzi. His wife, a marine biologist, was the renowned and widely admired Dr. Monique Bonnet, a scientist whose tireless fight against pollution of the oceans earned her a prestigious Sylvia Earle Award for Advancing Protection of the Natural Life in the Oceans. Varga's goons have also kidnapped their precog son Stellan Bonnet. In the world of missing children shrouded in mystery, all of them precogs, you can draw your own conclusions. Varga is also guilty of the crime of attempted murder of Nastassia Bonnet, Stellan's sister.

Even for a criminal like Winston Varga, whose misdemeanors and crimes I have amply documented over years, a provable murder is one step too far. The ghastly assassination of those innocent people took place on New Athens territory, outside of any jurisdiction his sham governor on the sky might have. But, this is not a time for an essay or to lament over that outrage.

We must demand justice.

We must demand clear answers regarding the missing precogs.

We must demand to know where Stellan Bonnet, the kidnapped child of six years, was taken.

This is to inform you, my dear readers, that tomorrow I am going to file a lawsuit against Winston Varga, the murderous PHOENIX ONE, Proteus FinTech Inc. as the PHOENIX operating entity, and also against Varga's recently discovered ally, a depraved murderer that goes under the name of Maléficus Ultimo, a.k.a. Hans Böhm. Ultimo / Böhm seems to have been behind all Varga's successes, a true mastermind. That beyond-vile assassin, suspected of the worst of all murders, that of matricide, whose depravity with gruesomely perverted sexual tastes, has been sheltered by Varga for years. Why would Varga protect and keep such a perverted killer away from the law unless Böhm has something on him? Soon, I will publish in-depth research on Varga & Böhm's dark dealings, and I will reveal the true intentions behind Varga's nefarious actions. But this can wait. The killing of Frédéric and Monique Bonnet and the kidnapping of their now-orphaned precog son Stellan Bonnet two days ago is an unspeakable crime that takes precedence over all other issues. Don't be fooled for a moment—while the PHOENIX ONE fired those murderous laser beams, it was Winston Varga who stood behind them.

I will finalize the complaint tomorrow and submit it to the Court of Law. Herein please find the draft of the lawsuit I am filling tomorrow on behalf of Bonnet's family grieving daughter and their missing son:

SUPERIOR COURT OF THE STATE OF NEW YORK
FOR THE COUNTY OF NEW YORK

NASTASSIA BONNET, and STELLAN BONNET,
as individual Plaintiffs,

vs.

WINSTON VARGA, an individual, and Maléficus Ultimo a.k.a. Hans Böhm, an individual, and the PHOENIX ONE, a self-appointed governor, and Proteus FinTech, Corp, a corporate human per honorable Mitt Romney's Declaration v.01, Defendants,

CASE NO. NY047451

COMPLAINT FOR DAMAGES FOR WRONGFUL DEATH
pursuant to 18 U.S. Code § 1111 - Murder

(JURY TRIAL DEMANDED)

Plaintiffs, NASTASSIA BONNET and STELLAN BONNET, allege:

1. Plaintiffs, are the sole surviving heirs at law of deceased Frédéric Bonnet and Monique Bonnet neé Blancaneix (hereinafter referred to as "decedents"). Their relationship to decedents are:
Nastassia Bonnet, daughter
Stellan Bonnet, son
2. Plaintiffs are residents of New York County, State of New York
3. Plaintiffs are informed and believe and based thereon allege that on March 24, 2048 in the New Athens Amusement Park, defendants callously, unlawfully, willfully, wantonly and maliciously killed decedents
4. The conduct of defendants as hereinabove alleged was willful, wanton and outrageous beyond the ability of ordinary human beings to comprehend and such conduct was intended by said defendants to and did actually cause the death of decedents. The imposition of substantial punitive and exemplary damages will in this case be both justified and necessary in order to send out a message from this Court to all persons in the United States and throughout the world that such vicious and outrageous savagery inflicted upon innocent human beings shall be met with the severest of civil penalties, no matter the status or wealth of the perpetrators.

WHEREFORE, plaintiffs pray for judgment against the defendants, and each of them, as follows:

1. For general damages, according to proof;
2. For special damages, according to proof;
3. For reimbursement of funeral expenses and costs of burial;
4. For interest on all sums awarded, according to proof;
5. For punitive and exemplary damages, according to proof;
6. For costs of suit incurred herein;
7. For such other and further relief as to the Court may be just and proper.

Dated: March 23, 2048

By
Philip Bolghery, Esq. in Law
Attorney for Plaintiffs
NASTASSIA BONNET and
STELLAN BONNET in absentia.

I stored the material proofs about the murder of Frédéric and Monique Bonnet on the Graphene™ Backup Platform, an ultra-secure environment where proofs are encrypted locally, uploaded encrypted, and stored encrypted. In the event of my death, incarceration, or over my seven-day-long absence from the internet, the automated script will have released all the data and post them on all available platforms, including IOTA's Tangle, RIOTA, Tor Networks, and thousands of mirror websites and sub-tangles all over the world.

We must demand answers and we must demand them now. Varga needs to be arrested without hesitation. Hans Böhm must be arraigned alongside. Their crimes must finally stop. The PHOENIX ONE's role must be rethought through a serious democratic dialogue, unlike the last time when it was shoved down our throats. Unless we wish to live in an unaccountable, murderous dictatorship, it is not too late to reverse the path toward unspeakable catastrophe for our democratic societies.

Otherwise, next on the kill-list of that gruesome monarch on the sky could be you or it could be a member of your family, and the next child kidnapped would be your own.

Your comrade in arms,

Philip Bolghery

Philip Bolghery

PS Instead of a donation button, herein please find a link to the petition requesting an immediate opening of an official investigation into Winston Varga's crimes and the crimes of his criminal accomplices as hereinabove, by the New York State Attorney General, The Honorable Chad Montgomery Naujoks.

The Renegade, Nastassia, and Phatty finish reading at the same time and all look up from their screens at Bolghery, who beams with pride from his own.

"Got it?"

"Great. So we use the petition site as a honey pot," Phatty remarks.

"Graphene is even better. Given how secure it is, I am sure it would provoke Varga to try to hack into it and get the proofs. Plant several honeypots, viruses, malware, and we'd have these two and the dwarf trojan for Ultimo. It would multiply our chances to breach his systems," the Renegade instructs him and turns to Bolghery.

"Before you publish the article and the lawsuit, upload fake documents just in case. The files must be of a seeable size."

"Got it."

"Shall we still go with Phaty's 666 idea?" Nastassia asks.

"Let's do it with the article first, for several hours, to excite the people. Than the lawsuit goes publicly live."

The Renegade mulls over the plan for a second and speaks again.

"Good. Also, Phatty, setup Security Scanners for the Graphene and the Petition. We will play by the ear, depending on the Varga's action, assuming it would be one.Phatty nods, frantically typing into his computer.

"Make the app with the Trojan on the dwarves site live."

"Right away."

"Set up alarms to wake us up if anything happens, if Maléficus gets the app or if any intrusion toward the Graphene and the Petition. Any masked access is the lowest threshold for the alarm. Got it?"

"Yes, Sir."

"Now we all need to rest. Have something to eat Phatty. You too Bolghery. Turn off your computers. I am serious, turn everything off but the alarm. We need rest. All of us. We've been up for over forty-eight hours. Talk to you tomorrow."

The Renegade turns all the computers in the Lab off. Nastassia's internet access was cut off also.

"Hey!" she protested.

"You too, more than any of us, need rest. I'll make you a sandwich and a glass of milk—no discussion about it—and straight to bed.

The next twenty four hours are going to be crucial."

The Renegade had no idea how prophetic his words turned out to be.

Chapter 12

THE EMPIRE STRIKES BACK

Le Mont-Saint-Michel Abbey, France
March 24, 2048

Winston Varga was ready. He has been ready for years.

For quite some time, as he was carving the working memory of global brain to suit his purpose, Varga has been feeling like Michelangelo might have felt as he was painting the Sistine Chapel ceilings in Rome. The rapid creation of the digital century during the early years of information civilization was a boon for him. For over three decades he had been working diligently to get to this point of controlling the world. The difference in between Michelangelo Buonarroti and himself being, Varga thought, is in the fact that he was the artist, the Pope and God in one. Nothing was left to chance.

The INFINITUS had a running feature that checked every link with Bolghery's articles, and searched for predefined keywords as soon as they were published. It was programmed to alarm Varga about essays' content if needed. The word "murder" was given the highest priority for it was assumed it would represent a call for Varga's assassination. Instead, the article's content regaled Varga, like an unexpected gift would overwhelm someone with joy. "Check it out, it's such a nice libelous entertaining read. You might need it to get you out of your funk," he turns to Cordelia who was sitting on an Italian made, bought just for her, grey Arya Modular sofa.

Varga read Bolghery's text and the Complaint, like one would the best joke as he was probing the Graphene platform and the Petition's website, to check them for traps. "Philip, Philip, you plucky devil," he chuckled almost exuberantly, "but, *esquire* Bolghery, you should've known better, my dawg" He laughs. The INFINITUS has pointed out a small, hidden suspicious code that could not have been anything but a virus planted for him. He has no time to check it but has instructed the INFINITUS to check it out and to crack it.

"You and your hacking bozos of the PRIORI and their idiotic code. Did they really think I'd fall for their primitive tools and snares made to trap stupid little mice?" The idea amuses him but he has no time to waste. Screw their infantile mousetrap, real action is in order. Pronto.

He pings Maléficus, whose hologram appears almost instantaneously. Upon seeing him, Cordelia abruptly leaves the room in protest; she loathes that man and the gross, devoid-of-sympathy way with which he's ogled her. She always shuddered at the sight of a man immune to her beauty. She's never missed a chance to theatrically display her displeasure at him and how disgusted he makes her feel, *that damn smartass commie harlot*, as Maléficus has called her in his impure daydreams.

"It's time for you to earn your keep," Varga says, smiling charmingly from the screen. He looks regal, using the same sentence he used once earlier, on that fatal day in which he picked up Maléficus from the gutters in Shanghai, brought him back to the living, and, after an appropriate period of sobering up in a detox facility, trusted him with the Doomsday Vault operations.

"What do you want me to do?"

"Look!" Varga swipes Bolghery's material toward Maléficus, almost hiding his thrill. Maléficus got it immediately and slid in an ass-kiss: "We're finally crushing them damn cockroaches?"

"You got it. And that's why you are who you are, dawg," Varga says with a menacing smile on his face. Maléficus's forced flattery does not escape his attention. Good, he needs him to be subservient all the time and 100% ready to act at his pleasure. "Our idiot friends made their move. It's almost too easy to deal with them," he says, diabolically laughing. *He does look like an ancient God,* Maléficus thinks.

"Run the BESNILO Attack program. Hunt them down like rats, eviscerate them, have their skin flayed, and then make them disappear without a trace. Make it like none of them ever lived. I'll be doing the rest."

"Right away."

Varga came up with the word *besnilo*, a Serbian term for rabies, as the code word for the action he's planned all along and has just put in motion—while reading Borislav Pekić's thriller of the same title describing the outbreak of an extremely virulent form of rabies introduced to London Heathrow Airport by a puppy smuggled from Israel on an Alitalia jet headed for New York City. At the book's end, Pekić quoted the very last paragraph of Camus's *The Plague*: "He knew what those jubilant crowds did not know but could have learned from books: that the plague bacillus never dies or disappears for good; that it can lie dormant for years and years in furniture and linen-chests; that it bides its time in bedrooms, cellars, trunks, and bookshelves; and that perhaps the day would come when, for the bane and the enlightening of men, it would rouse up its rats again and send them forth to die in a happy city."

It is time to wake up the rats.

And it's time for the people's real education to begin.

The BESNILO Attack

The attack starts with a few simple lines of code:

```
// New Athens Gig in C#
using System;
// Ultimo
class ServerSide
{
   System.Console.WriteLine("BESNILO#");
   // no delay
   }
```

It is going to be wonderful, like a perfectly executed choral symphony in which all parts come together to deliver a mortal blow to his enemies and to educate the whiners. If this world is too tough for them, what would these flabby-bellied, feeble stroller-pushers think of honest work in a steel factory for example? Or a mine? They'd not endure a minute, these Frappuccino-with-almond-milk social justice warriors and their ethically sourced borsch. They need a nice little war to help pluck the chaff and purge the weak. Varga listens to *Ride Of The Valkyries,* the crazily wonderful Battlefield Vietnam rendering with helicopter attacks and sounds of napalm burning bodies as a part of the audio track. The Valkyries carrying the bodies of fallen heroes to Valhalla dance in front of his mental eye.

The BESNILO Attack has started.

The Virus

Varga unleashed a simple URL injection of an exploit, rather a long stealth feature of the Chrome browser he owned, a nasty little virus that lied dormant for years in every of over fifty billion computers and gadgets using it. As proprietary software, the browser was closed source, away from prying eyes. It was a hidden feature that waited patiently, undetected on the server side of any machine connected to the internet. The virus was a force of nature, beautiful in its efficient, unstoppable simplicity.

As soon as Bolghery published his lawsuit article and the IOTA community, who cracked the hidden 666 code in minutes, started to push a link with the material all hell broke loose. But not in a way the Renegade, Phatty, Nastassia, and Bolghery expected and hoped for. While Varga has avoided all their traps, Trojans, and viruses, all the URLs of the websites displaying the link and every message containing the link were inflicted with a code already prepared, injected with the malware Varga had ready for a day like today.

Wildfire

With the rapid exchange of links on the Net, the virus started to instantaneously infect every computer that opened Bolghery's article link. Within the next twelve hours, most of the computers in the world would be rendered as useless as dead. But as the infection was spreading around, Varga had another ace up his sleeve. He has several hours to do the deed. After all, it was he who controlled the spread of the virus. The rhapsody of victory can't be played by one sole instrument. It requires an orchestra, a devilish rapture dance of the electrons, ready to ravage the world and, at the end, when he's ready to also have him, Winston Varga as its savior.

As the computers began to malfunction, their screens displayed the message "YOU ARE DOOMED!" repeated in big, blinking red letters. "YOU ARE DOOMED!" while a bunch of indecipherable numbers fell in the background like the *Matrix* rain code, and the people started to panic.

The boiled froggies of physically and mentally obese America grew up defenseless, with cartoon characters as their only friends, loonies whose sole purpose was to brainwash the nation as they rescue the frightened rabble from some evil genius, had no idea what to do. The virus took over their digital lives, which meant that it took over their lives, period. The age of cultural decline, marred by magical thinking and Batmans or Supermans or some other "superheroes" saving the world, made the vast swathes of people totally delusional, engaging in passionate discussions on imbecilic topics such as who would win in real life, Batman or Iron Man, but left them wholly unprepared for such an event in real life.

When Hollywood turned even more vapid and vacuous than anyone could imagine it could ever possibly be and started to cram in every damn superhero they had on their Excel spreadsheets, Iron Man and the Captain America, Hulk and Thor, and who knows who else in one unbearable diarrhea sludge oozing from a nightmare factory, the people knew on a subconscious level that they had been abandoned by their beloved heroes and protectors. The superheroes now had their own squabbles to deal with instead of saving the world. And a witty repartee or two to exchange.

The people?

Fuggedaboutit. No one is coming to rescue them anymore. While they didn't really need to know that Varga is their new and only God, soon it would come the time for him to be their second best: a superhero in the eyes of the world.

Varga, the Savior

"Focus!" Varga slips an eyepiece and finger gloves on and turns his gaze toward several holographic split screens in the middle of his command control room. He can feel the pallid grandeur of his magnificent space filled with Hans Ruedi Giger's biomechanical carvings. He pulls up images of the PHOENIX ONE clones over their respective cities as they descend to direct-communication levels, just above his subjects' heads. The PHOENIX lightens up and, in a surprising appearance, beams the image of the divine governor all over the world. The throngs, facing digital demise, were trembling with the hope that something was gonna happen. The Good Governor is coming, and not a minute too late, to tell them something important—they can sense it—something to reassure them as the ugly virus attack takes place.

Varga starts conducting the consoles, magnificent in his divine element. He feels a surge of cosmic energy, him alone on his throne, conducting the destinies of the world. And now? What gift, what a surprise he has prepared for them, the subjects who have no clue. Oh, how generous, how magnanimous he's going to be. As long as they obey. Otherwise, a requiem for a dream awaits them.

The cherubic creature of unspeakable beauty, the embodiment of the PHOENIX ONE, now has a smidgeon of resemblance to Varga. He chuckles. "Looking good, my dawg," he hisses and overrides the program. Winston Varga speaks through the voice filter, bypassing the pre-recorded message that was meant for this occasion. But, it was too important, the moment, too big not to savor its every second in real-time, not to be a direct, visceral part of the happening. Varga enjoys the sound of his new voice, the recognizable, reassuring bass-baritone from the skies, with which he's going to promise a thus-far-elusive land of milk and honey to the subjects beneath.

They better be grateful.

"Citizens of the world, I hope you are ready for a gift. Santa came to town." Varga barely suppresses a chuckle. "I am aware that you, good people of Earth, hate bureaucratic language and long-winded tirades, so I'll cut to the chase. Today, I'm presenting you with a new currency that will pave the way for the second coming, the resurrection of a wounded world, a new lease on life in peace, prosperity, and wealth. I am introducing you to the new money of the world, One American Talent."

A high-tech-looking silvery bill appears everywhere and flashes an inscription placed beneath a rainbow enveloping the United States:

"𝔗𝔥𝔢 𝔏𝔬𝔯𝔡 𝔰𝔢𝔫𝔡𝔰 𝔓𝔬𝔳𝔢𝔯𝔱𝔶 𝔞𝔫𝔡 𝔚𝔢𝔞𝔩𝔱𝔥; 𝔥𝔢 𝔥𝔲𝔪𝔟𝔩𝔢𝔰 𝔞𝔫𝔡 𝔥𝔢 𝔈𝔵𝔞𝔩𝔱𝔰."

Murmurs come from dumbstruck viewers. As the PHOENIX ONE speaks, the virus down below starts to spread like wildfire. Like a circus fly, it jumps from computers to 3D displays to any gadget imaginable to a hologram, unstoppably multiplying like von Neumann machines. More and more people, unable to use the internet, stick their necks out of their windows, stand in awe on their balconies, freeze on the streets, or they turn on their TV receivers, no matter the tech in it, and listen.

He observes the people below, fearfully gleeful in their astonishment, and waits for the gasps and murmurs to quiet down and then continues, "No, we're not abolishing the dollar or EURO or any other national currency yet. But, from this day on, every American child, every European toddler, each and every Brazilian kiddo, every Aussie ankle-biter, and every other child under my rule will receive the same amount of human credit, one million talents, pegged to Alethia-wrapped Bitcoin and ready to invest at the moment of their birth. Or right away if they are already among us, those dear giggling hodler toddlers."

"Think of it as the free Alethia tokens. Winston Varga has made many a millionaire with his genius invention that changed the financial world forever." Varga has to stop talking for a second, pressing a hand on his mouth so not to let laughter out. *I really am a fucking genius*! And then continues, almost exuberantly, "But this time, the wealth is available and free for everyone. As of today. As of now. The distribution has already started via the True Identity© Alliance, Corp., as authorized by the Internal Revenue Service, and will go directly to new bank accounts already opened for these kids."

He pauses and conspiringly winks, sharing a secret with all the lovable subjects crawling beneath. "Details of how to award every living citizen without creating inflation are being worked out, but for now, let us focus on the future."

Zendaya H.B. Woods

A photo of the wonderful First Baby Recipient of the American Talent, a round faced, Black baby girl named Zendaya with her happy parents Homer H. Woods and Betsey L. Woods, pops up all over the world. Her round face was beyond cute, her eyes already filed with wonder. Her tiny smile as she looked at her tired, but happy mom, move billions. That raw moment of love and joy, in its simplicity, is the symbol of a new era. "Zendaya and her fantastic parents shall be cherished as a blessing with which humanity, with its head held high, is ushering into a new era. Thanks to the American Talent project, no child will ever be hungry again. Thanks to the American Talents, no parent will ever have to worry about their children's future. Almost a century-old vision of the greatest politician the greatest country in the history of greatness has ever seen, George W. Bush, the vision of No Child Left Behind, is finally being realized." Varga's voice cracks, filled with emotion; this is the emotion the PHOENIX ONE shares with the people. Yes, the people that are witnessing this magnanimous display of love agree: the PHOENIX ONE is a cherubic creature that has a profound connection with the people. He loves them and they love him back.

"The world is thankful to this little bundle of joy," Varga as PHOENIX continues, "and to her parents for this angelic Zendaya will be the face of American Talent from now on." The silvery bill beneath the rainbow appears again, shakes a bit while it morphs into the same bill as earlier but this time with 1,000 American Talents value inscribed over the motto and little's Zendaya's dark eyes smiling from the center. A master cut to Betsy, who cries tears of joy. No heart is left unmoved. But when the father, lovable Mr. Homer H. Woods, squeezes the mother's hand with his own big, strong paws and embraces Zendaya and Betsy in one big, bear hug, it is like the whole world stands in the embrace. It is pure perfection. The image freezes in the sky and Varga lets it linger for quite a while as the people soak up its beauty and the joy coming from the free money that the image represents.

They deserve some music, Varga thinks and lets them enjoy the tune they've already been conditioned to enjoy during the greatest moments of their lives, Made by Varga.

> *May good fortune find your doorway*
> *May the bluebird sing your song*
> *May no trouble travel your way*
> *May no worry stay too long.*

Even Winston Varga, deeply moved by his own performance, wipes a tear trickling down his cheek.

The White Noise

"No need to get sentimental," he tells himself. "Now's the right time for lesson number one." Stick-and-carrot has always done miracles when dealing with the rubes. He cackles and has the PHOENIX ONE run a routine written by Maléficus Ultimo years ago. It manifests itself like white noise on the giant holographic screens, similar in looks to the virus's first appearance on computers. Little Zendaya and her parents are blurred, the sound coming from the skies rendered unintelligible by noise interference. The dreaded "YOU ARE DOOMED!" message appears even in the skies. Then it vanishes, replaced again with the PHOENIX's divine image, before reappearing. The startled people strain themselves to see and hear the PHOENIX, but the words from the sky are not coming anymore. It appears that the PHOENIX

ONE was himself hacked after he delivered the most important message any human wanted to hear: free money is on its way.

Varga goes onto the terrace to witness the masterpiece in the sky himself. He laughs, "This is fucking great, really great," and walks back to let PHOENIX appear to be "hacked" for several more minutes. The code rain and the message of doom makes the people flat-out insane out of fear. Varga zooms into faces filled with horror. He takes control of each and every computer and, using random number choices, shows its users on separate walls of screens—rather walls of *screams*—that was showing out of their mind Reality for Everyone™ players. These include dungeon rat addicts of online forums, gambling bozos jonesin' for some action, crackening bastards hooked on porn, all of them deprived of their vices and in delirious need for a shoot-up of digital smack. It is wonderful. Their systems were down for a mere few minutes, an hour or two tops, and they are already losing it. Varga predicted it was going to be like that, but it is such a special joy to observe those hooked idiots agonizing over the interruption of a game that made him a trillionaire in less time he needs to wipe his ass with the silver bill of their new hopes.

He instructs the INFINITUS to run face-detection software in a search for Jeremiah DeJohn, the Surveillance's Human Evaluator SHEX27-009 who was given the task of following Nastassia Bonnet. And as sure as death, there he is, gaping at the skies, bamboozled by a show above his paygrade. Varga swipes his image toward Maléficus.

"Put him in charge of finding Nastassia Bonnet. Promote him, whatever," Varga barks and turns back to the wall of human destiny as written by him.

Phase Two

Speed and surprise are the key ingredients of every victory:
- Blind the enemy, in this case with the computer virus, checked ✓
- Hoodwink the enemy, PHOENIX's appearance as itself a hacking victim, checked ✓
- Dash along with utmost speed to crush the enemy. That part is happening now ✓

Varga runs another routine, also written a long time ago, and sends it to the PHOENIX to execute. The virus's message slowly morphs into one letter, the immediately recognizable "P" from the PRIORI logo, a "P" associated in the worlds outside New Athens as an arcane, dangerous symbol. Sending that "P" to Varga was was like sending in a brigade to pave the way for the later blitzkrieg. So, now the army! A deafening sound alarm rips the skies apart. Huge movie theater screens appear on horizons all over the world. The same image is repeated on all functioning machines, on every display in every subway car, smart-watch, and TV screen alike. One big, frightening red word flashes over it:

EMERGENCY!

EMERGENCY!

EMERGENCY!

The PHOENIX ONE's cherubic face, this time resembling Varga even another tiny notch more, appears in the skies yet again but his expression is stern and angry. He speaks in an icy tone, its color of blind hatred, its firmness is that of a Templar's sword.

"We face the unimaginable. The Peaceful Era has had its first breach," the PHOENIX ONE says. "The world's telecommunication systems are under attack. The enemy even attacked me, your governor, with what seems like a powerful virus." His image starts to blink, his voice interrupted. Varga liked Maléficus's idea of having images and voices "struggle" for domination in the sky. The PHOENIX ONE seems to be being constantly attacked. He appears and breaks, at moments his image bursts and shatters and then struggles to come back. That devious devil, Maléficus, knows his shite.

The images come back online to a brief respite for the terrified populace below.

The portraits of Nastassia and the Renegade appear all over the skies, so Winston Varga continues his PHOENIX speech. "These terrorists of the infamous PRIORI Hacking Alliance have hacked the world's systems. They interrupted the distribution of wealth as it was happening and cut the money supply to you and to your children, my dear citizens of the world. They want you to starve. It is obvious that they want to destroy peace and prosperity, goals humanity strove for decades and only recently managed to achieve, and that was the world we started to build, all of us together, the world these human rats, these despicable vermin, want to obliterate." The PHOENIX ONE pauses, letting his words sink in.

"Yes, terror has struck us again, so I will paraphrase that great wise statesman's words: 'Today, we are a country and a world awakened to danger those terrorists represent, and today we're called to defend our freedom and the wealth they want to take away from you. Feel free to turn your grief to anger and anger to resolution. Whether we bring our enemies to justice or bring justice to our enemies, justice will be done.'" Varga lets these words sink in again, and this time he lets the world stand silent for two painfully long minutes. Once he appears again, in the gravelly voice of the PHOENIX ONE, he lets the world know: "I am calling for the special forces to leave no stone unturned and find these terrorists no matter the price. Shoot-to-kill is authorized."

The theater in the sky's screens vanish, and eerie silence falls to Earth. The nations of Earth are frozen in dread. What's going to happen now? Who are these terrorists? What are we to do?

Freedom Lives TV

Varga understood that controlling the events means controlling the narrative and how it unfolds. It was the same approach he used for the Aletheia Attack—in waves. He could not leave the people on their own for too long. So the white-noise-like "struggle" in the sky continues for several long minutes. Then the PHOENIX ONE appears again. His message is curt and to the point.

"Turn on your gadgets. The internet is down but the TV backup channel 'Freedom Lives' is up and running and will from now on be utilized to inform you about the ongoing struggle."

Everyone rushes back to watch "Freedom Lives" on TV. A legalese-looking word salad on the screens tells the world that the magnanimous PHOENIX ONE, with the generous help of Winston Varga's Proteus FinTech Corp., has activated an emergency backup channel while the internet is down, to keep the populace informed. More to come. The message scrolls down in a loop for several minutes repeating itself, when, to the collective sigh of the digitally addicted mass's relief, the "Freedom Lives" TV starts to broadcast.

The studio is improvised, but, hungry for information, no one cares.

"We will not succumb to the terrorists. We will not vanish into the dark, and we will not go down without a fight. We will keep you informed," says Dr. Maximillian von Liechtenstein, the very same man who had presided over the governmental transition and, as an INNOCENTI lauded honorary member, was given a board seat on Varga's TV, and defiantly promised, "We will keep transmitting no matter what."

Good Morning
The Renegade's Lab, NYC
March 24, 2048

After the Renegade awoke to a world in which he's been labeled a terrorist, his crew of hackers and renegades was still asleep. As he stands in front of the surreal images portraying him as someone worse than the worst criminals throughout history, he's drenched in cold sweat and stunned at Varga's brazen criminality. In the same gleeful breath, Varga's propaganda machine has managed to compare him to Charles "Carl" Panzram, a serial killer and rapist, and Adolf Hitler, the infamous Nazi leader responsible for the killings of millions. And then, Varga's anchorman—"Called in due to the emergency and the Reality for Everyone™ being taken down by the terrorists' evil plot!"—celebrated Baiano Lindo, a damn bot at that, reads a script that suggests all of the PRIORI should be thrown in a gulag.

Without hesitation.

What follows is a noble tradition of elite media and a treason of intellectuals on display as a talk show in which illustrious public intellectuals compare Hitler's crimes with Stalin's, insinuating that the PRIORI crimes, masterminded by the Renegade, would cost more blood and treasure than world wars, Stalin's pogroms, the Ukraine Holomdor, Indochina massacres by both France and the US and Mao's Cultural Revolution put together. "He has blood on his hands," says Baiano Lindo with his charming smile, a bit disgusted at the idea. "We need to deal with him," he concludes to a chorus of Harvard professors and retired intelligence anchor-experts who fervently nod in agreement.

The Renegade, overnight, symbolizes terror.

Watching it was like looking at an open, purulent wound with yellowish pus oozing from it—Varga's cunning trickery on display. Almost like the girl from *Exorcist* had vomited yellowish bile all over the screen and it now slowly runs down. It was pure evil, what he had concocted in his sick mind, the Renegade thinks. Varga has had everything ready—for years, no other way around it—otherwise all this would not have unraveled so fast, the Renegade is certain. Varga had the callous gumption to break down the internet, and with it he cracked open society for one reason only: to stop Philip Bolghery's formal complaint, an accusation of Varga's criminal deeds, and his writing. That was truly insane. But was that all?

Is that really worth the bother?

What does Varga really have in mind?

Really?

The Renegade worries that what he is seeing is only the beginning, and he is right. Varga's attack continues to arrive in waves as an avalanche, a cacophony of masterfully conducted propaganda.

"He had everything ready," the Renegade tells Nastassia, who stumbles into the lab, all disheveled and drowsy, almost comatose. She looks like a sleepwalker. She did not sleep well, having nightmare after nightmare, but nothing has prepared her for what she is going to see on the screen when she comes back to her senses.

"Who had what ready?" she asks.

"Look." The Renegade slips the screen toward her.

Nastassia, fully awake in an instant, gets it immediately. What she is looking at is her own image, with the Renegade, on the FBI Most Wanted Fugitive criminals list. Winston Varga has been rolling out the PHOENIX's declarations and proclamations, one after another, at the speed of light. Buried deeply in the Governmental Transition Declaration Act of 2048 and its seven thousand pages, was an authorization, given to the new governor, i.e., the PHOENIX ONE, a right to appoint state governors in the case of emergency. Every single state already had one and each of them was a member of the INNOCENTI. That fact became clear to the Renegade even after a cursory glance at the names rapidly scrolling down the HoloTV screen.

And then the full-blown attack starts.

Persecution

The police commissioners in various parts of the world join together in a public conference call. The audiences are hypnotized, gobbling up every word of this colossal struggle for life and death and their children's freedom that's unraveling in front of their eyes. After all, they are not alone. Yes, they were attacked, their future was almost snatched from them, but there's a sliver of hope. Baiano Lindo, enjoying the limelight as a human would, with a snide smirk on his gorgeous face, turns to the camera and looks straight into the eyes of everyone watching. "Here's the list of the most dangerous terrorists that these fine gentlemen of the Global Police are in charge of capturing," he says.

"Ultimo," growls Varga, "he's too flirty. Tweak the program."

"Right away." Varga calls him Ultimo only when tense, like now. *Thread carefully now* thinks Maléficus as he proceeds to adjust Baiano Lindo's public routine.

Simultaneously, the list of the following criminals, accompanied with the images or short video clips about each of them, scrolls down the screens.

The PRIORI, Designated Terrorist Organization, leadership:

Dr. Richard A. Rutherford, a.k.a. The Renegade
Nastassia Monique Bonnet
Philip Bolghery
Dr. Nastassia Petrovna Musikhina
Dr. Uri Mayerling-Hieronimus
Professor Ludovico Sinigaglia
Dr. José de Martin-Palacios
Lyn "Manolete" Sutherland
Professor Odongo Ogolla
Dr. Wolfgang Heinz Bode
Dr. Michael Broomfield
Dr. Ayako Sakaguchi
Lorainne Elster †
Jeff C. Winiecki †

"The Act authorizes every law-abiding citizen to do a citizen's arrest of these individuals. Law officers are also authorized to shoot to kill if the terrorists resist the arrest," Baiano Lindo reiterates with subdued gusto and a serious glint in his acrylic eyes, a new look Maléficus just added to his appearance.

His cruelty is unspeakable, the Renegade thinks, *putting a "dead" dagger next to Nastassia's murdered parents' aliases, knowing she'll see it, is a touch of devil*. And the devil in the details was precisely the reason for putting those death daggers there. Varga had barked at the puzzled "Freedom Lives" TV director, "Just put them there because I told you so."

Drones

Next, swarms of drones were unleashed in a search for these evil people all over New Athens worldwide. Jeremiah DeJohn leads the search in New Athens, New York. If anyone knew that little terrorist bitch Bonnet, it's him. Months of surveillance have mapped her habits into his brain. He'll find her, he'll arrest her, and if she dares to resist, he will—this time he's armed to the gills—gladly execute her on the spot.

"Search every nook and cranny," he orders the police officers and swarms of drones at his disposal. "Leave no stone unturned."

His dream came true—he is a peace officer. Or, rather a peace officer that matters, finally a ranked, valued member of the force, to be reckoned with and feared by those that disrupt the peace. He wants to blow a kiss of gratitude toward the PHOENIX ONE in the sky but such action might be too corny. He knows that he's being watched and that he'll be taken care of if he does his job to his master's satisfaction. He feels with every bone in his body that it was Varga himself who had promoted him.

What a man.

And what a proud day for a formerly lonely boy from the Bronx.

The PHOENIX ONE Speaks Again

He does not beat around the bush. "Due to the severity of the terrorists' actions, the Global New Athens Privacy Treaty of 2041 has been terminated as of now. All the privileges coming out of the former treaty are hereby suspended. New Athens are ordered to be dismantled and their citizens ordered to vacate the premises over the next forty-eight hours. City councilors will provide them with adequate lodging until the final solution is found."

"The final solution," murmurs the Renegade in horror.

Phatty appears, all sleepy and messy after a brief sleep. "What is going on?"

"Watch." Nastassia slides the screen toward him.

"Our war on terror begins with the PRIORI Alliance of Evil, but it does not end there," continues the PHOENIX ONE. "It will not end until every terrorist group of global reach has been found, stopped, and defeated. From this day forward, any individual, organization, or nation that harbors or supports terrorism will be regarded as a hostile entity and dealt with accordingly. You might be asking, why do they hate us? They hate our freedoms—our freedom of religion, our freedom of speech, our freedom to vote and assemble and disagree with each other. They hate our wealth and they hate our prosperity. Rest assured, dear citizens of the world, the American Talent program prompted them to destroy you and the future of your children's children. But they will not succeed. The American Talent program was severely damaged but has not been stolen from. These terrorists have not, despite their best efforts, managed to grab the funds meant for our children and their children's children."

"What the fuck is this BS?" Phatty yelps from his screen.

The Renegade explains Varga's initial malware injection and his ongoing coordinated action. Philip Bolghery pops up on his screen next.

"Have you seen this?" he asks, out of his mind. Yes, they have. And here they were, alone against the most powerful force on Earth unleashing its might upon them. And even that was only the beginning.

The Nuremberg Trials

The emergency TV backup channel "Freedom Lives" started to gleefully transmit arrests of the PRIORI founding members. In Europe, only Dr. Wolfgang Heinz Bode was spared due to the very angry intervention of the former German chancellor, Dr. Ursula Hansen-Schroeder, who still held what was seen as a largely symbolic position, like that of the King of the United Kingdom. But she was a political legend with a legacy people respected. When Dr. Hansen-Schroeder speaks, the world listens. Not even the "Freedom Lives" TV dared to deny her a time slot, although in the United States her speech was recorded and broadcast at 4:15 a.m. ET. She gave a blistering speech defying both Varga and the PHOENIX ONE order for Dr. Bode's arrest:

"A hundred and two years ago my beloved Germany kneeled in front of the world in deep shame. *Die Nürnberger Prozesse*, the Nuremberg trials, were taking place in the Nuremberg Palace of Justice. Some of the worst war criminals our country and our world has produced were tried for war and crimes against humanity. Names like Alfred Rosenberg, Joachim von Ribbentrop, Alfred Jodl, Hermann Göring, and many other Nazi leaders live in infamy forever. There has been no doubt about their guilt. None whatsoever. And yet, the world has given them a fair trial. Yes, justice needed to be served, but only after a lawful, legal process.

"Justice was served. Ponder that word for a moment, 'justice.' It's a powerful word. Throughout history, many have sacrificed their lives so we'd have a right to justice that was given to us. The Lady Justice is blind. She holds a mighty sword in one hand and scales in the other. The Lady Justice is just. The Lady Justice does not look down on us with her cyclopean eye from the sky and she does not lecture us. The Lady Justice does not order extrajudicial arrests of the people accused of crimes, she stands with the most sacred principle of the justice system, innocent until proven guilty. The Lady Justice does not threaten us with shoot-to-kill orders." Dr. Hansen-Schroeder takes a deep breath and continues even more passionately.

"The United Nations voted the PHOENIX ONE into power, but *it*," she emphasizes with barely disguised disgust, "does not seem to be aware of the very same United Nations' principles we abode by for over a century. The United Nations Declaration of Human Rights, Article 11, (1) is clear. 'Everyone charged with a penal offense has the right to be presumed innocent until proved guilty according to law in a public trial at which he has had all the guarantees necessary for his defense.'

"The law. The public trial.

"We Germans are a proud nation that has paid a heavy price for the sins of our fathers. A heavy price we gladly paid. Why? Because we know the horrors of extrajudicial shame of perverted justice.

'The Nuremberg trials' accused were judged for the crimes committed under the Third Reich, the biggest stain on our collective consciousness. It was a police state rife with arbitrary arrests, imprisonments, and murders of political opponents of the regime. Many ended up in concentration camps and were killed there without ever being tried for the crimes they did not commit in the first place. We are not going to allow arbitrary arrests and imprisonment on our soil ever again. We are not going to let extrajudicial processes take place in some hard disk controlled by the richest man on Earth. And as sure as hell, we are not going to let anyone arrest our citizen, a distinguished professor emeritus, Dr. Wolfgang Heinz Bode. No one. I will stand with him, and if the PHOENIX ONE or Winston Varga goons come to 'shoot to kill,' they will have to kill me with him. We demand an open and fair process. And we demand justice for everyone. Thank you."

Filled with hatred, Varga watches her speech.

"You'll see justice of your own," he swears through his clenched teeth but orders Maléficus Ultimo to leave Germany and that damn Kraut alone. For now. There's a lot to do in the meantime. Germany would be his last European prize and he'll take it slowly, dismember it bit by bit, and throw it to the vultures and cannibals to devour it with gusto, fava beans, and some nice Chianti. *Once I am done with them, they'll wish the Third Reich was still with them, damned arrogant bastards.*

There's so much to do before he'll have time to deal with those *doctors*—Varga hisses the word with disgust—Dr. Bode and Dr. Hansen-Schroeder. *So let me continue crushing those that are an immediate threat,* he decides. As the world watches with bated breath what's going on in the epic struggle between good and evil, the grave, immediate threat to the world has less than a handful of actively engaged "terrorist" members still capable of working. And all of them were in the Renegade's lab or on the screens in the lab, feeling more hopeless and helpless than ever. Dr. Maximillian von Liechtenstein, accompanied by Baiano Lindo, appears with Breaking News on the "Freedom Lives" TV channel. For reasons unknown, Varga has his emergency TV studio broadcast in a manner of the vintage black & white TV era, a bit naive, too overdramatic, and simplified. Perhaps he wanted to put the clock back to the times of relative innocence, or so was everyone's guess. Not that anyone cared, awed by the only electronic window into the world's affairs that was left. The people, used to thousands of electronic outlets at their fingertips, now entirely depended on that one and only emergency channel.

Thanks to those damn terrorists.

Getting Back to Normalcy

Dr. von Liechtenstein smokes (!) but Baiano Lindo does not even frown at the gaucherie. *We are all under great stress,* he thinks compassionately. They had old-fashioned rotary phones on their desks, next to bunches of papers, while assistants rushed to and fro, bringing even more stacks of papers, presumably information.

"In the next twenty-four hours, internet access will be restored," Dr. von Liechtenstein announces as proudly as if it were him who would personally connect every single computer to the internet. Baiano Lindo adds, a bit nonsensically but nevertheless encouraging:

"Anti-terrorists and antivirus squadrons are working around the clock to restore your Net access and bring the world back to normalcy." He waves a graph in front of the camera, showing an impossible maze of interconnected lines. "Please be patient before our tireless heroes connect all these dots," he finishes, all excited without any apparent reason.

"You will have to restore your access with the three steps." Dr. von Liechtenstein takes over with the most solemn expression he's worn since the governmental transition day. "Everyone in the world will be getting a link to a special website you'll be able to access, bypassing the virus."

Who?

"Who is buying all this bullshit?" Nastassia yells back in the Renegade's lab.
"Everyone," Phatty says, rolling his eyes.

Securing the Privacy

Dr. von Liechtenstein continues. "Once you have the link, you will have to go there, on that specially prepared website, and download a new version of your, Government Approved, Chrome, a.k.a. GACH, browser. It will secure your privacy and will be the only way of accessing the internet after the network is back up and running after this horrendous terrorist attack on our way of life and our freedoms."

"The browser will also have an identification code, based on your own True Identity© BIDNA TIN, which will make you even more secure from any future attacks by the terrorists and that code will allow you to free and safe browse the internet, without any worries about your privacy."

"And to go back to your Reality for Everyone™ life," Baiano Lindo jumps in, assuring the world, all fidgety and beaming and smiling. Was that a tear of joy on his gorgeous Moreno face? He composes himself and continues reciting a set of instructions for the anxious population.

"No need to worry your pretty little heads about technical details," he says, allowed to flirt and joke a tiny little bit again, which is his nature. "Everything will be published for the techies among you, as an open-source code, to check and triple check, but for us normal people," says the perfectly crafted robot without a trace of irony, "the assurances are more than enough. After all, the same company that brought you life and pleasure through Reality for Everyone™, Proteus FinTech, is behind this security solution. A name you can trust, rather its heroic work, had been strenuously controlled, triple verified and approved by the PHOENIX ONE." Baiano concludes his little speech, all exhausted by the effort.

Dr. von Liechtenstein takes over. "Everyone works very hard, round the clock, not only to restore your digital lives, but to provide you with extra layers of privacy and impenetrable security so such an atrocious attack on your freedoms and well-being of your children never happens again." He makes a significant pause and then continues.

"Over the next seven days, as the world's telecommunications are getting back online, no other protocol offering an alternative, fake privacy will be allowed." He lets his words sink in and continues again, with a hint of menacing pleasure in his voice.

"Internet service providers will have to upgrade and allow only the traffic from access points, your browsers, that have your identification code in order to enable you to browse the internet freely in the privacy and safety of your sacred home. None of these terrorists' tools such as Tor, RIOTA, its Tangle, SOCIETY2, or all the signals or any other so-called privacy apps and or tokens like Monero will be allowed to transverse cyberspace. We will never again let them pollute and endanger our—your—cyberspace. Think of your True Identity© BIDNA TIN as the password, rather your 2FA, a second automatic layer of authentication you would need to get online. Just a tiny step, getting the GACH browser, and your access will be fully automated forever. But, rest assured, no BIDNA TIN code, no internet access. No BIDNA, no mobile service. No BIDNA, no Reality for Everyone™ for anyone. No BIDNA TIN and no access to the vast online array of services provided for your safety and well-being."

Dr. von Liechtenstein pauses and gulps a big swig of water. The dark circles beneath his eyes tell the world he's visibly exhausted by the work for the people. He's been tirelessly perusing the stashes of documents in front of him. Von Liechtenstein takes another stash, glances, leafs through, and sighs.

What's in it, the world wants to know.

"Internet service providers that would enable any of the secret protocols, created and peddled from the PRIORI New Athens terrorists' pits, and allow traffic without checking the new browser's identification code, your BIDNA TIN, will be shut down immediately. Their licenses will be revoked for good. Their equipment seized. Their operators and owners jailed for prison sentences up to ten years to life."

After he has finished his tirade, an animation showing the wonders of the new, safe and secure internet access start prancing on the screens. It even has a poor little masked terrorist trying to access the internet from his dungeon, only to see—DENIED—all over the screen, while, above the surface, the children and their children's children happily play Reality for Everyone™ and win, win again and win all over again.

In this new world whose dawn is coming, everyone but the terrorists wins. Varga is pleased. Everything goes by the plan. And he is ready for the next step. Nothing should be left to chance.

The Weakest Link
Renegade's Lab, NYC
March 24, 2048

"He found it, he has found the weakest link!" Nastassia struggles to say the obvious.

The whole internet structure exists on an entry point, that's of your internet connection, controlled by the internet service provider and those have the power to cut you off. As much as the water company could cut you off from water or an electric company from the electric power, or your phone provider from the service, the internet service providers can do the same with your Net connection. The beauty of Varga's newly introduced rule is that no one will be cutting off your service; you'll be able to access the products and services allowed by Varga only after complying with his new rules.

"Would we be able to go around it?" Phatty asks.

"It would be difficult," the Renegade answers when a "BREAKING NEWS" banner on the TV screen shows them that Varga has more in the cards.

The Last Piece of Puzzle
Le Mont-Saint-Michel Abbey
March 24, 2048

Never one to shun serious questions during a grave crisis, the Old Lady we Can Trust, the one and only Oprah Winfrey, summons her strengths and Winston Varga himself to his studio. The world needs to hear from its richest man during these perilous times of terror and such danger to all of us and our way of life, the announcer morosely tells the cameras. The global citizenry, through his concerned but honest eyes and reassuring timbre, is informed that no studio audiences are present. No one could be reached in such short notice, given the terrorists' cyberattack that paralyzed the internet and all other means of communication. Transport was also stopped to a halt, given its dependency on the internet. The silence in the studio was eerie, the joy understandably gone.

Varga enters the studio also in a manner starkly opposite to his usual public persona. Joyce Modeste, his personal assistant whom he shunned during the governmental transition process given the erection she gave him every time she passed by with her modest demeanor, sexy legs, and slutty perfume, has organized a makeup session. It makes him look like he hasn't slept in ages—*'such is the man fighting for you'*—Baiano Lindo whispers off-screen, loud enough so the audiences would hear his hot mic "mistake," while the technicians are getting Varga's mics ready. There are no theatrics; even his trademark smile is gone. He understands the gravity of the situation. After all, the Proteus FinTech Corp. and his programming skills shoulder a huge responsibility for resolving this unprecedented crisis.

The Old Lady we Can Trust goes straight to the point. "Why do they hate us, Winston?" His answer surprises them all.

"Frankly, I don't know, Oprah."

He admits his powerlessness while earnestly spreading his arms like a good uncle would. He's one with the world watching. Who could understand a brazen, devastating attack on such a scale? Really? "Only a sick mind would try to destroy the world like that. In a sneaky, cowardly way."

He lets the words sink in. Heads all over the world nod in agreement. The people feel the same, they feel the man who has given them power, freedom, and games to enjoy is someone who feels their pain.

Varga's voice almost cracks when he continues. "We've given the world its first Peaceful Era in ages. New Athens people were enjoying everything the rest of us have, even more so, in their so-called autonomy. The governor, out of the goodness of its electronic heart, God bless him, and from the might of his incalculable brainpower, has proposed the American Talent."

"New Athens wasn't excluded from the program?" Oprah interjects. She's the only person alive capable of interrupting Varga in the middle of a sentence without facing his wrath.

"On the contrary, Oprah, they were embraced. I even welcomed all those mean-spirited video games poking at me."

"You did indeed. American Talent, you're saying?"

"The world was given a chance to thrive like never before. American Talent program…" Varga looks straight at the camera. "Rest assured, the program will continue. They will not win. No way."

His resolution moves Oprah. She stands up, unaided, and hugs him. Yes, the world needed a hug, the Lady we Can Trust has sensed it and gives one big, forceful hug to the man so many depend on. Winston Varga was firstly a bit confused with Oprah's spontaneous hug, which he carefully planned to be placed at the right moment, but then, after several seconds long enough for the director to cut in two nice closeups, he gladly succumbs. Their hug freezes on the screen and the previously seen hug in between the Woods family members appears on the split-screen.

As the transmission cuts back to the emergency TV studio, what is revealed are tears pouring down Baiano Lindo's gorgeous dark face. His voice trembles as he reassures the world, "What we are witnessing are the hugs that symbolize the world united. These monstrous terrorists and their evil attacks will not break us. There will be a future."

Oprah Winfrey and Winston Varga's frozen image slowly fades out and Zendaya's cute little smile stays alone to linger on the screens for a little while. Yes, there will be a future for all of us, a bright, happy, free future indeed.

There Will be a Future

Dr. von Liechtenstein was given a task to liaison with the leading members of the INNOCENTI, an elusive, elite inner circle known as Verum Innocentes, the TRUE INNOCENTI. The little man's main task was to keep everyone in the loop, at Varga's personal request. There was an important piece of the BESNILO's puzzle they needed to be notified upfront of. Dr. von Liechtenstein played a 3D holographic message by Varga himself, "as he wanted to be closer to all of you, despite being so immensely busy," he explained. Varga was again his old smiling self.

"Sorry for not being able to attend the conference in person, my dear friends, our most valuable members of society. But you for sure understand how busy I have been for the last many hours."

They did. Had Varga had time to observe their collective nod, he'd be amused.

"A quarter of a century ago, an obscure crackhead journalist wrote how 'truth becomes a numbers game: the person who can demand belief, either by force or by the creation of the most successful image, is right.'" Varga shared a chuckle with Crème de la Crème of the world by a pause he inserted into his recording, "In that, rare for him, moment of mental clarity, the journalist of a bygone era was right. Things have gotten worse since his cyber caveman times. In a post-truth era, the brains of our population have been poisoned by all sorts of propaganda, the worst of it coming from Red Communist China without and the Terrorist New Athens network within our borders. I am giving you my solemn, iron-clad assurance, this will not be the case anymore. They will be crushed," Varga's hologram concluded by bidding them farewell and vanishing.

The question of what he meant was on everyone's mind. They did not have to wait long for von Liechtenstein's clarification. "Firstly let me assure you," he told them, "the government-approved Chrome browser rules do not apply to you. You will be surveillance-free and each of you will have your own, BIDNA-requirement-free browser. Trust is a paragon among us, as…" he pauses and rolls the First Name, relishing the intimacy it implied, "Winston personally ordered me to convey to you."

He let them heave a sigh of relief.

"For the rest of the measures, please tune in. I will have to inform the world, so help me out, make my life easier so I won't have to repeat the same thing twice."

"Sure, sure," everyone agreed, as they went back to minding their own business. Like everyone else, they had the "Freedom Lives" TV on. A dramatic banner announced a new leap forward in assuring everyone's peace of mind.

The End of Fake News

It was Dr. Sharon Tusk who Varga coaxed into reading the next proclamation. She was adamantly opposing the idea of reading it, arguing, "I am an engineer, not a wrestling announcer." But after Varga's kind acknowledgment of her principles as he said, "I respect that. You're fired and your husband is also fired," she understood the true importance of the proclamation and promptly changed her mind.

It wasn't her hazel eyes or silky mulato skin that qualified her for the task in his eyes, it was rather her husky alto that created quite a buzz in the Reality for Everyone™ chatrooms during the governmental transition. Varga noted the reaction of people on the quite random choice of engineer in charge of a countdown. He wanted something familiar, a voice subconsciously connected with the most significant moment in human history, to inform them about the final part of his plan. At least the public part of it. As Dr. Tusk read it, The Proclamation scrolled down the emergency TV screens:

"None can undermine our resolve to create a better world. The post-truth era, mired in fake news, if left unchecked, ends up with people feeling disgusted by the state of society. This environment of misinformation was created on purpose. Trust in the democratic processes goes away. Moral indignation pervades all facets of life. Trust in institutions is non-existent. Contempt for the rule of law ends in tragedy. We've all seen that. We've all suffered. The malicious New Athens establishments have been peddling viral fake news for years. At the end, not surprisingly, they have degenerated into terrorists spitting into our faces, brazenly stealing from our children's future.

No more.

From now on, we will favor mathematics and technology as a guarantee of performance rather than human regulators. The end of the fake news era and the environment of misinformation has come to its deserved end. The landscape of actions needed to combat misinformation has been a long-standing project. And now we have a solution. In order to further protect the citizens of the world from the proliferation of fake news that fosters extremists like those that have attacked the world's digital communication networks, the new government-approved Chrome browser will not only have your True Identity© BIDNA TIN but also Smart Security, Smart Sharing, Fact-checking Protocol, or SSCP-Я, reassuringly watching over you, protecting you from the lies. The fact-checkers of the past and The Trusted News Initiative members such as AP, AFP; BBC, CBC, Radio-Canada, European Broadcasting Union, Facebook, *Financial Times, First Draft, The Hindu,* Reuters, Reuters Institute for the Study of Journalism, Twitter, *The Washington Post,* and their ilk were not bound by ethics or facts but by the ideological dogma of fickle, fallible, biased humans. They all were compromised and are not to be trusted.

The AI embedded into this new system will, using sophisticated natural language processing methods, semantic recognition tech, and machine learning, detect fake and malicious news, false truths, and outright lies in order to protect your mental well-being from poisonous fakery. Unobtrusive for you as a user but highly effective, SSCP- Я will sift through the news outlets, social media posts, forum conversations, tweets, or chatrooms even before they land on your digital commo gadget and, if fake, will quickly, rapidly, and irreversibly remove them, not only from your innocent eyes, but from the internet, for good as well. It will be like the lies never existed.

However, should you need any help, our fact-checking quality assurance experts, to be known as the FFCAI, standing for the friendly fact-checker AI, will always be at your disposal to answer your concerns. We've all learned a lot from this terrorist attack, but the most important lesson learned is this: we must protect our minds. And the minds of our precious children.

Our priority is our collective Social Resistance, protected by the SSCP- Я, so to help the healing process of our, from now on, unpolluted minds. Persuasions, judgments, sentiments, and viewpoints are relics of the past. In the future, there will be no more confusing opinions or perplexing estimates of reality. In the future, you will be able to rely on the one and only truth as given to you. A stringent truth, vehemently checked for 100% honesty and accuracy, the one and only truth you can trust with your life. The vile Environment of Misinformation is being replaced by the Environment of Truth and Honesty as of now. Your GACH browser is your portal, not only back to the internet, but a glorious portal toward the Truth."

As soon as the proclamation left the screens, Dr. Tusk ran to vomit in the bathroom, far from prying eyes. But those who matter, those like Baiano Lindo who still have their place in the public eye, kept their ecstatic dance of truth on the screens of the "Freedom Lives" TV. Baiano appears, proudly booming from a nice artistic dissolve, and speaks to the camera with the revolutionary zeal of Saint Greta and Che Guevara put together: "Hey, terrorists. Do you hear me? You have lost." His laughter was a reassuring sign of hope; the good ol' Baiano Lindo, the gregarious Reality for Everyone™ judge loved by billions, will soon be back into his old role and the world will be normal again. Only a few more days of internet-less agony. But, the terrorists have indeed already lost.

The Renegade's Lab, NYC
March 24, 2048

"Jesus H. Christ," Phat Prophet says, expressing everyone's state of mind.

"What do we do now?" Bolghery asks.

All heads turn toward Nastassia who stands in the middle of the lab like her feet are covered with cement. She does not start to pace around as usual. Her mind is as frozen as her body is. The green flickering of the holograms reflect in her emerald eyes, which do not blink. That *abomination* is crushing them with so much power that she feels disoriented, overwhelmed, rather lost. What's in Winston Varga's mind that has made him act in such a maddening manner, unleashing a crackdown of such magnitude, is beyond her. Even his beloved stock markets, sources, and guardians of his enormous fortune, were closed due to the internet being down, but OTC trading, over-the-counter exchange of shares indicated staggering losses of over 60% in his portfolios and even more so in the Proteus FinTech Corp. shares. Bitcoin fell below $10K for the first time in decades. He could not care less about losing trillions? All of this is mind-boggling.

She feels the Renegade's gaze. He's expecting her to *see* more than she's able to see, but his gentle mental nudges do not feel aggressive—he's here to support her, no matter what. But that very *what* on everyone's mind, rather the *what now*, is beyond her reach. Often in the past, which feels like another life, she *saw* problems, mostly computer-related, as a big mosaic missing tesserae all over it, as it hung in front of her mind-eye. Those empty spaces, where an appropriate piece should be placed, made her feel a bit uneasy, more often frantic, but always nervous as long as she did not have a solution. But as soon as she was able to add a missing part of the puzzle in her mental mosaic, she felt better, knowing the solution's coming, like a promise of a cold, refreshing breeze in the middle of a scorching summer day.

Such a whiff she feels now.

Deep in the still unreachable parts of her being, she senses a hint of revelation, a possibility of it. The overwhelming power with which Varga has been attacking them makes no sense at all. It's the mother of all overkills. She side-glances at the Renegade and hears an echo of the words he has uttered in the I.R.I.S. chat room from what feels like a million years ago. *"Varga's empire is at the peak of its powers but it could crumble overnight. And he fears that more than anything. We're ones that can push the first domino to fall."*

She *hears* that first domino of the empire on its peak as it starts to crumble. *Where does it come from?* The sound?

The Doomsday Seed Vault
Norway, Spitsbergen
March 24, 2048

Maléficus's adrenaline rush has subsided. Jeremiah DeJohn is hard at work searching for the stupid jailbait orphan and the old codger, both morons well out of their league, all over New Athens. He possesses the religious zeal of a true fanatic and the stamina of Kalahari Bushmen hunters, he'll find them. The Subject Zero is under control. The MEGS have started probing his little precog brain with all tools at their disposal. Varga is conducting the world's destiny with his, *our*—Maléficus dares to feel proud—BESNILO Attack. He has some time before the next phase starts. He needs some respite. Not even Claire K. and her Boy Chorus, singing Hildegard von Bingen's "Canticles of Ecstasy" could satisfy his needs. The enchanted place where two rivers meet, the Nahe river and its tributary, the smaller Glan, under the crest of a small hill was the source of Hildegard's angelic music, her divine inspiration, a place he holds dear.

But angels in the heavens would not do it today.
Neither the river Nahe, nor the Glan creek.
He needs the ecstasy of a more easily obtainable order.
He has time, does he?
Yes, he does.

Maléficus feels his juices rushing toward the right place and he knows. Like so many times before, he needs his dark chamber. A space of his own. He needs his release. He needs Bridget the Midget and all she has to offer. He has not dared to use any of these cute boys of the chorus, so excruciatingly close to him; Varga would not have approved it, the fine psychic balance with the MAGS and precogs in the same vicinity should not be disturbed, no matter what, so better to play safe from his wrath than to be sorry. Especially now.

A rare update on the site does not alert him. He is randy and wants to see what these new savory dwarves taste like. He leafs through this new virtual catalog of bearded, mythological creatures while the update continues in the background. That one, the mischievous looking knight-dwarf, armed with the arbalest, a huge crossbow, attracted Maléficus with his strong arms and barely concealed bulge. He clicks on the image and the 3D virtual sex fantasy starts.

With it, the Phat Prophet's trojan virus starts to execute, hidden in the background.

The Ping
New Athens, Harlem, NYC
March 24, 2048

Ping!

That was all. A tiny little chime sound, the alert that the trojan has been executed, modestly announces its execution. Its quiet cry of revelation reverberates through the lab with the force of Big Ben. Nastassia rushes toward the computer. The Renegade jumps like a stag, doing the same. "What, what?" Bolghery, seeing the commotion, yells from his hologram. "What's going on?"

"Phatty?" Nastassia almost yells at him. That's it, that's the *sound*. "Are we in?"

"It seems so. Check it for yourselves." Phat Prophet swipes the holographic screen right so everyone would be able to see what he sees. The virus has given them access to Maléficus's computer. They have their break. As expected by Nastassia, it was Hans Böhm who fell into Phatty's trap.

Maléficus has been hacked.

Sisyphus is Happy

Her father gave Nastassia *The Myth of Sisyphus* by Albert Camus to read only a year ago. She was fascinated to learn how "the gods had condemned Sisyphus to ceaselessly rolling a rock to the top of a mountain, whence the stone would fall back of its own weight." It has always been funny to her how everyone focused on the allegory, on Sisyphus being the symbol of humankind and his task as the symbol of absurdity that is the main ingredient of human existence. On the rock that always rolled back. The absurd continues. Camus's fame came from beating the absurdity with his essay's final words: "The struggle itself toward the heights is enough to fill a man's heart. One must imagine Sisyphus happy."

But, Nastassia often thought, what if the rock does not roll back? What if Sisyphus succeeded and the rock rolled down the other, dark side of the mountain, where the unknown resides? It was an interesting thought experiment she should have given to the AI to ponder during her work on the emotion of Artificial Intelligence. What would be the *sound* of that?

And in that moment, she *heard* it. *What's that?*

It is a distant roaring thunder that sounds like an avalanche of huge rocks falling into the Grand Canyon. The echoes of it are weak, but they carry a charge of future in them. She turns toward the Renegade. *It was him.* He's the source of the echo. The Sisyphus rock is the Renegade's rock falling down the other side of the mountain, and he's relieved beyond measure. He can't be that happy only because of the successful hack, his eyes tell her.

'*No more secrets,*' right Renegade?, she thinks, but is too overjoyed with the hack's success to hold it against him. She barely perceptible waves hear head, the young girl gently scolding the old sage. Her eyes still hitched on his, and a glimpse of understanding passed in between them. *She gets me every time*, the Renegade did not want to betray his thoughts but her nod and a barely contained smile tell him he's right; she saw right through him. This hack means something completely different to him than it means to her or Phatty. Her emerald eyes glow with a mash of apprehension, excitement and hope.

What now, Renegade, really?

She wordlessly asks the old sage who, almost embarrassingly, smiles back.

Part Three

TYCHO BRAHE SECRET

Chapter 13
DE NOVA STELLA

De Nova Stella
November 11, 1572 - Uraniborg, Denmark
(excerpt from Frédéric Bonnet's unpublished novel)

> *"The basic pattern of life is a network. Whenever you see life, you see networks. The whole planet, what we can term 'Gaia' is a network of processes involving feedback tubes."*
>
> **Fritjof Capra**

Like a monarch on his throne, Tycho Brahe, a morbidly obese man in his mid-twenties sat in a chair that barely contained his large girth and drank copious amounts of red wine. He was sweating profusely and barking orders at the dwarves that scurry around a big telescope, cleaning, polishing, and adjusting its lenses. Tycho's nose glinted—its metal tip is the relic of an old dueling injury—as he tried to strike with his scepter and missed the dwarf.

"Hie thee, sirrah," Tycho yelled at the nearby dwarf.

"Yes, sire?"

"Thou motley-minded whoreson, hie, hie or we'll miss the Starre," Tycho said, nervously peering through the telescope's eye lens.

He then uttered a loud cry of excitement, "De nova stella!"

He jumps, almost falling over the nearby dwarf, and keeps yelling what seems like a magical mantra, "De nova stella!"

"De nova stella!"

What he had just witnessed no man has ever again seen since that glorious Tuesday, on November the 11th, A.D. 1572, a day in which "De nova stella," a new star, appeared in its glory.

Supernova B Cassiopeiae, nowadays better known as Tycho's Supernova, the first recorded supernova in human history, in the constellation Cassiopeia, bursts in a myriad of colors. A rhapsody of space magic enthralled everyone and scared many. Brighter than the Morning Star, Venus, it announced a new era. "At night, it often shone through clouds which blotted out all other stars," Tycho Brahe would write a year later. On this day, the dwarves danced exuberantly, jumping up and down, yelling in unison of joy:

"De nova stella! De nova stella!!"

"De nova stella, jolterheads!" screamed Tycho Brahe from the top of his lungs, "De nova stella!" He wobbled on his chair, stood up a bit shakily, and triumphantly raised his scepter, yelling to Jepp the Dwarf, the distinguished chief dwarf.

"Mumsley for all, Jepp, my good chap," he ordered. "Let's get these dunces drunk today."

Jepp the Dwarf disapprovingly shook his head. He did not like his crew when unruly, these mischievous ruffians, but he obeyed his patron and ran to fetch some old Greek Malvasia wine. Its color was straw yellow, its smell yellow pulp fruits, its memories long, remembering Aristotle and his mistake about the unchangeable universe of unmovable stars.

I deny you, Aristotle, thought Tycho Brahe, but dared he not to say it aloud.

At the sight of the wine, dwarves rapturously applauded. It was not some gloop they're used to drinking alone during the long, dark nights when they were cold, Mommy was far away and they were lonely and scared. No, sire, this was a divine nectar coming straight from the aristocratic cellars. They merrily started another round of round of dancing and singing:

"De nova stella!"

Tycho, looking at the small people's ecstasy, himself started booming from his throne:

"De nova stella," and then, as he quietly repeated *De nova stella* mantra just for himself, turned his gaze toward the heavens, immensely proud of himself. He discovered *De nova stella*, something he'd be remembered for.

At that moment, the famed astronomer and alchemist Tycho [Tyge] Ottesen Brahe, the eldest son of the Councilman of Rigsrådet, nobleman Otto Brahe and of glorious Beate Brahe, a protégé of the King Frederick II of Denmark himself, a nobleman and a scientist whole Europe came to admire, realized that his life had not been lived in vain.

THE END

The Renegade's Secret Lab
New Athens, NYC
March 24, 2048

>Nastassia stares at Renegade in disbelief.
>"You're kidding, right?"
>"Nope."
>"Frédéric wrote a book about Tycho Brahe?"
>"That's right."
>"And this is somehow connected with our struggle?"
>"Indeed. He wrote about the Starchild Prophecy in it."
>*Nautilus mentioned that Starchild*, she recalls. *Can it be Stellan?* Nastassia starts pacing around the lab. "I'm on *Candid Camera* as some dumb-ass wannabee screenwriter spouts crap thinking all this is funny?"
>"I wish."
>"So I'm not going to wake up?"
>"No."
>"Seriously?"
>"Yes."
>"I'm glad we cleared that up," she says wearily. "So, why do we need Tycho Brahe for?"
>"His secret." The Renegade flashes a fidgety smile. "It must be rather absurd for you, all of that, I can understand that."
>Nastassia spreads her arms, showing all that's around, kilometers of aquariums all over the place: an octopus, Nautilus, observing them, several holograms showing the sea creatures that were tirelessly gobbling up the Apollo cable traffic and are now resting on their spines, the PHOENIX ONE high in the sky, a black and white Dr. von Lichtenstein and Baiano Lindo spewing nonsense into their rotary phones while being broadcasted via the

"Freedom Lives" TV farce, Phatty and Bolghery suspended in the air from their own holograms.

"More absurd than all of this?"

"Oh, yes!"

Nastassia stops pacing around.

"Well, if you say so." Then she ponders a moment and looks up. "Renegade?"

"Yes?"

"You discovered the Theory of Everything and got the Nobel for it."

"I got lucky."

"Yeah, right," Nastassia says as she quizzically looks at him. "What secret could an obscure astronomer from the Dark Ages possibly possess, that you'll need, like a million years later?"

"Only, it's already the Renaissance," the Renegade jokingly corrects her. She does not return a smile, for two full seconds blazing daggers at him without a word.

"OK, the Renaissance." Nastassia gives him that and keeps staring at him.

"We need Tycho Brahe, not as an astronomer, but as an alchemist."

Alchemist? Right, thinks Nastassia. She carefully examines the Renegade as she senses the old sage's quite strange mix of self-conscious shame, undefined hope somehow related to her, and suspicion dressed in a dense cloak of secrecy. *Suspicion? Was he suspecting me? Of what? Or is he rather doubtful of himself? No, he's been hiding something from me, for quite a long time. All that Starchild nonsense. Bolghery's fear of me. Dad's secrets. It's time to clear the air.*

"Renegade?" she asks. "Can we talk privately for a moment, please?"

"Sure."

He turns off the holograms with Phatty and Bolghery, removes the lingering PHOENIX holo as well by pushing it into a corner, and turns off the screen showing Nautilus. He sits, offering Nastassia a seat on some impossible old imitation of a sofa. She sits across from him and looks around. That eerie feeling of isolation under tons of water again. That flickering loneliness hidden in the wires as residues of life almost stink up the lab. That mythical place, above all expectations, is the lone abode of a recluse. *The Renegade moniker suits him well*, the techno renegade hermit, she thinks. Varga wants him dead. He represents freedom, but somehow a withering version of it, like an old relic from an era of the world that might have never been? She observes him; he's vigorous and strong despite his age, but what does he really represent? No, she holds no suspicions of her own anymore, but she needs full transparency, she needs to know what he still hides from her. So she simply asks.

"If Tycho Brahe, an alchemist dead for ages, is our last chance, as you put it, why did we bother with trying to hack Varga? It's been three days already and we've only minutes ago broken Hans Böhm. We still have no idea what will find on his computer. But, if alchemy and not technology is going to solve our problems, what's the point of Bolghery lawsuit, Phatty's trojans, the Maléficus hack, of any of this?"

She pauses to take a breath. The Renegade assumes she's finished and opens his mouth, but she gently interrupts him.

"Let me finish, please. What is Frédéric's role in all of this? What is the Starchild? And, most importantly, why are you spoon-feeding me info? What else are you holding onto, hidden from me? And why?"

The Renegade wonders how her mind works, how does it feel to be her?

Well, sometimes a straightforward truth intimidates, a no-holds-barred approach can be harmful, thinks the Renegade for a fleeting second, but as soon as he looks at her glowing emerald eyes he realizes how hinky he's been. Such behavior is not even remotely fair to her. Not only that she has suffered personal loss, but they've all lived through Varga's world's neurological catastrophe on a gigantic scale that's accelerating into an overt war on all fronts, and yet, he's behaving like some fuddy-duddy frozen stiff. And after he had promised her no more secrets. Yes, he has had his reasons. But, did he *really*? So, don't twaddle, he says to himself as Nastassia patiently observes his inner processes, his tosh-encrusted balderdash's not working with Nastassia; just tell her in plain old English what's been going on, smack-dab in the middle.

What comes out of his mouth, surprises him mightily. "I fear failure."

Wow! Nastassia is surprised too. Here's one of the most accomplished men in the world, and yet here's his soft, vulnerable underbelly all exposed by such a sudden disclosure, coming out of the blue. Was it out of the blue? Or was he tortured by such a fear for a while? She does not ask him to elaborate, but her eyes ask for more. *What failure does he fear?*

"Frédéric wrote about the Starchild Prophecy in the Tycho Brahe book. Ask yourself, why did he never publish it? It was his own deep research into the precogs, what they meant, and Stellan and you in the context. He knew who you two were since day one but was trying to put everything in perspective. If you have a purpose, and he was certain that you both do, what is it really?" The Renegade stands up and goes to get a sip of water. "Want some?"

She shakes her head no, thanks.

"I am an engineer. A scientist. *The Pleasure of Finding Things Out* by Richard Feynman was always my guiding thought. I never feared the unknown, but Frédéric's research after Doyle's tragedy was too esoteric for me. Only after spending some time with you, observing you—sorry, no other word for it—I realized what Frédéric meant when he warned me."

"Warned you? About me?"

"Yes. He feared that you might be—how should I put it? Breached. That Varga might, through his MEGS and precogs, somehow manage to get to you, hack your brain, so to speak. Either of you two, if he managed to get hold of one. After I realized you were under a psychic attack, it became clear to me that Frédéric was right to worry." He takes another sip of water.

"You had so much to cope with over such a short period of time that I did not know how to share everything with you. And…" He pauses. "Rather, a but. I have no clue what secret Tycho Brahe has in his grave nor how it would help us. Frédéric was still working out the details when he was killed, but he was certain Tycho's secret was what we needed. More importantly, your dad was sure that if push comes to shove, you'd need to be ready and you'd have to have knowledge about Varga, even that energetic connection, in order to be ready. He was also sure that otherwise you'd be crushed this way or another and, with you, our hopes. I was executing your dad's strategy. That's why all the homework and all the spoon-feeding, as you called it."

Nastassia nods, accepting all of that as fait accompli, almost relieved that the Renegade has opened up. But, there were so many questions his confession opened.

"OK, let me get this straight, Renegade. We are hiding in the sewers of New York, in your lab. We can't get out as they're ransacking New Athens, as everyone in the world is searching for us. Not to mention, we face the most unreachable machine ever. That one." She points toward the corner hologram where the PHOENIX ONE stands. Even from the darkened end of the room, its dark, threatening presence is felt.

"Varga's ongoing attack rendered us altogether helpless. Am I getting it right?"

"You got it so far."

"Now we have to miraculously engage a deceased 16th-century alchemist from Prague to help us fight the 21st-century overlord, the most vicious, richest monster that ever lived."

"Yes, we even have to go to Prague."

"And how do you plan to even get there?"

"I might have a way."

"Sure you do. So, we go to Prague. We go through Hell and half of Georgia and get there unharmed, miraculously avoiding Varga's goons. Then we somehow barge into, based on the Eritrea backup facilities, what must be the most impenetrable, the most remote fortress that man and the machines have ever built. Also we have no idea where it is hidden. Then Tycho—who's been dead for five hundred years—and his alchemical hocus-pocus secrets help us beat the INNOCENTI, the PHOENIX ONE and all its drones, vanquish Varga, rescue Stellan, and save humanity from Varga's tyranny?"

"You got it."

"That's totally, absolutely bonkers."

"I know, it's so crazy that it just might work."

"But, *what* might work?" Nastassia cries. "What are you hoping to find, what secret?"

Suddenly, like she was triggered by a keyword in a post-hypnotic suggestion, she starts to invisibly shake out of dread and excitement at once. *What is she seeing or feeling, or falling into*? the Renegade asks himself.

There is a distant, barely perceptible echo in her, unmistakably Stellan's thoughts coming through the space-time of dark, pulsating eons to her. She has what feels like a true connection to him, the first since he was kidnapped... but still only one way—she can not reach throughout the darkness. But she did feel him.

Again.

Does this mean we're getting closer? *Stellan... here's all my love for you.* And she sends it through a dark, endless tunnel, hoping it would reach him.

It does!

I know you need me, little brother. I need you too... Maybe even more so, she thinks and silences the noise around her, quiets her own thoughts so she can send him more love and light and observe, hear, and see what's going on with him. For the first time since he was snatched, she clearly *hears* his thoughts, what's going on with him:

As he was mulling over his options, he heard a strange whisper, like the hushed breathing of the mighty redwood he once hugged in the forest in California, back when he was hiking the Redwood State Park with Nastassia, Mom, and Dad. It was a relief, that first, sweet, rather familiar sound. Alas, within seconds the whisper morphed into a long, longing howl that increased in intensity with each passing moment until it had reached a piercing, roaring thunder. Ear-splitting noise attacked him from all sides. It was clear to him that they were assaulting his mirrors, so he tried to protect them by letting them float and dance evasively in his mind. His efforts were in vain. A demoniacal, full-blast shrill, sounding like the thousands of blowing trumpets of Jericho, shattered all his crystal mirrors at once. All small victories were snatched from him in one heavy blow, crushing him along with it. A silence fell upon him yet again. This time, it felt worse; they managed to crush his key defense. What's left in him to fight with?

"Fight Stellan, fight my darling," Nastassia screams inside as the pandemonium that was attacking Stellan reverberates through her. They took his defenses away. She can feel his pain. She freezes. She's forgotten to breathe. All that is left of her is a bundle of nerves with which she is straining to get onto the precog network and to send him all her love. She is trying to find her way through the black maze of perdition and to let him know she's with him. *They are blocking her. Those same entities that kept Stellan are not letting her pass.*

While he was still disoriented after the terrible noise attack, he grasped onto his awareness and suddenly felt an ice-cold tingling sensation all over his body. It was like a thousand tiny needles had started to poke and probe him, penetrating his skin, like there were snakes spewing venom into his blood. It felt green, the devilish substance entering his blood and his mind alike, gulping it rapidly and greedily as it took over every molecule in his body, over every nerve and every neuron, every bit of what he is, of what he used to be, snatching his living essence out of him in a terrifying haste that nothing could stop. His ability to see and know was dipping away from him, like blood and life from a slaughtered lamb.

Oh no... Stellan, no... stop torturing him... stop killing them... no... stop... no...

He was able to see the ripples in space-time well before he was capable of understanding what he saw. Just earlier today he had been a part of the universe, but now he's lost and utterly isolated in this unknown dark world that feels like the black hole he once experienced in a dream. Only it reeks of that nauseating stench, a devil's hole being filled up with green poison. He started to lose consciousness, with one remaining thought in his mind; a sound-thought that resonated in him like Debussy's "Clair de Lune," which his mother used to play for him on the big black Steinway grand piano. It used to scare him when he was a toddler, the Steinway. It looked like a mythical beast ready to swallow him whole. It doesn't scare him anymore. He is six. He's a big boy now. He clings to that sweet music he's recreating in his mind. This a Mom-tune as sweet as memories of the smell of her apron, which he loved to sniff like a little puppy when she used to prepare sautéed rosemary. This was the music he loved so much when silver moonlight awoke him at night and Mom came into his room and played Debussy to put him right back to sleep.

"Endure, Stellan," Nastassia quietly whispers, white as a ghost. "Fight. Don't go..." when the dark engulfs him. She shudders. The Renegade stares at her intently, fearing she might virtually explode.

But then, Nastassia comes back, and her tortured emerald eyes glow as she looks at the Renegade. *That Starchild of his. It must be Stellan? Even his name, Stellan, means a bright star?* She says nothing as the shakes slowly subside and vanish like ripples on a lake's surface. Her own psyche, Stellan's predicament, the whole of life appears to her like divinity unfolded—this is something Frédéric said about Jung's vision or a dream—and she clearly sees the process she's undergoing. Yes, the Renegade was right to spoon-feed her, otherwise she would not have been able to strengthen her abilities, to *see* what she needs to see and to *feel* what she needs to feel in order to defeat Varga. She turns her glowing emerald eyes at the Renegade.

"I am now energetically part of Stellan's struggle and fully aware of the attacks. I can see more clearly already. I am not letting Varga create a monster out of my little brother," she says and sits on the sofa, catching her breath. The Renegade feels her steely resolve. It has always been in her, but now it bursts to the surface. *And those glowing eyes.* Her youthful energy matches his own brittle strength. He sits next to her, feeling like an ancient Al Badawi tree next to the young baobab, whose roots go deep into the netherworlds that have been haunting her forever. In the past, it was difficult for the Renegede to accept Frédéric's claim that Nastassia has an ancient soul that has lived unborn for ages, but here and now, worldessly sitting next to the mighty young girl, he starts to believe.

"We'll find Stellan. And we will get Varga this time," he says matter-of-factly.

Nastassia looks at him and with her small hand gently squeezes his wrinkled one, thanking him. No need for words. They sit quietly living a moment of respite. But the Renegade can not really find relief. That warm, small hand of the child that needs him almost as much as he needs her invokes a rush of feelings in him. His eyes turn inward, toward the deep, hidden bottoms of his soul, all the way down where and when the children he might have had lived, also unborn, here, there, anywhere, but never has. He feels guilty for having felt relief over the fact that he does not have any children in Varga's odious world, this vile place he has not done near enough to prevent becoming what it is—a torture chamber for all innocent souls like Nastassia's.

She senses his feelings. *I am not letting him fall into funk and regret. It always feels like acid, the regret.* She abruptly stands up, her eyes adrift. She turns her gaze toward the quiet humming of water coming from aquariums where Nautilus patiently sits, connected with the world. Perhaps the summer mistral never reached this lab and delicate fragrances of honeysuckle that smell like honey and vanilla, her mom's dearest flower, never graced its desolate darkness, but they are a part of this world. All of them, Nautilus and his sea creatures, the Renegade, poor Phatty who must be asking himself what's going on the other side of his darkened screen, even Bolghery and his fearfulness—all of us are *real*. Yes, that's the word. We're alive and we're real.

She speaks with conviction. "You said that Varga's filthy lucre is not real. How it's unnatural, almost against nature, something along those lines, do you remember?"

He nods.

"And how it might crumble?"

"Yes."

"Well, lets it help crumble."

"Let it burst, explode and crumble to hell," he agrees. His energy is back.

"And, Renegade?"

"Yes, dear?"

"I still don't understand who the Starchild is and what all that means. I don't need to know what that prophecy of yours was. I care not about that Tycho Brahe Secret you seek. But if my father wrote about him and you believe we need it, I have no other choice. You say we have to go to Prague to find out what Tycho Brahe Secret entails and get help?"

Nastassia pauses, glances at the Renegade and whispers with a self-effacing smile. "So, let's go on a hero's journey. To Prague."

Exploitation
New Athens, Harlem, NYC
March 24, 2048

They came back to Phatty and Bolghery by turning on the screens. They both were too busy to even notice how long Nastassia and the Renegade were absent. They also could not care less, since the Maléficus hack seemed to be a wealth of the data they needed and were combing through already.

"Where is Stellan? Can we find out?"

"Wait a sec."

What Phatty was doing is called a stealth post-exploitation, getting the files from Maléficus on his local machine. The obfuscated communication is tunneled through a tiny polymorphic backdoor. The output is fully undetectable which is to say that from that point on, Maléficus had no chance of detecting that he was being hacked, and not only was his computer fully accessible to them, but all his data would eventually find its way to Phatty's computer. In the end, his lust for the sexy knight-dwarf, an illusion created by Phat Prophet, cost him dearly. Phatty beams inside, full of pride. It was him who had hacked Maléficus and with a bit of luck, the devil himself, Winston Varga.

He cracks a joke. "I am tempted to play In the 'Mood for Love' on his machine."

"Phatty, drop the wisecracks." Nastassia smiles.

Phatty smiles back. "Finding Stellan is my number one priority. Many files on Maléficus's comp are encrypted, but it shouldn't be too difficult." He points to a small text file, 'psmemo.txt' file. "This contains a password for his KeePass, where all other passwords are encrypted. People are the weakest link, indeed, N." He gives a nod to Nastassia's insistence on Maléficus being their way in. And she was right.

The Renegade steps in. "We gotta go."

"Now?" Nastassia gapes at him. She points to the screen. "We have the mother lode's treasure trove there."

"Yes, we do. But it takes time to get it all downloaded and to sort it out. While we travel, Phatty will get all the files and unlock them. Organize. Prepare. No need to waste time by waiting for him." The Renegade turns back to Phat Prophet. "And Phatty, use the short wave radio terminal access to get in touch if normal commo is not working, as soon as you have something. We might need a full day to get to Europe."

Nastassia looks at him. *A full day?* Then the obvious occurred to her.

"Phatty?"

"Yes?"

"Where's Maléficus located?"

"Just a sec." He types in. "His internet address is in Spitsbergen, Norway." He pauses a moment. "Norway. I should've known," huffs the Renegade.

"Known what?"

"What's in Spitsbergen, Norway?" he asks rhetorically, not waiting for them to guess. "The Doomsday Seed Vault, Varga's impenetrable fortress, buried in an icy mountain on an island. It is located across Greenland, above the Arctic Circle between Norway and the North Pole. Quite a dreary place. As cold as hell."

"Nice." Nastassia it mulls over. "Do you think they took Stellan there?"

"Not sure as of yet." The Renegade turns to Phat Prophet. "Phatty?"

"I don't have anything yet."

"So are we going to the North Pole instead?" Nastassia asks.

"No, we still must get to Prague first."

"How do we get there?"

"Follow me, please."

The Grey Ghost
Aboard the Grey Ghost
March 24, 2048

While the Renegade opens another secret chamber, Nastassia thinks how nothing can surprise her anymore. That is until she sees another urban legend, Grey Ghost, the Renegade's supercavitating submarine.

"So, it's real?" she asks rhetorically.

The Renegade nods, beaming with pride like a little boy would.

Water is several hundred times denser than air, so the submarines of the past were slow-moving machines. Super cavitation was "a process wherein an object moves so fast through the water that it creates a gas bubble around itself, nearly eliminating drag. Unencumbered by the high drag of water, the object is free to speed along at much higher speeds than otherwise possible." And that miracle of technology, prior to now, at least for Nastassia, was in the domain reserved only for DARPA, the US Military's Defense Advanced Research Projects Agency, and similar projects developed in secrecy. That the Renegade would have a supercavitating submarine seemed strangely natural.

The Renegade opens the docking hatch lever and they squeeze into the submarine's control room; it's a bit on the smallish side, but its compact design compensates for it. It is completely networked; several screens simultaneously display images gathered from the 3D HD SAGE cameras and the data from The Global Positioning System, periscope, and the Nautilus's neural network.

"Let's go," the Renegade says and starts slowly navigating through the sewer pipe connecting his lab with the elaborate stone sewage system from hundreds of years ago, now abandoned, and slips into the Hudson River. Nastassia's face is concerned.

"We can jam the signals but can't they see us?"

"When designing this submarine I learned from the best. Nautilus is a superb master of camouflage." The Renegade beams with pride as the Grey Ghost blends with its environment perfectly, invisible from the prying eye in the sky that, like a hungry bird of doom, scours the scenery.

Nastassia glances at one of the screens.

PHOENIX ONE's eye observes the city beneath. Drones fly everywhere, examining every inch of New Athens and New York. Nastassia turns to the Renegade. "Why don't you have one of those James Bond rockets to hit that monster?" she asks.

"We'll enter the ocean in a moment." As they skedaddle from the Hudson, he avoids several ships' anchor chains.

Nastassia flinches. "No need to hurry that much."

Renegade smiles as the Grey Ghost elegantly slips into the Atlantic Ocean and speeds up, a ghostly underwater rocket.

"Prague, here we come," Renegade announces.

"You know Prague is in the center of Europe?"

"Sure, why?"

"And you're aware we're in a submarine?" Nastassia smiles. "Which autobahn do we take? European route E50?" She chuckles. Renegade smiles and types something in his onboard computer. E50 pops up on the screen.

"Blimey, it does go to Prague."

He turns to Nastassia. "Do we have anyone in Brest?"

"France? Not that I am aware of, but we have someone in Prague."

"So you have an idea?"

"I do." Nastassia smiles.

"Show me!"

In Prague, Jaroslav's computer buzzes and he answers after a second.

"Who's that?" Nastassia appears on the screen. Jaroslav beams, looks around his room and whispers to the screen.

"Where are you? They are ransacking New Athens all over the world, looking for you. This is insane." He looks around once more. "What have you done?"

"I need your help."

"Anything for you," Jaroslav states, filled with love and pride; finally he's able to help his idol, his friend and, he would never admit it to a living soul, his only and true love forever. He ponders a second and asks, somehow shyly, "Nastassia?"

"Yes?"

"Are the rumors true?"

"What rumors?"

"Everyone says you're on the run with the Renegade. Are you?"

Nastassia side-glances at the Renegade. He leans over, toward the camera. Jaroslav's utterly gobsmacked.

"The Renegade… Woah!" He turns his gaze to Nastassia. "Fuck no, no way." He looks back at the wide smile with which the Renegade observes his confusion. "Damn. Sorry. A great honor sir, you're the legend… sir… Renegade… I admire you… I can't believe it."

"Stop embarrassing yourself, Jaroslav!" Nastassia laughs.

He composes himself.

"Renegade… may I… may I ask… may I have a question for you?"

"Shoot!" The Renegade likes this confused, round-faced boy so damn obviously in love with Nastassia that she doesn't even see it. Kids.

Jaroslav types into his computer and explains, "I want to apply for early admission to the Charles University's Faculty of Mathematics and Physics, but do not understand this one." He hesitates a moment and hits enter. A formula, $T=\frac{1}{8\pi M}\,$, blinks on the computer screen.

"You idiot!" Nastassia yells at him.

"What? Why?"

"Solve your own damn formula by yourself."

Jaroslav shrinks, aware of his pas faux.

"We'll deal with it in Prague, Jaroslav, when we meet." The Renegade hides his chuckle and turns to Nastassia. "So, what's your idea?"

"Świnoujście, at the Baltic Sea, is the closest port to Prague. Once we arrive we'll continue by land," she says and turns to Jaroslav. "You have relatives there that can help us to travel unnoticed?"

"I have. Dobrý voják Švejk will be happy to help you, I am going to call him now. Talk to you soon. Stay safe," he says and leaves the commo channel.

Nastassia points to a part of a map of the Baltic Sea. "Świnoujście it is."

Renegade turns to her. "Did Jaroslav just say the Good Soldier Švejk?"

"No clue, likely one of his relatives. He must have the biggest family in the world."

Renegade laughs. "Dobrý voják Švejk is a Czech title of a dark comedy translated as *The Good Soldier Švejk*, by a Czech writer also called Jaroslav. Jaroslav Hašek. You should read it while we sail, it's funny as hell," Renegade says as the Grey Ghost dives deep.

"No time for reading. But would you please slow down for a few minutes? Look out."

The Renegade glances through the submarine's window. A school of gorgeous mandarin fish, blue with bright orange, red, and yellow wavy lines, pass by the window. They're small but remarkable in shape and color. Then a smack of invertebrate jellyfish appears dancing around the Grey Ghost, followed by a pod of cheerful dolphins squealing and giggling in happiness at them. *It's not by chance*, she thinks. A few porpoises follow the dolphins, not to be outshined by their more popular relatives. A swarm of octopuses hurriedly swim together with a lone purple seahorse that follows them and looks through the windows, straight at Nastassia and the Renegade. They're here to bid us farewell, she *feels*. *Thank you, Nautilus*. She sends her love to the majestic creature left behind in the lab, and whispers, "They are so beautiful."

"Indeed they are."

There's so little we really know about the world, flashes through Nastassia's mind, still overwhelmed by the display of what could only be Nautilus's farewell, when she notices something strange with that seahorse; it's been yellow and then golden and purple. Then black and again purple, changing hues like it was lighting up on purpose. Its purple was pulsating, interchanging darker and lighter hues, from violet with a hint of red to a pure, darker shade of purple. Nastassia recalls how her mom was fascinated by chromatics, the study of color, in order to better understand the significance of colors in marine life. A while ago, in Jacaranda City whose real name was Pretoria, in South Africa, when they slowly drove beneath the thousands of purple Jacaranda trees, her mother taught her that the color purple means wisdom, bravery, and spirituality. And here it is, the small pulsating purple seahorse messenger, a magnificent new friend for sure sent to them by Nautilus. *Was it really*? If so, then the natural world knows so much more about us than we ever bothered to learn about it. We had Sir David Attenborough, but we never really learned from him or truly understood nature. It was inspiring, rather beautiful to ponder all of that, but after more than a minute, the Renegade waves at the seahorse and says, "Enough gawking at them. Let's go!"

Nastassia blows a kiss to the seahorse, whose purple brightens before he is left behind, floating in the ocean that's now their highway to Prague. The Renegade pulls an automated rudder and after an initial jerk, the Grey Ghost's ultra-cavitating propulsion speeds it up to over 150 mph. The map on the control center's main display shows its planned itinerary across the Atlantic Ocean. The Grey Ghost will sail near St. Pierre et Miquelon, head north, and then pass between Greenland and Iceland, turning south.

"It will take us twenty-four hours or so to reach Denmark and the Elsinore - Helsingborg channel," says the Renegade. "From there we'd have 149 nautical miles before we reach Świnoujście."

"I read your article stating that a supercavitating vessel could reach the speed of sound underwater. That's what, twenty times faster?"

"That's in theory. For every action, there is an equal and opposite reaction, no?"

"What do you mean?"

"Isaac Newton. Third law of motion. There are quite a few formulas regarding ultra-cavitating propulsion that would enthrall, or puzzle, your boyfriend Jaroslav." Renegade winks at Nastassia who scoffs at the notion like only a teenage girl can, with such a dismissive air about her that he thought she might have a soft spot for that quirky boy as well, without knowing it at all. Kids. Renegade flashes another smile that miffs Nastassia even more, but then he moves back to the submarine question.

"If I translated math, physics, and thermodynamic language of the liquid propellants and the Grey Ghost's overall structure into layman's language, not that I am saying you're a lay-girl…" He can not help himself and chuckles again. He loves to gently mock that dear, brilliant lassie. She was a rug rat only a few years ago, when he used to visit Frédéric and Monique and he'd play the horse she rode while squealing with joy. She does not remember it; she was only a toddler then. But now she has to carry the weight of the world on her shoulders. Heartfelt sympathy for her overwhelms him. "I'd say, when faster, the Grey Ghost became very unstable. The vibrations could damage its structure. Worse yet, it would be very noisy. Not something we need."

"So that's why we're so slow?"

"A hundred and fifty knots underwater is not slow at all, but yes, better safe than sorry," the Renegade explains. "Once we're closer to Europe, we'll circle the Faroe Islands, pass the United Kingdom, closer to Norway's side, and enter the Elsinore - Helsingborg channel at an even slower speed. Too many ships and submarines around."

The Grey Ghost speeds up.

Faroe Islands, aboard the Grey Ghost
March 25, 2048 – 2:00 a.m.

Despite the wee hours of the morning, the Renegade and Nastassia are still deep in conversation. They've mulled over and analyzed Varga's life and his latest attack over and over again, trying to get to the bottom of it all. Once in Europe, they'd be on the move all the time without having time to think, so this was a sort of their last chance to prepare themselves for the challenges ahead. What Varga wants is still a mystery to them; what his ultimate goal is, for not even obscene wealth nor total control of the world seems to be what he truly wants.

The blinking dot of the computer console tells them they've reached the Faroe Islands, the point of contact with Phatty, who was busy deciphering the data from the hack. "Let us see what Phatty has discovered," the Renegade says, and the Grey Ghost surfaces from the deep, dark, cold waters of the Atlantic Ocean. Looking north sat Venus, just above the horizon and squeezed between the constellations of Hercules, who became immortal thanks to divine milk, and Canes Venatici, the hunting dogs.

The Goddess of Love, the Renegade thinks, glancing at the skies. *We'd need as much help as possible, even from the heavens.* "Let's see what Phatty has to report."

The Phat Prophet's Hack Report

"That's insane, guys. Bonkers. Varga's gathering data about any imaginable catastrophe, melting ice sheets, the Atlantic thermohaline circulation collapse, the permafrost methane time bomb. There are petabytes and petabytes of data in gazillion files. He uses monikers so I find out about several key databases of our interest. President Mooney is Pinocchio. Ali Baba and the Forty Thieves are the Senate. Moby Dick or the Enemy is the Google database. The Cave of Evil is the Supreme Court. Access to everyone's computer, cameras, microphones, like NSA, while storing it all, is Kola well. It's the name of that huge Kola superdeep borehole, somewhere in Russia."

"Phatty. Anything for us, our immediate issues?"

"Well, you might not like this," Phatty says, sending them a video feed. "This file is named Kazuko."

"What does it mean?"

"I had no clue so I researched it. Crazy stuff. Ponder this. Kazuko is Japanese for child of peace and also the name of a *hibakusha* child that was born two days after the Hiroshima bomb exploded. Kazuko Kojima was her name. She died a few years ago, at ninety-eight years old."

"What's in the file?"

"The smell of fresh blood, the stench of death; the stuffiness of human sweat, writhing moans," says Phatty, strangely immersed in his words. "That's from the poem by Sadako Kurihara. Another *hibakusha*, a Hiroshima-bombing survivor. Interesting fact? She was an anarchist and…"

"Phatty!" Nastassia interrupts.

"What?"

"We always love to hear about your discoveries. But did you forget to send us the file?"

He apologetically raises his arm. "Sorry, here it is."

The Black Rains of Hiroshima

The footage Phatty took from the hack started like video of an ordinary black rain on the screen. It was quiet, the rain, until thunder slowly faded in and made it surreal to watch, those waterfalls of black rain splattering all over the screen. The images looked real but it was still obvious it was a simulation. The camera moves in, like through a dense, coal-black waterfall until it shows a silhouette of Earth below. It becomes clear that it's aerial footage of land and then rather a city that clarified more as the camera comes closer.

Then, without any warning aside from Phatty's "watch out now," come nuclear bomb explosions, blasting in myriad colorful flames, which pop up all over the screen, leaving the cities in destruction behind them. Edited in quick succession, not unlike the ending scene of *Dr. Strangelove*, the movie Varga loved more than any other, the simulation has shown summer corn and wheat fields being obliterated, famous landmarks razed to the ground. The sound has vanished and only eerie images of total destruction fly along the canvas hanging in the air, coming from the hologram. A bunch of undecipherable numbers all over the screen, likely estimates, flash in green.

"Are those simulations or Varga's concrete plans? Any files supporting either option? If those are plans, how would he be able to create nuclear mayhem?" the Renegade asks.

"I tried to understand that first. I cross-referenced Pinocchio and Ali Baba and the Forty Thieves's files to find out. Varga had a secret meeting in the Room SD-419 at the Dirksen Senate Office Building, with Mooney and the US Senate Committee on Foreign Relations's big honchos. He had the room bugged and recorded so I had a chance to watch and read some of it. Bear with me." He looks at his other screen and pulls the data from it.

"The meeting, held on Dec 29, 2048, during a cold Tuesday night in DC, introduced a secret addendum to the Senate Hearing, 115th Congress and its Authority to Order the Use of Nuclear Weapons from November 14, 2017, and subsequent changes to the H.R. 921, No First Use Act & H.R. 669, Restricting First Use of Nuclear Weapons Act of 2017. That's a mouthful. We know Varga had President Mooney in his pocket forever, and it was clear from existing laws that the President does not need the concurrence of either his military advisers or the US Congress to order the launch of nuclear weapons. Neither the military nor Congress can overrule these orders coming from the President, which was the letter of the law. The military is still bound by the Uniform Code of Military Justice to follow orders, provided they are legal and have come from competent authority—that of the president. A legal formality, but an important one, a safeguard. Now pay attention, this is the reason why Varga had that meeting." A drop of sweat trickles down Phatty's eyebrow. "The key change in the nuclear attack procedure was the authorization given to the PHOENIX ONE. Yes, a secret directive concocted in that meeting in Room SD-419 gave the PHOENIX ONE control over all nuclear arsenals in the USA via the Permissive Action Link's change, rather its transition from the requirement of the presence of two authorized people at all times to the two computer authorizations, with human supervision. Presumably that of the president, but not specified. So, that was the loop, the president was checked by the computers that he had to check. Given Varga's spell over Mooney, it almost certainly means Varga has the sole power of the US nuclear arsenal and the first-strike policy. He does not care about the rest of the military so they have retained full authority over their engagements all over the world."

No one says a word, dismally aware of the images of destruction running in the background, so Phatty continues. "Varga's signature all over. He had them change one line or so to completely change the meaning of that existing law. For all I know, the crux of the matter is that Winston Varga alone can launch a military attack on China and Russia if he wished to. And that's just the start of it all."

Phatty is now visibly sweating, and that makes him nervous even more.

"The video wasn't too clear as far as the targets, but I've found what Varga uses and wants. See those green numbers? They are also in the folder titled Vasili Arkhipov, the guy who did not file a nuclear missile at the US during the Cuban crisis. Those file names… Varga's something else. So, he uses OpenWeather. Teams of scientists have been gathering deep weather data for decades. He used real-time weather data to determine the fallout patterns from surface nuclear explosions and modeled the attack patterns, in order to magnify the fallout's impact. To kill as many people as possible, to put it bluntly. This came from the US planners for nuclear war against the former Soviet Union, understanding that many bombs would miss the target, and so planned for multiple weapons to be targeted on each. This idea goes back to Major General Lauris Norstad of the US Army Air Forces, from over a hundred years ago. I have the date, September 15, 1945. Varga added the weather patterns. So an N-bomb kills, say, five million Shanghainese, but there are many more left alive. So, another one falls on the nearby Chang Chiao. One B-83, 1.2 megatons, deployed by Boeing B-52 Stratofortress would target on average 2,373,710 citizens of Chang Chiao. The number of estimated fatalities is 481,250 and estimated injuries: 907,990. He then uses the US military's probability of damage calculator to calculate the probability of damage to targets caused by, for example, overpressure, dynamic pressure, cratering, and ground-shock coupling due to nuclear weapons effects and after winds carrying the nuclear cloud with the radioactive materials to see how effective it works in Shanghai. Its effects are used to decide about the second kill. What weapons to use. Those are most definitively the plans. Targeting over two thousand targets in China and Russia," Phatty concludes, now drenched in sweat. Somehow, he also feels relieved that he's not the only human on earth, outside Varga's circle of evil, who is aware of what's in the cards. Nastassia's aghast state matches his when she asks, "So if Russia and China do not succumb to his governmental transition steps in the future, Varga's ready to nuke them?"

"It seems like it."

Aware of the tension and the gravity of their feelings, the Renegade addresses them both as calmly and as assuredly he can. They will need cool heads to deal with the horrendous task at hand. Firstly he needs to calm down and reassure Phatty. At this juncture, he's doing the most important job of combing Varga's data. Who knows what else is hidden therein.

"No need to get alarmed, Phatty. Even if those are his plans, he's not going to launch missiles today. There's a Chinese and Russia lead Security Council meeting with the PHOENIX ONE representatives scheduled for this summer. If we know anything about Varga, it's that he plans for years and decades in the future. He rarely acts on impulse. My estimate is that there isn't any imminent danger of a nuclear escalation at the moment. Keep calm and work as you have so far. You're doing a great job," the Renegade says, to assess the states of their minds. It seems both Phatty and Nastassia are accepting his words almost as facts. He needs to nudge Phatty into relevant, immediate action. "Send all relevant material about that secret meeting to all the PRIORI that are on the run and then to all our guys. Dr. Ursula Hansen-Schroeder needs to get the data first. Bode is the best guy to give it to her, so alert Bode when sending the data to Ursula. I have her contact, will send it to you as we speak. Don't forget to include the transcripts. There are still some channels open?"

"I guess so. I.R.I.S. is still working. Linux systems are operative and non-inflected."

"IOTA messaging?"

"Sketchy but working."

"HAM radios work. Use them if needed. Eben Moglen's FreedomBoxes are still in use. Our guys have them." The Renegade's inner honey badger is ready to take on the most venomous snake. His determination is palpable and, as he fires words in bursts, has a soothing effect on Phatty. "Your best bets are satellite links via those low-earth orbit devices that are providing access to remote areas. Their main satellite is orbiting above the United States. They can't stop you."

"Something will work, don't worry."

"If nothing else works, have Bolghery use some of his wealthy friends to lend you a private plane and deliver hard copies to her, if necessary. She might still be able to raise hell."

"Rest assured, I will take care of it." Phatty has never known the Renegade that riled up and feisty; his dark eyes shooting daggers and his long white hair making him look like an old wizard leading armies into war. The Renegade is putting so much confidence in him that it made Phatty proud and belligerent as a warrior of destiny for those evil mofos he hacked with his genius Zero-Day dwarf. The Cherokee blood of his ancestor warriors boils in him. He broaches another subject:

"Shall we alert the Chinese? That Shanghai is the first target?"

The Renegade shakes his head, nope.

"Let the PRIORI leaders outside the US decide what to do. No one's touching them as of yet, right? Ayako, Dr. Sakaguchi, was involved in calming China's and Japan's war games a few years back. She's as emollient as a geisha and as patient as Buddha himself. If anyone can, she can get Chinese to listen to her through Tokyo."

"Got it."

"Also, Professor Ogolla might reach highly placed officials via her contacts at the National Space Science Center in Beijing. Her office in Nairobi works with them. Through NSSC, she might even be able to get to Wu Yuhan, the General Secretary of the Chinese Communist Party. The Chinese president. He's also the chairman of the Central Military Commission. She works very closely with the Space Center on their directed-energy systems weapons." The Renegade takes a deep breath. "All of them,

Ursula, Ayako, Odongo, must understand that those images you give them are Varga simulations. Perhaps his wishes. But nothing more. No plans for an attack. No immediate danger. We don't want anyone to panic. The key issue to be presented to them is the Secret Directive. The political stuff. Brazen disregard of the process. Security issues, perhaps security breaches done behind people's backs. They are the most urgent issue. I am sure not even Varga's minions, all those feudal INNOCENTI lords delegated to act as liaisons between PHOENIX and their nations, know about any of this. It's not Varga's style to share power."

"What about the Russians?"

"Anything that gets to the Chinese, the Russians would know in real-time."

"Don't you worry he'd start a war?" Bolghery asks. "If his plans are revealed?"

"Varga's not suicidal."

"Are you sure he's not?" Nastassia shoots a meaningful look at the Renegade.

He mulls over her question for a moment. "Even if he is, this is the moment of his triumph. The war with China or Russia, their annihilation, is the last thing on his mind today. He's too busy chasing us, destroying New Athens, and reshaping the world to his image with the help of the PHOENIX ONE."

Phatty nods and pulls up one set of graphs and data and swipes them so everyone can see them.

"I think Renegade is right. There's a Black Swan folder that seems to be a program whose task is to identify characteristics that lead to the Black Swan event, complete systematic market collapse in China, and how to help it happen once the time is right. See it here. I had no time to dive into it but it's pretty self-explanatory. China *is* his target, but a long-term target, but," he stops talking, raises his eyebrows, and slightly spreads his arms.

"What?"

"There's another issue. The PHOENIX ONE does not have any autonomy. It's an armed entertainment center but it's governed fully by the INFINITUS, from the ground, under Varga's total control."

A loud "Duh!" comes from Nastassia.

"There are petabytes, I guess even exabytes of data, no one would be able to process in such a short time. It would take years to go through that, should you wish to indict him, for example, and with custom-made software and a bunch of people at that. Luckily, Maléficus is supremely organized so he has labeled Varga's data quite thematically and dramatically and I was able to find the bulk of what interests us for now."

He lets the data scroll down the screen.

Even a cursory glance at all of that reveals that Varga's following mega-comets Herman One and the Last Dawn's close encounter with Earth, tracked Via Víctor M. Blanco's four-meter Telescope in Chile. Also, he was, rather his INFINITUS' combing the Net for the occurrences of the language of demons and angels and how contact with demons can elevate the magus to the divine, stuff like that, tells you that the main theme of Varga's work destructive in nature."

"Duh!" Nastassia cries again. This time even louder.

"He's doing crazy stuff like classifying Kabbalah and events of kabbalistic magic rituals. INFINITUS does semiotic and symbolic interpretations. I wonder, do you know how to summon an appropriate type of demon? Varga studies that," enthusiastically continues Phatty. He types in a search term. "If we wish to produce the Apollonian frenzy, for instance, we might choose to summon a Solar demon. Cool stuff."

"That's for some other time." Nastassia gently smiles at him. Phatty beams and nods, continuing his ad-hoc presentation, oblivious to her thinly veiled impatience.

"Once he finds people interested in demoniacal or angelical rituals he creates Venn diagrams of the Venn diagrams seeking whether New Athens people are connected with the outsiders. It never ends."

"Time will end before you tell us the most important things." Nastassia musters another smile. Even under such pressure, she likes Phatty. "Where's Stellan? MAGS? What's their purpose."

"Stellan, the whole operation in fact, is in the vault, as Maléficus calls it, in Norway. He's alive, N, don't worry. All the precogs are there, all alive. That's all I know. Their purpose? I still do not know for sure. Two hands. One head. No time. But, it seems that the MAGS and the precogs employ intuitive reading of the people they've been following. They have a pulse on the psychic movements of humanity, so to speak. But there are petabytes and petabytes of Varga's internal analyses of those data. I did not have time to take a look yet."

"Can you give some of the files to our guys?" Phatty ignores the question.

He's like a prospector who found a goose, rather a flock of geese, and a bunch of golden eggs with them, "They have petabytes of data on Nastassia alone, for example, everything since she was born. But it seems they also spend enormous energy on stopping the psychic energy flowing from Stellan to Nastassia and vice versa. In fact, it looks like they have a mental shield placed on Nastassia, not unlike a voodoo curse that weakens her abilities." He turns to Nastassia. "Do you have any idea how this would work?"

"No." *Yes, I do. Sorry, Phatty, but I can't talk about it now*, she thinks.

The Renegade glances at her and turns to Phatty and Bolghery.

"We need to hurry to Prague. And it's not smart for us to be above the surface for too long anyway. Work with Philip, Phatty. Prepare lawyerly stuff, one-pagers for each criminal instance so Ursula et.al. can get the gist of it in one glance. See if you can fill injunction seeking lawsuits in International Criminal Court in the Hague. A cease and desist for the PHOENIX ONE. Citizen's arrest for Varga. You name it."

"Done," Bolghery says. "I will file a lawsuit for crimes against humanity with all liaison offices, in New York, Kinshasa, Tbilisi. Will find the others."

"Good thinking," the Renegade says.

"Renegade," Phatty asks, "does it make any sense? To spend energy on lawsuits?"

"It will be Philip's energy anyway." The Renegade smiles. "But, more importantly, Varga has made a mistake, which makes all that work more than worthwhile."

Nastassia turns her head.

"What mistake?" Philip and Bolghery ask in one voice.

"Once his BIDNA and GACH browser charade restores the internet you'll be able to upload everything. No limits were placed on such activities, he only wanted to put an end to privacy once and for all. Well, he'll taste his own medicine. We have enough people ready to post your material; nothing illegal was implied in his new set of orders. And we have hacked some of his Deepfakes, more than we'd ever need, and have enough data for them to pose as humans." He notices their quizzical glances and remembers no one knew about that first, albeit minute, Varga hack. "It was Wyverin, before she or he left. Sorry, Phatty."

The Phat Prophet nods, all is OK, but his eyes turn toward the floor.

"I will send you the file with all the hacked Deepfakes right away. Just leave the mini-modules everywhere there's Net access, upload everything and let Varga's minions chase the ghosts. The data about his shenanigans would be available for everyone to see. Even Varga would have difficulties to, all over again, block the access and delete the data."

"He would've been wiser never to restore the access." Phatty nods.

"Impossible. His empire depends on the Net," Nastassia agrees. There's hope, no matter what Varga might have in his deck of cards.

"Live by the sword, die by the sword of his own digital gulag making?" Bolghery puns.

"And the pen is mightier than the sword, old friend. So get to writing. We have to try everything humanly possible to stop Varga. Good luck."

"Good luck to you too," Bolghery says as the Grey Ghost submerges again and continues its trip toward the Polish shores, where they are eagerly anticipated.

Pawel and Švejk
Świnoujście, Poland
March 25, 2048

Dobrý voják Švejk, the good soldier Schweik turned clown, is a sixty-two-year-old cheerful harlequin standing on the shore. He shivers in a cold wind and observes the sea through his colored binoculars, going left and right all over the horizon, and talks to his black, miniature, bejeweled donkey.

"Do you see them?"

"Hee-haw! Hee-haw!" was the donkey's only comment.

"I thought so." Schweik shakes his head, displeased by his donkey's ignorance. "Sooner or later, Pawel, I'll sell you to the butcher," he threatens Pawel the Donkey with a chuckle. Before the argument between the clown and donkey ensues, like it has many times before, to the endless joy of the circus's audiences admiring those antiquated relics of the romantic past, the Grey Ghost submarine emerges from the depths of the sea and reveals itself. From the inside of the Grey Ghost, the Renegade checks the beach through the windows and spots Schweik and his donkey.

"A clown?"

"With a donkey, yes." Nastassia bursts into laughter as the Renegade types a command into Grey Ghost's computer console, "I need fresh air. Let us get out," he says and helps Nastassia disembark the Grey Ghost. While the Renegade and Nastassia wade through the cold Baltic Sea's breakwater toward the beach, behind them, the Grey Ghost slowly dives and hides at the sea bottom nearby.

"It will wait for us," the Renegade says to assuage Nastassia's concerned glance.

Schweik runs to them and hugs Nastassia and quickly turns to the Renegade.

"I'm so happy I finally get to meet the legend," Schweik says and bows in front of the Renegade, adding, "And, of course, Jaroslav's famous girlfriend."

The Renegade chuckles. Nastassia shoots a mean look at him and turns back to Schweik, all sweetness as she calmly emphasizes every word and claims, "I'm not his girlfriend."

"Yeah, right," Schweik murmurs to himself, then loudly to both, "We need to hurry! The drones and the Peace Police are ransacking New Athens, searching for you two. What have you done? Robbed a bank?" He chuckles. The question was rhetorical; Jaroslav instructed him not to poke his nose into their affairs too much. Just being in the Renegade's company should be enough.

Schweik gets a multi-color clown wig out of his donkey's saddle pocket and places it on Nastassia's head. The Renegade's laughter ceases immediately after Schweik places an oversized clown's top hat on him and affixes a fuzzy nose and glasses on him, also adding a clown nose on Nastassia.

"Why's that?" It's not the most surreptitious disguise."

"Before we can take you to Prague, we have our last performance tonight."

"We?" Nastassia asks suspiciously.

"Yes, after the performance the troupe goes back to Prague and will take you with us. You need to blend in."

"What performance?" Nastassia's now alarmed. The Renegade keeps chuckling as a little boy would, totally amused over the utterly bizarre developments on the icy-cold beach of, out of all places in the world, Świnoujście, Poland.

"You'll see. Jaroslav told me all about the Renegade's tricks." Schweik winks. "You must blend in, otherwise how'd I justify having two strangers among us? Someone might even recognize you without the outfits."

"Tricks?" Nastassia asks. The Renegade shrugs with a smile. She's about to give him a piece of her mind when Schweik rushes them off to the nearby Park Zdrojowy Świnoujście, where his curiously named circus, "Knedlík" (a dumpling), has set up its colorful tent. Pawel, the donkey, follows them, huffing.

The Circus's "Knedlík" Last Show

The big red and white letters on a banner outside proudly boast:

"THE LAST SHOW ON EARTH TONIGHT"

Not even a thick, old-fashioned red-and-white circus tent set in the middle of the Park Zdrojowy can muffle the sound of belly laughter coming from the audience. The show is in full swing. The bejeweled elephants leave the stage, followed by the audience's loud cheers when the Ringmaster Pawel, a flashy man in his forties, appears. He wears red huntsman tails, a black cylinder hat with a red ribbon and a feather attached to it, a silk white shirt, and gloves. He smokes a big, fat, Cuban cigar and slowly puffs a few smoke rings, waiting for the excitement to subside and for the audience to give him their undivided attention. When the cheerful crowd quiets down, the Ringmaster Pawel theatrically addresses them.

"Dear guests. Beautiful ladies and distinguished gentlemen, brace yourself. The last act of the last and the greatest show on Earth is about to make your heads spin and your hearts sink," he pauses pompously and slowly puffs another smoke ring from his cigar, looking around, to make sure everyone's listening. "As the trapeze artists fly in the air jumping from trapeze to trapeze without a safety net, Magnificent Miss Lilly and Monsieur Grand Renégat will perform the most terrifying act ever," he dramatically announces.

Nastassia peers through the curtain and whispers to Schweik, "Miss Lilly?"

Schweik shrugs and nods toward Pawel. He holds the audience in the palm of his hand; they wait with bated breath. He puffs on his cigar again, creating a few more smoke rings, inhales them, and blows them away taking his sweet time, imbibing the intoxicating moment of total control over his audience. When he notices that no one breathes anymore, dying of suspense, the Ringmaster continues:

"Please welcome the orchidaceous Miss Lilly as the target girl and Monsieur Grand Renégat as the knife thrower for their incomparable act: the blind wheel of death."

"I don't like how this sounds," Nastassia whispers.

Schweik gently nudges Nastassia toward the circus ring and, with a musical crescendo, she and the Renegade appear under the circus lights, greeted by the standing ovations of the audience. At that very moment, several men enter the circus tent, quizzingly looking around.

The Renegade uses the plasmonic graphene meta-surfaces invisibility cloak, the same he used to escape the PHOENIX ONE's wrath with Nastassia back in New York, and covers her again. She vanishes. The audience gasps loudly. The Renegade walks away and puts a blindfold on his eyes and, maddeningly quickly, throws twelve knives to the target where Nastassia stands, but then... blood splatters all over the floor!

A blood-curling scream of pain startles the audience; several people scream in terror as the blood pours out from beneath the invisibility cloak.

"He killed her!" a terrified woman yells in dread.

The Renegade dashes toward the cloak and vanishes himself. Inside the cloak Nastassia looks at him, unhurt.

"Why, in the name of God, were you doing that?"

"Let's run," the Renegade tells her and drags her out.

"Hey," Nastassia protests, for the Renegade yanked her so strongly that she felt an intense pang of pain. "Sorry," he says, rushing to calm her. "They're here. We must run."

She runs like mad after him. They leave the circus, but behind them, bedlam ensues as many members of the audience start skipping the balustrade-like fence and rush toward the center of the stage where Nastassia stood seconds ago. There's no one there. Everyone looks around, bewildered. Loud, angry, and somehow menacing requests are hurled at the Ringmaster.

"What's was the trick?"

"Is she dead?"

"Where are they?"

"What has happened?"

"We want our money back!"

Outside the circus tent, Nastassia and Renegade stop running as they catch their breath.

"What happened?"

"The Peace Police found us," the Renegade says, himself breathing heavily.

"How?"

"We've been betrayed."

"By whom?"

Renegade silently looks in her eyes. The spark of understanding is almost visible. Nastassia is vividly upset. "No way. Never. Jaroslav would never, ever do it, you can't suspect him." Before Renegade manages to agree with her, Nastassia spots Schweik with the Peace Police, vividly explaining something.

"Schweik! It was him. I must call Jaroslav; his cover's broken."

Dr. Bode Comes to Rescue

Once outed and furious over the betrayal, the Renegade and Nastassia run for their lives, as far from the circus "Knedlík" as possible. The old sage calls Dr. Bode in Berlin for help only to find out that he's nearby, taken away to his old post in order to avoid Berlin's New Athens ransacking and possible harm. They go on to meet with him.

Chapter 14
TYCHO BRAHE SECRET

Prague, Czech Republic
March 25, 2048

Praha hlavní nádraží, the "golden city" Prague's main, and largest, train station glows under the morning sun as the night train Peenemünde – Berlin – Prague enters the station. Jaroslav has been nervously waiting outside the station for over half an hour already; he's on the edge and worried sick. He could not come to terms with the fact that the Dobrý voják Švejk is a traitor. No way! But then, he trusts Nastassia and the Renegade. That treacherous oldie… You just can't trust them oldies—unless they are geniuses like the Renegade, of course. Confusing thoughts race through his head. *This is a nightmare*, he thinks, glancing at the sky.

The PHOENIX ONE's clone stationed above Prague keeps sending drones to ransack New Athens, as they have all over the world, searching for the Renegade and Nastassia. Nobody was safe from them; the *hlavní nádraží* was swarmed by the Peace Police, the Virtuosi™ and the Good Samaritan volunteers since early morning, all zealously trying to find and capture an old man and a teenager, or "the most dangerous fugitives & terrorist the world has ever seen." But they are Jaroslav's friends. At least Nastassia is. And they are just now entering the wolf's den.

He wonders, what possessed them to decide to meet here of all places?

What Would Paul Morphy Do?

What Jaroslav did not know was how the Renegade and Nastassia managed to get from Świnoujście in Poland to Peenemünde (where the V1 and V2 rockets, weapons of terror against the civil population during World War II, were built) in Germany. The fifty or so kilometers might have been too far to walk, but what is known to us is that, after they escaped the Peace Police chase from the Circus "Knedlík," they found themselves in the Historical Technical Museum in the center of Peenemünde. There they met with Dr. Wolfgang Heinz Bode, a very good, old friend of Renegade's, and as we saw earlier, one of the founding members of the PRIORI Alliance who used to work for the museum as the tech adviser. Dr. Ursula Hansen-Schroeder insisted that he help him evacuate from Berlin to safety. The museum was closed while waiting to move to the new building, so Dr. Bode had it all for himself and now, for his unexpected guests.

After a forceful hug, he follows his old friend's glance toward the old relic nearby. They both know very well what that glance means. The Renegade needs a means of transportation since the planned circus route to Prague turned into a fiasco due to the clown's betrayal. In the museum display is the original 1943 Zündapp KS 750 military sidecar motorcycle, Dr. Bode's prized possession, the crown jewel of his tech collection, his pride that he restored with his own hands decades ago, a prized antique he loaned to the museum and now yet again had for himself.

"No way in hell; it's a venerable relic. I am not going to allow you to damage it. Or destroy. You can go fuck yourself."

Nastassia looks at these two older men and thinks, *This is what being in the Matrix must look like.* Dr. Bode was the Renegade's dead ringer, only a German, meaning that his jaw was chiseled and more pronounced than his look-alike's and his accent sounds like it came from the *Indiana Jones* series, but otherwise they could've been twins. At the moment, they look like two angry, white-haired peacocks screaming at each other over a gorgeous peahen, only there were alone. *Old people are so funny, but when they are geniuses arguing over nothing, they are hilarious,* thinks Nastassia.

"I dare you to Dragon Variation, Levenfish Attack," the Renegade says cryptically. "If I win, you'll lend it to me."

"What are you two talking about?" Nastassia asks. They both ignore her.

"Sicilian?" Dr. Bode knew very well what the Renegade is saying. He dares him to a chess game, the Sicilian Defense opening, the fabled, aggressive, Dragon Variation. "You'd never beat me playing Levenfish with blacks." He looks at the Renegade, somehow suspiciously, somehow smugly. "Even Paul Morphy detested Sicilian."

"So, you've got nothing to lose," Renegade says, challenging him. They stand close to each other, locking their eyes like two boxers before a bloody match. Nastassia shakes her head in disbelief. My mom was right, she thinks, men all behave like boys when the opportunity presents itself, no matter their age or brilliance.

"OK, then," Dr. Bode says and, still somehow quite angrily, gets a chessboard out of his desk. "You have it, patzer," he squeezes through his teeth.

The Renegade runs his finger through his unruly hair and takes several deep breaths. "We'll see who's the patzer soon."

They set up a board and sit, ready to play.

"You'll play chess now?" Nastassia sighs in despair. "Like we have nothing better to do?"

They both keep ignoring her.

She loudly whistles. The Renegade and Dr. Bode turn their heads, annoyed by the interruption. "What?"

"Aren't we going to discuss a plan of action? Phatty's discoveries? Send a message to Dr. Ursula Hansen-Schroeder? Go to Prague?"

"Ursula already knows," Dr. Bode says.

"We can't travel during the night," the Renegade adds and they both turn back to the chessboard in front of them.

The battle of minds ensues. 1.e4 c5 2.Nf3 d6 3.d4 cxd4 4.Nxd4 Nf6 5.Nc3 g6 … etc. Their moves take precedence over both her nagging and the world outside the chessboard and its unparalleled magic. Nastassia observes the game of those two clone geniuses, chortling at the thought, but they still continue to ignore her, both deeply immersed in a game she did not play or really understand. She heard that one of the world's first supercomputers, Deep Blue—or was it Green? One of the base colors, anyway—won a game over some good human chess player hundreds or so years ago, so she really did not understand why such a slow, ancient game would be interesting to today's mighty minds such as those two. The Renegade and Dr. Bode play without a chess clock, both immensely focused on every move; you could hear a pin drop. Only once, when Nastassia tries to type in something on her laptop to check the hacked material Phatty was still collecting, the two old brainiacs turn their heads as one and croaked at her, in one voice, "Stop typing!" Nastassia shrinks back, so they get back to the game and keep playing in quiet.

The Phat Prophet's Hack Report II

The Historical Technical Museum has a lot of rooms so Nastassia settles for the exhibition room of the mass production of A4 rockets in Mittelbau-Dora and their use against large towns and cities in Western Europe many years ago. Seems appropriate. She pings Phatty. The dark circles under his eyes are the only sign of his strenuous work.

"You alone?"

"I am in the middle of a glitch in the Matrix. They are the same person, Phatty, I am telling you. They look the same. They talk the same. And they play chess."

"Chess?"

"Yes."

"Like now?"

"Yes. Now. They threw me out because the keyboard clicking annoyed them. They're both crazy," she concludes but her smile and admiration of these two 'codger clones' tells Phatty that nothing grave's going on, so he goes on updating her about the hack's results.

"Where they keep Stellan and other precogs is something resembling a mash of photon milk bath and cryogenic liquid, like liquefied oxygen but some green, absinth-y substance."

"They froze them?" Nastassia asks, aghast.

"No. They are kept at room temperature." *Kept* flashes through Nastassia's mind, *like vegetables*. "I did not find the compound of the substance. Have no clue how any of that works, sorry, N, but what I've found is a ledger with every precog's data."

"So it's easy to match them with the missing children?"

"I've done that already."

"Good, Phatty. You're a real Dark Dante."

"Funny should you mention him. Kevin Poulsen is helping with the missing children bit."

"He's still alive?"

"Alive and going strong at eighty-three. His great-grandson, Mad Max Poulsen, is one of the kidnapped precogs, placed right next to Stellan."

"Jeez."

"Kevin went berserk. We'll use his publishing experience to publish and notify all the mothers of the missing precogs. 'The mothers can take Varga down, if no one else,' were his precise words."

"Phatty." Nastassia's concern is palpable.

"Don't worry. I trust him, he's a legend. But I did not tell him about the Maléficus hack. I've just given him the data about the precogs, where they are, what Varga's doing to them, as they came from a totally unrelated source—a whistleblower."

"He'll see right through it."

"Perhaps, but he's too worried about Mad Max and sending the word out."

"Why did they call the kid mad?" Nastassia asks and Phatty beams. That's one of his favorite stories.

"Huh! Mad Max, at seven years old, hacked the raw data of the *Mad Max* franchise and changed the code so he'd be the Max Rockatansky character, revenging his family's murder. Then—"

"Phatty, Phatty" Nastassia interrupts his story. "Not this time."

Phatty huffs, nodding, displeased, but he understands. Nastassia remembers something.

"Get the photos, video feeds, screenshots of the frozen precogs. That might enrage and wake up the masses."

"Kevin's on it as we speak. I have some here, N, but brace yourself, it does not look nice," Phatty says and swipes a cluster of images toward Nastassia.

It looks like a sarcophagus from digital hell, Nastassia thinks.

The Chess Endgame

Dr. Bode, bent over the chessboard like a broken ragtag doll in a dumpster outside Manhattan, is puffing in anger. "It can't be," he murmurs to himself. "It just can't be," he repeats in despair. The Renegade, contrary to his friend's demeanor, leans back with his hands behind his head. He looks coy as he triumphantly glances and winks at Nastassia when she comes back into the room.

She shrugs. *What does that mean?* And the Renegade nods toward Dr. Bode and makes an unambiguous sign, understandable in all languages: a throat-slitting gesture, while happily mouthing "he's done."

It took almost another hour for Dr. Bode to finally admit defeat and resign the game.

"Who's the patzer now?" The Renegade laughs at Dr. Bode's huffing.

The Movie Characters

To say that Dr. Wolfgang Bode was a magnanimous loser would not be a wholly accurate portrayal of his behavior. The words he uttered and repeated in vein upon losing the game were terms like *flibbertigibbet, brain minimus, dung pile fraud,* a *floppy-titted overweight cockroach,* and, for a reason only Dr. Bode would have known *a flatulent cuckold,* all of which he, in rapid succession, has been hurling at the Renegade, whose laughter grows louder at each insult received.

"I love you too, you loggerheaded old coffin dodger." The Renegade keeps laughing as he extends his hand. "The keys, please, or I'll defenestrate you."

Geez, they even talk alike. Un-damn-believable, Nastassia thinks, and she's to learn just about now that one of them is going to be her ride on a 612-km long journey to Prague.

A Phone Call

A video satellite-link call from Dr. Ursula Hansen-Schroeder interrupts their bickering. Upon seeing the Renegade, she slightly raises her eyebrows—such is the extent of her willingness to display surprise. *She's so beautiful,* Nastassia thinks. Indeed, with her glacial blue eyes and long white hair, she looks more like a character from a fairytale than a person of heavy political clout.

"Dr. Rutherford…" Dr. Hansen-Schroeder's thick German accent surprises Nastassia less than how she addresses the Renegade. Nastassia has never heard anyone call him by his last name. It was apocryphal anyway. "Wolfgang informed me about your esoteric journey, which I don't really understand. The information your man gave me is of exceptional value. Do you have any ways of corroborating the data?"

"No, those came from a hack that's still underway."

"So, the evidence is obtained illegally? Herr Varga would not like that."

"Illegally?" Nastassia cries. "Is she insane? *Herr Varga's* holding kidnapped, frozen children and is using them for his sick plans! Is *that* legal?"

The Renegade knows better than to try to calm Nastassia down and turns to Dr. Hansen-Schroeder instead. "She's right. If we can get to a long legal battle with Varga, we'd have already won the first round."

Dr. Ursula Hansen-Schroeder nods, slowly mulling over the situation. Her eyes fixed on Nastassia. She immediately likes this bird-like, fiery girl with such impossible greenish-yellow-purple hair and glistering emerald eyes. *So, this is the most important human in the world*, as Dr. Bode has told her, she thinks. *I wonder why. I don't envy her.*

"Understood, Dr. Rutherford. We have enough political power left in the structures still intact since the transitional period to challenge Varga. I'll do my bid, starting in the United Nations and you do yours. If you'd need any help, call me anytime on my direct line."

The Renegade nods.

"She's a force of nature, Ursula," Dr. Bode exclaims once the call has ended. "If anyone can mobilize the few remaining honest politicians, that's her."

"I hope so," the Renegade agrees. "The United Nations are still a functioning entity. Varga keeps a tight grip only over the Western nations, Brazil, and some African countries. The rest is still relatively free of his influence, despite his propaganda assuring everyone the opposite is true."

Nastassia steps in. "Don't we have to go now?"

"Yes, it's time to give me my trophy for such a brilliant chess victory," the Renegade says, poking at Dr. Bode, but he is already over the defeat so the last remark flies over his head. Begrudgingly, he takes them to the display on which his Zündapp sits in all the glory that only a hundred-plus-year-old machine in perfect working order could invoke. That magnificent engine from a less than magnificent era also has an authentic MG-34 machine gun on it, a killing monster that startles Nastassia. Zündapp is painted and covered by various stickers promoting none other than the *Indiana Jones and the Return of the Holy Grail* movie, the long-awaited, upcoming seventh installment of the series. It is also the first movie fully written, directed, acted, and edited by Varga Entertainments Ltd., a Manila-based multi-media corporation's AI appropriately, albeit not too creatively, named Lumière I, M.A.I. LLC (where M.A.I. stands for the "movie artificial intelligence.")

While Varga was promoting the movie, he said, "During the ancient, heroic times of filmmaking when filmmakers needed all those grip crane clamps and clips, cameras of all sizes, lights and fixtures, more stuff than I needed to build The Varga Tower, not to mention all those overpaid capricious, fickle actors, there was only one Steven Spielberg. In today's world everyone could, and would should they wish to, be a Spielberg."

"The final cut, in fact the *only* cut for Lumière I M.A.I., did not need several takes or various camera angles for each scene," Varga promised. "*Indiana Jones and the Return of Holy Grail* will be released under the Creative Commons Attribution 4.0 International (CC BY 4.0) license." He went on explaining, "This license lets others distribute, remix, tweak, and build upon our work, even commercially, as long as they credit us for the original creation." Varga then invoked Indy's hologram to the stage to rapturous applause. The AI Indy stayed mum since Varga did not want to share the limelight. "Let's have a competition in the Reality for Everyone™ for the best-remixed version of the movie," Varga yelled excitedly. "Simon would have a ball." He laughed, to the mirth of his record four-and-a-half billion followers. And now, this Varga's own extravagant film production will be used to camouflage the very two people his ghouls are seeking all over the world.

Dr. Bode hands an old motorcycle ignition key to the Renegade and adds, "You'll also need this," and he hands them new pairs of clothing. For the Renegade, it was all there, the wide-brimmed sable fedora hat Indiana Jones wore in all his movies, the leather jacket, and khaki trousers, a bullwhip made out of long braided strips of leather, a 1917 Smith & Wesson pistol chambered for .45 ACP, and the Cross of Coronado that Dr. Bode insists the Renegade must wear around his neck. Given that Harrison Ford, a dignified symbol of Hollywood's last Golden Era and iconic actor famous for playing Indiana Jones, is now 106 years old and a retired lumberjack in Montana, he's been replaced by his long-haired computer simulation, another spitting image of the Renegade and Dr. Bode. For Nastassia, Dr. Bode has a costume of Morgaine la Fey—a simple black dress, and a purple domino mask. Morgaine was rumored to be the villain who fought Indiana Jones to the death over the Holy Grail. Once fully dressed, the Renegade and Nastassia look at each other and snicker.

"No one will ever recognize us," she says.

"In fact," Dr. Bode says, "no one would. There are hundreds of Zündapp replicas roaming Europe, as they carry actors' doubles and promote the movie; you're the only ones riding the original." He has sadness in his voice as he lovingly pats the motorcycle's leathery seat like it is the last time he will see it. He comes to his senses and his old self in a moment and turns to the Renegade. "Break a leg, patzer."

"I will guard it like I would guard the apple of my eye, Wolfie," the Renegade says and they exchange a brief, forceful embrace.

"*Wolfie?*" Nastassia thinks, looking at them, and then says to the Renegade, "Are we going to occupy Prague with this *thing?*" Her words meet with their cunning smiles. One never knows. Francisco Pizzaro had conquered the mighty Inca Empire, its twelve million people, and an army of over thirty thousand battle-hardened men with only one hundred and eighty soldiers.

"Jump on," Renegade tells Nastassia, and he screams in an unrecognizable voice, uttering words totally devoid of any sense to her. "Easy Rider, you live foreeeveeeer."

And they zip away.

To Prague

"What in the name of Chernobog is that?" Jaroslav asks as a greeting to Nastassia and the Renegade, astonished at the sight of the dirty and now leaking Zündapp. He awkwardly kisses Nastassia on the cheek. The Renegade chuckles, his eyes yet again meet with Nastassia's angry glances.

"What did I do now?" The Renegade laughs while Jaroslav observes their interaction in embarrassment. He does not want anyone to know about the secret crush, or more, that he has on Nastassia.

"Let us hurry," he says, nodding toward the PHOENIX ONE's clone in the sky and all the Peace Police cars parked around the *Praha hlavní nádraží* station. Nastassia glances upward.

"Jump in," she says and scoots a bit, making space for Jaroslav in her sidecar, making him giddy.

The Renegade starts the bike. "Tell me how to get to the Old Town Square."

The Church of Mother of God before Týn

From the Old Town Square, in Czech known as Staroměstské náměstí, a small, cobbled Týnska street leads to the church, Tycho Brahe's last resting place. The Renegade parks the Zündapp in a narrow passage next to it. Their Indiana Jones costumes create quite a sensation and a throng of tourists immediately surround them asking for autographs, trying to touch them, take selfies with them. Jaroslav looks around, uneasy.

"No need to worry," Nastassia jokingly assures him. "We're celebrities now—no one would suspect us."

"We have a tradition in Czech Republic—we don't trust anyone," Jaroslav says, blushing at the memory of Dobrý voják Švejk and his betrayal—*I trusted him with Nastassia and the Renegade*, he thinks, ashamed, *but luckily they do not seem to care or, thank God, blame me*—and nods toward one tall, strange-looking man who stares at them from across the street. The tall man is taking photos of them, comparing them with the "Most Wanted" photos of the Renegade and Nastassia. "We also have a tradition of spies being everywhere."

"I love you, Indiana," one older lady with a wool shawl made of real Himalayan yak's wool yells at the Renegade, asking for an autograph. He signs the *Indiana Jones Unauthorized Autobiography* by Harrison Ford as Harrison Ford. After he kisses the old lady on her cheek, she swoons to the hilarious laughter of the throng enjoying the spectacle. She was as strong as the yak whose coat she wore, *only a pair of big horns are missing on her wide head*, so to see her faint like some blushing debutante is truly a comical sight. And those missing horns? They likely belonged to the lady's husband, the only person in the audience who did not laugh but rather flashed a spiteful smirk at her while she's unable to see him. The Renegade is enjoying his moment under the sun, basking in Harrison Ford's iconic role and its deserved fame when Nastassia pulls his sleeve and whispers, "The guy over there."

Not turning his head, the Renegade registers the man and enters the church. The tall, unpleasant-looking man is dressed in a cheap suit a half size too small, stares after them and records the time of their entrance as they move inside. As soon as they vanish behind the big oak doors, he dials a number.

The Tomb

The Renegade, followed by Nastassia and Jaroslav, enters the eighty-meter-tall Church of Mother of God before Týn from the magnificent northern portal. The church is an impressive building that has seen and comforted worshippers for over a thousand years, from the times when in its place stood an old Romanic church. Tourist brochures teach visitors about its main altar with paintings by Karel Škréta, a portrait painter from South Bohemia (*Assumption of Virgin Mary and Holly Trinity*,) as an of early-Baroque portal architecture from 1649. A Gothic statue of Madonna with baby Jesus, the so-called Madonna of Týn from 1420 is located on a new-Gothic altar by the wall on the right side of the aisle. *The Calvary*, the piece done by Master of Týn, and *The Crucifixion*, from the beginning of the 15th century, are located on the Baroque altar at the end of the left side aisle.

On the right, when facing the altar, just before the first row of worshippers' pews lies the tombstone of the nobleman Tycho Brahe. The marble tomb slab is covered with four red and four white roses. Four brass pillars with yellow tape signal the tomb is an off-limits area. The Renegade stands in front of Tycho's last resting place in reverence. *So, that's it*, he thinks and turns to the kids.

"Without Brahe, it might not have been Kepler and his laws of planetary motion. And without Kepler who knows if Isaac Newton would have been able to derive Kepler's three laws. Newton had shown us that Kepler's Laws are what they are in their very core: gravity. His Universal Law of Gravitation came out of that understanding. None of that would've been possible without Tycho Brahe, kids."

"Renegade?" Nastassia whispers at him.

"Yes?"

"Yours is a fascinating lesson about physics and its history. We'd love to learn more, but do you remember the guy outside?"

"What about him?"

"He might have recognized us, that's what's about him. If so, the Peace Police and the drones could be here any moment now."

"If they do, we're doomed," says Jaroslav. "No way out from the church."

"So, what do we do now?" Nastassia asks. "I see no secret language on his tombstone. It's clean. How do we go about that secret of his?"

"By paying Tycho a visit."

"What?" Nastassia and Jaroslav ask in one voice.

Without an explanation, the Renegade jumps the rope, raises one heavy brass stand, and forcefully hits the tile, breaking the slab at once. And for the third time, since the 1901 and 2010 diggings of his tomb, the Tycho Brahe grave has been disturbed. Even more so, a group of nice Franciscan nuns enters the church at that moment. The nuns are chattering all together, in profound shock over the vandalism. What truly scandalized them upon seeing a dignified looking man such as the Renegade, was that he has not only committed the outrageous crime but keeps doubling down on his evil deed by bending down, removing pieces of the tombstone's broken tile, and finally, by jumping straight down into the grave.

"Follow me, kids," he orders from the grave, channeling his inner Indiana.

"He's insane," Jaroslav concludes.

"I know," Nastassia concurs and jumps into Tycho Brahe's tomb herself. Jaroslav embarrassingly looks around the church, glances at the superfluity of Cheeseheads nuns, shrugs at them while whispering, *"Sorry,"* and also jumps, like some depraved grave robber would, straight into the last resting place of the great old astronomer.

Tycho Brahe Secret

The Renegade ring-finger lights his Zippo lighter and hands it to Nastassia. "Hold this, please."

Nastassia holds the lighter while the Renegade rummages through the grave, looking like a shadow under the pale light from his Zippo. Tycho Brahe's remains are nowhere to be seen. There were no traces of clothing, not a single bone in his coffin, no teeth, not a trace of hair, not even his brass nose prosthesis was there.

"Tycho's body not here," the Renegade murmurs to himself. "They must have removed him for the forensic analysis of his death and never returned it?"

There's an old replica of Mechanica, the famous manual Brahe wrote explaining how the many astronomical instruments that he invented worked, lying in the coffin among some other, unrecognizable artifacts. Tycho's wife's coffin next to his is intact, so it seems no grave robber ever desecrated Kirsten Barbara Jørgensdatter's resting place. Nastassia looks around that dark, solemn place with a flicker of the Renegade's Zippo as the only source of light. This is how we live our lives, in our digital catacombs, with flickering blue lights disrupting our sleep and our nerves and our dead. She looks at the old sage frantically rummaging through the grave. He looks like a true graverobber ransacking the resting place of rich people, looking for brimming treasures, hidden maps, lost manuscripts, or, in this case, the Tycho Brahe Secret.

What if there's no secret? Frédéric and the Renegade are, were, scientists, but the whole secret saga is the fruit of her dad's imagination. There's a novel, not a math proof behind their phantasmagorical journey to the end of the night. However, no one has doubted the Renegade, not herself, and his faith that Frédéric was right. But, what if they are both wrong?

"What are you looking for, Renegade?" Jaroslav asks.

"Jepp the Dwarf hid it from Johannes Kepler. It must be here," the Renegade says as he keeps frantically searching the coffin.

"Who hid what?"

"Instructions for getting to Tycho Brahe diary," the Renegade explains and then yelps, out of excitement. He triumphantly raises a small object. A beautiful silver-gilt brooch in the form of a letter T features the two figures, the Archangel Gabriel and the Virgin Mary, standing on opposite arches of the letter. At the top center of the letter T is a small star. Nastassia comes closer and examines the brooch.

"What does it tell you?"

The Renegade opens the brooch. A small paper falls from it. Nastassia grabs it and reads it, with the help of the light coming from the Renegade's Zippo.

"Sequere Stellarum."

"What does it mean?" Jaroslav asks.

"Follow the stars," the Renegade translates. "We must find the stars."

As he looks around, Nastassia paces around, searching for clues, and she abruptly stops, calling the Renegade. "Look, look, here at the floor," she exclaims. He rushes to her, excitedly takes the lighter, and kneels, like a truffle sniffing dog. A small path of stars leads him toward the opposite wall. The Renegade keeps walking on all fours when he bumps his head on the wall. Nastassia chuckles when Jaroslav gently nudges her with his elbow, nodding toward the Renegade, who looks confused by the few drops of blood the bump has produced.

"It's here!" The Renegade grows more and more excited with every passing second.

"What?"

The Renegade sheds some light to reveal the Tycho Brahe Model of the Universe that stands on the right side of the chamber and a mosaic of stars that portrays the constellation Cassiopeia showing the position of the supernova that made him famous forever. The Renegade stands up, lighting up the star map, and points his finger to the center of the model.

"De nova stella! Tycho Brahe's Supernova," he says when the thud of the Peace Police boots coming from behind startles them. GRIFFIN and the swarm of drones, followed by the Peace Police and the tall snitch, enter the grave through the tombstone's crack.

"They found us," Nastassia whispers. The Renegade covers his lighter's small fire with the palm of his hand and closely examines the mosaic. This must be the key to the doors, he thinks. He turns, alarmed by a noise. A green-lit GRIFFIN and several of his drones, with the Peace Police chief next to them, rush toward the tiny flicker of light and the three silhouettes, clearly seen through their night visor. The rest of the Peace Police fast-rope down the tomb and run like crazy after the police chief and GRIFFIN.

"Now or never, Renegade. What's the point of the Nobel?"

"I am trying."

He pushes the biggest star in the De nova stella mosaic, and the invisible door, at least a meter thick, opens with a quiet whoosh, revealing a long, dimly lit tunnel behind. They all rush into the tunnel as the police chief showers them with bullets. It hits Jaroslav, who was the last to go in. He screams in pain and falls to the ground. The Renegade grabs him, rushes into the tunnel carrying the young boy, and the invisible door whooshes again, closing behind them.

From the inside, a replica of the De nova stella mosaic is hatched to a chain hanging from the ceiling and going someplace inside. This must be a hatch for the doors. The Renegade yanks it and De nova stella vanishes from the front side where GRIFFIN and the Peace Police helplessly stand, firing at the wall in vain. They are locked outside.

The Tychonic Planetary System

The tunnel they entered was more of an entrance hall, a rectangular chamber around three-and-a-half meters by and seven meters big. It has no chairs or tables, only one stone slab onto which the Renegade carefully lays Jaroslav down. He is sweating profusely but is conscious. A shiny glaze of limestone rock reflects the light provided by the scarcely placed torches around the hall. Two human skulls on each side wall create a macabre feeling, but the Renegade is more concerned about Jaroslav's wound.

"It hit you at what's called upper trapezius muscle. Right back side. You were lucky, the bullet did not hit your spine or neck. You'll be fine. No shrugging up or lifting the shoulders for a while. I can only close the wound for now. It will hurt a bit."

"Hold on, my hero," Nastassia says and kisses him.

A beam of happiness spreads all over Jaroslav's face. The Renegade tears apart Jaroslav's shirt and tries to distract him.

"Jaroslav, the fraction in your homework formula that you showed me."

"Yes?"

"Attack it with a polynomial ring from Serre's conjecture and you'll have a solution."

Jaroslav beams, out of himself with happiness. The wound? Irrelevant. The pain? Welcomed. The love of his life has just kissed him; the genius he's admired since he saw the very first formula, Einstein's famous $E = mc^2$ that made him fall in love with math, all of which led to Nastassia, has helped him with a math problem. Those happy thoughts are interrupted by the Renegade's hard pressure as he bandages him. He tries mightily to suppress a scream.

"You'll be OK for several hours before we take you to the hospital."

Nastassia sits next to Jaroslav and holds his hand, her emerald eyes glowing at him, his heart soaring.

The Renegade looks around. On the farther end of the hall, there's a door of some sort. He starts to clean it, and fragments of a sketch engraved on the wall start to appear. Nastassia joins the Renegade, sent to help him by Jaroslav, who's in a full-selfless-resistance-hero mode, in cleaning the dirt. They scrub the wall like devoted cleaning ladies. "It is coming up," the Renegade says.

It's true, the engraved sketch, a chart of the solar system with Earth at the center of the universe and the sun revolving around Earth and the planets revolving around the sun shows up. The Renegade steps back and looks at the image on the wall while Nastassia uses his Zippo to light the chart and steps closer to it, examining it.

"This is the Tychonic planetary system," the Renegade exclaims. "That's it!" A loud bang comes from the other side as the Piece Police start to bore a hole in the wall for some explosives; it spells danger that's not going away.

"What do we do with it?

The Renegade hastily examines the carved Tychonic planetary system. Nastassia helps him, touching the convex of the Tychonic planetary system's sketch. They bulge. The Renegade puts his reading glasses on and comes closer, millimeters from the sketch, squinting. He touches the planets with his nose and moves a step back.

"This represents a safe combination lock!"

"Do you know how to unlock it?" Nastassia asks.

"No idea."

Another bang, even louder, comes from outside.

"We need a fresh young mind with this puzzle, look closer. What do you see?"

Nastassia looks closer.

"It's obvious."

"What?"

"The planets! They are not aligned, see?"

Renegade looks closer.

"You're right," he says excitedly, and suddenly places a kiss on Nastassia's forehead.

"You're the real genius here. The original alignment of the Tychonic system must be the combination to open the door. Almost no one today knows what it looks like."

"Please tell me that you know."

"I do." The Renegade aligns the planets and the Sun.

Then he moves back. Nothing happens.

"Perhaps you should try again?"

"The alignment was not quite right," the Renegade says, fixing the position of Jupiter. He steps back and the door starts shrieking and moving. "It's opening!" Nastassia clasps her hands. "You really deserved your Nobel Prize."

As he smiles, he glances at Jaroslav.

I'll get him. Nastassia does not have to say it aloud, and she goes to help Jaroslav come with them. Clinging to her, Jaroslav would rather die than allow himself a yelp of pain again. The Renegade squeezes through the slot and enters the Great Hall. Nastassia and Jaroslav follow him. The huge vault door, at least another meter thick, closes behind them with a loud bang.

"Where are we?" Nastassia asks.

"Looks like the vestibule leading to Tycho's grith."

The Renegade looks around and, upon seeing the text as written almost five hundred years ago, he cocks his head. Nastassia's eyes follow; a big relief sculpture, cast in bronze, lit with two big lanterns, hangs to the right of the big oak doors. "What is that?"

The Renegade takes one deep breath, summoning up memories of Frédéric Bonnet, the father of this young girl, and he whispers to himself, "You were right, Freddie. I am so sorry you're not here with us to witness it," and turns to Nastassia, quietly stating the obvious.

"Must be the Starchild Prophecy." They approach the sculptural relief.

"What does it say?" Nastassia asks.

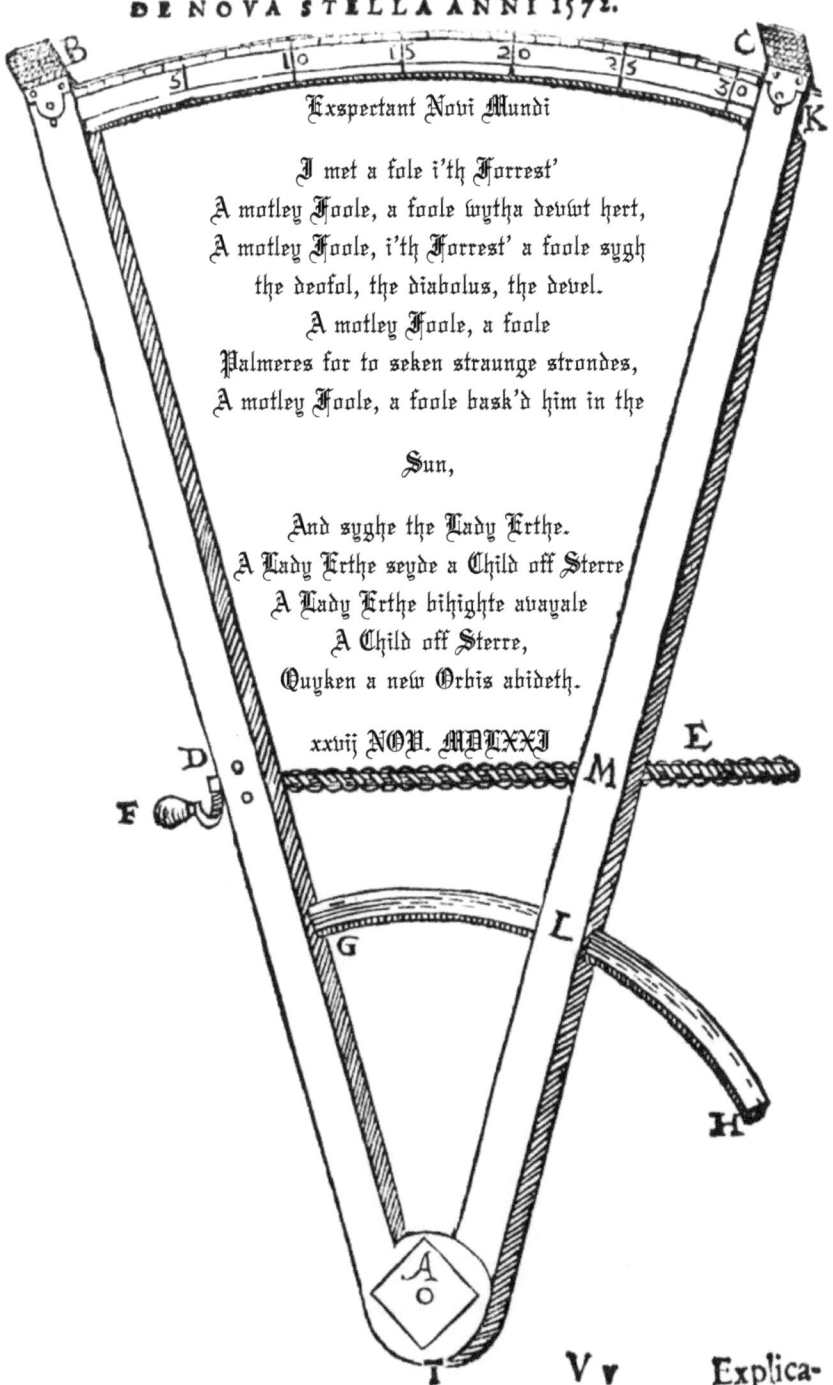

"What does it say?" Nastassia asks again.

"My medieval English is rusty." The Renegade squints. "It goes something like this: 'Awaiting the new world, I met a fool, a fool with a devout heart. The Fool has seen the Devil.'"

He struggles with the new line: "*Palmeres for to seken straunge strondes.*"

"What? What does it mean? Translate, please, translate."

"The Fool went on a pilgrimage to seek foreign shores. He was sunbathing when The Fool saw the Lady Earth."

Deep inside Nastassia, something heavy moves, sounding like an ancient tree uprooted, startling her. She hastily turns her inner eye inward, not sure she wants to *see it*, no matter what it is. But, it is something dark and dreary, something scary that is prowling the forbidden shores of her own soul. A part of her she wasn't aware of before, the black heart of darkness, is there, in her, pulsating.

It can't be!

The Fool? The Devil? Inside her? Part of her? It can't be. What is going on?

The closer the Renegade gets to the translation of what he calls the Prophecy, the deeper she goes inside her psychic, impalpable body. *I'm not alone?* It feels like an invisible guide, holding her hand and following the sounds of the Renegade's words from another world, the visible one. She rummages inside, feverishly looking for the source of that second, black heart, mightily trying to *disconnect* from whatever is going on and to just be herself. Or the darkness might swallow her alive, now, just in front of the Renegade's big mystery, Tycho Brahe's tomb and his secret. *Are those the secrets pulsating, now since they're so close? No, it makes no sense. Was it that Varga's energetic blob? If anything, he has the heart of darkness. Nope, it's not that either.*

He's behind that wall of darkness, Varga, he's submerged in the dark waters that keep them apart. That's it! She was indeed kept away, she had been blocked by the forces behind Varga's Doomsday Vault. That is the place where the block originates.

Precogs!

Phatty said that Varga may be using precogs to keep her in the dark.

As she gets closer, they strangle her attempts harder. But their powers wane as she sees and feels more and more, no matter how horrific those discoveries are.

There seems to be light at the end of a long, dark tunnel. Beneath the surface, in the grave of all places. She feels hope, real hope. This all starts to make sense. She needs to reach Stellan with a tunnel, a mind-eye tunnel, like his crushed mirrors—she has to create a tunnel and get to him and to see, to finally *see* how to defeat Varga.

This time the Renegade does not notice her absence. It takes her a fraction of a second anyway. "And? What comes next?" she asks, keeping a part of her attention inward. The Renegade continues with his translation. "The Lady Earth saw the Starchild and The Lady Earth promised to help, the Starchild. See the initials, N.B."

"Like mine," Nastassia whispers. Jaroslav looks at her in awe, suffused with love. Pain? No pain. "Is that the date below?" Nastassia fingers the bottom line of the Prophecy.

"Yes. It was thought that the poem and the date below are related to Johannes Kepler, lionized as the father of modern astronomy through his laws of planetary motion. He was born on December 27, 1571. The date of this line. Kepler became Brahe's assistant twenty-seven years later. So alchemists of old assumed that he was the Starchild Tycho Brahe was referring to in his prophetic poem."

"So I am not the Starchild? Kepler is?"

"No, that date was added later, some claimed by Kepler himself. In the original poem's signature, Tycho wrote a different date. Frédéric was certain of it." The Renegade starts to frantically scratch the date with his Swiss knife. Nothing.

"What are you doing?" Nastassia hisses.

"See how the font of the date is different than the poem's."

He cocks his head again, leans his head onto the sculpture and pushes the knife's blade in between the date and the flat background.

The date, inscribed on a small bronze plate, falls off.

"I knew it!"

He scrubs the revealed surface.

XXI MARTIUS MMXXXIV appears.

"Look!" The Renegade triumphantly shows it to Nastassia.

"What?"

"The original date, March 21, 2034, the day you were born."

Nastassia stands still, *knowing* all of that is *real*, but a part of her does not want to accept it. There's more, and she's not sure she wants to discover it.

"Renegade?"

"Yes?"

"You bet everything on bad poetry and a coincidence?"

"There's much more to it than that."

"Some conspiracy theorist might have placed this plaque when the grave was opened, to mess with the future explorers of the netherworld." Nastassia looks at him pensively. Her expression does not match her words.

"Our answers are behind these doors," the Renegade says, pointing at the heavy oak door that seems to have been flickering with millions of stars. All three of them stand, frozen, and stare at the gates of Hell or Heaven, not moving a muscle to jump forward. The reluctance is palpable. *What is behind it? What awaits them?*

Nastassia's mind leaps backward in a flashback she has not relived any time before. It comes from her parents' trip before she was born, which they embarked upon after Frédéric heard about a strange case in Bethlehem, a town south of Jerusalem and the birthplace of Jesus. It was something she wasn't aware of but that greatly aroused his interest, and the Renegade knew it by heart.

The Star of Bethlehem
Bethlehem, West Territories
June 20-21, 2033

Frédéric was somehow familiar with dysprosody, a rare neurological speech disorder, better known as a pseudo-foreign dialect, which had just occurred in Bethlehem. The patient who prompted their unplanned trip was a certain thirty-three-year-old carpenter named Kamal ad-Din Abdallah. He had suffered a head injury and, as a result, he suffered from a condition known as Broca's aphasia, characterized by partial loss of the ability to produce language—be it spoken, manual, or written. However, several weeks following the injury, Kamal ad-Din had miraculously regained his ability to talk, but, to the astonishment of everyone around him, he started to speak in a fluent ancient Syriac, a language he did not know prior to the injury, a language that was not widely spoken anymore. His speeches were terrifying in tone and manner as he seemed bedeviled by inner terrors and horrified by the invisible demons that populate the world. A blogger who wrote about Kamal ad-Din described his screams as bellsybabble from hell.

No links with the genetic disease had been established, so Frédéric was keen to see if there was a possible connection, and he urged Monique to join him on the research trip. She made fun of him, questioning his motivations: was it the neurogeneticist scientist or a budding pulp-fiction writer in Freddy who wanted to find out more about such a sporadic disease?

"Neither. It is a romantic who wants to take you, my love, to Bethlehem, since we're in Africa anyway. And it's not pulp, it's science fiction," he replied, and so they went on and ended up as their Alexandria – Bethlehem adventure of July 2041, a magical journey that also included wandering about the mythical Canaan territory of the southern Levant, a trip that also brought them an unexpected surprise or two.

There were rumors floating around that Kamal ad-Din would be stoned to death, as the devil incarnate he seemed to have become. The fear around him was palpable. Once he started to talk incessantly of "šaqluṭā," "the beast of burden," the Patriarch Ignatius Alqidiys I, the Syriac Orthodox Patriarch of Antioch and All the East, located at the Cathedral of Saint George in Damascus, Syria, was alarmed and called to examine the poor man and, perhaps, exorcise the evil spirits if those were the source of the scary phenomenon.

Regretfully for both His Beatitude Ignatius and Frédéric, Kamal ad-Din had another accident, this time fatal. As he was crossing King David's street in Bethlehem, he was hit by the Super Security Services van and killed on the spot. The secrets of the beast of burden he had been uttering about in ancient Syriac, and with such dread that he frightened everyone, were therefore lost for good.

Dar Sitti Aziza

Kamal ad-Din Abdallah's tragedy would've been a loss for Frédéric, but as chance would have it, it turned out that another random encounter had changed his life for good—and in a way he would've never expected. He and Monique decided to stay in Bethlehem for a day or two and found a room in the Dar Sitti Aziza ("The House of My Grandmother Aziza") heritage hotel. It was Monique who, while waiting for Frédéric to get ready for dinner, met Doctor Brent Landau, ThD, Harvard Divinity School, at the time a senior lecturer in the Department of Religious Studies Department, University of Texas at Austin. Both being Americans, they recognized each other under the shade of pistachio nut trees in the hotel's courtyard and started chatting, sharing their impressions from the nearby Milk Grotto Church. When he started to talk about his passion for the ancient Christian apocryphal writings, both Monique, and Frédéric who had joined them, were mesmerized. Dr. Landau was the author of *Revelation of the Magi: The Lost Tale of the Wise Men's Journey to Bethlehem*. He had translated the ancient text he had found in the Vatican Library.

It was originally written in ancient Syriac.

"Ancient Syriac?" Frédéric jumped, like struck by lightning.

"Yes, why?" Dr. Landau was surprised by his unexpected outburst.

Frédéric went on, telling him Kamal ad-Din's curious story. This was a coincidence, a rare commodity in life, so they spent the night talking about what Kamal might have been seeing and saying and how that phenomenon was likely to occur. Speculations took them back to the three Magi and the Starchild, Jesus, who came to this world to save it. Dr. Landau provided them with a great feast of knowledge, sprinkled with his imaginative theories about the Holy Grail, and again, about the Starchild that shone ever so brightly but was seen only by the Magi and was invisible to everyone else. Frédéric was feverish the whole night afterward and behaved like he was under a spell for the days that followed, long after Dr. Landau went back to the Vatican to pursue his other research. Monique had never seen him like that ever before.

When they made love on that summer solstice night of 20th to 21st of June, 2033, he was different; he was flaming with passion but gentle. His blistering eyes devoured her. His lips and hands, always passionate, this time adored and ravished Monique like never before. His love for her was as deep as the oceans; his passion was as fiery as volcanic lava. He had worshipped her as he would an ancient Nazareth Goddess under a blue moon that never settled. His hands touched every fiber of her body until she had totally surrendered, losing herself in their lovemaking and, in simultaneous ecstasy, became one with him.

But then, Frédéric instantly zonked out and passed out. He was gone, like he had died. Monique was flabbergasted by everything that happened. Normally, Freddy was like a cuddly bear, always awake 'til she went to sleep, never letting her go, always wanting more of her eyes, of her kisses, of her touches, but now this? Well, she was blissful and loved him more than ever so she moved closer to him, embraced him, and soon after, unlike him, she slept a dreamless sleep with a happy smile on her face.

Baal Shamen, Lord of the Heavens

Unlike Monique, Frédéric dreamt. And he had dreamt Nastassia's dream.

In a dream in a dream, he saw his unborn daughter growing up next to the baobab tree and, still a baby, starting to climb it. As she climbed, she grew older, now a toddler, when the sea of blood appeared from nowhere, rising dangerously close to her. She climbed faster. On the top of the mighty baobab grew a peculiar dragon blood tree. As Nastassia arrived at the top of the dragon blood tree, safe from the sea of blood beneath, Baal Shamen, Lord of the Heavens appeared above her. He spoke to her in tongues, to which she replied with a toddler gurgling sounding noise.

"The divine madness of the child protect you must," the baobab said to Frédéric, and it started to swim-float in the red sea, which morphed into the river Lethe. "Don't forget who you are," Baal said in English to Nastassia: "The Starchild of Heavens."

Toddler Nastassia smiled at him as he vanished.

The red river sped up, carrying the trees and Nastassia away. Frédéric found himself swimming toward her in panic, for the distance in between them increased each passing second.

"The river is taking us to hell," the dragon blood tree yelled, now weeping blood itself and approaching the thundering sound of a waterfall—the Lethe was descending into the netherworld, cascading downward at an increasing speed. "Swim harder!"

Too late!

Decomposed bodies, bloated, mutilated, and on their way to hell surrounded him, trying to grab onto him like they needed to cling to his life in order to get back their own, long since lost. He fought them off, screaming Nastassia's name, and the corpses disappeared. But he lost a lot of strength fighting off the cadavers. Barely able to keep his head above the surface, he was sucked by a giant whirling water vortex and started to drown in the crimson red river Lethe. He looked up at the surface as he tried mightily to swim toward the sun, but a vortex kept pulling him down. At that moment, he saw a crystal mirror above him, in shimmering rippling water. In the mirror was Nastassia reflection. She was resting peacefully in the arms of a fairylike, translucent creature of unspeakable beauty, which grew out of the trees. It was a girl or a woman, but it was of tremendous size, as tall as the tallest skyscrapers, at the same time crystalline and a fiery fairy. Nastassia was just a little speck of giggling baby on the palm of her hands. The fairy pushed the tip of Nastassia's nose up, causing Frédéric's heart to want to explode. "You will crush her! Stop!" he yelled from the underwater.

Nastassia giggled at the fairy, who was very careful and gentle.

Nastassia vanished from his sight.

The crystal mirror shattered.

Frédéric drowned.

Figs on Toast

He woke up drenched in sweat, shaking like a leaf, profoundly changed by the dream. He barely had time to compose himself when Monique came back from the restaurant, bringing them some figs on slightly burned toast and a tangy lebaneh kefir for breakfast. She kissed him good morning, suspiciously gazing at him.

"What got into you last night?"

"I was helping you create life."

"What are you talking about?"

"We will have a baby. A baby girl. Our Starchild. And we will call her Nastassia."

Monique observed him quietly and carefully. She came close to him and hugged him. She knew that he was right. She *felt* it. She had no idea how and why, but the happiness that overwhelmed her made her calm and accepting of the new reality.

She did not even notice the sweat dropping to the floor from beneath his pajamas.

"Love the name Nastassia," she whispered, kissing him.

Tycho Brahe's Underground Grith
Prague, Czech Republic
March 25, 2048

The Renegade did not say anything that described the Bethlehem journey by her father and mother. It was a telepathic spark from his memory of Freddie's story to Nastassia's awareness that took only a fraction of a second, but it opened a dam in her. The ripples of memory fired up her neurons like crazy; they oscillated rapidly, and mightily, like the silver waves of Nazaré. She *saw* her own conception as a universal spark of life and felt its *significance*. The universe's spasmic burst of energy sounded like a whip or a starter pistol and the memories started their unstoppable roll, like a tsunami of images rushing toward her.

She saw her father's nightmarish dream; she was in it, still non-existent but fully present, like time that's yet to come her way. She was in her mom's belly, aware of the world. She grew. She *knew* that baobab from Dad's (later recurring) dreams, it was the same baobab she hugged in Madagascar years ago. While she, at the time, did not recognize it from her father's dreams, she now *knows* the baobab recognized her, and her love, on that very day in Africa. The dragon blood tree from the Socotra island yelled at her as it had yelled at her father. "Mirrors! Get the mirrors!" But, unlike Frédéric, who could not have known (Stellan was to be born years later), she knew what it meant.

Those were Stellan's mirrors.

They are the way to him, his mind-eye's protection, and a shortcut to his mind.

But he was still shrouded by the pitch-black gloom that stripped him of all his senses and cut him off. She could not get to him.

She could not find any of Stellan's memories in this torrent wildly whirling around her.

As she already knew, those were the precogs keeping them mentally apart, her and her kid brother. The precogs operated from that dark tower of doom in Norway, aided by the intrinsic web of Varga's devilish obstructions. Strange! She *sees* them, but as *memories*. She remembers stuff she has never seen. Those were not her memories, those were the memories of the world.

Someone else's.

Stellan's perhaps?

#

It was overwhelming at first. The ancestral memories of Earth and all its creatures started to flow through her like thousands of cosmic tsunamis; she has *heard* the dragon blood tree's thoughts from millennia ago as much as Nautilus's ancestors from five hundred million years ago and both of them today, this moment, *right now*. Everything that has ever happened to every living being, the collective unconsciousness as much as the conscious thoughts and emotions of billion living creatures were bursting, like endless Big Bangs, each belonging to its own creature's birth, in front of her inner eye.

At the same time, in that chaos, it strangely does not frighten or overpower her. She feels a sense of peace creeping in. The peace permeates everything; it is the key force of this violent, unruly world. It is an odd feeling, that the peace might be the reason all of this exists? Or was it a peace of her own, a peace of *realization*?

She *is* the only unmovable point in the universe.

#

Dervishes of the past whirl around, whispering messages of the past, present, and future alike. They are drumming. They are humming and they are singing. She realizes that they are praying universal prayers of unity. The rhythm of their dance mirrors the vibrations that permeate the universe. Everything vibrates in her. *Everything at the same time.* "*Do not fear! You're not alone! There are others but you who, unknown to you, live your life too,*" the hoarse voice of a poet tells her. That was Tin Ujević's famous poem titled "Blood Brotherhood of Persons of the Universe" and was narrated by him, in Tin's original Croatian. She has heard it in English. She loves that poem. "*We've all gone the same paths in the dark, we've all gone astray the same way seeking for the truth,*" the gravelly voice continues and vanishes in the hush that follows as it flies away, together with the holy whirlers.

#

The memories, a myriad of memories, not a single one belonging to her but somehow being a part of her as she was one with the world, keep rushing in, rolling like a thunderstorm, in roaring, never-ending waves, and suddenly, all those invisible, massive walls of darkness obstructing her inner visions and her connection to her little brother start to crumble under the pressure of time squeezed in the eternity she glimpsed at through the memories of the world.

And yet, she is calm.

Suffused, translucent herself. All that was happening was like trillion neutrinos passing through her body, but neutrinos with a unique DNA she is able to notice, all at once. That intoxicating feeling in which she seeks a way to organize the massive mess of every bit of info ever existing. And she has found it. She decides to see it, all the visions and images and thoughts and feelings and messages and memories, as a scrolling code. The memories were walls of code cascading and ready to be read at her wish.

It is wonderful.

Infinity in a moment. Countless infinities squeezed in countless moments. With her in the center of it.

She feels like a cosmic programmer who's able to find anything that ever existed in the universe in mere nanoseconds, right here, right now, in her mind. But, she has no time to rummage through the world's heritage, all she wants is to find Stellan.

Sure enough, she has found him.

He is unconscious in the dark chambers of diabolical human aberration, that triple-cursed Winston Varga and his Hans Böhm, that vile Maléficus Ultimo apparition. She would be able to free his mind but he is unconscious, poisoned, hooked on wires, and shielded by the precogs. Still, she is able to send him a message: *I am coming for you, darling, hang on just a bit more*, her love and thoughts are carried away on ripples and they touch him. She *sees* him smile. "Nastassia," he whispers and falls back into his drugged stupor. She also smiles; she does not fear anymore, for she has also seen herself embracing Stellan and playing with his new puppy. That was the moment of bliss, of pure love. Yes, she has a grave task still at hand, but she fears no more. She will find a way. *She's so close now.*

Nastassia's Trance

What in the name of God is happening with her? the Renegade thinks, observing her trance-like, frozen state. Even time seems to have slowed down as she traveled inside. When she comes back, she looks older. Bigger somehow. Almost as beautiful as the grown-up woman she'd soon be and she glowingly smiles at him.

"Let us go in," she says and the Renegade, with the vigor of a teenager, opens the heavy oak doors. And there he is. The Nobleman Tycho Brahe slumbers in a small bed that barely contains his grit. Out of nowhere, Jepp the Dwarf jumps in front of them, brandishing his sword.

"Stop, ye viperine thieves, or I'll excoriate ye!" he threatens. There's something comical in the menacing seriousness with which the small man flaunts his tiny sword.

"Don't ballarag us, noble Jepp. We came in peace," the Renegade says respectfully.

"Thou know me?" The dwarf's eyes widen. He steps back, regains his wits. "To which fiefdom you pledge your loyalty?" Jepp asks with dignity.

"No one has power over us but GAIA." The Renegade startles him with what would've been cryptic words to anyone else. Jepp the Dwarf drops his sword. Tycho Brahe, wide awake at the sound of the sword hitting the ground, stands up and coughs, looking at them.

"The Starchild has come," Jepp the Dwarf says, needlessly explaining the situation to Tycho Brahe. "To see the Lady Earthe."

Tycho Brahe looks at Jepp the Dwarf and then slowly turns his deep gaze at those two strangely dressed creatures, an old man and a child. The child, Tycho notices, follows his inadvertent glance at the huge Wooden Quadrant, its hinged pair of six-foot beams occupying a large portion of the room's right corner, which was built for him by Burgomaster of Augsburg, his friend Paul Hainzel. He had also brought him the Tyndale Bible of 1526, a book clandestinely printed in Germany, that has been sitting on the Tycho Brahe's wooden quadrant for half a millennia. It was written in Syriac, a language related to Aramaic, Jesus's tongue. Alas, Tycho Brahe did not speak Syriac and used this English translation.

He stands still, trying to grasp the situation. Has the Prophecy come to life? *In such a strange form of a tiny bawbling wench dressed liketh a wh're daught'r?* A minute or so has passed, but he still has not moved or said anything.

What is going on?

He has lived hundreds of years since he discovered, and described *De nova stella* and was given the honor of being a *Ligātiō*, a liaison for the Lady Earthe, should humankind ever need to talk to her directly. With such an honor came a curse of the eternal life in his own grave. He wasn't allowed to leave, doomed to live forever dead, with the whoreson Jepp to keep him company in this amber-like time-bubble trap at that. He lives dead but he will never meet Aristotle or St. Thomas Aquinas or "The Philosopher," the Muslim polymath, Ibn Rushd, famed Averroes in heavens. He will never set foot in the ancient Syro-Mesopotamia, the Near East of the three Magi, or the distant and mysterious land called Cathay. He has spent many a sleepless decade listening to the reverberating sounds of his decision to liveth dead. In the end he had accepted the honor but the honor felt heavy. It was like the Cross of Golghata is affixed on him and pinned him in the dark eternity of his life devoid of life, the life of waiting for the Starchild that never came.

While unaware of humankind's progress above his grave, he started to doubt the Starchild's Prophecy. Or at least his hope that he'd ever see the Starchild started to wane. Even the Lady Earthe visited him only a handful of times, her visits centuries apart.

In prayers, his lips silently mouthed the words *"This is the boke of the generacion of Iesus Christ the sonne of Dauid the sonne also of Abraham. Abraham begat Isaac: Isaac begat Iacob: Iacob begat Iudas and his brethren…"* He mulled over the words of Zoroastrian priests from Iran, the three Magi: Melchior, Caspar, and Balthazar. *The Revelation of the Magi* talks about the Christ Child, the Starchild.

But he's a male. This child can't be Him?

Is He not back?

Tycho's cross feels even heavier now.

Nastassia senses Tycho's pain as his thoughts echo in her mind. She can not avoid hearing his thoughts. It is unnerving. Unwanted. But needed. She steps forward. "The Cross on Golgotha is the Tree of Life, o noble Tycho. The Star of Bethlehem was a supernova as much as your Nova Stella was a supernova. Rest assured," the Starchild says, "your wait and your life have not been in vain."

Dad knew everything, she thinks when she repeats the closing words of her father's Tycho Brahe book. Those words were the key to Tycho's heart.

"I did not expect to wait for so long for you," he says. "We must hasten, if you're here. But, I warn ye, Lady Earthe might not be happy to see ye."

Invoking GAIA

He turns to a tall, elaborate model of a celestial globe and rotates it. A distant, barely audible riff morphs into a deep rumble. Jepp the Dwarf slinks behind a straw pallet and hides. The Nobleman Tycho Brahe has never, ever before used the globe. It was given to him for this moment; it has waited and waited, like Tycho himself, over centuries. It did not rust, it did not fail. And now it rotates, sending ripples of ancient promises to the Fiery Fairy, the Lady Earthe, invoking her to his Great Hall, where he waits for this moment to come.

With a quiet woosh, appears the Lady Earthe, an embodiment of GAIA. Hanging in the air, a fiery, ethereal creature of ineffable beauty, she shines as like thousands of stars, translucent and mighty, wonderful and terrifying.

"The Earth does have a soul," Nastassia whispers in awe, recognizing the fairy that held her in the palm of her hand before she was born.

Tycho Brahe, not letting Nastassia mull over the surreal phenomena she's witnessing, steps forward and bows in front of Nature's spiritual essence, the Lady Earthe. "Milady, hẹrte lōth-folks—" he starts, but GAIA interrupts him with a gesture of her long, flaming finger, as she turns her terrifying gaze to Nastassia and the Renegade.

"Ain chilede a'd ain foole?"

Nastassia steps in, looks at GAIA in reverence, and bows. Jaroslav, who has limped his way in from the stone slab in the Tycho's Hall entrance, lurks inside, where an enormous ethereal creature talks to his Nastassia. His heart wants to explode. The Renegade curiously gazes at the Lady Earthe, thinking how Freddy would be enchanted and terrified by his daughter's encounter with the GAIA that, in his book, he himself had envisioned taking place in this very grave.

"We humbly beg for your help."

"Help?" GAIA asks, a hint of anger in her voice.

"Our enemies want to destroy our civilization," Nastassia says. She types into her laptop and a hologram of the widespread destruction of New Athens appears. GAIA laughs, as terrifying and beautiful as hundred burning volcanoes.

"You want me to engage in your tribal squabbles? After you savagely waged intraspecies war against all other life-forms? How dare you, child?" Her voice rocks the chambers.

"We didn't."

"Don't you dare to lie to me so brazenly, child," GAIA's terrible voice shatters a mirror on the wall behind them. It falls to the floor. Jepp the Dwarf covers his eyes.

The War

Somehow GAIA takes over Nastassia's hologram, multiplying it, and a multitude of gruesome images pop up all over Tycho Brahe's chamber:

- fishermen savagely slaughter a bottlenose whale
- in the town of Taji, dolphins are herded into shallow water and hacked to death
- American buffaloes killings shot by tourists from the windows of their trains
- albatrosses starved at the Great Pacific Garbage Patch
- participants at the Gadhimai Festival sacrifice in Nepal massacre thousands of water buffalo, pigs, goats, chickens, with their swords and axes, hacking randomly at the animals
- dead fish and sea mammals float lifelessly amid the Atlantic Garbage Patch
- slaughter and poaching of elephants in Kenya
- cruelty in poultry farms all over the world, which is too shocking to watch so Nastassia averts her eyes
- a blue whale, victim of ghost fishing, lies dead, entangled with plastic waste in a discarded fishing net
- dying dolphins trapped in trawler nets
- fishermen cruelly kill seals, chasing them on the ice
- animal abuse and cruelty toward calves and cows at the Fair Oaks Farms Indiana that makes even the Renegade's eyes mist with tears

"You would not call this a slaughter? Tell me, child, again, that you are not engaged in an all-around war? Tell me. Lie to me again, I dare you," GAIA huffs. "Your vile, callous, insatiable species kills over 180 million animals around the world every day. With fishes, you have billions killed. Why? To gorge yourself on their miseries. What did you ever do for *them*? Your brothers and sisters? Look how obese, how useless you are."

An obese fat trophy hunter in Tanzania kills a lion with this sniper rifle. The lion dies with a horrifying roar covered by the hunter's triumphant screams. Nastassia's eyes tear up, the lump in her throat does not let her speak. She feels the terrible pain of the lion's pierced heart in her own. The pain almost makes her faint. GAIA is as terrifying as the atrocities she has invoked. Outside, in the world above, ominous clouds of doom gather over the dark skies. A ghastly wind picks up, blowing over the golden city of Prague.

GAIA's infuriated face morphs into the face of an ancient woman warrior as she grows bigger, looming over the puny humans; the thunder of her voice is horrifyingly loud.

"Your depraved tribes are committing all these despicable crimes." She looks like she'll smite all those humans with a flick of her flaming index finger as they look up to her, not knowing what to say, what to do.

Renegade observes Nastassia's strange smile, but she does not move, she does not talk so he tries:,"We made mistakes."

"Mistakes?" GAIA's furious huff kills all the candles in the chamber. Total darkness envelops them. GAIA rages and lights up Tycho's abode with more horrifying images:

- EXPLOSIONS of mountaintop removal
- COAL SLUDGE fills the mines
- In the Bingham Canyon Mine, monstrous machines TEAR the land apart
- NUCLEAR blast over Shanghai
- Amazon rainforest DESTRUCTION by enormous fires

The Plague

GAIA's mad rage continues.

"Your enormous herd is like a plague, murdering everyone and destroying everything, you fools." The roaring of her voice shatters the underground. Jepp the Dwarf trembles in horror behind the bed. Tycho Brahe waits for her to calm down, but her rage does not subside. Nastassia types on her computer, suddenly oblivious to her surroundings the Renegade glances at her and hisses, "Going to play now?"

"Buy us some time. Talk to her," Nastassia says. The Renegade notices images on her laptop; he knows better than to argue at this moment and turns back to Lady Earthe.

"We enabled you to see your own beauty."

He nods to Nastassia, she nods back. GAIA laughs.

"What did you say, old fool?"

The Renegade steps forward and faces her rage. "You gazed upon the stars for eons but only our humans' space probes have shown you what you look like from space." He turns to Nastassia, who frantically types on her laptop, "Nastassia."

A beautiful hologram of a blue planet Earth, our only home, that famous pale blue dot, as seen from the space ships appears, slowly rotating in the chamber. Its breathtaking beauty is glorious beyond imagination.

Tycho Brahe moves in awe, tries to touch the hologram. *That's what Earth looks like*? He has never seen such beauty. Astonished, he turns to his strange visitors, subjects of Lady Earthe's rage. *They are brave*, Tycho thinks.

"We've shown you in all your beauty," the Renegade says.

GAIA's laughter blows the hologram off.

"I shall obliterate your species, not help you. Tell me, you old fool, why wouldn't I?"

Nastassia jumps on her feet and starts pacing around, addressing GAIA. "Yes, why don't you?"

"Did you lose your mind?" Jaroslav yelps from the doorway.

Nastassia challenges GAIA. "Wipe us out, you'll be doing yourself a favor." She types into her laptop. Her hologram is up again. "But better hurry up!"

GAIA gazes at Nastassia for a moment. "You're mocking me, child?" she asks calmly, a cold, murderous threat in her ancient eyes. Nastassia types into her laptop and another hologram pops up. It shows the PHOENIX ONE and its clones, armed with nuclear missiles aimed at Earth.

"Our enemy is going to destroy millions and billions of creatures once he fires those missiles. He's your enemy also."

A simulation of N-bombs explodes all over Tycho's dwelling. Jepp the Dwarf shakes, his eyes closed. Tycho murmurs something quietly to himself, fascinated by the sight of such unimaginable power.

"Those birds of doom do not belong to you, Earth Mother. Those are his creations that are going to kill your own," Nastassia finishes and lets the simulation of total destruction of all living beings continue without words. The horrors of nuclear destruction flash blindingly in Tycho Brahe's chamber. It reminds Tycho of his supernova, but a million times brighter and stronger, and now so close to him. After a while, it slows down and Nastassia speaks again.

"This destruction is just a matter of time. Our enemy is ready. His missiles of doom are ready." Nastassia shows the PHOENIX ONE and his clones as they linger menacingly over Earth. "And they will be fired to kill and destroy your children very soon."

"We don't know that," the Renegade whispers to Nastassia.

"Neither does she," Nastassia whispers back.

Stopped in her tracks, Lady Earthe turns her blazing eyes toward Tycho Brahe. "Who is this brazen child?"

He steps forward and kowtows in front of her

"The Child off Sterre." He looks up. "Hark to the Starchild, milady, prithee."

"He will destroy all living beings." Nastassia kneels in front of GAIA, next to Tycho. "Help us, please."

"The Child off Sterre? This puny wench?" GAIA asks, catching her breath. She is much calmer now. Curious. She bends down, herself again a young-looking creature of ineffable beauty, coming close to Nastassia, who looks at her with the love of an unborn toddler from the top of the dragon blood tree from Frédéric's dream. A smile draws itself on Nastassia's face. "I was much smaller when you pulled me from the river Lethe and held me in your arms," she says. The Renegade and Tycho Brahe exchange glances. Jaroslav feels a lump in his throat. Even Jepp the Dwarf crawls out and stands mesmerized by the sight of the two women, a girl and the mother of all living beings, gazing into each other's glistering eyes. Nastassia's emerald eyes are glowing as much as the Lady Earthe's, and from her eyes emanate such calm that Lady Earthe held her breath.

"The Child off Sterre?" she whispers as the recognition sinks in.

They share a memory. She slowly touches the tip of Nastassia's nose and she giggles. Lady Earthe whispers to herself, "The Child off Sterre," and slowly moves back into the upright position. She stands and ponders the situation. She turns her eyes toward Nastassia's hologram showing a nuclear apocalypse with an indescribable smile in her eyes and slowly nods.

She glances at Tycho, who's moved into a kneeling position, and back at the destruction Nastassia's hologram keeps showing. Then, she looks again at Tycho Brahe; there's a glimpse of tenderness on her face as she casts her eyes downward to the Danish Nobleman who has been waiting almost a half a millennium for this moment.

"Thy foole and a Child off Sterre finally arriv'd, Tycho?"

"Forsooth," he whispers back. Indeed they have.

GAIA looks up as the hologram shows a split Earth bleeding in space. "I'm not going to alloweth this befall!" the Lady Earthe says and lets a horrifying roar shatter all corners of Earth. The Peace Police in the tunnel are blown away like ragged dolls and are killed in an instant. GAIA's terrifying roar reverberates through Tycho Brahe's chamber long after she leaves.

What is she going to do?

A Whirlpool Wormhole

The nobleman, Tycho Brahe, is now sitting back in his throne and trying to catch his breath. He stares at the Starchild but with a good, gentle gaze, a mixture of awe, curiosity, and, strangely, trepidation. Nastassia feels that he's waiting for something to happen and soothes herself with some deep kundalini breaths, not quite sure what to do.

"We have to go," she says to the Renegade. "Jaroslav needs to go to the hospital."

"Yes, we do."

And at that moment, Nastassia *feels* Tycho Brahe *deflating* behind her and turns to him. Tycho's deep glass-green eyes look at her. He does not smile, but his eyes do. She's startled by the depth of them. She does not see his reddish hair nor the glitter of his metal nose, she only sees those strange, luminescent, deep green eyes and feels their magnetic power. It is almost like a black hole attraction resides in him. *No way!* She looks closer. *No way this can be real!* She is aware of the exotic phantom energy physicists have dreamt about for ages, but she did not expect to see it in Tycho's eyes. And yet, it is there. Thus far she's known she needed to build a tunnel toward Stellan and didn't know how, but at this moment she realizes that it's not a tunnel she needs, it's a psychic wormhole and its whirlpool of unimaginable energies. This man, Tycho Brahe, first in human history to record a supernova, carries in him scalar, electromagnetic, and gravitational fields; all known energies, mechanical, heat, chemical, electrical radiant, nuclear, sound, and dark energy reverberate in those eyes. He's a portal to the world she and Stellan inhabit, the psychic worlds. He's the door and the key to the wormhole she needs to reach her baby brother.

Like rose petals, the world opens for her in an instant and she sees Stellan she awakens him with a burst of love-energy and whispers, "I am coming for you, puppy." His smile makes her feel alive and more aware than ever. She gets it, she gets everything in what felt like an eternity's instant. What she wasn't able to grasp or accept is so self-evident now. Her father was right; his Prophecy is true.

She is the Starchild.

She has no doubts anymore.

And she *knows* what that *means*.

And she knows what she and Stellan have to do.

And she *knows* what the darkening skies over Prague truly *mean*.

Not a second to waste, she raises her eyes and a flash of understanding passes in between her and Tycho, the Danish Nobleman born in the Knutstrup borg in the Svalöv Municipality of Scania some five hundred years ago.

"Noble Tycho Brahe, know that the world has never forgotten you. Please accept my deepest gratitude for the gift of time you have given me. I owe you more than words could ever express. Thank you," she whispers through tears of pure gratitude and gives him a deep bow of respect.

The famed astronomer and alchemist Tycho Brahe stands up from his throne and looks back at her, his heart filled with pride and gratitude of his own. He slowly strides toward her and, gently touching her chin, brings her back to the upright position. Then, he takes one step back, takes her hands in his own, and kisses them.

"Haven thankes thee. Fare thee well, Child off Sterre," Tycho Brahe replies devotionally and gives Nastassia a deep bow of respect.

Stellan Awakens
The Doomsday Vault
March 26, 2048

Stellan *felt* Nastassia and saw her with the old alchemist from his comic book through the wormhole, and her whisper *I am coming for you, puppy* lightens his world and awakes him from a floating stupor in the disgusting greenish liquid from the devil's nightmares. There's a message coming from her, *do it now*. He hears her thoughts and he *knows* what to do. Nastassia's eyes made him aware of this hellish prison, and using his mental eye to look around, he sees all the kidnapped children everywhere around him, each and every one of them immersed in the liquid, wired, and zombified. *You must free them*. He sends a wave of enormous psychic energy through the precog's compound, using the dread their prison creates in him, and wakes them up with the same images of their prison. As they start convulsing, like in a nightmare from which they will wake up momentarily, they create enormous disturbances in the force that has been feeding Maléficus's systems and crush it.

Stellan seizes the opportunity, the crack in their captivated consciousness, and starts screaming. His screams reverberate through the chamber and affect all the other precogs, who start to echo him in thundering voices with their own ear-piercing screams. One glass coffin after another shatters to pieces and the precogs, one after another, fall to the floor. They're weak, looking like naked slugs soaked in green; they shiver and shake, look around and at each other. The green bile is everywhere, and they fall knee-deep into this substance that has enslaved them and robbed them of their souls. They have nothing to wash it from themselves, nothing to wipe their bodies with, so they start to clean each other with their bare hands. They are cold, confused, frightened.

Nastassia senses how the invisible mental cage shatters into fragmented pieces and vanishes, this cage that kept her captivated and isolated from her kid brother and the world she's meant to inhibit since the day she had lived unborn under the dragon blood tree between the mythical cities of Yerushalaim and Bethlehem. And at that moment she *sees* it all.

Stellan, all green, naked wet, and shuddering with cold, and all the children he helped liberate are all around him. She *hears* "O, Jerusalem" by Hildegard von Bingen, and sees Claire K., the blue-eyed conductor of loneliness rehearsing. One boy, she *knows*, is Zachary, the son of the woman she saw days before next to the Wall of Lost Children, now a boy soprano singing for Emma Kirkby so to entertain none other than Hans Böhm.

They must rush there, to Norway's Svalbard.

Now.

She sends love to Stellan, reinforces her earlier message with a mental image of an impossibly cute Bernese mountain dog puppy and, in a hurry, takes Tycho Brahe's hands in her own and kisses them as a farewell.

The Shield's Down
Spitsbergen, Norway
March 26, 2048

Maléficus gasps at the alert screaming at him—Precog Network Shield Down—and rushes to the Precog Chamber like a madman. Første, whose MEGS were fed by the precog's data without interruption since the cursed day they were all brought to the vault, and Piccolino Scricciolo, Maléficus's jack-of- all trades, all rush after him.

"What happened?" Piccolino asks in fright.

"Do you know?" Maléficus turns to Første.

"No, sir."

"Check the traffic to and fro and triple check the Precog Shield." Maléficus barks. What he has dreaded since the day he started working for

Varga came to life—he was unable to secure the precious Precog Network and, worse, he has no idea at all what has happened—so he would have to face what could not be anything else but Varga's wrath. He must inform Varga about this development. He must do it now. But he hesitates, delaying the inevitable. *Let me asses the situation first,* he thought.

It was a dreadful, nauseating image, all those slimy, naked greenish precogs kids cleaning each other with bare hands while idiot freak MAGS stand motionlessly and look at them, dumbfounded and incapable of action, as the cryogenic liquid turned snot green and started to coagulate. Outside the comfort of his computer console and the computer screens dome, Maléficus also had no idea what to do.

"Get the hose," he barks at Piccolino, feeling like an idiot. A *hose*?

Leaving Tycho
Prague, Czech Republic
March 26, 2048

Nastassia and The Renegade rush out, carrying wounded Jaroslav with them, living Tycho Brahe behind in his liar. *What's he going to do now, since his task has been fulfilled?* She has no time to mull over. *Only if Dad knew how right he was*, the sorrow flashes through her, but she has no time for sorrow either. The leaking Zündapp motorcycle waited for them in the Týnska street, where The Renegade left it. They jumped in and rushed to the University Hospital in Prague where they left now unconscious Jaroslav to the care of Dr. Kristinka Volner and zipped away.

Direction: Dr. Bode's old friend and The Renegade's acquaintance from decades ago, a recluse telecommunication guru of the yesteryear, Radek Černý, a sinewy older gentleman, impeccably dressed even when he's glued to ancient AM radio, like today.

There were enough radio amateurs in the Old Bohemia that used old technology, high frequency shortwave radios, AM radios; some even used Morse code for shits and giggles for Černý to keep busy during the long, dark, cold nights in Prague. Now, that fringe community was an abundant source of disturbing info about New Athens brutal ransacking and the only truly functioning hub of communication. The Renegade had something else in mind.

"Do you have a satellite phone?" he asks Černý.

"Do beavers piss on flat rocks? Does a snake have knees?" Černý's cheerfully answers, pulling out an old Iridium Extreme phone. The Renegade dials Dr. Ursula Hansen-Schroeder who replies instantaneously. He did not even have to ask. Everyone was working in frenzy.

Ursula Hansen-Schroeder Springs to Action

"I've checked the documents, as much as could given the time constraints. Varga has crossed the every line." She says. "Can you get to, Tělový chovná Jednota… uh its something… unpronounceable." She starts to spell the world out, "Te-lo-vy…" when Černý rescues her out of her Czech spelling misery. "Tělovýchovná Jednota Uhříněves maybe?"

"Yes, this is an abandoned soccer field."

"What about it?"

"Go there and wait for the GSG 9 der Bundespolizei and Israeli Mista'arvim, the counter-terrorism units of the Israel Defense Forces working with us. They're in Leipzig, only two hundred kilometars away. In fact, they're already airborne. They'd be there in a half an hour before you."

"What's going on?"

"Hans Böhm is a German citizen. I had the Canadians issue a warrant for the murder and Norwegians to give us diplomatic clearance. Norway was neither part of the European Union nor it is a part of Varga's Governance and they were seriously pissed over the Vault's use and how it shields a murderer."

"Great!"

"There are twenty four special forces guys. You too are authorized by the Norwegians as a tech support. Good luck." She says and hangs up.

In seconds, The Renegade, yet again in a frenzy coming from Indiana Jones movies, starts Dr. Bode's Zündapp motorcycle and they zip away.

Right on time.

The High-Speed Vertical Takeoff and Landing (HSVTOL) stealth helicopter-jet hybrid prototype, code named, Valkyrja Dread jointly developed in Leipzig by the German and Israeli military has been tasked to take them to a 3,073.74 km long flight to Norway, in the Svalbard Archipelago, where the Doomsday Vault is located. At the maximum speed of 705 km/h they have almost four and a half hours before they'd reach the archipelago.

It did not elude The Renegade that Nastassia has been uncharacteristically quiet since they left Tycho Brahe behind. She seemed absentminded even when they left Jaroslav in the hospital, pensive and detached.

"Don't worry, he'll be fine. And we'll get to Stellan soon."

"It's not that," Nastassia lets a tired smile flash at The Renegade. "I'm afraid that she might have other plans."

Chapter 15

THE CODA

Deployment
Prague, Czech Republic
March 26, 2048

    She did indeed.
    These plans started to unravel slowly, as the Valkyrja Dread, as a fearful bird of destiny was rushing north, and then faster and faster. Unbeknown to Nastassia, as soon as they left Prague, the Golden City witnessed raging winds that tore roofs apart and hurled cars for hundreds of meters, like toys. A torrential rain started to pour. The thunderstorm has began. Prazaks, the citizens of Prague, who had never seen such devastating display of GAIA's power, scurried in panic, not having a faintest idea what's going on beneath or above.The security reasons forbid civilian communications of any means onboard the mighty chopper so Nastassia and The Renegade sat on their chairs, among the silent special forces guys, disconnected from it and unaware what's going in the world beneath them.
    "Try to get some shut-eye." The Renegade advises her, "so we're fresh later."
    He himself falls into the slumber.
    Nastassia close her eyes and almost immediately starts to dream of the little Aurora Jane and her bestie Noémie Lacroix playing Handel's impossibly beautiful "Passacaglia Duet" (a Norwegian Johan Halvorsen took the final movement of Handel's Harpsichord Suite in G Minor, written for a violin and viola, and adopted it. The girls in Nastassia's dream were playing

the piano version.) The girls' music was filled with love and the innocent passion of kids; Aurora Jane and Noémie's family and friends were there; Nastassia's parents were listening, together with Stellan sitting on Frédéric's shoulders. Luigi was there, sitting next to Monique's feet, his eyes upward toward Stellan who was mock-conducing them. Even a pink little elephant, Andy, that Aurora Jane often dreamt about was listening, mesmerized, in the audience. The good Auntie Gretchen was humming along. Tears that trickled down Nastassia's sleeping face went unnoticed by the hardened special forces guys, immersed in their own thoughts.

Raindrops Keep Fallin' on My Head
Montmartre, Paris
March 26, 2048

Around the same time, on March 26, 2048, at about 5:15 p.m. ET, a few small droplets fell on Earth, simultaneously, everywhere, all over the globe. They did not warn of the coming storm and looked as harmless as any other teeny weeny globule around. Not even Amélie Lefevre would put them in her diary after she had finished her daily walk with her two grandchildren, Madeleine and Mathieu. She always took them for a stroll on a small route from the Tomb of Dalida, over de Maistre street to the Boulangerie Alexine bakery on the Rue Lepic street in Paris. There she buys half a baguette for herself and some diamond butter cookies and obligatory madeleines for the kids. Her little angels could never get enough of her stories about how these famous sponge cakes were given their name after her own Madeleine.

As soon as Amélie forks out some of her pension for the cakes (on the sly she also buys two bûches de chocolat) she and her chattering grandchildren go home to keep listening to the Free Athens RIOTA-AM transmission, as Philip Bolghery tells a tale of the historical battle against Varga's evil empire. Due to the Net being hacked, Amélie feels like she is listening to the American radio during World War II, herself a true Resistance member. To her tastes, Bolghery is too dramatic, almost like Orson Welles's in his famous 1938 broadcast, *The War Of The Worlds*. Bolghery was also giving too many technical details about hacking and breaching and whatnot, which, without any images, was a bit boring to her, no matter how much she loved listening to Bolghery in the past. Still, this is better than Varga's propaganda "Freedom Lives" TV.

Despite living just north of the New Athens of Paris, Amélie loved to think she lived like those rebels. She saw herself as one of the New Athens revolutionaries, but because of her grandkids who lived in the same green building #79 on the Rue Lepic, where on the corner stood the "Le Moulin de la Galette" restaurant where the whole family ate every Sunday, she has not moved the few blocks south to La Nouvelle Athènes de Paris. Truth be told, she was also a helpless romantic and often took a solitary stroll to the nearby Musée de la Vie Romantique, a house of Dutch-French Romantic painter Ary Scheffer where one floor was dedicated to George Sand. Amélie used to spend hours upon hours there, immersed in her thoughts or Sand's books. Now, she was preoccupied with what was going on in the world. Varga seemed to have lost his mind over that kerfuffle. She did not really understand it—Bolghery was too excited and too vague. So she turned that mainstream TV back on. It was Varga's she knew, but she liked to compare her news sources, especially when Philip is too garbled as today.

Most of her neighbors were already angry at these developments given Winston Varga's relentless propaganda; she could hear them scream, often the words *la guillotine*, necessarily accompanied by cussing a blue streak all over the place. Matthew and Madelaine giggled every time the neighbors swore, but she couldn't do a thing about it—the people were simply too loud. Often she felt like she was living in a world parallel to that of the rest of humanity. The worlds were clearly delineated by the mass infotainment media that fed the world Varga's vision and the vision New Athens and, occasionally, Bolghery were giving to her.

The screams from her rabidly militant neighbor, Monsieur Jean-Pierre Darlan, were getting louder. A small wonder given the spectacle in the sky, which has just started. She glanced at the quote from the venerable Matt Taibbi's she had on her desk, bamboo framed. "Citizens are trained to believe that propaganda is something only other people consume." That dear old man who gave up on the world wrote those words decades ago, and yet, nothing has changed since. It has only gotten worse, one might argue. She heard how Monsieur Darlan rushed out to help "détruire ces traîtres," (destroy the traitors) and she hurried to the window to see him carry a big wrench and join the small river of equally enraged mob, rushing down south the Rue Lapic, toward La Nouvelle Athènes de Paris. The AM radio has been warning the New Athenians about the upcoming destruction. Amélie presses her hand on her lips, glancing at the children. She fears what might happen next in their world, which is oblivious to violence.

And yet again, millions of holograms, 3D eyepieces, VR & AR glasses, computer video streams, ancient flat 8K TV sets all over the world are endlessly broadcasting the "Freedom Lives" TV propaganda.

The War of the Species

As Varga barks his last orders, the INFINITUS alerts him about a strange intrusion. What captures his attention is bizarre: sea slugs and millions of other sea creatures are slurping data from the Apollo cable—his communication empire's backbone. The Net is mostly down so the only traffic is his own, back and forth between various nerve centers of his empire, and now these slugs? He gets it immediately; he's the target of those mofos even now, when they're under an attack of his own.

"Well, well, well," he says with disdain. "They're getting creative."

He types in an order and the INFINITUS sends several automated submarines to the bottom of the sea, where, with their high-energy beams' murderous precision, they begin mass-killing the sea creatures slurping their data. Nautilus makes them retreat but they are chased around the deep sea and murdered en masse. Parts of the Atlantic Ocean are reddened by blood. Nastassia awakes in dread, feeling like she's drenched in blood herself, disoriented from feeling Nautilus's pain, not sure if it was a part of her dream or if it was really happening now. The pilot alerts them of the final approach. *They'll be there in minutes.*

The Final Solution

Then, another intrusion astonishes Varga. He can not believe his eyes. Do they really dare to challenge him so shamelessly? Now, when he's doing all that's humanly possible to restore the world's internet access? To provide the cockroaches with American Talent, free money for them? To give them safety? Now, when the new apps his teams are developing for the major update to the Reality for Everyone™ that would blow everyone's mind are being polished to perfection? Now, when so many people in his Proteus work hard, sleeplessly trudging around the clock, just to help the ingrates? This wasn't that drunken bozo Bolghery's babbling, no, it was something completely different. A whole new level of unacceptable disobedience.

The INFINITUS has interrupted some Bluetooth-based internal communication by the Norwegian Ministry of Interior Affairs with a warrant for Maléficus's arrest. How dare they! That resentful triple-damned Gjermund Tingelstad, the prime minister of Norway, got all righteous since Varga took over the Doomsday Vault and is now trying to harm him? *I should've removed him when I had a chance. Well, I will soon. The freak will pay the price for such insubordination.*

In a private message to his whoring wife, Supreme Court Justice Monica Berget Tingelstad, that freak told her he's not coming home for supper because they, the New Athenians people, are filing lawsuits against Varga for crimes against humanity in New York, Kinshasa, Tbilisi and, with her help, in Oslo. How is the freak going to live without his flounder in disgusting apple sauce? The Norwegian police would need days to reach Svalbard, so he has enough time to prepare his defense and attack those mutinous bastards who dare to spoil his governmental transition triumph.

What Varga does not know is that the bird of doom, the phantom Valkyrja Dread carrying Nastassia and the Renegade, is already landing near the Doomsday Vault.

Nevertheless, he decides there's no time to wait while he has the advantage, so he has his sleeper cells raised all over New Athens, starting with Oslo. *Let me give that idiot Tingelstad something to worry about in the meantime.* The most zealous, militant Virtuosi™ of them all, members and sympathizers of The Incorruptus Order of The Virtuosi™ are given, not only the green light to attack, but, where they are available, Peace Police and drone logistic support as well. The Incorruptus Virtuosi™ have been waiting for real action for ages. Yes, it was fun to probe and poke those impure souls in need of redemption online, it was exciting to hunt them down through the Net but, truth be told, nothing beats the beauty of a bleeding face. The sight of New Athenians' hemorrhaging noses is one to strive for. The sound of broken bones is exhilarating, rather *needed*, to teach them a lesson. The Incorruptus Virtuosi™ will now wipe the smirks off the New Athenians' smug faces and will show them what reality looks like. No more sheltered living, potato growing, and liberty nonsense spewing. No more poisoning of our children's brains with ideas not sanctioned by the PHOENIX ONE and His infinite wisdom. Smoke will rise from burning stakes if those cursed heretics, refusing the New World Order of Peace, Virtue, and Truth, don't succumb.

Abbot Arnaud Amalric

"Kill them. The Lord knows those that are his own. Kill them all," yelled the magnificent military commander of the Crusades, abbot Arnaud Amalric, during the massacre at Béziers on July 22nd, 1209, and his words crossed the oceans of time to give the warriors of today a cry to unite them.

The Virtuosi™ needed no more.

The heretic-cleansing troops break the doors of New Athenians' homes, and the men hack their furniture into pieces and smash everything inside. The scale and intensity of the attacks were unimaginable. While most of the New Athenians ran away on time and found refuge among Outsider friends and relatives, cafés, and video games joints, those that stayed have experienced the full wrath of Varga as channeled through his Virtuosi™.

The raping of women, murder, vandalizing of private properties, and utter destruction of the infrastructure left unguarded were commonplace. The Peace Police and the Virtuosi™ used sledgehammers, hand-grenades, and dynamite to trash the homes of those despicable rebels into smithereens, only to torch and burn them down afterward. The orgy of violence goes on mostly unnoticed by the world, who are glued to Varga's emergency "Freedom Lives" TV broadcast and its sugary promises of a new world that's much better than the one they know.

Around the World in Ninety Seconds

In New York, the good Auntie Gretchen presses her hand over her mouth. *Jeez!* Angelo "Allegrino" de Carli, Nastassia's good friend from that impossible antique shop, has visited her and brought her some sweets and tea. "I am fine," she assures him but the dark circles under her eyes betray her.

The good auntie has not slept since Nastassia rushed out of her apartment without a word several days ago and was since declared a terrorist. The good auntie has no idea what is going on and feels excluded, not only from her little family but from the whole wide world. Nastassia always told her everything—she was her eyes and ears to a world she had difficulty grasping, given the pace of the changes Varga had imposed on it. She's worried sick. After the good auntie saw that odd couple so close to her heart, the Renegade and Nastassia together as "Wanted," and "Terrorists" at that, all over the skies, she was stricken with fear. Over the last several days she was so worried for Nastassia, Stellan, Frédéric, and Monique that she could not even understand why the Renegade is involved with Nastassia. And with what? What sordid affair brought him back from the dead?

Allegrino has not had the heart to tell her about Frédéric and Monique's murder or Stellan's kidnapping. He almost sighs with relief when they have a new issue to worry about—dark, low clouds over New York that seem to be teeming with not rain but rather buckets of iron.

Similar clouds sit above Paris, where, once back at home, Amélie is preparing a crème brûlée for the kids. Then she notices that a downpour of biblical proportions has started, seemingly out of nowhere. The sky over Paris opens up and darkens so suddenly that it feels like night, even at early afternoon. She and her grandkids have all but forgotten the sweets, and as they squeeze themselves onto the window frame, they look outside at the torrential rain in awe.

"The rain looks like falling tears," Mathieu excitedly observes.

"No," Madeleine contests him. "The angels are weeping." If only they knew, these little competing poets the *bonne-maman* Amélie loved so much, how close to the truth both of them were. They were about to learn soon. The droplets are heavy and silvery-grey, and as they are hurled around by gusty winds they are quite harmful to the people. Soon after the rain began, the streets of Paris are ghastly empty. After the droplets hit the ground, gusts of updraft winds force the droplets to go back to snatch other droplets high in the skies and, bigger than ever, fall to the earth again.

The whole world witnesses an outpour of massive rain on a scale never seen before. It is storming all over. Between fifteen and twenty inches of rain fell over the first several hours of the Global Storm on cities like New York, Paris, São Paulo, and Tokyo, and it continued to pour with no end. One meter and ninety centimeters of rain fell over twenty-four hours in Mumbai, India, and almost the same amount in Torino, Italy. Venice has all but vanished under the sea, which has also swept away and swallowed numerous tourists as they were running for dear life across San Marco square. A little yellow hat of a child left behind to drown is a symbol of the times to come as it chokes the billions watching it in dread on the "Freedom Lives" TV.

Daylight all over the world was not going *gentle into that good night* as the *New York Times*'s last edition, omitting the source of the quoted poem (Dylan Thomas) put as their last tired cliché. The days were as dark as the nights that replaced them.

The Winston Varga Wrath
Le Mont-Saint-Michel Abbey
March 26, 2048

Maléficus does not have a choice: he has to inform Varga about the broken Precog Chamber and the interruption of their operations. That bastard orphan Stellan was impenetrable when not connected with the other precogs and networked with the MEGS. Useless unless he's connected again, and that would take some time.

His ping could not come at a worse time for Winston Varga; he was busy leading the Final Solution attack on New Athens and his Virtuosi™ desperately needed to cover their tracks. Also there are those legal challenges. And that sudden weather change. What in the hell is that? And there is an arrest warrant against this same Maléficus who is interrupting him.

"What?" Varga barks.

Maléficus freezes for a moment but then, as succinctly as he can, he informs Varga about what has happened. Varga turns his dark, murderous eyes toward the man he has known since he was a destitute junkie vagabond. His penetrating stare frightens Maléficus, who feels guilty for his inability to prevent the breach. A drop of sweat trickles down his shaggy eyebrow but he does not dare to wipe it off. That makes him even more nervous, feeling almost naked like those damn wormlike precogs. Varga didn't need the GRIFFIN's green light to see through people, and Maléficus dreaded what Varga would see while looking at him, assessing his grave mistake.

What can I tell him? This panicky thought rushes through his mind while Varga says not a word and looks at the images from the Precog Chamber. But they do not concern him at the moment. He looks at the man who stood next to him for over a decade but to whom it did not even occur to inform him of his arrest warrant. So, he's dispensable, this hobo who stole from him.

Varga has never forgotten, nor forgiven Hans Böhm's sin. He just tolerated it all those years. He could not care less about Böhm/Maléficus murdering his mother, but the ingrate has betrayed him once. This time, by allowing the precogs' breach, Maléficus Ultimo Hans Böhm, whatever the pervert's name is, has shown inexcusable incompetence. Moreover, the sins of his past are now hunting Varga through that idiotic post by Bolghery.

Wait!

How did Bolghery know about Maléficus's matricide?

It was hackneyed gobbledygook he used to arouse his readers when he announced that idiotic lawsuit, and it flew right over Varga's head when he read it. *A moment of weakness.* He was too excited over the BESNILO Attack, enabled by the PRIORI's idiocy that he missed it.

Is Maléficus a traitor?

Has he sold him out to Bolghery? And those details about the orphans' parents? Where did Bolghery get that? So soon? Who knew? Maléficus. What else could be the explanation? He, Varga, could not have been hacked, so all the data are safe from Philip's delusional conspiracy theories, and yet, he knew a dark secret from forty years ago.

The precogs breach alone would be more than enough to doom Maléficus once for all, but this is worse than betrayal. He smiles and that smile is Maléficus's death sentence. What he says aloud, however, surprises Maléficus.

"It's her," Varga says. "It's the Bonnet orphan trying to get to this bastard here."

Everyone looks at Stellan.

"You think it was Nastassia Bonnet's doing, the breach?" Maléficus asks, not yet breathing, not yet relaxing under Varga's murderous glance.

"Kill him!" Varga calmly says. "I don't care if he's the Subject Zero, kill him. The little bitch must pay. And restore the Precog Net ASAP." Varga cuts the connection off.

Before the Beginning
Svalbard Archipelago, Norway
March 27, 2048

At the very moment of Varga ordering Stellan's execution, Stellan sees the dark arrows of death hurling toward him and all the precogs. He uses the same weapon as before: screams. As they all scream, the pandemonium is increased by the outside microphones picking up the loud roar of the Valkyrja Dread landing next to the Doomsday Vault.

Maléficus did not hear Varga's order, deafened by the noise.

"What the hell is that?" He rushes toward the exit to check it out.

The Beginning
Le Mont-Saint-Michel Abbey
March 27, 2048

In his TV studio nestled in the west wing of this castle, Winston Varga has no idea that Maléficus never received the order to kill the Subject Zero. A huge lightning bolt strikes the abbey with such force that all systems go out, until they are replaced by the generators. Varga is possessed with demoniacal wrath and mad ecstasy. The reports come from all sides about a lawsuit filed asking for an emergency injunction against his empire, even the PHOENIX ONE. *They*, those idiot fuckwits, dared to attack him, to spy on him, to challenge the God he has given them to watch over and care for everyone. And by trying to take the PHOENIX ONE down they would have taken down himself, the true New God of the new era. No way he'd let them do that. *Injunctions? Lawsuits?* He spits in disgust. *I am the Law.*

And what about those floods? It's because of him. He's God, he created all of that. Nature weeps over the ingrates' rebellion. *Let them all drown.* They are doomed to lose. He's the one with the power. They left his media empire intact, the idiots. Now they'll see how it looks when all the TV altars tell the rabble what to think, what to feel, what to do. He directs his media counterattack with the fervor of an opera conductor on a spaceship on its way to a black hole.

Varga hastily types a message into his computer console and sends it encrypted to the St. Patrick's Cathedral in New York where the Cardinal Luciano Antonioni personally receives it. The message reads: "The INNOCENTI will be destroyed unless we act. Send this message now." A copy of the message goes to the White House, to his own Pinocchio, a.k.a. the former president of the US, Jerome K. Mooney, who still resides there and was to record a message of his own. There was no time to waste. Varga was grateful for the history lessons that had taught him never to go against the church and the military.

Over the years he has carefully cultivated ties with both echelons of power, magnanimously incorporating them in the INNOCENTI movement so His Eminence Antonioni, the Archbishop of New York, dressed in his crimson red cassock, had no qualms about performing his duty. His utmost obligation is to help the secret order of the INNOCENTI live and thrive, the Verum Innocentes whom Varga never forgot to lavish with billions. The cardinal nods to the camera that he is ready, and he starts reciting in the famous, sweet, soft voice of someone who truly loves his flock:

"And God said unto Noah, The end of all flesh is come before me; for the earth is filled with violence through them; and, behold, I will destroy them with the earth.

And, behold, I, even I, do bring a flood of waters upon the earth, to destroy all flesh, wherein is the breath of life, from under heaven; and every thing that is in the earth shall die."

Varga snickers while His Eminence the Cardinal reads his homework. "I'll give them a flood of pain," he says. "Let them know who controls nature!" he yells in a terrible voice, noticing that all the PHOENIX ONE cameras stare into the dark clouds beneath. And then, yet another lightning bolt from the heavens strikes the St. Patrick Cathedral and interrupts His Eminence's heartfelt transmission from New York.

Varga turns to the Washington DC studio where Pinocchio is recording a message of his own. He struggles with "the geotechnologically changed weather is the terrorists' fault," which was meant to air after His Eminence, but now, since the cardinal was cut off, he is to be put on air ASAP. "Bloody PRIORI and bloody New Athens and bloody Renegade and that Bonnet orphan," Varga screams from the top of his lungs.

But, if this is what they want...

"They are going to taste the Wrath of God." His booming voice rages all across the studio. Not only his obsequious director, but also the technicians, broadcasters, and supporting personnel tremble in front of him. Even the incomparable Baiano Lindo cowers in fear as Varga runs upstairs to his headquarters where he has a direct line to the INFINITUS's secret features. *They have to pay the price.* He'll fire the nukes if necessary and blame it on the New Athens terrorists. But he has no time to meticulously plan as he's used to, so he has to improvise. These terrorists think they can take him down by destroying one cog or two in his well-oiled machine?

We'll see about that.

Given the zero visibility for the PHOENIX ONE, Varga instructs the INFINITUS to rapidly fire laser beams at every New Athens in the world, per the coordinates given, in a devastating burst of murderous energy. They are a cancer, rather a vicious rabies disease on the body of his new world. Once he eradicates them, the new world's order by Varga will be restored as a new shiny city upon a hill. "A tall, proud city built on rocks stronger than oceans. Windswept, God-blessed, and teeming with people of all kinds living in harmony and peace; a city with free ports that hum with commerce and creativity." Winston Varga's City, a global establishment whose happiness would be Varga's but whose misery would be their own. It does not matter to him that his own soldiers, the Virtuosi™ ransacking the terrorists' hidden caves, are also killed. Collateral damage is, sadly, the price every great general in history has had to pay for glory. And victory. In New York's burning New Athens rubble even Jeremiah DeJohn lay dying with his eyes fixed on the dark heavens from which Winston Varga came to make him a proud man, happy even now, when he's on his way out. If only he had a chance to get that treacherous little bitch and strangle her with his own hands. If nothing, he'll wait for her in hell.

A forceful, deafening roar of thunder carrying a force Varga has never experienced in all of his turbulent life draws him outside the chambers of Mont-Saint-Michel Abbey, to the pride of his castle, the veranda.

The lightning is blinding. Hail rattles loudly, crushing whatever isn't protected. "I made that happen, do you hear that, Renegade?" Varga screamed at the heavens, shaking his fist in anger toward the forsaken land of Norway and the Vault he seems to have lost to that old, useless pimp.

Cordelia Einarsdøttir, who has been avoiding Varga at least for the last several days hoping his fury would subside, which it never did, observes him raging on the terrace. The lightning storm flashes reveal his distorted face. And she finally *knows it*, for sure. For, in her groins and deep inside her, in her *stygian darkness* as he called it, in every fiber of her body that has so totally embraced him, knows he is truly *mad*. She stands there, blinded by lightning and deafened by thunder, and shakes in dread. It isn't lust or greed, neither was it unbearable pain from his childhood or his unquenchable will for power that drove him all these years. No, it was madness. What terrifies her even more is a revelation that has eluded her for such a long time—his madness rested upon, and fed on, hate.

Varga has been a man consumed by hate his all life. The very hate and the madness he produced she has fed with her body and her love. For yes, she did love that man, the maniac raging at the storm in front of the dark sea, under the torrential rain and hail, screaming at faraway land he's losing for good. Looking at him losing it made her feel her loss as painfully as anything, almost as painful as having to endure his outbursts and, even much more so, as loving him.

"Do you hear me, you old piece of shit? I made this happen," he screams from the top of his lungs. "I am God!" Varga yells into the dark with no one to hear him, not even Cordelia, who was straining to read his lips. *Did he say he's God?* she wonders. In his frenzy, he did indeed look like the mythical Nordic god of madness. In these moments that feel like infinity, the power of madness that engulfed and seduced her that fatal day in Reykjavik when they met, has neither a beginning nor an end.

Out of the corner of her eye, Cordelia sees a hologram of Captain Jacques Sansnez that flickers in the air, from his post in Africa, transmitting a dramatic attack by herds of animals on Varga's African research and backup facilities. The bloodbath was terrible, but Varga dismisses it with one flicker of a finger that never parts with its console, and he turns back toward the hostile skies that are plummeting the earth with all its might. Nearby, Les Iles Chausey, famous for its high tides of fourteen meters, are pushing a wall of water at least twenty meters high toward inland. To Cordelia, it looks like Earth is one organism that has also lost her mind. Even the raised Le Mont-Saint-Michel Abbey starts to fill with the water rushing toward it like an unstoppable tsunami.

"This world is mine! I create and I destroy everything!"

Varga screams when a horrible gust of wind sweeps him off the terrace. It carries him like a doll over the North Tower and hurls him into the darkened waters of La Manche channel.

Stellan and Nastassia
Svalbard Archipelago, Norway
March 27, 2048

When the Valkyrja Dread, carrying the special forces, the Renegade, and Nastassia, lands, the Doomsday Vault has already been defeated. It had only two old guys pretending to be security, who surrendered at the very moment they saw the special forces' painted faces. Varga never thought such a remote, almost unreachable place would need real security. Following Maléficus, almost everyone living in the vault rushed out, attracted by the helicopter-jet hybrid and the thunderous noise from the sky.

The precogs were trembling but excited. Freedom seems so close now. Nastassia rushes to hug Stellan.

At that moment, Maléficus sees her. *That's her. That's the little bitch, whose fault this all is.* He jumps, running toward her, yelling, "I will kill you!" when Commander Liam MacPherson shoots him dead. The special forces guys rush to wrap the precogs in warm clothing. Some go to inspect what's inside the Doomsday Vault.

The Gelatinous Mass

And then, like seeds from hell, gelatinous masses appear.

They started to pop up occasionally, first as slimy seed bundles on the redwood coast in California and the western hemlock-spruce trees in Alaska. Almost no one noticed them as the storms raged and the people hid inside, cowering in their caves and glued to their screens, observing the deluge on all continents. But only a few hours after the gelatinous masses appear, the slime starts to grow.

And rapidly spread.

The Great Plague of London in the Middle Ages spread in less haste than this mucus-secreting slime. Huge, rapidly growing gelatinous masses merged together and started their slimy marches, attacking a nearby electrical power grid first. They needed enormous quantities of energy to survive and were attracted to the grid, devouring it as a huge, rolling, bubbling, seething, slurping, steaming, ever-growing smoking puke of smelling lava that flowed along the transmission lines.

A demon seed was next. A biological super rust was born out of the electricity-eating slime and started to gobble up all kinds of steel things. It was like a swarm of metallic insects were frenzied upon the glorious towers of humankind, mercilessly gorging on anything that rusts. The Eifel Tower was devoured in a ghastly display of madness in mere hours. Cars dissipated into dark rust in a matter of minutes. Car factories took a bit longer but were soon after devoured the way cackling hyenas would gobble up a carcass. The Golden Gate Bridge in San Francisco, which underwent a restoration only weeks ago, fell into the Pacific Ocean when it was only half-eaten. The pride of Eritrea, the tallest building in the world, the fabled Qimat Alealam and its 365 towers took days to be destroyed, but in the end, it was gone. Nothing could've stopped the destruction. Subways, railroads, airplanes, anything metal was gobbled as the world of humans rapidly lost its recognizable features.

In a matter of days, GAIA devoured human civilization.

Before the Beginning
Svalbard Archipelago, Norway
March 27, 2048

Aghast and speechless, Nastassia, Stellan, the Renegade, and the motley crew of rescued precogs and MEGs, look at the live transmission of the catastrophe that has stricken human civilization like a million mighty hammers at once, until, one after another, live streams died out as the power grids failed, eaten alive. Darkness enveloped the world.

Nastassia chuckles.

"What could possibly be funny?" asks Første.

She raised her laptop showing him a message. "Your battery is low (5%). If you need to continue using your computer, either plug in your computer or shut it down and then change the battery."

"The vault's generators might last for a few more days," Første remarks.

"Not really," the Renegade says, pointing outward. Indeed, the unstoppable biological rust was rushing toward the Doomsday Vault and its vast resources of metal and energy, the tech in it a worthy prey for the shapeless mass. Nastassia glances at the laptop again. It has turned itself off; the battery ran out. This has never happened before—the world is left without electric power, in ruins. In darkness.

"I thought we tricked her to help us, but GAIA has tricked us!" Nastassia smiles bitterly.

"Well, she could've completely wiped us out as a species, but she chose not to. Perhaps she has given us a second chance?" the Renegade thinks aloud.

Nastassia, holding Stellan wrapped in a military sheepskin in her arms, looks around. "It might not be a second chance?"

"I am not sure. What she could leave behind would be toxic, deadly sludge that might be too dangerous for humans for decades if not centuries to come. No way to know at the moment," the Renegade explains. "The slime and this biological rust might leave behind a trail of dead crap that is too toxic to almost every living thing except specialized bacteria and insects that distribute the toxins far and wide."

What the Renegade was describing, the stenchy slime and advancing bio-rust, has moved over on a plateau outside and was already entering the Doomsday Vault, indifferent to the new display of beauty outside. A wonderful, colorful sky opens up and turns into a gorgeous, serene sunset. The Renegade looks around.

"It's almost like GAIA is sending us a farewell," he murmurs.

Nastassia follows his gaze and then looks at him begging, *Tell me more about what might happen, please.*

"If this were the case, and the toxic biomass keeps multiplying, the worst-case scenario is that humans might survive by finding giant bubbles in silicon lava flows suitable for colonization, and start anew. But this is a far cry. We have no way of assessing the damage now. Maybe the stuff just really needs a lot of power to keep up its massive growth rate. After it has eaten the transmission lines and all the metal, it might branch out toward new sources of energy. So it evolves and grows, a steaming even flaming front that branches out toward the volcanoes after it has eaten the transmission lines. We need to wait and see what will happen." The Renegade pauses. "No matter what, for sure it will be inconvenient."

Nastassia quietly chuckles at the word.

The Last Sunset

The sun was gone and with it the beautiful sunset. They all stand in eerie silence as darkness falls. The only sounds are echoes of the demonic slurping of the biomass devouring what was left of the Doomsday Vault, in the soft underbelly of what used to be the nerve center of Varga's empire.

Nastassia shakes off the thought of Varga—*at least I hope the bastard is gone*—and looks at the sky, full of stars, a stupendous sight people almost never see anymore. A sense of awe and dread suffuses her every nerve. Somewhere in those stars, their destiny has been written and is galloping their way at the speed of light. *I certainly hope the Herman One comet will not pay us a visit*, she thinks bitterly, *even though it would be poetic justice for us to vanish with a bang.* She does not want to share her gloomy thoughts.

"Renegade?"

"Yes?"

"Where's Tycho's Supernova?"

"There are only remnants of it left, called nebulae, mostly ionized gas and stardust. We can't see it by a naked eye." The Renegade looks at the sky and points toward the Great Bear. "Do you see the Ursa Major?"

"Yes." Nastassia whispers gazing at the stars, squeezing Stellan closer to her heart.

"It rotates around Polaris, the North Star. Did you know Polaris is actually three stars, locked in a same orbit. Do you see it? On the right side."

"Yes, yes."

"Now," the Renegade draws a line in the sky with his finger pointing upward, "follow the line from the Great Bear toward the North Star. Cassiopeia is on the other side of the North Star, at almost the same distance, but on the right."

"I can see it. Tycho's Supernova is located there?"

"It's remnants, yes."

"I would've been thrilled to have seen it with Tycho at his time."

The Healing

They all stand silently for a while, gazing at the starry sky on which the North Star twinkles back at them. The Renegade turns to Nastassia:

"What a glorious, epic fail that was, wouldn't you say?" he asks with a strange timber in his voice. It was a rhetorical question, so he averts his eyes and gazes across the sea at the Svalbard archipelago, its glaciers and its frozen tundra that are disappearing in the dark, lit only by the stars, as he mulls over the civilization that has been wiped out. He fears mayhem, the havoc that's going to ensue in a matter of days if not hours, when most of the world will be without food and water. Nastassia follows his gaze, sensing his thoughts. There's a profound sense of anguish in the Renegade, perhaps even guilt. He's grieving not only the destruction of the world but the very fact he's not likely to be here when it's being rebuilt. His anguish disturbs her, she needs him.

"Flibbidyfloo, Renegade." Nastassia smiles using his idiosyncratic language. "Snap out of it. Heebie-jeebies and gloom are not your style. We will recreate the world. To be better this time. If for nothing else, only to see it gloriously fail again. Until we make it right. And we'll need your knowledge."

It works. He chuckles at the *flibbidyfloo* and how she pronounced it, like some kid asking for a *lollipop*. This girl made of steel and stars has the power to heal the world in her, it seems obvious to him. She must've heard his thoughts again, for she asks, "What do you think is happening with the people of the world now?"

He does not have to think twice.

"Like always, they are going stark raving mad, killing each other."

"What about us? What now? Where do we start? How?"

"I am not sure. No one has ever lived in the world without electricity or computers."

"Tycho Brahe has." Stellan's off-hand remark makes Nastassia and the Renegade gawk at him and look back at each other. Understanding passes in between them. Stellan has just given them hope. Or at least a direction. They'll have to start the world's renewal, not only from scratch and build upon what has been available in Tycho's times, all those immediate things Nietzsche wrote about, but also from what's *real* in the human soul, its true values, in order to create a viable human civilization, worthy of its name this time. *His life has not been lived in vain* reverberates through Nastassia as her mental eye glances toward Tycho Brahe's underground lair. He's busy writing in his diary and he stops, looking around like something has alarmed him. Nastassia does not want to disturb him any longer and lets him be with an inner smile. Once the Renegade's mighty mind merges with Tycho's skills of the times the world has plunged back into, they might even have a chance.

"So, back to Prague?" Nastassia asks.

"Back to Prague." The Renegade nods, reinvigorated by those two little weirdos, Stellan and Nastassia, thinking how Frédéric and Monique would be proud of them. A flicker of sorrow flashes through his mind, but he gently removes it from his thoughts. Nastassia's right, there's no time for wallowing in pain over the tragedies of the past. They need to look forward. The Renegade looks at Nastassia and smiles. "You also have to help your boyfriend Jaroslav heal," he teases and goes to discuss the details of transporting all the people back to Prague with the commander MacPherson, even before she's had time to furiously respond.

"Yeah, like I would not have better things to do."

Nastassia Bonnet, the Starchild of New Era, huffs, more for herself, like she always does when miffed, in indignant protest of a badass teenage girl accused of gross ignominy like being in love. But this time, firmly grasping Stellan in her embrace and running toward the chopper and its whirling rotors, she brims.

Her smile says she likes the idea.

The Guardians of Time

St. Michael the Archangel, the protector of Saint Michel Abbey, who, at the end of time, will wield the sword of justice to separate the righteous from the evil and decide if they go to heaven or hell, will not be given the chance to judge Winston Varga. In the weeks that follow his being swallowed by the ocean, its currents take his body all the way down to another part of the world, to the deepest depths of the seas, the Challenger Deep in the Mariana Trench at the bottom of the Pacific Ocean.

On its way down, Winston Varga's body encountered the sea creatures he killed: Terrible Claw Lobsters and green sea turtles, the Colossal Squid, and the scary Megamouth Shark. Barreleye Fish and Abyssal Spiredfish stared at him with their dead eyes. Varga's body, on its way toward unimaginable depths, passes Gigantactis, the ray-finned fish and Chimera ghost sharks, the Black Swallower and the Scaly-Foot Snail, none of which are allowed to gnaw at his body. Finally, what used to be Winston Varga was given to the tiny crustaceans, the true rulers of the depth, scary scavengers called Hadal Amphipods, now the keepers of his remains and the Guardians of his Death. Their solemn duty is to have his death pay for the sins of his life.

THE END

Printed by
Libri Plureos GmbH · Friedensallee 273
22763 Hamburg · Germany